The Magician'

HDA Robe. ..

Chapter 1

My brother threw a fireball. His opponent raised her hand, and a single gesture sent it ricocheting back towards him. He waved his hands frantically, trying to dispel.

Idiot.

The ball was moving too fast, and his counter-spells have always been too slow. He should have dodged and cast another attack spell; his only advantage in the match was his raw power. Belle was just too quick and far too smart to fence with. Ah, he's got the fire out and... Belle hits him in the face with an ice-ball.

Desmond's shield glowed, but enough force was transferred that he hit the floor (with an amusingly solid thump), match over.

They were in the bigger gymnasium, the standard room for a practice duel, with bleachers along one wall and a neglected set of basketball hoops at either end. The difference between this gym and the ones that 'normal' students used was the heavily enchanted metal circle built right into the wooden floor, which surrounded the two combatants and kept their spells contained. Both of them were dressed in P.E. kit, with a heavy black leather vambrace strapped around their left forearm and hand, a focus tied to the circle designed to absorb offensive magic and prevent anyone getting hurt (the cuff was the only reason there wasn't a ice-ball shaped hole where my brother's head used to be).

There was a small crowd in the stands, mostly girls, mostly staring at my brother, the lucky bastard. I sat at the far edge, away from the crowd, waiting with barely disguised impatience for the farce to be over with.

The room finally broke into applause, and somewhat muted at that. Belle beating my brother had become something of a habit by this point. The girl took a bow, offering Desmond a cheeky grin before offering him her hand. He took it with a smile and allowed himself to be pulled to his feet, lingering in Belle's proximity just a little longer than necessary; his free hand running over her thigh in what I am sure was meant to be a subtle gesture.

Subtle is not my brother's strong suit, as you may have guessed.

He was tall and broad at the shoulder, though more wiry than beefy, he had high cheekbones, guileless bright eyes and a good chin that gives his face a certain gravitas.

He's also my twin, and while we had technically started off identical, that had been a very long time ago. His hair went golden blonde when his powers manifested; we both have one blue eye and one brown, but my blue is left, his is right. My hair is dark and short, he wears his like an 80's rock icon, which is to say, tacky. I'm also shorter, less muscular.

He's also a Wizard. That is the technical term, by the way, there are categories based on power level (the government made the categories, I think they're stupid). Wizard is the middle one, I won't bore you with the details of the others, they're not important right now.

Ever since Magicians (their word) came out into the open fifteen years ago, the world has gone from loving to hating to loving them again several times. At the moment they're loving, because of the duels.

No, excuse me, that's !**DUELS**!, as the marketing ads like to call them. Think along the lines of the Ultimate Fighting Championship with fire and lightning and you are maybe one tenth of the way there. Of course, everyone wears Mage-designed safety gear that is supposed to prevent serious injury, but occasionally "accidents" do happen.

Naturally my idiot brother thinks he's going to be the next great champion.

"Well Matty, someone has to hold up the family honour, and since you can't use magic, that leaves me!" that's what the brain-donor says whenever I try to point out the fact that duelling is dangerous.

He's also quite wrong.

I just choose not to use magic, that's all.

Well, nothing flashy anyway.

See, I have a problem.

Every magician has a specialty; for your adept (the lowest rung on the magical ladder), it's often little more than a single spell, lighting a fire, for example. For your Wizards and Sorcerers, it can be an entire element or even two. For the less powerful, that's often all they have, but your stronger mages are able, with enough practice, to cast a wide variety of spells, as long as you have the skill to craft it and the power to charge it. But your specialty will always come easiest to you.

For me, it's Shadow.

Otherwise known as Umbrakinesis. Now, that sounds fun, doesn't it? The very darkness itself jumps up and does what it's told, what could be more fun?

Very good questions, and of course I might well agree with you... if I wasn't afraid of the dark.

It's a holdover from my youngest years, when I was lying in the darkness, and the shadows started creeping towards me, and the more afraid I got, the closer the shadows came, responding to my fear, moving to protect me. Naturally, I discovered this in (relatively) short order, but by then it was too late, I was terrified and my affinity was the cause.

And here is where I discovered the difference between an affinity and a speciality. With a speciality, the spell comes easily, but it's still an effort to cast it; with an affinity, the effort is more in stopping it from responding, as the power ties in heavily with the subconscious, making the power more versatile, but also more prone to inadvertent action.

So I kept it quiet, afraid someone might try to make me use the thing, and I guess the secrecy just stuck, well past the point where I'd (mostly) got over my phobia. So now my brother is a budding battle mage and I am the class bookworm. Which is good for Desmond as I help him study his magical textbooks and prepare for duels (though he has no inkling that I read, absorbed and mastered those same books some time ago).

I'm a quicker study than my brother, definitely smarter, but he has magical power coming out his ears, he only barely missed the grade for Sorcerer, and he'll likely make that in a few years when he get older and stronger. If it ever came to a fight, he'd mop the floor with me, I simply don't have any practice at battle magic, in fact I'd always thought it a little vulgar.

Which is why I'd dropped an Asimov in his head.

Mind magic is a hobby of mine. It's fun because I can use it with hilarious results and complete anonymity. Focus, link, enchant; easy as that, but it takes finesse, and practice, to do it without causing an injury. I learned by practicing on my Uncle Thatcher. Don't worry, he's not a nice guy (wife beater, doesn't do *that* anymore), and he's more or less fine (I'm told that he still has to be reminded to take off his underwear before using the loo, but you can't have everything).

Anyway, an Asimov. Named after Isaac Asimov who created those three rules for robotics. Well, I put the same basic thing in Desmond, buried deep in his motor cortex. It's not that I don't trust my brother; it's just that I'd rather not have to worry about his hormonal exuberance getting the best of him.

Take today for example. Desmond's speciality is Light magic (the worrying polar opposite of mine), and a single blast of light would have dropped Belle like a bad habit, but since he's... oh let's call it "in a relationship" with her he lets her win. Bad practice, bad thinking, bad precedent in a duel. I've read every book there is on the subject, and he who hesitates over a shapely opponent isn't just lost, but found, charred and served up as an aperitif to the loser's table.

Dumbarse.

She likes him too, and that was adorable, but she was getting a false sense of her own skill from the practices, these two being the strongest of the schools five mages (out of eight hundred students, not including me), which meant that there really wasn't anyone else for them to practice with. They'd won a couple of matches against rival schools, but they were against acolytes (one down from Wizard), so they'd never had to face someone on their own level in earnest. Might end badly for one (or both) of them.

Might also be funny for me.

So maybe it wouldn't be the worst thing in the world for him to take a loss or two...

I know, I'm a terrible person, but you try listening to your brother's variations on "I'm a conduit for the universe's awesome majesty" for seventeen years and see how saintly you turn out.

Anyway, the bout was over and it was time for a little chat with my brother.

He'd finally separated from Belle, who was still grinning. She was pretty and tall, with delicate features, black hair all the way down to the small of her back and a pair of dazzling green eyes. Smart too; not as smart as me, but who is?

Yes, I realise I'm just as bad as Desmond in my own way, but we are twins, there have to be *some* similarities, and at least I have the decency to *pretend* to be modest.

"Matty! Did you see me?"

"Yeah, Matty, did you see him?" Belle chimed in.

Never liked that girl. She takes liberties, and is a snarky cow if ever there was one. I chose not to rise to the bait... this time.

"Yes, I saw you, but that's not why I'm here. You're five prep assignments behind and your teachers are hassling me again. They say that if you don't complete these by the weekend, they won't let you compete next Wednesday."

I dropped the assignments into his hands, glared once at Belle for form's sake, and turned around to leave. The teachers won't yell at Des, he's simply too useful to the school. Would you believe that magicians have an equal rights group? That's right, people who control the elemental powers of the universe have a group who complain about equal rights. As a Wizard-class magician, and a competing one at that, Des gets a lot of positive press for Windward Academy- "Look how progressive we are, we allow girls *and* magicians in here!"

Bleuch.

Anyway, because they won't yell at him, that means that any bad news (such as detention, late work or incomplete nonsense) gets dropped in my lap to pass on. And like a sap, I often end up just doing the work for him. I'm pretty sure that's it's only due to extreme luck (and a very tricky set of memory enchantments that took me a week to perfect) that he got enough GCSEs to continue on at the school.

Today though, I was in a mood, and Belle had irritated me, so he could damn well do his own prep for a change. I stalked off, vaguely in a huff, and was making a pretty good exit of it too, when the wooden floor in front of me froze for a few feet in every direction. I stopped abruptly, nearly slipping and falling on my arse.

"Where do you think you're going?" Belle asked, a nasty edge to her voice.

"Annabelle," said a low, menacing, gravelly voice from the far corner of the gymnasium.

You may wonder how safe it is for hormonal adolescents with magical powers to be among normal children (or Pureborn, if you prefer. That's the Magical Community's polite name for regular people; there are others, less polite), what with the worry of potential immolation due to hurt feelings.

Well, the government was worried too, and thus was born the Magical Supervisor, which kids have been calling "Leopolds" for years. Named after that scary teacher's assistant from an early episode of the Simpsons, a Leopold is a designated member of staff, trained in a special course by the government to deal with, and provide discipline for, the magical kids.

He was a great ox of a man called Mister Koenig. He wore one of the vambraces around his wrist for the practice and carried an amulet around his neck. These are very special amulets; they're made by Sorcerers, (which is to say the mystical equivalent of Mike Tyson), to absorb and stop dead any spell cast at the wearer.

I have a couple of theoretical ways around that thing, but I've never actually had a chance (or the need) to test them, and Koenig's always been nice enough to me; I think he realises that living in my brother's extensive shadow is not great fun for me.

"Sorry Mister Koenig," she said, glaring at me. I ignored her, nodded once at Koenig, a gesture he returned, before heading towards the main doors, my brother hot on my heels. As I walked through the doors, moving at the back of the small crowd, Des kept up, trying to keep the stack of papers and folders in some sort of order.

"Matty! Will you wait up?"

I sighed, knowing that there really wasn't much point in trying to outrun him now that my dramatic storm-off had been interrupted. I slowed to a halt, the rest of the kids moving off and away. We'd just exited the gym and were standing in one of the smaller squares. The sports building was behind us, and the other three sides were occupied by large Edwardian buildings, red brick with dark grey slate and delicately carved stone decorations running along the edges and roofs.

"Yes?" I asked, trying to keep the irritation from my voice, and mostly succeeding.

"I can't do all this by Saturday, there's too much!"

There was maybe four hours work there, not an insignificant heap, but hardly an insurmountable one. It was only Wednesday evening, for heaven's sake.

"And why would that be?" I asked, trying to be reasonable about the whole thing.

"Not enough time, I already have an essay due, and I haven't even started my art project yet."

"Des..." I started, rubbing my eyes, my brother was going to give me an ulcer if he carried on like this.

"I know Matty, I'm sorry. Can't you help, please? I can't miss that match next week, I just can't."

I already had a heap of my own work to do, and the teachers didn't cut *me* any slack if it was late.

"Give me the English and the History," I said with a resigned sigh.

Des flashed me a smile and pulled a pair of folders from the pile.

"That's art," I pointed out in exasperation, handing one back.

He handed me the correct one and smiled again.

"I owe you, little brother," he said, smacking me on the shoulder before running off after his girlfriend.

I'm exactly six seconds younger than him, but he still calls me that.

"Do that essay!" I yelled after him, trying to salvage some part of my dignity, "Tonight!"

"I will, scout's honour!" he called back over his shoulder.

He was never a scout.

Chapter 2

An hour later, and I was sitting on the roof of the chapel, hidden from the wind and sight by the crenulations and statuary. The door leading up here was pitifully easy to magically unlock and then relock behind me, and a small alarm spell would let me know if I was about to get caught.

I loved it up there, especially on warm nights like that one. I had Des' English prep leaning up against the roof, and I had a pair of reference books open next to it. His class was three sets below mine, so the work wasn't difficult, just time consuming; more so because one has to show an argument to these sorts of analytical questions. Our handwriting is quite similar, and questions about Romeo and Juliet aren't exactly tasking as long as you've read the damned book, so we can get this sort of thing by his teachers quite easily. The only catch is making enough deliberate mistakes so that he passes, but not by so much as to arouse suspicion.

I groaned in irritation, and more than a little frustration, and dropped my fountain pen on the pad I'd been using, leaning back against the roof to rub my head. I was thinking of taking a little nap when I was distracted by a rumbling noise followed by a weary sigh.

"Doing the brother's homework again?" asked a voice that rightly belonged to an aristocrat or a judge, but was actually coming from a moving statue. A gargoyle to be precise.

Have you ever walked under the eaves of a really old church? Ever looked up at a gargoyle and asked "Is that creepy little thing watching me?"

Well, some of them are. They're quite harmless, well most of them, and they are great illusionists, they can appear like worn little statues of monsters, blending in with the aged stones. They don't do any harm, they just like to watch the world go by, and they're terrific gossips. There are about three of them flying around the school grounds at any one time, and to date no one ever noticed that they rarely appeared in the same place twice.

Except me.

This one's name was Jeremiah (his real name is both difficult to spell and impossible for a human to pronounce, so he always insisted I call him Jeremiah). He was about three feet tall with grey skin, there were four small, bone coloured horns protruding from his skull above his orange eyes. Two large, bat-like wings protruded from his shoulders, exiting through two neat holes in what appeared to be a Savile Row hand-tailored suit.

Jeremiah is my friend, and he loves to show off. He's a great one for an "I know something you don't know", and his information is always bang on the money. He's helped me to avoid having my head forcefully introduced to a toilet on more than one occasion.

"Yes, but he has a good excuse, this time," I replied as the dapper little creature dropped down into the little cubby I was hiding in. He pulled a white handkerchief from his pocket and dusted off a small step before sitting on it gingerly.

"Doesn't he always?" he countered, a sardonic look on his face.

This wasn't the first time we'd discussed my brother, or my perennial inability to just leave him to it. The gargoyle does not approve of my coddling him. Can't say I really like it much either, but if anything ever happened to the half-wit, it would upset my mother.

"He's working hard tonight, writing an essay," I replied, picking a chocolate bar out of my bag and offering it to him, "I'm just helping to get a couple of the little things off his plate while he's dealing with the big stuff."

Jeremiah stared at the chocolate with naked desire. Gargoyles have something of a sweet tooth, and Jeremiah's was worse than most. He took it from me as fast as decorum would allow, offering me a muttered thank-you before pulling the wrapper off and swallowing it in a couple of bites.

"You quite sure about that?" he asked finally, using his hanky to wipe a small spot of chocolate from the corner of his mouth.

"About what?" I asked, turning back Romeo's misadventures in romance.

"That he's actually working."

I sagged in my spot, placing the pen lid carefully over the nib and putting it down. The smug little creature just stared at me with an exaggerated, long-suffering, look on his face.

"What's he done now?" I asked, already feeling the exasperation growing.

Jeremiah explained. I closed my eyes and smacked my head gently off a nearby slate.

The son-of-a-bitch did it to me again!

Chapter 3

This was, in fact, far the first time he'd sold me a bill of goods. It's always the same: he has a pressing commitment preventing him from doing a certain piece or pieces of work, would I please help? And every time I do, it turns out that his pressing commitment was at a party or game or even just sleeping.

Tonight it was a party. Jeremiah told me where.

Any other day, I'd just do the work and yell at him the next day, but tonight I was just mad enough to actually go down there and let him have it.

I should explain some things. Windward Academy is a boarding school. It has very strict rules about curfew (though they are not exactly harsh, and the older students don't really have a lights-out time at all, it's just a matter of location, really), but those rules are enforced by prefects, and those prefects can be bought, usually with an invitation to the next party, when they're off duty. Thus, as long as the gathering doesn't cause true havoc, and nobody gets pregnant, the teachers turn a blind eye, as they neither want to have to discipline the kids that actually frequent the parties, much less their prefects.

Normally they restrict their high jinks to weekends, but tonight there was a birthday or something; one of the older kids, the school's rugby captain I believe, I didn't (and still don't) keep track of that crap.

The school is a wide complex bordered on one side by fields, a second by farmland and the others by woodland containing a wide river and several small lakes. It's actually quite idyllic. This idiocy was taking place in the woods.

It was already dark when I made my way towards the party. I called the shadows to me, just like opening a door in my mind. It's the easiest magic in the world to me, and just that simple act of linking made the world appear in greys and whites as I saw the darkness wrapped around everything. I could feel it surrounding me, almost like a warm blanket. It had taken me a very long time to get used to that, and to reconcile it with the crippling terror that used to come from the dark.

I heard loud music and turned towards it, following the happy sounds. I was going to give Desmond such a mouthful. I really was sick of him lying to me. For heaven's sake, twins are not supposed to pull this shit on each other (yes, I'm aware of the hypocrisy, shut up).

There was a crowd of them, maybe thirty or forty. The light gave them colour in my eyes, and I saw our navy uniforms mixed in with the more conservative grey clothing worn by St James's College, a Catholic school a couple of miles away.

And then I spotted Des, dancing with his girlfriend. I took a deliberate step towards him, a torrent of abuse ready to hurl his way, but then they turned. And I saw that he was smiling. I opened my mind a little, creating a link to his. And I stopped. He was happy. I saw that he wanted to freeze that moment, make it last forever. I envied him his simple happiness, the joy he felt. Mad as I was, I didn't want to be the guy who ruined that for my brother.

With a muttered curse at my own weakness, I turned away, thinking that I'd yell at him tomorrow, and that's when I saw the creature.

I took a double take, not sure what I was seeing. For a second there, I was sure I was seeing things. And then it looked at me, and I nearly crapped myself.

It was a good eight feet tall, wrapped in a deep grey energy, merged with the shadows. Its eyes were glowing, a dark red, almost purple, two pinpricks that were barely visible. It was like it was almost made of darkness, but it wasn't part of *my* shadows. It scared the hell out of me.

I almost ran there and then.

And then it winked at me, which stopped me in my tracks in simple shock. Before I could digest that, it turned its head slowly to look towards the fire. At my brother. It looked back at me for a second, and I swear I saw the shadow creature's face shift into a smile before it leapt forward, heading straight for Desmond. I called my shadows, almost in a panic.

My commands weren't complex, the best translation would be *'Kill it!'*, more or less, focussing the darkness on the figure as it charged. The shadows became barbed and spiked, great waves of darkness lurching after the creature. They wrapped around it and... slid off.

I tried again, making the darkness sharper, heavier. But my shadows couldn't get a grip on it. It burst through the constructs, not even slowed by my attack.

It started roaring in triumph, its eyes locked onto my brother. The sound was awful, pure predatory glee. It was going to kill Des, I was certain of that fact. And I panicked, drawing in energy from all around me, focusing it into a point around the outstretched fingers of my right hand. It was crude and dangerous, and I felt a stray burst of energy leech out of the spell I was casting to scorch the back of my hand.

I hissed in pain and refocused, using a valuable half-second to stabilise the spell's shape. The other kids were looking around them in terror, searching for the source of the sound. Some saw it in the flickering firelight and screamed. Des and Belle saw it too. In that second, neither of them could manage so much as a cantrip to defend themselves. They weren't battle mages in training right then, they were just kids, standing in a dark forest, waiting for the monster to come get them.

The creature bunched its legs and leapt.

I finished my spell, just in the barest nick of time. The energy gathered at the tips of my right index and middle fingers, blue, green, white and orange light flickered and glowed brightly, lighting up the forest in a kaleidoscope of wasted energy from my improperly built spell.

I pointed, prayed for my aim to be accurate, and released the attack.

It was clumsy, the spell imperfect, born of panic and terror. It was a hodgepodge, an unbalanced mix of every energy type within easy reach of me, thermal, kinetic, chemical, static, even a little atomic and gravitational, all wrapped up and condensed into a single lance of power.

The energy crossed the distance between me and the creature in less than the blink of an eye. The image was seared into my mind; the creature looked like it was crouched in mid-air, its long, barbed claws reaching out to claw my brother's heart out in what would have been a single rending strike. Everything seemed to slow for me as the lance seared for the creature and struck it below the ribcage. In a flash of light and a crack of power, everything between the monster's sternum and pelvis exploded into a shower of black flesh and smoke.

The creature's remaining pieces fell to the ground, thrown away from the crowd by the force of the spell (not that such a hodgepodged mess can really be described as a spell, but I digress). Des and Belle looked at the still-twitching remains in shock, while I fell to the ground, a massive headache smacking me between the eyes as my nose started bleeding. The shadows fell away from me, and I was left in the darkness, surrounded by the terrible black.

Magical feedback from a crude spell, and it serves me right. I'd tried to shove too much energy of too many different types into a single construct that wasn't designed to handle them. Magic is essentially simple. A magician uses the store of pure magic inside him to create the framework of a spell with his imagination and willpower, a shell of intent and will into which he draws the energy that will generate the required effect. It's all about balance and concentration, making and breaking links and channelling energy. If you do it right, and you're skilful enough, you can do anything you can imagine, from conjuring a witchlight to re-growing a limb (just for example).

But if you do it *wrong*, or you lose control of what you're doing at the wrong moment, then you can quite easily kill yourself with the uncontrolled energy. With the sheer unbalanced panic I was working from, it was a miracle that I still had a head.

I groaned at the pain, and then the back of my hand seemed to catch fire as the feedback burn made its presence known, I pulled it closer to me, gritting my teeth against a very unmanly sound of distress, but being careful not to touch it.

The crowd was starting to recover their wits, and now they were looking for the thing that had stopped the beast. It wasn't long before they'd be looking my way. I shoved myself to my feet, fighting off a wave of dizziness and nausea and walked back the way I'd come, shoving a paper hanky to my nose to stem the sudden bleeding.

I was just in time, as Des ran into the woods, and ball of bright light held in his hand, Belle just behind him, ice coating her hands. The woods lit up, and I was just able to dart behind a bush before the light found me.

"You see anything?" Des asked.

"No, you?" Belle replied looking around.

Thank God neither of them ever took the trouble to learn Mage-sight, or they'd have seen my life force cowering behind the shrubbery, and this was no time to out myself as a magician.

I allowed the barest trickle of magic to flow, and my headache intensified horribly, but I managed to cast my own mage-sight (which I *had* bothered to learn) and looked around carefully, past Des and Belle, through the party and into the woods around us, sifting through everything, searching for anything else that could hurt someone.

I saw nothing, so I thought it would be alright to leave. Not that I could have done much more to help in my current state. I shut down the sight, and my headache pain went down several notches. I moved quietly into a gully and scuttled along it until I felt that I was firmly out of sight. I climbed out again and started heading back towards the school, falling over several times.

I thought of calling a light, or my shadows back, but my headache was a throbbing warning about what would happen to me if I didn't recover first, so I stumbled through the dark, finally breaking through the tree line, burnt, muddy and sore.

I made a beeline for my House, only wanting to lie down and sleep (or just die, whichever got rid of the headache quicker). Much to my annoyance, my room was three floors up in Kimmel House (named after some past worthy of the school), which is home to about eighty other boys, centrally located, near the dining hall and chapel, which I found convenient. I stumbled through the corridors, moving around the back of the TV room, which was still half full, even at quarter to eleven. The prefect who should have emptied the place of juniors an hour ago was sitting in the front row watching TV with the rest. Idiot. Though it did make my coming in late easier to conceal.

I dragged myself up the stairs, unlocked my door and fell into bed fully clothed, too tired to change and too sore to care about dirt. My throbbing head stopped me from sleeping for a little while, but eventually exhaustion won out and I fell asleep, the image of two purple eyes floating in front of me, following me into my dreams.

Chapter 4

"Matty! Matty! Wake up! You won't believe what happened!"

I was shaken into wakefulness after what felt like ten minutes of sleep. Sometimes, I swear, it's as if my brother is trying to kill me. My head felt like there was a demented drummer pounding at the inside of my skull with a pickaxe, and my brother's grating voice wasn't improving the sensation.

"What is it?" I asked groggily, sitting up as gently as I could. My clock said three am, what had taken him so long? Not that I was complaining, any sleep was precious sleep.

He filled me in on the story from his side. I knew it all right up until I left, which was naturally the point at which he noticed that I wasn't looking well.

"Matty, what happened?" he said, lurching towards me, looking me over none too gently. Knew I should have showered.

"Nothing important," I replied, noticing that the back of my right hand was now covered in a delightful collection of yellow blisters, surrounded by a nice streak of red skin. Lovely. Unfortunately, Des noticed too.

"We've got to get you to the matron, now!" he said, panicking a little.

For all my brother's faults, and they are plentiful, he does put family first.

"In the morning," I replied, "finish your story."

I stood and went to the sink, running my hand under the cold water before washing the blood off my nose and face.

"Well, after the *thing* just exploded, Belle and I went looking for the guy who saved us, and we couldn't find a thing. I was gonna come back and ask if you knew what it was, you always retain more of those books than I do, but Belle had called the rozzers, and they'd told us all to stay put until they arrived. Like, ten cars showed up, and one of those black vans, you know, mage coppers."

I did know about them. They were one of the reasons I kept my powers under wraps. They just reminded me too much of storm troopers (Nazi, not Star Wars) for me to be really comfortable with them knowing about me, or Des for that matter, I'd warned him when he started duelling that he'd eventually draw their attention, but he hadn't listened.

"They called the school and Mister Kenilworth came down along with three other teachers. They rounded us up, and then the police took our statements one by one; the mage cops spoke to Belle and me."

"Belle and I," I corrected in an automatic gesture. I'd been doing that since we were ten, it still hadn't penetrated his stone-hard skull.

"Anyway, they became much more friendly when they realised that neither of us had used any magic, and they went nuts when they saw the creature, or what was left of it. Everyone conjured fireballs and shields and started spreading out. I was listening in when they found a "hotspot", where they think the mage who saved us was standing. They said that the spell was clumsy, but wicked strong, they found a ring of ice and dead plants where all the heat and energy had just been leeched out."

"They have any idea who it was?" I asked as casually as I could, my burnt hand shaking a little.

"No, but they said that the creature should have been nigh-indestructible, and the guy who killed it got lucky to a stupid degree. That thing should have gutted us!"

"So, no idea who saved your lives?"

"None, but they found tracks leading from the ice-circle thing up to the school, and they're coming back tomorrow to canvas the students. They want to ask this guy some questions."

"They think it's a student?" I asked.

He nodded, "From the shoe size."

"You heard a lot," I said, trying to slow my heart rate , while thinking through what steps I needed to take to conceal myself. It's not like I was an obvious person of interest or anything, but there were some ways to conceal magic that I could use if I had to.

"And just what were you doing in the woods when you should have been writing an essay?" I asked, as an aside. I just had to get that in there.

Des' eyes went wide as he realised he'd just confessed to promise-breaking. He got to his feet, spluttering and muttering as he tried to form a coherent excuse.

I smiled tiredly, letting him off the hook. I hugged my brother tight, and he returned the gesture.

"I'm just glad you're safe, Des," I said, really meaning it. I don't know what I'd have done if something had happened to him.

"So you're not mad?" he asked, a little timidly.

"You're off the hook this time. Near death experiences get you a pass."

He sniggered before turning serious.

"When they come back tomorrow, will you come with me? To the interview, I mean? I don't like those guys."

"Of course I will," I said, patting his arm.

We chatted for a while longer before he started yawning and headed off to his room. I showered quickly and changed into pyjamas, now that I had recovered some energy, before tumbling back into bed for a few more hours' desperately needed sleep. I was out like a light, and this time I didn't see the purple eyes, for which I was very grateful.

Chapter 5

My alarm woke me three hours later at 7:30. My head was much better, though my hand was still painful enough for me to avoid moving it too much. I dressed in a striped shirt, house tie (red and white stripe), charcoal trousers, blue v-neck sweater and school blazer. I looked out the window as I got ready, seeing a light drizzle splattering on everything. England in February; the occasional warm night aside, the drizzle was likely as good as it was going to get for a while.

Des was at my door fifteen minutes later, dressed much the same as I was, though his tie was rarely done properly. I fixed it before leading the way to the dining hall, knowing that the damn thing would be flying at its usual socially acceptable half mast before we were three steps from the house's front door.

"You see the matron yet?" Des asked, gesturing at my hand.

"It's fine," I replied, not wanting attention drawn to it

"You sure? It looks painful."

"It is, but I don't want that ham-fisted troglodyte poking it with a tongue depressor before roughly applying some sort of foul-smelling crap that'll sting like hell and end up making it worse."

"Honestly Matty, one time she messed up cleaning out a cut and you hold it against her for life?"

"She used pure ethanol on a deep cut that didn't even have any dirt in it," I replied. That had bloody hurt, and since then I simply went without medical care. That bitch was a frigging monster.

"Fine, fine," he said, knowing he was losing. We'd had this conversation before.

A gaggle of chattering girls wondered past, heading in the opposite direction, dressed for PE. The outfits on some were... interestingly fitted, shall we say.

Des' eyes followed them, raising some giggles from the group who waved coquettishly at him. He waved back, not looking where he was going, tripped, and in his flailing caused me to stumble and fall flat on my face, knocking the wind out of me.

"Oh crap! Sorry, Matty!" he said, moving to help me up.

"You suck," I replied without heat, allowing myself to be hauled up to the giggles of the girls, who'd stopped to watch the show. He brushed me off, and we carried on, me with a red face and him with a wide grin.

"You have a girlfriend," I reminded him as I shook off a slight limp.

"Doesn't mean I don't like the attention," he said, elbowing me in the side and making me jump.

"Just remember that she knows magic, and she's faster than you," I said.

He expression turned sour.

"I hadn't thought of that," he said.

That should be his bloody motto. Maybe I should pop an Asimov into *her* head, just in case she ever catches Des leering...

We got to the dining hall, filled our trays from the canteen and sat at one of the fourth year tables. The room was about half full, and my group was already there. I say group, there are just the three of us, all in the chess club, debate team, maths challenge and gamers' club. Bill was about my height, brown haired and skinny, always willing to smile. He loved a dirty joke and had a repertoire that would make a sailor blush.

Cathy was pretty and sweet, with delicate features and short, blonde, curly hair; but she was quiet. She'd talk to me and Bill, but not many others. She was also the only person I knew who could actually beat me at chess from time to time. She also had a wicked crush on my brother, something which annoyed me rather more than it really should have.

Naturally Des' social group was a little further up the school hierarchy, but he still ate with me, and thus my friends, from time to time.

Bill and Cathy were chatting about movies, the staple of our normal morning conversation, and Cathy stopped mid-sentence as she saw us coming, culminating in a strangled squeak that made Bill go wide-eyed with worry for a second before he turned around, saw us and rolled his eyes.

"Morning Gravestones!" he said with his customary morning cheer (the bastard). Our last name is Graves, so naturally a fellow with Bill's sense of humour would come up with something like that.

"Bill, we've talked about excessive morning enthusiasm," I said with a warning glare.

"Sorry. Shit! What happened to your hand?" he asked as I sat down.

Cathy took a look, too, and went wide eyed looking at the damage. She reached out tentatively and pulled my hand forward so she could to see, squinting through her heavy glasses to get a good look.

"Spilled some hot water, wasn't paying attention," I answered.

Cathy raised a quizzical eyebrow, looking at the burn pattern, but said nothing. It would take a few minutes in Des' company before she could speak again without squeaking.

I started eating my breakfast, idly picking at the scrambled eggs while the conversation picked up around me. What with the headache and the adrenaline, I hadn't really had a chance to just sit and think things through. There was no getting around the fact that something had come after my brother. The question was, did it come on its own, or was it sent? Was it attacking at a moment of opportunity, or had it planned to attack then?

I supposed that It could have been after Belle, but I didn't think so. The way the thing looked at me was very deliberate, and the way it had jumped hadn't left much doubt as to its target. But that left the question: Why?

Why would anyone or anything go after Desmond? He was essentially harmless, as good natured as a person can get.

He talks a good game in the duelling ring, but he'd never actually hurt anyone or anything, not on purpose. So why?

I needed more information. I needed to find out just what the creature was, and I couldn't do that at Windward. The school library only had a few magical texts, and most of the books Desmond had were rather restricted in what they told us, it was all government approved stuff, after all.

I needed more a more varied selection, and I knew where to get them, it was just a matter of getting away, which might take a while.

I suppose I could have just left things to the authorities, but what are the chances of them telling me anything useful? I wanted to *know* what was going on, and how to make sure this didn't happen again. God, what if I hadn't been there?

But, before I do any snooping, first things first; a day of schooling. What fun.

The school was abuzz with rumours about what had happened. There was talk, speculation, gossip (oh, the gossip...). Everyone wanted to know who the mysterious saviour was. You'd really think that they'd have better things to talk about.

Physics followed Chemistry and then Maths before the morning break. I was on the way to my room for some ibuprophen (I have a small medical kit and a modest collection of medication) as my hand had been killing me all day. It made writing a real chore and was a constant distraction. I'd normally cast a small healing charm in a situation like this, but I was still a little wary after last night, what with the magic police around. Who knows what they can see if they're looking?

I was almost there when I got a text. I'd had the phone on since breakfast so that Des could tell me when he was about to be interviewed.

Desmond> NOW, Kenilworth's office.

Me> On my way, say nothing before I get there.

I muted the phone and stuffed it in my pocket, jogging across the school to the headmaster's office. It was located on the second floor of the main building. It had been my main ambition in that school *not* to end up there.

I arrived to find a man in a black suit standing guard at the door. He put up a hand as I approached, then took a double take, no doubt as he recognised my face as being already inside the room. Our eyes and faces are distinctive enough that sometimes the differences don't register as much as they should.

"The headmaster's busy," he said abruptly.

"I know; I'm here to see my brother."

He relaxed slightly, but held his ground.

"He's being interviewed."

"Not without me present he isn't," I said, pulling my phone from my pocket, "I have my family's lawyer on speed-dial. If you are interrogating my brother without a family member present, or if you deny my request to see him immediately, I will call, and bad, press-related things will begin to happen."

"Now look here, you little-"

"I'm also recording our conversation."

His mouth slammed shut with an audible clack. He glared at me, his cheek twitching slightly as he thought it through for a moment.

"Wait here," he said finally before turning around and walking through the door, closing it behind him with a none too gentle thud.

My heart was pounding already, I wasn't cut out for this crap. I liked the quiet life, reading and playing chess, maybe getting an eyeful of a tightly-clothed girl from the gymnastics team from time to time; you know, the simple pleasures. Dealing with the government is just not for me.

The door opened again and a young woman appeared.

"Mister Graves? Won't you come in?" she said pleasantly. The guard came out, glaring at me all the way. I tried to conceal a grin as I walked past him.

The headmaster's office was quite impressive, a good fifteen steps from wall to wall, another ten wide, it occupied the space on the floor above as well, every wall lined with books. His desk was wide and impressive, a dark wood bound by gold with a leather-inlaid top. Everything was neat and precisely placed, from the monitor on the table to the exact angle of the other pieces of furniture.

There were three other people in the room apart from myself and Des. There was Mister Kenilworth, naturally, he'd be acting as an advocate-slash-guardian. He would almost certainly have called our parents to make sure that this was alright. Naturally they didn't bother to give me a heads-up. Mister Kenilworth was tall and thin, greying at the temples, dressed in a tweed suit with a chequered blue and white tie. He was a reasonable man, fair and kind. I could trust him to look out for Des, but not so much that I wouldn't be doing the job myself.

There was an older man sitting on the sofa opposite Des, who had a smaller sofa all to himself. The man looked strong, his blue eyes were bright and intelligent; he looked like he was in his late forties, his hair a dark grey, white at the temples. He wore a tailored suit not dissimilar to the ones Jeremiah the Gargoyle likes. He looked intelligent, which was worrying, I'd prefer an idiot I could manipulate.

The woman was younger, closer to my age than his, but still a little older, maybe early twenties. She was attractive, wearing a sympathetic look on her face. Her eyes were brown and warm, she looked like someone who preferred to smile. I liked her immediately. It helped that she wore a low-cut blouse. If I were a suspicious fellow, I might guess that her outfit and demeanour were meant to be disarming, particularly to the male of the species.

The man stood, offering his hand and I shook it.

"Bernhardt Kraab," he said, "this is my colleague Vanessa Knowles. I'm told that you wish to be present during your brother's statement. Normally we don't allow that sort of thing but he says he won't talk without you here."

"My brother was simply wanting a familiar face around while he answered questions, someone to help him remember the details of what happened," I said.

"But you weren't there?" Vanessa asked, taking a seat next to Kraab.

"No, but Des told me all about it soon after, so I may be able to help clarify some of his memories."

"Is that true? Does Mathew need to do your talking for you, Desmond?" Vanessa asked, turning her attention to him.

I was about to answer when I felt the spell. She was gathering it, it was subtle, gentle. Almost certainly mind magic if I was any judge (or Telepathy, if you prefer). She was focussed on Des, I could feel the spell coalesce, she was ready to cast.

Some mages are more sensitive than others to magic used around them. I seem to have a pretty low threshold for magical detection; it doesn't take more than a whisper for me to notice.

I moved my hand closer to Des, allowing the barest flicker of energy to travel between us, bolstering his mind's defences with a simple shield. She released the spell, and it flew invisibly across the room, impacting the shield and fizzing out without latching on.

No one noticed a thing, though Vanessa looked surprised when Des remained as rational as ever. I decided it was time to rattle the cage a little.

"Ms. Knowles, did you just attempt to hex my brother?" I asked, my voice calm and low.

"What?" Vanessa and Desmond asked simultaneously, almost identical looks of horror passing over their features, though naturally the motivations were different.

"That's quite the accusation, young man," Kraab said, getting to his feet, "I hope you can back it up."

"Of course I can't," I replied, staying seated, "but I've watched my brother practice magic for more than a decade, and I know the look, the posture and the inflections that come from someone casting a spell. I can't stop you from doing so, or prove that she did, but I wanted you to know right out of the gate that I saw that, and if you wish this interview to continue, then I must insist that you not attempt anything similar again."

I think my reasonable tone took the wind out of their sails a little bit.

Kraab looked over at Vanessa and he gestured at her to sit back down. Des looked livid, but he followed my lead.

"That's quite the eye you have there, young man, and you've never manifested any magical ability?" Kraab asked.

"Afraid not," I lied carefully, keeping a wary eye on both of the interrogators.

"Unusual. Well, let's press on then," Kraab said, pulling a folder from a black leather briefcase and setting it on his lap, as if I hadn't just caught them attempting to commit anything from a misdemeanour all the way up to a crime, depending on the nature of the attempted hex.

"We have examined the testimony of the five primary witnesses, our mages have examined the scene, and we are comfortable concluding that the perpetrator was indeed after you, Mister Graves. At the moment, however, we are unable to determine why this is the case because what is left of the creature barely fills a pedal bin bag."

He set the folder down on the coffee table between us and pulled out a picture of the creature. It was grainy and fuzzy, but the overall shape looked all too familiar. In death the creature looked vaguely human, though the features were elongated and its skin was jet black; a gaping mouth lay open, displaying three rows of shark-like teeth, also black. The eyes were black, now, devoid of that purple energy, for which I was glad.

"Would you know anything about that, Desmond?" Kraab asked.

"About what?" he asked, transfixed by the pictures.

"About how the creature was stopped, who did it, and why they would go to so much effort to protect you?"

"I have no idea," he answered.

"Please think, has anyone used magic to protect you in the past?"

"No, but then I've never been in danger before."

Not true, but what he doesn't know can't get me into trouble.

"Nothing at all?" Vanessa asked.

"No, nothing," Des replied, getting frustrated now.

"Would you mind if my colleague took a quick look at you?" Kraab asked.

"For what?" I asked, alarm bells going off in my head.

"Magical signatures," Vanessa answered, "if he's ever used magic to help or protect you, there may be a trace of it in your aura or on your body, it will help us to get a feel for the guy, so we can find him."

"Out of the question," I said immediately, "you already tried to mess with his head once-"

"Alright, I'll do it," Des interrupted.

"Des, that's not a good idea," I said quickly.

"Look, this guy saved my life; don't you want to know why? Or what he was doing there in the middle of the night?"

"An old phrase about gift horses springs to mind," I said sardonically, fear tightening in my gut.

"Let's get it over with," Des said, leaning forward.

What could I say? If I protested any more I might arouse suspicion, there might be a chance that I can deny everything later, as long as I stayed calm.

Vanessa stood up and then knelt down in front of Des, I stood out of the way while she focussed. I saw her gather a sizable chunk of energy into a complex spell, focussed on her eyes and mind. She looked at Desmond, focussing hard, and then gasped.

"My God," she said.

Uh oh.

Chapter 6

"What is it?" Kraab asked, getting up to stand next to her.

"The subject's power is everywhere, I see the remnants of dozens of enchantments and charms, and one complex spell still buried deep in his mind. Whoever he is, this guy's been around Desmond for years."

"What kind of spells?" Des asked, terror filling his voice. Oh boy...

"Healing charms, luck charms, protection spells, memory enhancements. Someone has been looking out for you, keeping you safe and healthy."

She hissed, looking at his chest. She waved her hands, almost like you would to clear condensation from a window.

"He's saved your life before. There's evidence of someone using some serious magic to close a chest wound. Damn, he used a life-link spell, must have nearly killed him too, judging by the depth of the signature."

I tried not to swallow unnaturally loudly. My twit of a brother had fallen into a gorge about two years ago, and when he landed, he'd gotten himself impaled on a hidden fence post. I'd had to use my own life force to keep him alive while I tried desperately to fix what was wrong using basic first aid magic never meant for that.

I'd nearly died too, and truth be told I'd never fully recovered. Ever since, I'd been slower, more easily tired, got sick easier. Naturally Desmond was just fine, better than new, the lucky bastard. He didn't remember anything about it, he thought he'd had a lucky escape, just got knocked out and woke up with a bit of a headache and his now sickly brother crouching next to him. He thought I'd had a panic attack.

"I don't remember anything like that," Desmond said.

"Well there's an active spell in your mind, but... no, it's not it's not in memory, it's in motion. God, it's a variation of Kerkoff's protective hex!"

Ha! No it isn't, Kerkoff's is completely different you semi-competent, nosy, besom. Oh, how I wanted to say that, but of course I couldn't, though it would almost be worth the trouble it would bring down on my head.

"A variation?" Kraab asked.

She peered into Des' mind.

"No, not Kerkoff's," she said after a minute's squinting. Damn, I hate it when people I'm trying to dodge turn out to be clever. "This is something else. The subject has implanted a pair of commands, *don't harm* and *don't allow harm to come to.*"

"Who, Agent Knowles?" Kraab was agitated now.

"Wait a minute," I said, "Agent? Agent of what?"

"Not now," Kraab barked.

"I can't tell," she said, answering his question, "the activation part of the hex is bound up in sensory input and decision making, it's too fragmented to reverse engineer the trigger."

Ha, ha. Not that it was intentional, but still a happy outcome for yours truly.

"Can you remove it?" Kraab asked.

"Maybe, but it'll take hours for me to prepare for that, the spell's really in there and very well designed, subtle enough to be slippery."

Well, I don't like to brag...

"Please," Desmond said, "you've got to get it out of me, it's not right."

Oh, for heaven's sake, what a baby.

"I'll prepare, and we'll do it after the rest of our interviews, alright?" she said, placing a gentle hand on Desmond's arm.

He nodded, his lower lip wobbling a little.

"Agent of what?" I asked again while they were distracted.

Kraab turned to look at me with a glare.

"The SCA," he said.

I swallowed hard, there was no disguising it that time. It felt like the bottom had dropped out of my stomach.

In Britain there are three agencies that police magicians. There's the Super-normal branch of the police service, which is essentially people like Mister Koenig, trained to handle low level problems and misdemeanours, coupled with a few mages here and there against any rapidly evolving problems. The second is the Conclave, which is more of a judiciary, really, handling your more serious magic crime. They have so-called 'hunter teams' that deal with murders, assaults, grand thefts and the like.

Then there's the SCA. The Supernatural Crime Authority. They handle magical threats to national security and beyond. Essentially, they're MI-5 with Sorcerers. They turn up when something needs turning to ash. If I had to guess, the lads that turned up last night were Conclave. And they took one look at that creature and bumped it several notches up the ladder.

The SCA is not known for dealing with mage-related problems peacefully. Generally they blast first and try to ask the questions only if the remains are large enough for a scrying. I didn't want my brother anywhere near these people.

"Desmond, we're leaving," I said, getting to my feet and backing away. Desmond got up too, and I put him behind me. I shoved him towards the door.

"I see you've heard of us," Kraab said sadly. Vanessa was also on her feet, and took a step towards us. No doubt meant to placate us, the gesture seemed quite sinister now that I knew who they were.

"Mister Kenilworth, were you aware of this?" I asked our headmaster, trying to keep the naked fear out my voice.

"Well, the government, you see, they were quite insistent on the subject, little I could do, you know..."

"My brother has committed no crimes, and he will not be alone with any of you. He refuses consent now, in front of witnesses, to be taken to any facility outside of this school. Don't you?"

"Um," said Des, still confused and scared.

"Close enough, off we go, Des," I said, shimmying him out of the door.

"Mister Graves?" Kraab said as we left.

"Which one?" I asked.

"You. Your brother is not who we're looking for. We mean him no harm, don't let our reputation for efficiency block him from what's best for him."

"Your reputation is for bloodshed, Agent Kraab. He's answered your questions as best he can. Do not approach him again."

I slammed the door behind me and almost had to drag Des out of there. The guard looked dumbstruck for a moment there (that seemed to be his default), but let us pass. We jogged down the stairs, Desmond's mouth opening and closing rapidly as his brain tried to get into gear and stalled, but he followed me anyway.

This was definitely not good. The country's premier witch hunters were looking for me. And they were trying to use my brother to do it. Maybe I should just come clean? After all I hadn't done anything illegal, well except for the Asimov, and some other stuff that doesn't need mentioning, but that was explicable-ish.

Which reminds me...

I focussed, crafting a little spell which I dropped into Desmond's mind. The spell's tendrils found my Asimov's attachment points and pulled it free, the spell fell apart and drifted away. That, at least, should mean that they didn't need to go rooting around in his head, they're be no excuse for th-

There was a bang of displaced air and we fell to the ground in the resulting blast. Kraab appeared out of nowhere, his form shimmering with energy, his hands lit up with harsh blue-white light, eyes casting around for threats.

"Nobody move!" he bellowed.

Well... that's not what you want.

Chapter 7

We stayed on the ground, it seemed the only sensible thing to do. I had an arm over my brother and so was interposed between him and the angry mage (who had just proven himself a Sorcerer, teleportation isn't something a Wizard can manage on the fly).

"Where is he?" Kraab asked.

Oh, thank God, he still doesn't know it's me.

"Where's who?" I asked.

"The mage! The one who just removed your brother's obedience hex! Knowles just felt him cast the counter-spell."

"He removed it?" Des asked, feeling his head. I shook my head in exasperation. Wants to be a battle mage, can't respond to unexpected situations. He'll go far...

"There's no one here but us, Mister Kraab," I said, still keeping myself between my brother and harm (and a couple of defensive spells I know held ready in my mind, though who knew what use they'd be against a fully trained Sorcerer?).

"You see him?" Vanessa had come skittering down the stairs, electricity coiled around her right hand as she turned the corner.

"Nothing," Kraab said, dropping his shield and recycling his attack spells.

I moved slowly, getting Desmond to his feet and leading him away. I said nothing, but I had an all-new respect for the SCA, and the firepower at their command. I wasn't tangling with them. I got Des moving, keeping them in sight in case they did something esle.

Vanessa was looking at me strangely, I didn't like it. Kraab moved towards us, offering his apologies for the scare. I simply nodded and kept Desmond moving. We exited the building and moved into the fresh air, leaving the dangerous pair behind us. I led the way to the square, sitting down on one of the wooden benches. I started shaking. Des seemed to be fine though, but then, what did he have to be afraid of?

So, no more magic for me for a while, at least until these... people were gone. Until today I only had the barest idea that a mage could be tracked by their magical signature. Could have lived without that knowledge if I'm honest. Thank goodness my file says I'm non-magical, or Mulder and Scully might have taken a closer look at me, and the jig would have been thoroughly up.

My heart was pounding and I was sweating like I'd run a marathon. Des seemed fine, almost completely recovered.

"Well, at least I'm not being mind controlled anymore," he said.

"There is that," I replied, sitting upright, "you alright?"

"Yeah. It's weird, but I wasn't surprised. I can't explain it, it's like I already knew that there was someone looking out for me. Is that strange?"

"You're a magician, it would be strange if you didn't know."

"And you never spotted anyone?"

"I think that I'd have noticed something like that."

Des laughed, patted my back and got up.

"I have Art next, see you later?"

"Yeah," I replied, dragging myself up as well. He smiled again and wandered off. I decided that I could comfortably miss the last few minutes of English Literature and stayed where I was, taking a seat on the grass under the oak that grows in the centre of the square.

I closed my eyes for a minute.

Chapter 8

And woke up ninety minutes later. I swore and ran for
the dining hall. I arrived as they were putting out the last tray
of stew. I took a seat at one of the quiet tables. I was still
sleepy, and ate almost mechanically. I caught a few snippets of
conversation, everyone was talking about Des and the SCA,
and that information could only have come from one place. He
just can't keep his trap shut, always with the attention.

"...he's got a war-mage bodyguard..."

"...protecting him for years..."

"...guardian angel..."

"...they say he's right here in school..."

"...wish I could do magic..."

"...who could it be?"

Stuff like that, it makes you nuts.

I finished my lunch and made my way towards Kimmel,
thinking to have a nap before chess club. I was nearly
recovered from my stupidity the previous night, but I needed a
little more rest before I'd be back to my normal self.

I unlocked the door to my room, dropped my book bag
on the chair and flopped down on top of the duvet. I almost
used a little magic to shut the curtains before I remembered
what might well happen, and I did it my damn self.

I set my alarm and closed my eyes.

I swear I was asleep for five seconds before someone
knocked on my bloody door. I groaned and rolled over, hoping
they'd go away. Of course they didn't. The door clicked open.

"Mathew? You in here?" Cathy asked.

Now this was unusual, and just plain odd. It was strongly
frowned upon for a member of the opposite sex to come into
the other's houses (though this rule was more for the boys). I
can count on one hand the number of times Cathy's been in
this building, this making three.

"Cathy?" I asked, still foggy in the head department.

"I heard the rumours; your brother has a mysterious
benefactor?"

"Evidently," I said, rubbing my face. I sat up and she sat down on a comfortable chair. "What have you heard?" I asked.

She recounted pretty accurately everything that had been said in the recent interview. It seemed my brother had been even more prolific with his blabbering than I thought.

"So, what do you think?" I asked, "Spotted anyone that fits the bill?"

She sat there for a second. She pulled her glasses off and cleaned them carefully before popping them back onto her cute nose.

"It's you," she said simply.

"What, now?" I asked, nearly panicking right on the spot.

"You're the one who's been keeping your brother safe," she clarified.

I tried to calm down, because now I was in a pickle. I had a memory spell that could deal with this, but I had no way to use it without bringing the law down on me.

"I'm not going to tell anyone," she said, she probably noticed something in my posture. Also my dumbstruck silence can't have been helping my case any.

"I'm not even a mage, Cath, how can I be the guy?"

That's right, stay on topic, keep to the story...

She raised an eyebrow quizzically.

"Brothers, twins, one has power, the other doesn't? Metaphysics still new subject, but this is unlikely. Differences in personality, disposition, certainly, magical alteration of physiology likely. Hair colour, eye colour, ergo magic in both, altering phenotype. Therefore unlikely you have no magic of your own. Also, your ability to teach your brother to use his own magic; success likely to be considerably less without practical understanding of magic. Brother poor student, yet passes GCSE. Lacking in sufficient skill to alter own memory, therefore outside influence. Person who most wants brother to succeed is you, likely conclusion drawn."

She rattled off these ideas and conclusions clinically, like she was making a presentation.

I was speechless for a moment. I told you that girl was smart. It would seem I wasn't as subtle as I thought, I said as much.

"Getting less careful as time went by with no discovery. Began using magic to help your friends. Easier to notice."

"How long have you known?" I asked.

"Suspected after my stutter went away. Supposed magic, speech therapy unsuccessful, thought it was your brother, hypothesis disproved after information received today. And he wouldn't have noticed my impediment. Wouldn't have cared enough to try fixing it. Wouldn't have the skill, if I'm right?"

I shrugged non-committally.

"So, someone close, someone wanting to remain undetected, using magic to aid *your* friends and *your* brother. Common denominator: you. Occam's Razor produced conclusion based on evidence."

She sat there, hands clasped together, waiting for my answer.

I didn't really know what to say to that.

Outed in one afternoon because my blasted brother couldn't keep his fat mouth shut! More than a decade of secrecy gone. You know, it's true: no good deed ever goes unpunished. I sighed, leaning back against the wall.

"No one else knows," I said finally, "and I would really rather keep it that way."

"It's true, then?"

I nodded once.

She came over to me and put her arms around my neck, hugging me tight. I was so surprised it was a second before I returned the gesture.

"Thank you," she whispered in my ear, "thank you so much. You don't know how much you changed my life."

That was the first time anyone had ever thanked me for magic I'd done.

Naturally Des picked that moment to turn up for a visit. The door snapped open.

"Matty, you won't believe what just ha-" he started before taking in the scene and stopping dead

Cathy jumped away, bright red from chin to ears.

"Sorry, bro. I'll come back later," he said with a smirk and a wink before darting out again.

"Oh, no, no, no!" Cathy said, pacing back and forth on the spot, "What's everyone going to think?"

Well, I didn't know what it would do for Cathy, but it couldn't do my reputation any harm. But that wasn't the pressing issue.

"Don't worry, Des may be cavalier with his own secrets, but he knows I like my privacy. He'll keep quiet."

"You think so?" she asked.

"I do, don't worry, your reputation is quite safe."

She nodded, checking her watch. "Wanna come for a walk?" she asked.

Hell no, I wanted to sleep, but she was being very decent about the whole "hidden-magic" thing, so I could hardly refuse.

It was a surprisingly cathartic walk. I told her things that I'd never told anyone else before, about what it had been like to learn magic in secret, to help my brother, try and keep him safe, all the while keeping my own abilities under wraps.

I told her about my first reasons for reluctance (afraid of the dark), and she laughed; the reason why I wasn't as physically formidable as my brother and she held my hand.

By the time we'd come back around to the school, approaching one of the free classrooms where the chess club meets, I felt a certain lightness that I hadn't really felt before.

"So, are you going to be a duellist one day, like your brother?" she asked.

"God, no. It's dangerous, and I've never really been one for battle magic."

"So what are you going to do? You can't hide forever."

"I can try," I replied.

She gave me a look that practically screamed "bullshit", but she had the decency to pretend to believe me.

"So what about the creature-thing? Any idea why it would go after Des?"

"Not a one, but I do have a source or two, I thought I'd poke around a little."

"Is that... wise?" she replied, looking worried.

"Probably not, but it's not like I can just wait for the SCA to kill their way to an answer, which they probably wouldn't share with me anyway."

"You will be careful, won't you Matty?" she asked in a small voice.

"Please, Cath, you're talking to one of England's premier cowards. I wouldn't even go *near* it if it were dangerous."

She sniggered, "Your statement would carry more weight if you weren't sporting a war wound," she said, gesturing at my blistered hand.

Well, she had a point.

Chapter 9

Securing an afternoon pass was... difficult. In the wake of the "incident" (as it had become known), the school was wary about security. I had to beg and plead for that thing, it was annoying.

Before I left, I checked in with Des, apparently that blasted Vanessa woman was now following him around as "security", yet another thing I had to worry about.

I hopped the only bus into town. Stonebridge was small as cities went, about the same size as Oxford, and similar in appearance, a blend of ancient with small blocks of encroaching modernisation, but the temperament of the city was very different. There was an edge to the place, a certain tension; something in the air. It was supposedly the most magical city in Britain, it had the largest population of magicians and other supernaturals, including a wide sampling of human-compatible creatures such as ghouls, vampires and weres of one stripe or another (all monitored by the government, so don't worry; nobody's getting eaten). I loved it; the place was so delightfully weird.

The bus stopped in the town centre, and I hopped off, pulling my hoodie over my head against the chill before heading off. I wore a simple blue raincoat over the hoodie, keeping my uniform shirt, trousers and tie (too lazy to change).

I made my way into the most ancient part of the old town, where the streets narrowed to three or four feet, no room for cars down there. The buildings were light stone, stained grey and black with age and soot, dark slate hanging over the alleys and paths. Arches and iron gates blocked private streets, and everything had an air of mystery. It's a warren of curiosity shops and arcana. Much of it is utter crap, but if you know what you're looking for, there are a few shops where a mage can do some discreet shopping.

Curios Books was my favourite of these. It's big for the location, stacked floor to ceiling with anything and everything from *'The Illiad'* to *'Alice's Adventures in Wonderland'*, all antiques of course. The shelves were wooden and beautifully carved, older than most of the books they held. Everything in that shop is special in some way, from the rugs on the floor (Persian, 400 years old), to the antique cash register (made in 1898 and still working in shillings) on the marble-top counter (allegedly once part of the Parthenon, according to the proprietress).

The owner was a friend of mine, just as special as the store she owned. Her name was Ming (so she says), but she's even more Caucasian than me and I'm one summer in the shade away from being albino-white. Her hair was also a bright strawberry-blonde, so make of that what you will. If she doesn't have what you're looking for, she can get it (for a relatively reasonable price).

The little copper bell above the door tinkled as I came in and Ming looked up from her ledger to greet me. I pulled the hoody back and she flashed me a wide smile, which I returned.

"Mathew, long time, no see!" she said, bustling around to shake my hand. She was in her mid-thirties, her hair pulled back into a loose bun, her short spectacles perched on the end of her nose. She wore her usual woollen-skirt, green cardigan combo which made her look like someone's favourite aunt.

"Hi Ming, how's business?" I asked.

"Same old, same old. You need the next set of spell-books?"

Des's books were government-approved spell manuals, but they weren't too easy to get, generally only a few suppliers bothered to stock them, Ming was one of them. I suppose I could have got them online somewhere, but I preferred shopping in little places like Ming's.

"Not this time," I said, "I need something a little stranger."

"Oh really?" she said, "Points for drama, lay it on me."

I described the creature I'd seen as best I could, and as I did I saw Ming's complexion go steadily paler, until I was worried she was going to pass out.

"I have a little, but I don't think I can help you, Mathew,' she said, heading into the back of her shop. She returned a minute later with a wide tome, placing it carefully on the counter. She opened the book and turned a few pages, until she got to the part she wanted. She turned it around so I could read the passage under her finger.

"And while searching for the Dark King's final fortress I came upon a battlefield. One of our advanced parties had been slaughtered, almost to a man. The single survivor described the King's terrible revenge, a demon, moving with the shadows themselves. Emerging from the night, it attacked two full companies of mages and their servants.

"Neither spell nor blade could harm it, it tore the men to pieces and devoured the mages' strength one by one before attacking again and again. Only the bright light of day drove it off but by then it had completed its bloody work.

"The survivor died three hours later, his body filled with the demon's corruption."

Translated from the last journal entry of Denias the Vigilant, Defender of the Realm. Found on his body two days later amongst the remains of a last stand, April, 1102 A.D.

I looked at the spine of the book. The Rise and Fall of Nekarand, the Dark King.

"Anything else? That's a little vague," I said.

"I've only heard of them in passing, the only people to come near one of these things die, thus information is somewhat thin."

"Ah, right," I said, closing the book carefully.

"I might have one lead for you, though," she said with a grimace on her face, "but I'm not sure you want to go down this road."

"Why's that?" I asked.

"These things, whatever they are, are monsters in the truest sense, utterly evil. The people who know about them are the people who use them, or know the people who do, and that's dangerous, especially for a mundane, no offence."

"None taken," I said thinking it over. If I had any smarts at all, I would drop this matter right now, leave it to the professionals and go back to school. But I didn't trust the SCA, how could I? Even if they solved this, they wouldn't tell Des and I anything, and I'd be looking over our shoulders for years, if not forever.

I had to know what was going on.

"Alright, where do I go?"

Chapter 10

It took me half an hour to walk to my next stop from *Curios*. The address was a three story mansion wedged into the old town's residential district. The roads here were a little wider, enough to admit a car or even two in places. The mansion itself was amazing, the building was all basalt crenulations and gothic carvings. Gargoyles glared down at me as I approached. I took a peek through my mage-sight and saw four of the sentient variety. I smiled and waved at them before heading up to the door.

There was no doorbell, but there was a heavy brass knocker. I knocked. As I watched, a series of numbers appeared on the door, written in orange light.

1, 1, 2, 3, 5, 8, 13, 21.

That was certainly new. You'd think a simple "Who is it?" would have done the trick, but Magicians are an eccentric lot. I stared at what I assumed was a puzzle for a minute before it clicked.

"Fibonacci," I said. The numbers stayed there.

"34?" I said hopefully. Nothing. I scratched my head for a minute, then I tried tracing 34 next to the numbers with my finger. Orange light shone and the number stayed in place. The numbers disappeared.

Correct, the door flashed, and then:

Igor's first law of universal entropy states?

Oh, that's obscure, and I had to be looking fairly idiotic to anyone watching by now. Igor was a man who tried to reconcile magic and physics. He failed dismally, but he had some good ideas that other mages used as a basis for their own more successful work.

He thought that magic was energy that decayed at a faster rate due to entropy, allowing it to bypass the normal laws governing energy because it ceased to exist once used. What was that damn equation?

I scribbled something down on the door.

Close enough.

What is knowledge?

Easy one, it's in every magical textbook. I scratched "The path to wisdom" into the door.

Cliché, but I suppose it's correct enough. Fine, come on in.

There was the sound of heavy locks clicking, and the door opened on its own. I walked in, still somewhat concerned about my course of action, but convinced of the necessity. It opened onto a wide hallway, where there were old wooden doors, three a side, and a mahogany staircase at the end, curving back on itself.

The furthest door on the right opened and a young woman came out. Late twenties, brown hair and eyes, pretty enough. She had a slightly crooked front tooth and a pierced eyebrow. She wore a loose fitting cotton suit, black edged in gold with a rearing lion embroidered over her left breast. She didn't look happy.

"Yes?" she asked in a voice filled with hostility.

"I'm here to see Professor Wilks," I said, "Ming sent me."

"Oh, her," she said in a resigned voice, "Come along, then."

She led me through the door she'd come through and into a large study. It was *packed* with every sort of knickknack and gewgaw you could imagine. There were cuckoo clocks with imps in place of the birds, books that turned their own pages, a mechanical rat made of gold that skittered around the periphery, chasing after something only it could see.

And the books, oh the books! Every magical tome I'd ever heard of but had never had a chance to read, they were all right there; Megry's *'Circles and Cycles'*, Odrogast's *'Study of the Blacke'*, dozens more. I could spend a year in here and still not have fully explored the wonders I'd just glimpsed.

"You can tell a lot about a man by what he looks at first in a room like this," said a voice from next to the fireplace. There were two high-backed chairs covered in red leather, pointed towards the fire at an angle. The man's face was out of my line of sight, but he sounded cultured and his hand bore a heavy gold signet ring as well as a crystal snifter filled a third with brandy. The same rearing lion from the woman's suit was picked out on the side of the glass.

"And what can you tell about me?" I asked, hoping I wasn't looking too much like a kid in a candy store.

"Most young men your age and some women I could mention, would notice the staves and the other weapons."

He stood, turning to face me. He looked like he was in his late forties, maybe early fifties, he was straight-backed and poised, handsome in a paternal way. He had a sharp nose and bright, curious eyes.

"Not you, though. You went straight for the books, and for Tabitha."

"Tabitha?"

"The rat," he answered with a grin.

"I've never seen anything like her before," I said, "so lifelike."

"Six hundred years old, runs as well as she did the day she was assembled. But I suspect that you aren't here to discuss my esoteric collection." He sat down in his chair and waved me to the one opposite him.

"Tea, coffee?" he asked.

"Tea, please," I replied, trying to be polite, really I try to avoid caffeine, it makes me jittery.

"Melanie, tea for our guest," he said. The woman nodded and darted out the door.

"So, you're a mage?" he asked, "You have certainly read our books, and know what you're looking at when you see others."

"My brother's the real mage in the family," I answered carefully, "I just read his books for the sake of the knowledge."

He looked at me for a moment before smiling.

"So, you're *that* brother."

"You've heard of Desmond?" I asked.

"Yes, but only in passing. Battle mages are a penny a dozen these days, what with the mundane community's current fascination. Scholars, however. They are considerably rarer. I have so been hoping to meet you, Mister Graves. It's been a long time since I had a chance to talk with someone who practices magic for understanding instead of profit."

"Practices?" I asked warily.

"Oh yes, I should be honest up front. Your gargoyle talks to my gargoyles."

Damn it, Jeremiah!

"Ah," I said articulately.

"I'm actually quite impressed. Do you know how many of us bother to look at gargoyles, much less try to talk to one?"

"Not many, I would guess," I replied.

"Very true. But a lesson for the future, anything that will gossip *to* you will gossip *about* you."

"Evidently," I said, just as articulately.

"So, a Shadow Mage? That's a rare talent."

"Was there anything that creature didn't blab?" I asked.

"You mustn't be too hard on him. If you hadn't shown up on my doorstep, I'd never have known you. I certainly wouldn't have been able to locate you from what he'd told my associate."

If the last twenty-four hours had taught me anything at all, it's that I had to be far more careful. I was getting sloppy, letting things slip. This now made two people who knew I had magic, and that was two more than I was comfortable with.

"It's my own fault. I knew he was a talker going in," I said finally.

"So it's true, then? You are a Shadow Mage?" he asked.

"Is that a problem?" I asked. I discovered some time ago that my particular speciality is not well liked among other mages, it's one of the reasons I kept it quiet.

"Not for me, young man, but you have my condolences, just the same."

"Condolences?" I asked, a tingle of fear passing down my spine.

His eyes went wide.

"Sorry, forget I said anything."

"After "condolences"?" I asked with a small grin.

He chuckled.

"Just my poor wit, young man. I don't mean to make light of your condition."

"What condition? I'm fine," I asked, now *very* worried.

Wilks' brow furrowed.

"You don't mean... surely you *know*?" he asked.

"I don't have the foggiest idea, Sir. Am I in some sort of trouble?" I asked, now getting very apprehensive.

He nibbled his thumb, like he was debating something internally, but eventually he looked me in the eye again.

"Alright. Shadow Mages. They go bad. All of them. May take a month, may take a century. You all go bad eventually."

"What do you mean, "bad"?" I asked, not really sure what to make of that.

"Evil. Monstrous. Murderous, megalomaniacal. Hitler without the impulse control. You get the picture. All sorts of magicians can use the shadows, as weapon or tool, they tend to be alright, but those who are born to them, Shadowborn, if you prefer, you have the darkness in you, a part of you. And one day it gets too far in, and your soul merges with it."

I had a sudden, clear image of the creature. The way it had recognised me, the way it had looked at me.

Wilks was still speaking.

"A Shadowborn Wizard or acolyte becomes a Shaadre. A creature of shadow. Monstrously powerful, part of the darkness, but feral, animalistic, nothing human remains. A Sorcerer, like you, however-"

"Sorry to interrupt, Professor, but I'm not a Sorcerer. My brother's a Wizard, I would think that I'd be similarly able."

"Oh, sorry, my boy. The Gargoyle's been exaggerating again! But it's probably for the best. A Sorcerer would be that much worse."

"Worse than animalistic horror?"

"Much. An intelligent horror. There would come a point, and he'd barely notice at first, but it'd be like a little switch just went off in his head. And then he'd feel it, deep in his core. Black magic, the really bad stuff, and he'd love it, he'd want to use it. And then one day he would and that would be that."

Just what the hell was I supposed to say to *that*?

Chapter 11

"If it's any consolation, most don't live long enough to go bad. Other mages kill them off. Especially Light Mages, they really don't like you."

Light Mages like my brother.

And no, that was *not* a consolation.

"I think I saw a Shaadre last night," I said, laying it out for him.

"You destroyed it? On your own?" he asked after I'd completed my story.

"I still don't know how," I replied.

"It was the combination. All those different energy types in a single spell, it overwhelmed the creature's natural resistances, allowed enough power to get through. Though you don't need to worry too much for yourself. Shaadre are no more able to get a grip on you than you could on them, they're made of shadow, you're physically harmless to each other."

"Good, I'm not really that competent with battle-magic," I said, "I'm just looking for where it came from, and why it was there."

Wilks sat back and puffed the air out of his cheeks. Melanie came back with the tea, pouring me a cup and stepping back, it gave the Professor time to think.

"That's a tall order. It could be that the creature was simply there because your brother and his girlfriend were there. They feed on magic, and younger magicians make easier prey."

"Do you think that's likely?" I asked, hopefully.

He smiled sadly, and shook his head.

"It's likely someone wanted your brother out of the way. A Light Mage is a terrible threat to many groups, and they tend to be more prolific than your kind, so any dent made is a happy one as far as they are concerned."

I tried not to wince at the "your kind" remark.

"So, can you help me find out who sent it?"

He sighed, "I can't, but I know of exactly one person in the city who *might* be able to help you."

"But?" I asked.

"She's eccentric," he said with a shrug, "and she doesn't share information, you'll have to buy it, and even then, asking about what you're planning to ask about would be dangerous. Are you sure you want to carry on?"

I thought about it for a moment. A long moment. I almost said no. That afternoon's revelations were not doing anything good for my digestion.

"Where?" I finally asked.

I took a cab to this one; it was all the way across town.

I found myself in front of a newer building in a more affluent commercial area, trees poked up through carefully cut holes in the pavement; the buildings were clean, the streets busy, but not crowded. The building I stood before was glass-fronted and bound in bright steel, but that wasn't where I was headed. There was a slim gap in the railings, where I could see a set of marble stairs, heading down.

It was already dark out. I'd missed dinner, and I was getting tired, but hopefully this would be my last stop before I could head back. There was a bouncer on the door who tried to stop me entering. I didn't blame him, it was a gentleman's club, and I was seventeen.

I cast a simple mental block on him, and suddenly he didn't even notice I was there. He also wouldn't remember I'd even spoken to him. I sidled past and into the "Purple Pussycat". I know; they didn't break any records for inventiveness with that name, did they?

The interior was... a new experience for me. There was a wide stage in front of me where three women danced in various stages of undress. There was comfortable seating everywhere and smaller circular raised areas dotted around the large room, stainless steel poles connecting them to the ceiling. There were women there, too.

It smelled strange in there, and I started to feel a little dizzy. It took a minute for me to recognise the subtle enchantment for what it was and protect myself. It was mostly mental, carried through sensory input, the smell, very clever, very subtle. I put up a mind-shield and carried on. I noticed that all the staff were women, which was a necessity, no doubt, as the enchantment in here, I'm guessing, was designed to make men pliable and free with their bank cards.

I walked over to the bar and attracted the attention of the bartender.

"Hey honey, what'll you have?" she asked.

"I need to see Tethys," I said, "I have business for her."

"Sorry, sweetie, she's not in today. But if you leave your name and number, I'll have her call you when she comes back."

I'd been keeping a surreptitious watch on her mind, and saw the lie immediately as a band of red spreading through her psyche. I increased the strength of the link between us, and I could hear her inner voice dimly in my head.

"Where is she now?" I asked.

"I don't know," she said.

Office, she thought.

"Where's her office?" I asked.

"I can't tell you that!" she replied, getting mad now.

Door behind me.

Another simple charm and I disappeared from her sight and memory. She blinked and went back to her inventory. I focussed hard and created a little spell. Nothing drastic, just enough for a distraction. A tiny sphere of dull light appeared in my hand, and I placed it carefully on the floor. I released it and it rolled away, skittering around patrons and waitresses before it arrived at the speaker system.

It did a little jump and a leap and there was an explosion of sparks. While the staff turned to stare, I darted past the bartender and through the swing door.

The door shut behind me with a muted thump, and the sounds from the club immediately cut out. To be replaced by other, even less wholesome sounds coming from a slightly ajar door at the end of a long corridor. There were other doors and niches to be seen, but they were all wide open. The rooms behind the doors and contained alcohol and other "supplies" that such a place would need, I won't go into detail, but they were certainly festive (and revealing).

I headed for the door at the end. I opened it the rest of the way and saw a well-furnished office; comfortable seating lined the walls, and there was a large stainless steel desk at the far end, covered in papers and other paraphernalia.

The sounds were coming from a sofa at the far end, where three women were engaged in some rather acrobatic sexual activity. I caught a glimpse of scattered under-things before I turned away. Damn, but today was providing me with quite the education.

I coughed suggestively, and when I got no reaction, I coughed even louder. I heard squeaks of embarrassment, followed by a grunt of frustration, and then the sound of women scampering past me.

"Can I help you with something?" said an irate female voice from behind me. This was not going according to plan.

"Professor Wilks sent me," I said, "he said you might have some information for sale."

"Did he also tell you to break into my office?"

"My apologies, Ms Tethys, but time was, and is, of the essence," I turned around, and the rest of my words fell out of my head.

She was the kind of beautiful that has caused *wars* in less civilised times. Long black hair that seemed almost purple, full, red lips that were inviting and sensuous; her eyes were violet and piercing. And she was completely naked. I won't go into detail, but good grief, that body was ridiculously difficult not to stare at.

"Take a picture, it'll last longer," she said with a smile. I turned away again with a red face and I heard a chuckle. I heard the rustle of soft cloth and the gentle scrunch of leather.

"Alright, I'm decent," she said. I turned again. She was sat behind her desk wearing a black silk robe that frankly made her look less covered somehow, if that makes any sense. She waved me towards a chair. I pulled a sealed note from my pocket and placed it on the table in front of her before I sat.

Wilks had given it to me to give to her by way of an introduction. She snapped off the seal (an actual red-wax seal with the rearing lion on it, made by that heavy signet ring I'd seen him wearing; I'd actually been quite impressed by that) and read the note. Her eyes twitched for a second, and then she smiled at me widely. There was something predatory in that smile. Wilks had mentioned that she wasn't quite human, but that he'd never had the courage to ask what else she might be.

She pressed a button on her phone and leaned back in her chair, looking me over.

"So, information. Would you care to tell me what that is, and if I have it, then we can discuss payment."

"Alright. Yesterday night I encountered what I have been informed is called a Shaadre. I would like to know who sent it, why, and what can be done to ensure that something similar doesn't happen again."

She tapped a perfectly manicured index finger on her chin before looking at me with a grin.

"You don't want much, do you?" she asked.

"Can you do it?" I asked.

"I can, but I won't. That information would be dangerous even to acquire, much less disseminate. It's simply not worth my trouble. Sorry."

"There's nothing I can say to change your mind?" I asked.

"No."

"Can you at least tell me where I could begin my own enquiries?"

"No," she said it with a satisfied smile, rocking back and forth in her chair.

"Sorry to have wasted your time, then, and for the interruption of your evening," I stood up. Disappointed, but also relieved. I'd done my best, and now I could go back to school with a clear conscience.

"One thing, though," she said, and the tone of her voice immediately put me on edge. My heart started thumping, and the shadows responded. I could feel them coalescing at the edges of the room. She didn't notice.

"Yes?" I asked, trying to make my voice steady.

She tossed Wilks' letter to me. I caught it and turned it over so I could read it:

My Dear Thethys,

Please find with this note one Wizard-class practitioner, young and vital. Make your preparations properly and your accountant should be very pleased with the sale. Oh, he's Shadowborn, but a novice in battle magic, so I wouldn't worry. I trust this settles all accounts?

Warmest regards,

Samuel Wilks.
MD, PhD, BSc, MSc, FACS.

"This doesn't mean anything good for me, does it?" I asked, feeling terror well up inside me.

She chuckled at me, a genuine laugh this time.

"If you weren't worth so much money, I'd let you go just for that answer, but alas..." She pressed the button on the phone again, and three large burly men came in, they were dressed all in black, and they carried tasers.

But that wasn't all. They wore Spelleater amulets, all of them.

She stood up behind me, the robe falling away from her body. As I watched, she changed, her skin going paler until it was whiter than ivory, her hands and feet grew scaly and black, until it seemed like she was wearing gloves and boots of black bone. Large black wings sprouted from her shoulder blades, horns from her head and a long, bony tail from the small of her back.

She smiled again, revealing long fangs, and I was gripped with the sudden, awful truth that I was well and truly screwed.

Crap...

Chapter 12

I was in trouble. Big, big trouble. I had a single second in which to think before someone did something nasty to me. I guessed that it would come from the tasers, first. These people were obviously prepared for magical resistance, hence the amulets. So, they were my greatest threat, as they were largely immune to a direct attack.

I needed to buy time to think of something that would get me out of this.

Tethys jumped for me in the same instant that I called my shadows. My shadows arrived first, thankfully, surging through the room like a great black wave, blocking all the light before coiling protectively around me. I sent a command through my link to them, and they pulled me out of her way, enclosing me in a cocoon of darkness before dropping me safely onto a sofa at the far side of the room.

The whole space was now pitch-dark, my shadows smothering the lights, returning the advantage to me. The darkness stopped short of the three thugs, about a foot away from each, but they, along with Tethys, were still blind. The Spelleaters' effective range was nowhere near enough to return the light to them.

Tethys knew that I wasn't where I used to be, but the guards didn't even have that clue, they were still pointing their tasers at the spot where I'd just been standing. I had my breathing room.

So now what do I do?

Tethys hadn't seen my face, thanks to my hoodie, but I couldn't imagine that it would take an information broker very long to come up with an identity or at least a place to start looking for me. I had to do something here, now, to throw her off, and that meant that I couldn't just run, like I wanted.

While I was thinking, Tethys was busy sniffing. To my surprise, and horror, her head suddenly turned, and her eyes pointed right at me, even though she couldn't possibly see through the darkness.

"Come out, come out, wherever you are..." she sang, that predatory smirk in full force.

Then she jumped at me.

My shadows acted on my desperate instincts and caught her in a suddenly solid tendril as thick as my leg before tossing her away from me like a bag of rice. She spun head over heels and hit the far wall with a wet crack that told of breaking bone and made me feel queasy. A quick look through my mage sight told me that she was unconscious not dead, thank goodness. I don't think I could have handled killing someone, even a monster.

That still left the three guards, who now seemed to be growing a bit frantic after the unpleasant sounds they'd heard.

"Mistress?" the one in the middle asked, his free hand casting out in front of him, "Are you still there?"

Now that I'd had a chance to ponder the problem, I felt that I had a solution. It was one of the ideas I'd been contemplating about Mister Koenig's Spelleater, though my current answer was a touch more violent, bearing in mind the additional unpleasantness of my present situation. The crux of the idea was a reliance on simple physics. I couldn't directly affect anything inside the effect of the amulets, but there was plenty outside that I *could* affect. And throw. With great force.

I started with Tethys' *very* expensive touch screen computer monitor. I applied a simple piece of mental magic that linked my imagination to my Will and gave it form, think in terms of planes of force shaped by my imagination, effectively hands made of energy controlled by my mind.

I might have preferred to use my shadows for this, but the effort of keeping them up and running while so close to three Spelleaters was making them a little tricky to control with precision, which was important in a situation where hitting these people too hard with a heavy object would kill them (which I still didn't want on my conscience).

I seized the screen with my Will, and with a mental flick, I tossed it across the room at the first guard, the one closest to me, sheared cables flying behind it like some bizarre streamers. My mental grip failed at the edge of the field, but Sir Isaac Newton would be the first to tell you that an object in motion tends to stay in motion...

The screen hit the thug hard in the head, causing an instant concussion that knocked him out cold. The screen continued on for a bit before smashing into the ground, startling the remaining two guards.

They immediately became more agitated, spinning in place, looking for a target which wouldn't present itself.

"Show yourself!" one shouted, causing his friend to jump. The second one swore and started backing in the general direction of the door, which I Willed shut with a heavy bang. The thugs jumped at the sound and one turned, firing his taser. He missed completely; I was nowhere near that door.

The sofa flew next, aimed at the pair of them. I hoped that I hadn't thrown it too hard. One moved at just the wrong moment, though, but I got the other one, and he crumpled under the furniture, unconscious. There had been another wet crack; I think I broke his collar bone.

I shuddered a little, feeling my gorge try to rise. I really wasn't cut out for this sort of thing. If I have to defend myself, I prefer *mental* magic, for heaven's sake. I put people to sleep, I don't break their bones!

But in for a penny, in for a pound. I Willed up another sofa. I would have preferred to use one of the tasers, but leaving aside the fact that I was just as likely to electrocute myself as one of the guards, I wasn't willing to risk getting any closer to one of those amulets.

So I hurled furniture again, and unfortunately misjudged the trajectory. It tumbled from the air at the edge of his barrier, which had been a little larger than the other two, and hit his legs instead of something that would have knocked him out immediately. I heard his limbs break, and then the man started screaming.

He dropped his weapon, hands going to his mangled legs. The noise he was making was dreadful, so I did the best I could to stop it, which turned out to be dropping the ten grand, custom made, Fritz Hansen desk chair on his head from a fair height, and the screaming stopped with a thud. My stomach churned again as blood flowed from his nose and broken teeth, nearly causing a mishap, but I held it together somehow.

I took a moment to breathe and make sure that everyone was out before I finally sent my shadows away. The colours came back to the room, which suddenly had a lot more red in the decor. I checked Tethys first, and she was still out of it. I placed a sleeping charm on her to keep her that way for a few minutes. Then I went for the guards. I took their amulets, cast more quick sleeping charms, and went out the door, looking for a bathroom.

I found one behind the door opposite and flushed the talismans like they were toxic, removing them as a threat. Then I went back in and placed more firm sleeping charms on the thugs. They wouldn't wake at all unless I removed them. Probably for the best, they all had broken bones of some sort, and I felt surprisingly awful about that, which was strange. After all, they were planning to kidnap me.

I brought my shadows back and wrapped them around the... whatever Tethys was, propping her up against the wall. I felt the darkness swirling around my legs and feet, fed from the dark patches all over the room, it was even under my clothing, but for once it didn't feel creepy. It made me feel safe.

I touched her forehead and removed the sleep charm, inverting it momentarily so that she would wake up. She was bound shoulder to ankle in darkness, those wings pressed to her back; though naturally the shadow was only shades of grey mist to me, I could see right through it. I had to shake my head a little, because she really was stunning.

"You can stop faking, I know you're awake," I said.

"Fine," she replied, those lovely eyes sliding open. She looked down at her bindings, and the shimmering oily formations of darkness that flowed around me.

"It would appear that the situation has changed somewhat," she said.

I couldn't help but laugh at that.

"If you didn't have the information I need, I'd let you go just for that answer, but alas..." I said, echoing her words from earlier. So sue me, I have a sense of the dramatic.

"Touché," she said, "so, what now?"

"Well, there are two ways that this ends. Either we part as friends... or we don't."

"Say for the sake of argument that I'd prefer to part as friends," she said, "what would that entail?"

"I will let you go, and you will find that information for me, and needless to say I would prefer it if something like *this* never had to happen again."

"Tempting. But here's the thing, the worse you will do is kill me. They'll do far, far worse if they catch me poking into their affairs."

"There must be some information you can glean, some source that you can tap. I would accept a low risk result," I said, clutching at straws, really. I was pretty sure that she was about to call my bluff. There was no way I was actually going to kill anyone.

"I suppose that there may be one source. We don't know anything about each other, so the risk for me would be minimal. But that will take some time, and I would naturally need to be alive to make contact."

"Acceptable," I said, "by the way, just who were you going to sell me to?"

"Auction. You'd be amazed what people are willing to pay to get themselves on a fresh mage that they can mould, sacrifice, indoctrinate or eat."

"Eat?!" I said, my voice almost as squeak. The shadows swirled at my pulse of fear and anger, growing barbed and jittery.

"Don't worry, Shadowborn don't make good eating, I'm told. More likely it would have been one of the end-time cults, they're always looking for good shock troops."

"Leaving that aside for the moment," I said with some anger, "how are you this bad at kidnapping? Shouldn't you have mopped the floor with me?"

"Yes. We really should. Shadowborn aren't usually this strong, normally any light is enough to weaken them. Seems you're a little different. It's annoying, to say the least, but then they'se the breaks."

"You seem remarkably sanguine about all this," I said, "bearing in mind your situation."

"When you've been around as long as I have, you learn to read people, and now that we've had a chance to chat a little, I'm pretty sure you're not a killer. I was fairly sure about that the instant you walked in, but now I'm certain. Sometimes the mages I meet are vicious, or unstable. I leave them alone, because if they get the upper hand, they might well kill me. But you are just too civilised for that. You're not even willing to torture me a little, are you?"

"No," I admitted after a moment's thought, "but I am willing to put you to sleep for a year or two, shall we see how your business thrives without you?"

"Must say I hadn't thought of that," she said, "fine, we have a deal. Let me go, and I'll see what I can do."

"Your word on it?" I asked, taking a quick peek with a mind-reading spell.

"Oh, fine. My word." She was telling the truth. I just had to hope she wasn't the sort to change her mind.

"Now, it goes without saying that you shouldn't engage in any shenanigans when I let you go," I pointed out.

"Of course not, as if I would!" she said in such an innocent tone of voice that I was instantly worried. I shook my head, but I released the shadows anyway, withdrawing them slowly so that she could keep her feet. She stretched, and I took a few steps back. Her body shifted back to fully human, and she bent over to retrieve her robe, sliding it back on.

"We good?" I asked.

"Sure," she said, smiling again, "you have a way that I can contact you?"

I moved to the desk and wrote down one of my e-mail addresses on a convenient pad. I turned to find her right next to me, I jumped, shadows leaping from every nook and cranny.

"Easy, tiger," she said with a smile, "a deal is a deal."

I calmed down, and the shadows slithered away again.

"Let me see your face," she said, still a little close for my comfort.

"Nope, you know enough already, thanks very much," I took a step away, she followed. I could feel whatever subtle magic she used pushing against my mental shields, and she was making progress. I concentrated for a second to increase the strength of the barrier, and in that time she was on me.

She had her arms around my neck before I could stop her.

Damn it. Round 2, I guess.

Chapter 13

My shadows were coming. They would be too slow. I was anticipating some sort of strangulation, or a neck-break type situation, so I was already sending them that way to brace the bones.

Instead she brought her face up to mine and kissed me.

Wasn't expecting that...

And wow.

I knew with an absolute certainty that this was very, very bad for me, and yet I was having trouble caring. Her scent was intoxicating, and I felt my heart rate triple as by body responded to her closeness.

My mental defences were crumbling with every moment she was in contact with me, and I barely noticed, she was all there was.

My first kiss. I know, mixed boarding school, and still hadn't been kissed. I wasn't happy about it either, and it's not something I'm proud of, I don't want to go into it right now.

But there it was. And as far as kisses go, it was one in a billion (I'm guessing). But still... My first kiss and it was in a monster's lair behind a strip club? That wasn't right.

And that made me just that little bit mad.

That anger was like a light shining on my mind. It let me see what she was doing. It likely saved my life, certainly my soul. I rebuilt my defences around that anger, laying the foundations of a massive wall around my mind.

Little by little she faded from my perceptions until I came out of it to find her still kissing me. Only seconds had elapsed. My shadows had come. And we were pissed. They were all around me, coating my skin. My hands were black with it, it covered my neck and in a second it was between me and Tethys, finally breaking the kiss.

She looked up into my eyes and I saw fear flicker across her features. I raised my hand, and barbs sprouted from the darkness, bladed and vicious, matching my mood. She stepped back, tripping to bang her bottom against the desk. I followed, standing as close to her as she'd been to me earlier. I leaned down, and in as menacing a voice as I could manage I said, "Don't do that again."

Still wasn't willing to hurt anyone, but the shadows meant that I can look intimidating as hell when I want to. She nodded hurriedly, and I picked up the piece of paper with my e-mail address on it, placing it in her hand.

"I'll be waiting," I said. I turned on my heel and walked away.

Then I ruined the effect by telling her that her people needed medical attention before I released their sleeping enchantments. They woke up and started screaming, I ran for it, my heart still pounding.

I left as nonchalantly as I could, though neither the bartender or the bouncer would even be able to see me until the mental block wore off in a few hours, so I wasn't too worried about being waylaid. I climbed up into the night and as soon as I was out of sight, I ran for as long as I could, which isn't far, as you might guess. Eventually I slumped against a convenient house and threw up everything I'd eaten in the last few days.

Alright. I passed "in over my head" some time ago, right about the time I left Ming's as a matter of fact. So, what do I do now? I stood there panting and dry-heaving for a while. I heard ambulances in the distance, no doubt heading for the Purple Pussycat. I walked away slowly, my stomach cramps not making it any easier. Once I was upright again, I flagged down a cab and it took me back towards Windward. Before I did anything else, I needed a cold shower and a long rest.

I made it back half an hour after my curfew. No one noticed. I was tired and frightened and still a little bit aroused, if I'm honest. This is not a good combination, FYI.

I got my shower, and stumbled into bed. I fell asleep instantly, so much the better. If I'd had a chance to think about the insane risks I'd taken that day, there was a good chance I'd start throwing up again.

Chapter 14

I woke up the next morning when my door slammed open and my brother piled in looking excessively pleased with himself.

"I finished all my prep!" he said by way of an ice-breaker and with too much cheer, "I can fight next week!"

"Hooray," I muttered, pulling the duvet over my head.

It didn't work; the rat bastard just started shaking me.

"Breakfast time! Up an' at 'em!"

"Sod off," I replied; my legendary wit at work, I think you'll agree.

"Come on Matty, tell me what you found," he said in a whiny voice. I'd told him where I was going the day before, but not the specifics of what I'd be doing. It would appear as if his curiosity has finally gotten the better of him (I'd been mostly convinced that he didn't have any natural inquisitiveness).

"Nothing yet, I'm waiting for a source to get back to me," I said.

"What kind of source?" he said, wrestling the bedclothes off me at last.

"The kind that can't be rushed," I explained, "and that values their privacy."

"But you can tell me, right?" he asked, a pleading look in his eyes.

"You've never been this interested in my wheelings and dealings before," I said, hefting myself up and heading for the sink.

"Well, life on the line and all that," he said.

My eyes narrowed. Seventeen years, and he's never shown this sort of interest in anything I've done for him. He's never asked for details before, ever. He simply accepted and trusted. Des is just not an ideas man.

"Des, are you interrogating me?" I asked, watching him for a reaction. I had a nasty suspicion all of a sudden.

"What? No, no, no. Of course not."

He looked away, idly scratching his hand.

"Des!" I said, turning to face him, "You tell me what you're up to, and you do it now."

"Aw, come on Matty, don't be like that. Vanessa just wanted me to ask you who your sources were."

"And how, pray, does Vanessa know that I have sources at all?"

"Um," he said, rubbing the back of his head.

"God damn it, Des! These people trust me!"

I wasn't too worried about either Wilks or Tethys, let both of them rot (though preferably *after* I got my information), it was Ming, and the other fifteen or so people from magical society that I am in contact with from time to time. None of them deserved a government-sponsored prostate exam.

"She doesn't mean any harm," Des said, a sheepish look on his face, "she only wants to know what you know."

"I don't know anything, I discovered nothing and I don't know anyone. That's what you tell her. Now go away."

"Matty..."

"Don't Matty me. You just tried to make me betray a confidence. I can't believe you did that. I'm so disappointed in you Des, I thought you would know better."

"And just who the hell are you to be disappointed?!" he said, jumping to his feet. He was yelling at me. Desmond doesn't yell at me. I frowned as I saw something in his eyes. Something alien, something I'd never seen there before. It was as if he were a stranger in that moment.

"I'm the one who's been taking care of you since the day you couldn't figure out how to use the potty, that's who I am!" I said, shouting just as loudly, my own temper flaring.

"Oh, really? It wasn't you who's been keeping me alive. It wasn't you who brought down a creature that would have eaten me!"

"So, what are you saying? That now you know about this guy, you don't need me anymore? That everything I've done for you over the years doesn't matter because someone else was doing a more important job?"

"Of course not, but I need to find this guy! I need to know why he's been following me around, and you're stopping me from doing that!"

"I just spent yesterday sifting through filth in an attempt to get information for you. Information about the people that are after you! The one that's saving you is not important; we need to stop assassins, not protectors!"

"But if we can find him, he can tell us who's after me!"

I wouldn't bet on that, I thought.

"I'm not giving you their names," I said, a final note in my voice.

"You tell me!" he said, grabbing a handful of my shirt.

"Get off me, this instant!" I said, trying to pry his hand away. He was so much stronger than I was, but I managed to lever a finger off and pulled it hard enough to get him to let me go. He yelped.

And then he hit me.

His balled his fist and punched me hard in the gut. I folded over, the breath shoved from my body. I think it was the shock and betrayal that hurt more than the actual blow. I fell to my knees, gasping for air. He'd never hit me before! He'd never even accidentally hurt me before.

He stood back, looming over me, an expression of shock on his own face, now, the foreign look seemed to clear from his eyes as he realised what he'd done. But he was in too deep in his position now, his pride wouldn't allow him to back down.

And I wasn't too happy either.

"So that's it then," I said after a few more gasps, "the first piece of arse that comes along and asks you to do something, and you turn your back on your own brother?"

"She is not a piece of arse! She's a government officer."

"Not the important part of the question, you imbecile!" I pointed out.

Then he kicked me!

While I was down. My brother actually kicked someone when they were down.

"What the hell happened to you?" I asked, despair welling up inside of me.

"I'm growing up," he said coldly, "Why don't you do the same? Who are you to look down on me? You're not even a magician."

"That never mattered to you before," I said in a small voice.

"Well, maybe it does now," he said, his expression showing a little doubt.

"I'm not going to tell you anything. Not now. Not after this. And I wouldn't hit me again, if I were you."

"Really? And just what are you going to do about it?" he asked, a nasty tone in his voice. *That* look was back in his eye; this wasn't Desmond. This kid was a bully, pure and simple, and nasty with it.

I was at just the right height. And he was asking for it.

I've never hit anyone before. Ever. I've never had the need, and I'm just not good at fisticuffs.

But then you don't really need to be when you're punching someone in the groin. He doubled over twice as fast as I had, gasping for air and groaning in pain. I pulled myself up by a chest of drawers and pulled on a clean set of clothes. He stopped gasping and gagging as I was tying my shoes.

"You little shit," he said as he dragged himself up. He took a step towards me. I was still sitting.

"Going to hit me again, then, are you? Well, at least I'm sitting and not lying down. Make you feel big, did it? Beating on your little brother?"

He stopped for a second, and there was something like shame in his eyes for a moment before he left the room. I sagged, seeing heads poked out of bedrooms. Everyone had heard that. Terrific.

I could already feel a bruise coming up on my chest and another on my leg where he'd kicked me. And I couldn't use magic to help fix them up.

And that is why I placed an Asimov to begin with, I thought, as I rubbed my sore parts. My heart was still pounding, and I was as miserable as I'd ever been. I'd never really thought about this before, but Des had always been a constant, always good natured, always agreeable. He'd always listened, or pretended to, at least. He'd never been hostile, never seen me as the enemy.

He'd always been there with a reassuring word. And now...

I just didn't know what to do.

Chapter 15

Ninety minutes later, I stumbled into English and nearly fell into my seat. This was becoming just a little bit too much. Everything was falling apart, and I wasn't sure what to do about it. Hell, I wasn't even sure that there was anything that I could do.

Bill sat next to me, concern all over his face.

"I heard," he said.

"Already?" I asked.

"Gossip, mate, the only thing that travels faster than light."

"Crap," I said.

"Don't worry about it. You come out looking pretty good," he said with a grin.

"How's that?" I asked.

"Well, the rumour around the dining hall this morning is that you made out with your brother's girlfriend, and that when he came to kick your arse you kicked him in the balls and tore him a new one for picking on a weaker kid."

"Oh, no," I said, laying my head in my hands.

"You stud, you!" he said, elbowing me in the side.

"Not what happened!" I said, "Not even slightly what happened!"

"The cool kids are saying that your brother finally got tired of you dragging him down, and kicked your arse so you'd know who's boss."

"Not what happened either, but still closer than the first one."

I rubbed my eyes and tried to wake up from this bad dream. Mister Kendler came in with his notes, and started talking about Shakespeare. I didn't hear much and understood less, so thank goodness Bill was paying attention.

The lesson ended, and Bill and I met up with Cathy for our free period. I filled them both in on what happened yesterday and today (minus the magic parts, but Cathy met my eyes, and knew that I was leaving a few bits out).

"That's intense," Bill said when I'd finished the retelling.

"Tell me about it," I replied. We sat there for a while, my two friends reiterating the point that my brother is a bit of a tool, until Vanessa and Kraab appeared at the edge of the square and made a beeline for us.

"Uh oh," Cathy said.

I couldn't help but agree.

"Mister Graves, could we have a word?" Kraab asked.

"May I ask what this is regarding?" I asked, trying to be polite.

"We'd rather discuss that in private," Vanessa said, her voice very deliberately neutral to my ears.

"Alright," I said, standing up, all the while hoping that I wasn't making a terrible mistake by not running for my life.

They led me into the administrative building, to one of the smaller rooms used for conferences and guest lectures. Kraab unlocked it and ushered me in. He gestured for me to sit me down on one side of a wide table. Kraab sat opposite me, and Vanessa stood behind him.

He stared at me for a minute and made a brief gesture. Vanessa took a stack of folders from the end of the table and placed them in front of Kraab.

"No headmaster this time," I mentioned as she did that.

"No," said Kraab.

"Is that legal?" I asked.

"If we were interrogating you, no, but we're just having an informal chat at the moment."

"I see," I said, "and just what are we chatting about?"

"Why don't we start with your whereabouts yesterday between the hours of five and ten p.m."

"I was out walking in Stonebridge. The Old Town."

"For five hours?"

"Something wrong with that?" I asked.

"Your brother is under the impression that you spoke to some people yesterday, people you know who might shed some light on the events leading up to the attempt on Desmond's life two nights previous," Kraab said.

"My brother is mistaken," I replied.

"Really? And how would he come to be so... mistaken."

"I don't know."

Kraab leaned back in his chair, steepling his long fingers while staring at me very intently.

"Right now we're having a chat," he said, "the only reason this isn't something a bit more unpleasant is because your brother is important to us. He's our hope for the future, and as of this morning, we are no longer concerned about mistreating you having an adverse effect on him."

"*That* was the only thing preventing you from mistreating a minor?" I asked sardonically.

"Don't get cute with me, Graves. You know something, and I will have that information. Either you give it to me, or Agent Knowles will take it from your mind."

"Now I *know* that's illegal," I said.

"Not for us," Kraab replied.

"Only if you get a signed warrant, and those are never granted in cases involving minors. I took the liberty of looking you guys up after you attempted to hex my brother yesterday."

I did a brief set of internet searches during a free moment, surprisingly useful as it turned out.

Vanessa took a piece of paper from a folder and placed it in front of me. I looked down at the neatly typed words.

It was a warrant authorising the telepathic interrogation of any and all subjects which might provide relevant information, blah, blah... *restrictions on minors lifted*, etc., etc., *protection of an innocent life taking precedence...*

"Ah," I said, pushing the paper back towards them.

"Would you like to volunteer that information, now?" Vanessa said, sitting down opposite me. I didn't bother answering, I was already building my mental walls. It's more difficult when you can't use magic; I was having to use pure imagination and sheer bloody-mindedness.

"Do it," Kraab said, and I felt Knowles slam into my defences like a battering ram, a whole battalion of them, actually, hammering from all sides, smashing at my walls. I kept building, creating a massive maze around a colossal fortress in my mind's eye, walls within walls, false keeps and pitfalls.

The pressure kept mounting, and I kept building, jumbling my thoughts, focussing intently on the images of the defences I was building.

"He's blocking me," she said, an impressed tone in her voice.

"How?" Kraab asked, sounding surprised.

"Simple blocks and mental shields, all of it mundane, but there's just a lot of them, and every time I get through a wall he puts up another one and shifts the entire mental architecture around to keep the defences in the way. It's maddening."

"Push harder," he said.

"I already am, he's tricky. Distract him," she said, sweat beading her brow.

"With pleasure," he said in an ugly tone. He pulled back his hand and slapped me hard in the face.

I lost concentration with the sharp spike of pain, and a whole bunch of my defences disappeared. I felt her advance, pushing hard against my inner walls. I fought hard to rebuild, shifting and twisting the defences like my brain was a snake with its tail in a trap.

I was starting to regain ground when he hit me again, lighter this time, but a straight shot that made my nose bleed and my eyes water. The inner walls crumbled, and she made it into the keep.

I focussed carefully, twisting the internal architecture. I went full Escher on her, making stairs and floors that twisted around on themselves before finally leading to nowhere, traps and pitfalls that caused huge sections to collapse, I brought her probes into dead ends and blocked them off, smashed the walls apart onto her attacks. I was scorching the earth as she walked on it, and it was painful for both of us.

But I was clawing my way back.

"Again, quickly. I can't hold this much longer," Knowles said.

Not to worry, neither could I. I was pretty much exhausted.

He slapped me again. The pain ripped through my keep and it fell. She got what she was looking for. My head hit the table and I breathed raggedly. I was sweating all over, and my face was aching.

Knowles (not thinking of her as Vanessa anymore) wasn't in any better shape. She was panting in exhaustion, staring at me with something resembling respect.

"Sorry," she said, and I actually thought she meant it.

"You can go now, Mister Graves," Kraab said, giving nothing away. I staggered to my feet, barely able to stand. I was furious at the violation, but I was damned if I'd ask these two for help. I weaved slightly for the door and grabbed the handle. I yanked it open to see my brother waiting there, a neutral expression on his face.

I couldn't look at him, and brushed past without a word. He took in my appearance and looked like he was about to say something, but then he saw Knowles, that anger returned to his face and he went in, leaving me alone. I made it out and into the square, but that was as far as I got.

The last thing I saw before I passed out was Bill and Cathy jogging towards me and the ground rushing up to meet me as I keeled over. You'd think I might have earned enough karmic good will to land on the grass, but no. I hit the gravel path *surrounding* the grass cheek first (ouch). Just before my lights went out, I took a little nugget of comfort from the fact that all those two shit-heels got was the name and address of Professor Julian Wilks.

Even if they got in the door, there's no way he'd even admit to having seen me, seeing as how he'd tried to sell me to a flesh-peddler.

So, I guess that I could call this one a draw? Meh, I'll figure it out when I wake up.

Chapter 16

I woke up to find my mother staring down at me. She looked worried. I could understand that...

"Mother?" I asked, a little groggy.

"Hi sweetheart," she said, stroking my hair, "How are you feeling?"

"Sore," I said, trying to sit up. My head protested and I laid back down again.

I was in the infirmary, in one of their two wards. Sunlight was streaming through the wide windows, and I was lying in a clean, white bed under warm blankets. I was still wearing my uniform.

"Ow," I said as my skull throbbed.

She chuckled, her eyes worried even as she tried to smile for me. She squeezed my hand gently. She looked tired, dark circles under her eyes. I thought she was in Egypt with Father. Archaeologists, you see. She was tall and a little heavy-set, carrying a few holiday pounds. She had green eyes and blonde hair, and was dressed in a practical suit. She was generally a warm, happy person, Desmond takes after her, I think. Or he used to.

"When did you get back?" I asked.

"This morning. Your father wanted to be here, but the dig's at a critical stage, so only one of us could get away. I came as soon as your brother told us about what happened at the party the other night."

"You spoken to him yet?" I asked.

"I came straight to you. Mister Kenilworth called and told me you'd collapsed. You scared the living daylights out of me, Matty. You're the good one; we normally don't have to worry about you."

"Sorry," I said.

"Oh stop that," she said, giving me a crushing hug, which I returned. I'd missed her.

"Now, why don't you tell me what happened."

I did, leaving out the magic, Des beating the crap out of me, the almost getting taken by human traffickers, and of course the strip club.

She stopped smiling about half way through my story. By the end she looked livid.

"Would you excuse me a minute, Matty? I'll be right back," her voice was suddenly arctic-cold.

"Sure," I said.

She left and shut the door to the ward behind her.

The shouting started a few seconds later. I heard the words "headmaster" and "shove someone's head up" among some other epithets that showed Mother's mood. And then silence. I assumed that meant that she was on her way to see Mister Kenilworth, the poor bastard. It really wasn't his fault.

I closed my eyes for a minute. My whole head felt like it was a giant pulsing wound, and I was still exhausted from my little mental fight. I figured I'd nap for a few minutes...

Turns out it was a few more than that.

When I woke up it was dark outside. There was a note on the table. My mother had left it. She was off to sue the SCA, best of luck to her was all I could say. In the meantime, they'd left the school and weren't coming back, which is always reassuring.

She said she'd be back in a while.

I got to my feet slowly. My headache had faded, and I wasn't too tired anymore. I wondered out to find one of the matrons reading a book in her office.

"Can I go, Matron?" I asked.

"What are you doing up?" she replied with a frown.

What followed was a discussion I won't bore you with, but suffice to say it was irritating and eventually meant that I could go. I was able to glean a certain amount of what had happened from her needless clucking.

I'd passed out (it was at this point that I started hoping that no one was calling it fainting), and Cathy had immediately run for help. She'd come back with two teachers, who'd called a matron and Mister Kenilworth.

He'd been in the process of calling an ambulance when Knowles and Kraab came along to tell them that it was unnecessary, and that I'd be fine with a little bed rest, "just a simple procedure," they'd said.

So they'd carried me up to the infirmary, where I'd been watched carefully while Kenilworth called my parents. Two hours after that, my mother had arrived and come to see me, which was when I'd woken up. As you know, I fell asleep, and while I was doing *that,* my mother was raising a hell that the matron would not go into too much detail about.

Evidently Mister Kenilworth had managed to persuade her that it hadn't been his fault, because the school was still standing (I exaggerate a little here for effect, Mother's not a mage, she just has a temper). After this, he'd spilled the beans and directed her fury at the government, and off she went after leaving me the note.

And that was a whole day wasted.

Chapter 17

Saturday. Normally this is a half day, not so much for me, on account of being badly behind on an entire day's work.

Oh, and it turned out that the descriptor of choice was indeed "fainting".

I heard it first at breakfast and then twenty times every hour after that. I also noted a growing hostility from the upper echelons of the student body, which made me a little nervous.

Before I go further, I should explain how that place worked. There was a social hierarchy at Windward, something that wouldn't even exist but for the fact that the school was mixed, thus everything immediately became about status (and impressing the opposite sex). At the top you had the sportsmen, anyone who took part in team games. Rugby was at the top, then football, then rowing, then everything else, including mages. For girls the top tiers were gymnastics, ballet and drama. Naturally, the older you were, the higher up the ladder you were.

After that, everyone else fell into the two categories of weird or normal. If you were "normal", then you were alright, just not part of the in-crowd. If you were considered "weird", and had no redeeming qualities useful to the in-crowd, then God help you, because you just became fair game to anyone above you in the pecking order.

As the day went on, I noticed that people were starting to look more and more in my direction, and it wasn't in a good way. The looks were hostile, challenging, and even the older kids seemed to be looking at me funny.

It wasn't until lunch that Bill shed some light on the situation.

"It looks like your brother's been bad-mouthing you," he said, looking at me with something like pity in his eyes.

"How's that?" I asked.

"I don't know the specifics, but it looks like you've been moved into the Weird Pile."

"You mean I wasn't there already?"

"Debate and Chess Teams, they got you a pass."

That's where I got my information from. Bill had made it his personal project to understand the ins and outs of the social structure of that school. He had it down to a point system based on interests, attractiveness and social contacts. It really was quite impressive.

"But not anymore. Your brother was keeping you cool by proxy, now he's shifted the balance the other way, and the big kids are smelling fresh blood in the water."

"How bad?" I asked.

"We may be looking at a Carrie situation here."

I hissed. His class-system of identifying someone's social standing was based on pop culture. At the top was "Ferris Bueller" (kings of the school), at the bottom was "Lord of the Flies" (where someone could get seriously hurt). One tiny notch up from that was a "Carrie".

So, I wasn't going to die, but some very bad shit was likely to happen to me, and probably soon, and then repeatedly afterwards.

"I take it then, that this is the last I'll be seeing of you for a while?" I asked, only half joking, I knew he valued his "Marty McFly" rating, and how desperate he was to keep it. But he surprised me.

"Don't be dense," he said, "you, me and Cathy are a team. We ride together, we fall together."

"That was beautiful, mate," I said, wiping a fake tear from my eye.

"Shut up," he said with a grin, "Besides, who else is going to help me with Shakespeare? The man's incomprehensible."

I actually was quite touched by that. Bill really was a good friend. I grinned back at him and resumed my lunch, feeling a little better.

So the day had started well enough, but from there it went horribly downhill. The bad stuff started in the library. The library! Is no place sacred?

A ball hit me square in the head as I was heading for one of the reading rooms. It hit hard enough that I stumbled, tripped and fell flat on my face, dropping books and papers everywhere.

There was laughing and cackling. I sat there red-faced as a group from my year came along, snorting and pointing.

It occurred to me at that point that I had really led a very sheltered life. I'd never had to deal with this sort of thing before. Hell, I'd rarely even seen it happen to other people. This occurred to me because, up until that moment, I'd never really considered the idea of using magic to hurt someone outside of self-defence.

And the fact that I was now scared the hell out of me more than anything else. One does not have the power that I do and allow oneself to become a bully (much less a sadist).

"Looks like he fainted again, huh guys?" one of the girls said. The group laughed even harder. Courtney Wilcox. She was just a little shorter than me, sporting a sunbed-tan, her hair was blonde and curly, she had blue eyes and perfect teeth. Everyone with a y-chromosome had at least a little crush on her (even me at some point). Bill calls her the grand high witch of the school (he likes Roald Dahl. And that's his *most* polite name for her).

This wasn't the brightest group, I thought of replying, but there was nothing to be gained by engaging this shower of Twits (if you got that second reference, good for you).

I pulled my things together and stood up, not saying a word.

"Oh, look at that, he's heading off to cry. What's the matter, don't like the taste of carpet?" this was Charlie Oxley, "the Ox", he's the captain of the second-fifteen rugby team. He's a dick.

"Of course I don't. It's carpet, it's not meant to be eaten," I said dryly, walking away.

I think I actually confused them for a minute.

"You trying to be smart with me?" the Ox said, following me, with the rest of the group in hot pursuit.

"I *am* smart, it's only you that has to try," I replied, passing the librarian's desk, where my comment had raised a snicker from Mrs Falstowe, the kindly, middle aged lady who runs the library.

"What did you just say?" he said, growing red in the face.

But I was already gone, I'd turned the corner, made sure I was out of sight, and bolted through a nearby door, going down a set of stairs, down a corridor connecting the main building to one of the science blocks, before ducking through an archway and out the other side.

Oh, that was going to cost me one day. And probably soon. I've spent too long getting away with murder, getting by on other people's apathy and a little nudge of mental magic. But now, unless I was willing to start enchanting vast swathes of the student body, I was going to have to find a way to solve this problem, and soon, or I was going to get myself lynched.

That was it for my Saturday. I stayed hidden like a sensible person, attending to my backlog, and checking my e-mail. I even had a chance to look through Onbridge House's duel roster for next week (Des' upcoming duel opponents). I finished my work in time for dinner, and ate that in a hurry. I shoved my tray into the wash rack and had started back for my room when I saw Belle walking towards the quad, on her own for once.

I wondered if she'd seen the roster and if she knew what she was up against. What did I lose by asking? I followed and called her name, she turned with a smile, which left her face as soon as she saw me instead of Desmond. We sound similar, as you might guess.

"What do *you* want?" she sneered, looking at me with naked hostility.

"Have you seen Onbridge's team, yet?" I asked, cutting straight to the chase.

"No, why would I?" she replied, crossing her arms and glaring at me.

"Because you're duelling them next week?"

"What's your point?" she said, growing obviously impatient.

"There are three of them, which means that one of you will have to go twice. Two aren't anything to worry about, adepts with a single element; but the third is a Wizard and a well-known turtler."

"A what?" she asked, an unpleasant expression appearing on her face.

"A turtler, it's a gaming term. They build up an impenetrable defence, wearing the opponent down before a single overwhelming strike to win the match."

"And?" she asked, glancing at her watch.

"And neither of you are have any practice at a long term duel. And neither of you can dispel for toffee."

"We do just fine," she said, turning away.

"He hurts people Annabelle," I said, which made her stop walking, "it always looks like an accident, but he's found a way to penetrate the wards. You and Des need to work on your shield-breakers and defences. Des will know what I mean. Just don't tell him it came from me. He'll refuse to look at it just to spite me, and one of you will get hurt."

She turned around to face me, looking me over.

"Why should I believe you?" she asked, "You and your brother aren't getting along right now, maybe you want him to fail."

I felt my eyes narrow in anger and I took a step towards her.

"He's my *brother*!" I hissed; she took a step back, "Whether he's acting like a child or not, he's still my twin, the other half of me! I wouldn't see him hurt for the world. If you don't believe me, fine, don't. Go check their website. They have *videos* for God's sake!"

I turned and stalked away, leaving her to it. She'd either believe me or she wouldn't. I'd done what I could.

Chapter 18

Sunday was quiet. Lie in followed by chapel, followed by indolence. Bill, Cathy and I spent the better part of the afternoon playing Starcraft II on a network Cathy'd set up between us. We sat on the grass under the shade for hours, forming and breaking alliances, laughing and generally wasting a whole day. It was great.

Monday dawned bright and breezy, but almost immediately the good weather of the weekend evaporated in sheets of rain that soaked everything and everyone to the bone. Des hadn't spoken to me since our little spat, and that looked like it wasn't going to change any time soon.

He wouldn't even *look* at me. I'd tried to approach him and he just walked away; I wasn't fast enough to chase him. The first part of that week passed very slowly, I was growing steadily more morose and worried as the day of the duels approached. The increasing hostility of the other kids didn't help with that.

Would you believe that people were now trying to trip me up as I walked down the corridor? And it was working, too. I'd taken three almost serious falls between Sunday and Wednesday morning.

Wednesday was quite sunny, no rain for a change. I spent the day in a barely controlled panic, to the extent that I could hardly eat my lunch. Bill and Cathy were looking at me in concern.

"He'll be fine," Cathy said.

"I know," I replied, trying to smile, "I just don't like the idea of him fighting someone who actually tries to injure their opponents, that's all."

"It's just a duel. The government wouldn't let kids do it if they could get seriously hurt, would they?" Bill asked.

I knew that. And nobody had ever died in the school championships. The worst that had ever happened was a broken bone, thankfully never a neck, and some third degree burns once, but that last one was more due to faulty equipment than anything else.

Desmond would be fine, he always was.

"You guys gonna come to the duel?" I asked hopefully.

"Wouldn't miss it," Cathy said.

"Naturally," said Bill.

I smiled, and tried to focus on my casserole.

It was another couple of hours before the duel. I did my best to distract myself. I was with Bill and Cathy when the Onbridge minibus finally turned up. Two skinny teenagers hopped out. One was tall, the other short, both boys, no more than sixteen. My mage sight spell showed two acolytes, both about midrange, neither trying to hide their power the way I do.

Then the Wizard dropped out of the van, and he was a monster! About average-sized, but broad like a bull. He looked almost like a shaved Neanderthal, completely bald, but with a single hairy eyebrow stretching from ear to ear.

From the looks of him I'd have thought him to be stupid, but then I saw his eyes, and there was an evil cunning there, brutal and harsh. I could practically feel kinetic power radiating from him, and the faintest hint of fire in his aura. Dangerous, very dangerous. Force Magic can form a very strong base for battle spells, if you know what you're doing. And he did, I would have placed money on it.

He glared around him, eyes lancing hostility into the crowd. This was not a friendly kid. Mr Koenig met them and shook hands with the Onbridge coach before leading them towards the changing rooms.

"Come on," Bill said, "we should go now if we want good seats."

Cathy and I followed, after I threw a last glance back at the ogre my brother or his girlfriend was going to have to face in the ring.

We filed into the gym, where the circle had been polished after yesterday's practice. The stands were quite full already, but we managed to find seats up at the front.

"Are they using the standard rules?" Bill asked, his leg jumping up and down in anticipation.

"Yes," said Cathy as she stared intently at the circle.

In case you don't know, the rules are quite simple. There's a coin toss at the beginning. Whoever wins gets to decide who chooses the first combatant. That means that you can force your opponent to pick first, which can effectively allow you to pit your water mage against their pyro for example. Each match is the played to touches. The first duellist to get three attacks, of any type, physical or magical, past their opponent's defence wins; simple as that.

The gym had finally filled up, all five hundred seats, with the staff in a roped off area at the back. The coaches led their teams in, and the crowd went berserk. It was quite surprising how much the public had taken to watching magicians' duels. Tickets to the last world championship were sold out fifteen minutes after they went on sale. Scalpers were able to charge five figures for tickets, it was insane.

Anyway, the two teams came out. Des and Belle wore Windward's white and sky-blue horizontal striped shirts and white tracksuit bottoms, the ogre and his hangers on wore the black and gold quartered shirts of Onbridge. They all wore the absorbent cuffs.

Koenig, as host, introduced the contestants to cheers, first the guests, and then our lot, at which point the cheers got so loud they hurt my ears.

"First round is Albert Taas versus Annabelle Warren!" Koenig bellowed, and then he explained the rules again for everyone.

The two contestants lined up at two red lines made of tape, facing each other, side on to the stands.

"Windward ready?" Koenig asked.

Belle nodded.

"Onbridge ready?"

Taas nodded.

"Duel!"

Belle had her hand up before Tass had even started to move. He ice bolt seared across the circle and slammed into his chest. The ice exploded on contact with the gauntlet's protective enchantments, Taas' gauntlet glowed bright red, showing a hit and a few shards of ice splattered on the floor.

"One-Nil Windward," Koening shouted over the roar of the crowd.

They lined up again. This time Taas was slightly faster and threw out a wall of flames that Belle desperately darted away from. Her second ice bolt died as she redirected her power into a hasty shield. The flames lapped around and Belle's gauntlet glowed red as it absorbed the heat.

"Two-one, Onbridge," Koening bellowed. As an acolyte against a Wizard, Taas got double points for his side with every strike, meaning that he could lose the duel, and Onbridge could still win the match.

They lined back up again.

This time Belle brought up a shield first, dodging to her left to avoid the next blast of fire. She kept her left hand pointing towards Taas and started calling ice to her right. Her hand glowed a very pale blue and ice crystals started forming. She started hurling tiny bullets of ice that forced Taas to shift his fire back to defend himself. She threw her ice lower and lower, until Taas' head was exposed, and then she concentrated the last of her stored ice into a single lance that flew straight for his chest.

"Two all."

It was essentially over. The last round was over in a flash as the acolyte was almost out of power, he threw a single fiery spear at Belle, which she easily deflected and then followed up with a token bullet at half speed to end the match in her favour.

"Three-two Windward. Warren wins the bout."

There was riotous applause, and Belle took a bow with a wide grin on her face. She shook the guy's hand, I saw her mouth "good match", and her opponent replied, "get you next time," with a smile.

The next match was Belle again, this time against an Asian acolyte named Chan. When Koenig gave the word, Chan gestured and his whole body lit up with arcing electrical energy, covering him head to foot in a powerful shield.

Belle conjured a shield of her own just as the first arc blasted from Chan. It bounced off, arced from the floor to the surrounding barrier and back to Chan, who caught it and threw three more from different directions as Belle threw an ice bolt.

Chan's defences caught it, and Belle took a hit to her rear.

"Four-three Onbridge. Chan one-nil."

Belle hissed in annoyance and got ready again. This time Chan attacked immediately, and threw three bolts of lightning before Belle could do anything. She dodged, but too late.

"Six-three Onbridge. Chan two-nil."

This time Belle was mad, and hurled a wall of ice at Chan as she dove away, bringing a shield up to block his riposte, which bounced into the ground and exploded in sparks. The wall of ice smashed his defence away and Belle followed up with a trio of bullets that smacked into him.

"Six-four Onbridge. Chan two-one."

The next point went to Belle too, a simple rapid attack that Chan couldn't move out of the way of.

It came down to the last point. Belle was brutal, fast and untouchable. She jumped and rolled, coming up with a shield surrounding her body in ice. She darted forward, sheets of ablative ice-shielding shooting forwards to absorb the electrical attacks in explosions of steam and lightning.

Then she was close and lashed out with her ice covered fists, lances of energy battering Chan's shields down before she finished him off with a single swipe to his chest.

The crowd went wild.

All tied up, six-six.

And now it was my brother's turn...

Chapter 19

"Final round. Desmond Graves versus Adam Trench."

They faced off. The ogre was almost twice as broad as my brother. Trench planted his feet and spread his arms, Des put his left arm forward, bracing his body like he was holding a tackling pad in Rugby practice.

"Duel!"

Des struck first. A small burst of light that smacked into Trench's quick-cast shield (which was not unimpressive. Casting shields quickly is not easy unless you go with energy-intensive pure-Will barriers, which Trench's was not). Des cast another burst, and then another, with increasing power, until he realised he wasn't making progress and threw out a continuous beam that scorched the Force-based shield and made it glow brighter and brighter before it finally collapsed with a crack.

Des took the first point.

Trench didn't look like he cared. It was worrying me.

Round two. This time it took even more of Des' power to break the barrier, and by the time he was done he was breathing hard, his reserves greatly depleted.

Second round to Des, and Trench hadn't thrown a single attack spell yet, nor had he bothered to build a strong defence, or use any of the tricks I'd seen him use in his videos. And then it hit me. It was so simple! He was making Des tire himself out, and it was working. Des hadn't bothered with a dispel, or any of the other simple ways to dismantle a one-dimensional shield like Trench's, he'd simply attacked with raw power.

And now Des was probably going to pay for it...

Round three started much the same way, but this time Trench started by raising more powerful shields. It began with a simple force field, facing forwards, layered and strong enough to withstand the intermittent blasts of light and fire Desmond was throwing Trench's way. With that in place, he expanded the shield to cover his body, until he was covered in flickering blue light.

Trench started walking towards Des, who started to get desperate as his opponent closed the distance. His spellwork became sloppy, wasted energy flaring uselessly throughout the circle.

It didn't take Trench long to close with Des, and his main barrier had barely been scratched. Trench backed Des up to the edge of the circle, and threw a single punch at Des' very weak forward shields, pulling a whole mess of his own shields' force into his fist. The safety gauntlet caught most of it, everything magical in fact, but that still left a meaty fist on the end of a very muscular arm, which hit Des right in the face. The gauntlet was only designed to stop magic based attacks, not a simple physical one.

Des lost three teeth from that hit, and got a long gash on his cheek when he hit the ground face-first. I was on my feet and running before Koenig could call it. Des was still on the ground when I arrived, spitting blood onto the floor.

"You can't do that!" Chang shouted at me.

I may have said something trite, likely inviting him to do something anatomically improbable.

Then I was at Des' side, looking at the wound with my mage sight. It was deep, but no permanent damage had been done. Apart from the teeth. I collected those, in case a dentist could put them back in, or something.

"Matron!" I shouted, pulling his chin up gently so the blood wouldn't run into his eye.

"Get off," he said, "duel's not done."

"Are you insane, he's beating you to a pulp! Mister Koenig?!"

"How are you, son?" Koenig said, kneeling down by Des. Belle was there too, holding his hand.

"I'm fine. I want to carry on," Des said.

"Des, please, you've got nothing to prove!" I said.

"Get away from me!" he said, backhanding me and sending me to the floor with a split lip.

"Desmond!" Koenig said, anger crossing his features.

And all the while Trench was standing there, looking on with a slick smile on his face.

"Oh look, their fighter would rather pick on the other kids than duel a mage. Oh well, I guess it's true what they say about light mages: all flash, no substance."

Oh it was so on. I stood up and was a good two steps towards the ape before I felt strong arms around my shoulders, dragging me back.

"Matty, keep away from that thing, it's not worth it," Belle said.

"Listen to her, son," said Koenig from my other side.

They were bodily dragging me back towards the stands; probably for the best. Trench would have mopped the floor with me in that state. I hadn't called a single spark of magic. I was going to go up against a Will and Force Wizard with my weak little fists.

And then he laughed.

"Even the mundane has more spirit than your mages," he said.

"Mister Trench! Mind your manners!" his coach said in a sharp tone.

"Sorry, sir," he said, meaning it not at all.

Des stood up.

"I can continue," he said, his eyes blazing with rage.

Trench smiled.

"Mister Koenig, stop this!" I bellowed. Belle may have said something similar, I wasn't really paying attention to much except the incoming act of stupidity.

Koenig had a talk with the matron who looked Des over. They muttered, but in the end, Koenig decided to allow the match to continue.

He stood near me along with Belle, all of us next to the ring. I was petrified.

The next round went just like the previous. Des giving it all he was worth, and Trench taking one ponderous step after another to deliver a crushing blow. This time he hit Des square in the gut, dropping him to the ground again. I winced, but Des soon got back to his feet, not too worse for wear, and I let out a breath I'd been holding.

They lined up again.

I felt a hand grab my own and looked over to see Belle wearing a look of fear on her face. I squeezed back and reassure her, but I wasn't too confident. Then I took a look at Trench and I felt even worse. The look on his face... and that nasty, smug smile. I knew on the spot that he was going to do his utmost to hurt my brother in this last round. I had to stop it. Somehow I had to.

Screw my secret. I started assembling a spell.

The final round. All scores tied, this one would take the duel and the whole evening for the winner. This time Des didn't attack. He brought up his own shield and started layering it. No dispels still, why didn't he listen? His shield was fire based, a large square of static flames, bound up with kinetic energy.

While Des was erecting his clumsy carrier, Trench was already finishing his own standard spells. Just as Des finished, Trench started that inexorable damned march of his. This time Des went to meet him, a coil of fire around his right hand, which he sent searing towards his enemy. Trench's main barrier absorbed it, and he kept coming, barely slowed.

Des didn't have the chance to cast another attack spell before Trench hit him. The force of the strike shattered Des' shield and sent shards of flame cascading around the circle, raising sparks on the barrier protecting the crowd. Des flew back a couple of steps and fell, almost all his shields gone. Trench came forward, raising his meaty fists, covered in power, aiming a blow at my brother's head.

Des was readying an attack, but it would be too late. If he hit Des like that, his head would hit the hard floor, and his skull would crack, no two ways about it. I waited until Trench started to bring those hands down, and then I acted.

Here's the problem with using Will as a base for your spells the way Trench was. It's all part of a single enchantment, the one connecting Magic to mind. Everything else is built on that single continuous spell. When you craft a Will based spell, you should create smaller, separate shells for each one, which prevents anyone doing to you what I was about to do to Trench.

And what Des could have done to Trench if he'd listened to my bloody advice.

The fists came down.

And a barrier of bright, blue light flashed into existence between Des and Trench, sparkling with intricate shapes and clusters of power. Trench's fists hit, and twelve layers of dispels detonated in his face.

Dispels are immensely difficult to produce, but there are a couple of ways to do it. The simpler one involves a spell that interacts with and dismantles another spell. This can fail, as the spells can be incompatible. The second is a 'pure' dispel. Magic that is perfectly neutral, designed to neutralise the magic of another spell. The problem is in *conjuring* that type of magic. It takes concentration and practice to strip some of your innate power down to a neutral state. That also makes dispels very power-costly.

Generally worth it, though, as without the underlying Will, every spell wrapped around Trench immediately collapsed. All that energy was suddenly released, and Trench was blasted out of the ring by the kinetic energy contained in his own shields. Even if the energy hitting him hadn't been enough to cost him the point, stepping (or being thrown) from the circle costs a point too.

I heard Belle gasp as she saw what had happened. She looked at me for a moment in shock, still holding my hand. And then the cheering began. Trench hauled himself to his feet, mostly unharmed, if a little dazed, and promptly fell over again.

I breathed a sigh of relief as Koenig marched into the ring.

"Graves wins, three-two! Windward victory, nine-eight!"

The room exploded with noise. I pressed the hanky with Des' teeth in it into Belle's hand.

"Get these to him a.s.a.p., a dentist may be able to put them back!" I shouted over the noise.

"Okay!" she shouted back, still looking at me strangely. She let go and went with the swirling crowd of people that had hefted my brother up onto their shoulders. He was grinning like an idiot, no doubt under the same impression as the crowd, that he had won that duel. I let them flow around me and sat back down on the benches, where Cathy and Bill were waiting for me.

"Holy shit!" Bill said once the majority of the crowd was gone "How the hell did he pull off that last minute miracle?"

"Yes," Cathy said, turning to look at me with suspicious eyes, "how do you suppose that happened, Matty?"

I hadn't fooled her for a second. I smiled at her sadly, and went back to looking at my shoes. Well, all things considered, the night wasn't a complete disaster. Des was alright, Belle was alright, the ogre's been knocked down a peg or two. He was still having trouble remaining conscious, in fact.

That's good, I wouldn't want him permanently harmed... yet. But one day, I was going to have to pay him a little visit about what happened tonight.

But that was another day. One problem at a time.

Chapter 20

The three of us went back to the dining hall and had dinner in a quiet corner; all the while the rest of the crowd was chattering and practically shrieking with excitement, something that got even louder when Belle came in. She came over to us and set her tray down for a second.

"One of the matrons took him to an emergency dentist," she said without preamble.

"Good," I said, feeling blue again, as I should have been with him. Des hates the dentist.

"I..." she started, looking right at me, but then she seemed to think better of it, "I'll see you later."

She scuttled off to her adoring fans. Bill looked after her with longing in his eyes.

"I could show her some magic, if only she'd give me the chance..." Bill said wistfully.

"Billy!" Cathy said, going bright red. That kind of talk makes her uncomfortable. So naturally Bill did it as often as he could.

"What? I'm just saying that if she really wanted to learn magic, I have a wand she could practice on..."

"Whoa! Even I have to call creepy on that one," I said, trying to look disgusted. Cathy's redness had spread to her ears.

"Sorry, sorry. You know the magnetic effect I have on the ladies works both ways," he said, waggling his eyebrows at Cathy, who went an interesting shade of vermillion, and lost the ability to speak.

"Mate, look what you did," I said, as Cathy started sweating, "feel the room, huh? Cathy, you want an ice-pack?"

"Nope," she squeaked, slowly recovering, but still unable to look up from her pasta.

"New topic," Bill said, "did anyone see the flyer?"

"What flyer?" I asked, eager for a conversational change.

"Main board. A lecture series on "The History of Magic, and its Relevance to Modern Society". Anyone wanna go?"

"I already know more than is good for my health," I replied.

"I'll go," Cathy said, her interest piqued. That's the thing about Cathy, when she has an interest in something, she *inhales* every piece of information on or about it; it's ridiculous.

We chatted for a while longer and then made our way out of the dining hall before going our separate ways. I headed back to my room, where I intended to sleep until all this crap was a bad memory.

The next few days passed slowly for me. Des was back in class the next day, the hero of the hour, and very confident in his own skills and prowess. The dentist had managed to fit his teeth back in without too much fuss. The gash on his cheek had needed a couple of stitches and still looked a little ugly. If he'd let me near him, I probably could have fixed all those injuries right up with a little surreptitious casting.

But he still wasn't having anything to do with me. I got all this information second hand through Belle, who was being much more agreeable with me lately, which was a pleasant surprise.

But it wasn't until Saturday that things started to move forward, because that evening I finally received an email from Tethys.

My new friend,

The only Shaadre to be recently sold was done so three years ago to an organisation calling themselves the Sons of the Dark Moon. A group of Magicians and Pureborn desperate to usher in what they call the "Reign of Shadows". No one knows what that is, what they plan to do to get it going or who their members are.

My contact knew only one mage, who acted as a go-between. A mutual friend of ours, the good Professor.

If you will take some advice, don't attempt to invade his home. Even a magician as "interesting" as yourself would have trouble dealing with him behind his own walls.

To my knowledge, the Sons are the only active group insane enough to use a Shaadre as a weapon. Also, the creatures themselves are quite rare according to my source, you may, in fact, have killed off the last one. Attempts to domesticate them have almost universally met with calamity. This allows me to greatly narrow down the possibilities for you.

This is as far as I am willing to go. There's no way I'm crossing them, not even for my dear new friend.

Should you require my services in the future, no doubt we can come to an equitable arrangement, and you know where to find me. I'll leave a VIP pass for you.

Yours,

Tethys.

Even with an e-mail, that woman can tantalise...

So, now I had a lead, but how to go about exploiting it? Wilks was a Sorcerer, that's what he said anyway, and I had no reason to doubt his word on *that* (even if he was a duplicitous bastard on everything else). So I would need to think, and plan carefully, before confronting him again. At the very least he was complicit in human trafficking and maybe the slave trade, so caution was the order of the day.

Tonight, though, I could start with a little observation.

I left the computer lab, already making plans for my excursion, and started making my way back to Kimmel. I was yawning by this point, I hadn't been sleeping well lately. I was a few feet from the door when I heard someone call my name.

"Hey Mathew!" she said, and I turned to see Courtney Wilcox smiling at me.

I was surprised and confused for a moment. This was... unusual. Forget that, unprecedented! The only pretty girl to give me the time of day in the last four years has been Cathy.

"Hello," I replied stupidly, turning to face her. She kept that dazzling smile pointed at me as she walked up to me. She was wearing home clothes, tight shirt and jeans, a hint of makeup. She was stunning.

"Wanna see something awesome?" she asked playfully, taking my hand.

Now, in my defence, I was seventeen. Pretty girls do not smile at me often. I was flustered.

She dragged me into the night, and I followed like a lemming. She was laughing, and it seemed to be genuinely cheerful. It made me smile. She led me out towards the rugby pitches, past the cricket pavilion, and it was only at *this* point that I started to smell a rat. So much for my vaunted intelligence.

"Where are we going?" I asked, now a little nervous.

"It's amazing," she said, giggling as she led me towards the copse of trees that marked the boundary of the school grounds.

"What is?"

We passed a shed, and were about ten good steps from the trees when her posture changed.

"How gullible you are," she answered with an evil smile. She dropped my hand and stepped away. Dark shapes seemed to detach themselves from the shadows, they moved in, surrounding me. I even think that someone was hiding behind a set of Rugby posts nearby.

About fifteen kids, all told. Nine guys, six girls, including Courtney, and... yes, there was the Ox, looking smug.

"Not so smart now, are you?" he asked as torches blazed to life all around me.

I have to admit, he rather had a point.

Chapter 21

Wow. I literally fell for the oldest trick in the book. There were *cavemen* who knew better than to fall for that.

Courtney had her arm around the Ox's neck, and everyone was smiling. It would appear that I took the baby step required to get from "Carrie" to "Lord of the Flies", after all.

"I guess that makes you Jack," I said, looking at Ox.

"What? The name's Charles!"

"Jack as in Lord of the Flies," I explained.

"What?" he said again, now looking irritated.

"Really? No one here knows Lord of the Flies?" I asked, looking around. Blank stares.

"Seriously, pick up a book sometime, you might be surprised at the parallels to your daily lives in the classics."

I was just talking, trying to buy myself some time to think my way out of my latest mess. Also it doesn't do to show fear to predators, it makes them think you're food. And this lot were as close to a pack as you can get and still be considered human.

Alright, options.

I could run. They would chase me, they would catch me, and that would be that. I could fight, and I would lose. I could use magic, and lose a lot more. The only subtle magic I had was the mental stuff, and I simply wasn't good enough to use it on the fly without considerable risk of injury to the target. I could probably knock up an Asimov in a quarter of an hour, but that would stop one of them, what about the other fourteen? And that was assuming they'd give me the quarter-hour. I could use a sleep spell, or a memory charm, like I'd used on the bouncer and the bartender, but there were just too many for that to go unnoticed, and we're back to discovery.

Horrible though the idea was, if I had any hope of getting out of that mess, I was going to have to *talk* my way out, and that just has "teenager's body found in ditch" headlines written all over it. Still, I can always atomise them if push comes to shove.

So, needs must.

"We're not here to talk about books," Ox said, taking a heavy step forward, no doubt meaning to appear intimidating, but just coming across as clumsy.

"Movies, then?" I said, stepping towards him lightly, keeping my expression calm and neutral.

"What? No. We're not here to talk!"

"Well, I can't dance," I said. A look of bovine confusion crossed his face and he actually stopped for a second, trying to puzzle through my reactions. I don't think he was expecting the conversation to go quite like this.

"No one's asking you to dance!" he said finally.

"Oh, alright then, I guess I'll see you later," I said, and just walked past him through a gap in the group.

I kept on walking, heading for the copse of trees, it wasn't deep, but it was dark, and my shadows could hide me once I was out of sight of the pack. I figured I had a couple of seconds before Ox recovered his wits enough to-"

"Don't just stand there, stop him!" Courtney yelled.

Oh shit. I *hate* that girl. I ran. I called the shadows, and they waited for me on the far side of the nearest tree. It should be safe enough to vanish as long as I was out of line-of-sight when I did. I was five steps away when she yelled.

I started sprinting. Four steps, three. Then two...

I felt a colossal impact as Ox hit me in the small of my back in a perfect rugby tackle. I hit the ground like a sack of potatoes. My shadows were there, tantalisingly out of reach. A tiny coil slithered towards me, so I exerted my will and sent it away. I shoved my elbow back and my arm went numb and then tingly as I smacked my funny bone into the Ox's face.

He yelped and let go, I shoved myself to my feet. But too slow. I felt a set of impacts as three of Ox's brutes landed on me. I felt the air rush out of my lungs again (this was happening far too often lately), and an awful burning wrench in my left shoulder as they grabbed my arm and pulled.

I yelped in pain and started thumping and kicking with my remaining limbs. I hit a few soft parts, but I think I was just pissing them off. And then they started hitting me back. And trust me, what those cretins lacked in brains they more than made up for in pure brawn. There was nothing I could do to stop them from punching and kicking me until I couldn't easily get up anymore.

I was in so much pain that all I could do was try to protect myself. I wrapped my arms around my head, curled up into a protective ball and tried to ride it out as best I could. Any attempt to get away just resulted in more pain. I managed to keep my ribs and skull intact, but everywhere else took repeated hits and kicks, and my face took a couple of good smacks despite my best efforts. My nose bled, there were a couple of deep cuts above my eye and my lips split again before they gave up and just held me there.

Now that they weren't hitting me I noticed that there were five of them on me, so I needn't have felt too bad about losing, even if I was badly bruised and I had about twelve or thirteen pulled muscles sending spikes of pain around my body with every movement. They hauled me to my feet, and I was too hurt to stop them.

Two of them held me with my arms behind my back. Blood ran into my left eye, so I couldn't see out of it. Everything hurt, and I was a little punch-drunk. Even if I'd wanted to use magic, it would be an awful idea now, I might actually kill someone.

No. I *would* kill someone. When you can't concentrate, and you're that angry, Magic will kill, it's that simple. And I was truly furious.

I spat blood out of my mouth, swallowing some had made me queasy. I could feel my throat swelling up a little.

Ox stood in front of me, barely a scratch on him, maybe a small mark on his cheek. I am so bad at this, it's ridiculous.

"Pathetic," he said, punching me in the solar plexus. I responded by gasping, and when he dragged my head up by my hair, I kneed him in the groin. He made a sound half way between a mouse that's had its tail stepped on, and a water buffalo that's been surprised by a lioness.

I found it greatly comforting.... right up until the point that he stood up and punched me hard enough in the head that I saw sparks, and things got a little fuzzy after that. I think I'd got a mild concussion, and even been knocked out for a while. I faded in and out of consciousness, I felt rough hands grabbing me, and then I was propped up against something cold; which soon became bitterly cold. I saw a brief flare of light that may have been fire, but I was too out of it to be sure at that point, and I slid into a welcoming darkness.

I came back to my senses after what felt like seconds but was probably more like half an hour. I was hard up against a set of rugby posts, these ones much closer to the school than the ones those idiots had been hiding behind. I would be in full view of one of the girl's houses once the sun came up. I was tied to it by rough rope, my mouth was gagged by a strip of cloth, and but for my Spiderman boxer shorts (such a bad day to be wearing those), I was completely naked.

Nearby was a smouldering pile which was all that was left of my clothes. I was in considerable pain from my feet (which had been stomped on, and were now lacking circulation) to my head (which had been pounded on like a tough piece of beef). I felt awful, but my mind was working.

I called my shadows. They came and ripped the rope apart. I would have fallen, but they caught me, holding me up and wrapping around my freezing body. I pulled the gag from my mouth and had to spit out more blood. My legs wouldn't work on their own, they were numb from the cold, and the muscles felt like they'd been ripped to pieces, besides.

So I used the shadows again to get me back to Kimmel, letting the darkness engulf everything, so that I'd go unseen. I felt utterly humiliated and livid with anger that I couldn't get rid of. I felt my face grow hotter with every shaky step I took. I even felt tears of shame and helplessness fall from my eyes and down my swollen cheeks.

By the time I got back to my room, I was ready to collapse. I washed briefly and lowered myself gingerly onto the bed. I pulled my covers tight over my head and stifled a single enraged sob before thumping the wall, which only hurt me more, as it sent a chain reaction of agony down my knotted back.

Surveillance would have to wait a while. A very long while.

Chapter 22

I woke up unable see a thing. I flew into a blind panic for a minute (ooh, bad choice of words) until my hands went to my face and I discovered that I wasn't *actually* blind. My right eye was just swollen shut, and my left was sealed by a small puddle of dried blood. I went to the sink by memory and washed the blood from my face with some care. And then I saw myself and wished I hadn't.

My body was a giant bruise. There were few patches from my hairline to my feet that weren't the wrong colour, even purple in places. My muscles ached, and I could barely stay upright without squealing (in a thoroughly manly way, of course). My legs started to shake after only a few seconds on my feet, and I had to sit down again.

I would have preferred to start some basic healing spells, but I'd woken up too late, and I didn't have time before the morning services started. I'd already missed breakfast, so I dressed quickly in my Sunday best and limped for the chapel as quickly as I could, which wasn't very.

I drew quite a few glances on the way there, and more as I took my customary seat with Bill and Cathy. The chapel was quite beautiful. It was larger than some cathedrals, high ceilinged and wood panelled, lit by candle-bulbs under white shades. The wooden panels were carved beautifully, leading the eye forward to a beautiful fresco behind the altar, showing a scene of the crucifixion.

My friends looked at me like they didn't recognise me for a second, and then Cathy squeaked, and Bill turned slightly green. Before they could ask me what had happened, the organ started playing the opening hymn. Bill had to help me stand up, and Cathy looked like she was about to cry for the first half hour.

It seemed like a longer service than usual, and through it all both Bill and Cathy kept looking at me like I was going to keel over at any moment. I also discovered that I'd lost my voice, which came out as an anaemic croak, not that I was much of a singer to begin with.

Damn, but that was a very bad morning.

Finally the service was over, and I limped out of the chapel with my friends. The muttering and staring continued as we walked, but I ignored it. As soon as we were clear the questions began. I told them what had happened in my rasping voice, and they immediately started swearing, calling the buggers for blind. It made me smile.

We settled down in the square while everyone else went back to their rooms to change.

"Have you had anything looked at yet?" Cathy asked, "Some of that looks pretty bad."

"It's fine," I replied, "besides, I don't want to have to answer questions, it's embarrassing enough."

"What?! It's them who should be embarrassed, picking on you like a pack of animals," Bill said.

"Yep, but I still fell for it."

"That was pretty stupid," Bill agreed.

"Billy!" Cathy snapped.

"Sorry," Bill said.

"It's not Pooh's fault that he got his head stuck in the honey pot," she added.

Bill laughed so hard he nearly fell off his seat, the bastard.

"Oh ha ha," I said, glaring one-eyed at Cathy, who was sniggering, "it's not funny."

"I'll grant you that the beating's not all that funny, but the fact that you were tricked by a group of people whose combined IQ isn't a match for yours because one of them was wearing tight jeans and a low-cut top is kind'a hilarious," Bill offered.

"I want you to know that I've given it some thought, and I hate both of you," I replied, though I was grinning like an idiot.

"Lunch?" Bill said.

"I could eat," I replied.

And just like that I felt a little better.

The rest of the day passed pleasantly enough, and I allowed myself to think that things were going to be alright. None of the teachers had asked how I'd come by my injuries, so that was something.

Naturally I'd put off going to look for Wilks again. I was in no state for it, and it would be a while before I was. At the end of the day I spent some time casting healing spells on myself that would last the night and help to repair some of the damage. I knew other, more powerful spells for triage, but they would work too effectively removing my injuries overnight, which would raise awkward questions. So the weaker ones would have to do.

Monday, however, proved to be something of a bad day.

It started off alright, and some of my aches and pains had been soothed by a night of sleeping and healing. I was actually optimistic... and then I saw the first of the posters. They were A1-sized and glossy. They showed (and rather clearly, too) an image of me, bloody, beaten and gagged, tied to the rugby posts.

They were *everywhere*, at least five in the corridor I was standing in. I yanked down the one in front of me, and the others I passed on the way to the dining hall, even as I knew that it wouldn't help. There would be more. I felt my face go red again as I thought through the possibilities of what I could do to get my own back for this.

I felt a nasty rage building up inside me, and the corridor went dark around me, solid shadows scraping against the wooden walls. I heard a wrenching crack before I got my emotions under control and the shadows dissolved. One of the heavy oak panels had been ripped open. Splinters were lying on the floor, revealing the light-grey stonework behind what was left of the panel. I shook my head to clear my thoughts and calm myself down.

That was unforgivable of me. What if there'd been someone around? My heart was pounding and my sore head was throbbing as a result. So I breathed and thought it through. It was just a few pictures, a small addition to my humiliation, no great problem, all things considered. What with the gossip around this place, it was likely everyone already knew anyway, so nothing lost there.

It was best just to carry on and do my best to ignore it.

I went to breakfast, and it was still early, so not that many people there. I sat down with Cathy and started eating. Bill hadn't arrived yet.

"Saw the posters," she said.

"And?" I asked.

"Not good," she replied.

"You can say that again."

Chapter 23

The next three days introduced me to an interesting blend of pity and amusement. I had five separate visits from housemasters and headmasters insisting that I tell them what had happened to me. I said I couldn't remember. The answer seemed to satisfy them.

You might wonder why I didn't just turn the bastards in, and you know, I'm not sure. If I'm honest, it might well be because somewhere in the back of my mind was the idea that I wanted to deal with them myself one day, and I couldn't make them suffer if they were expelled (at least not without a lot more effort than I was willing to expend).

I must say that Ox and his crowd kept quiet in the days that followed, whether from gratitude over my silence or in fear of my speaking, I'm not sure, but they left me alone.

Des even came to check on me.

It was an awkward conversation. I think he felt bad about the way he'd treated me, but he couldn't find a way to make things right without his pride taking a hit. I tried to meet him half way, but he wouldn't reconcile without me revealing my source, so I gave him Wilks' name, and he went off relatively happy.

I wanted the rift between us repaired, and I lost nothing by giving him a name the SCA already had. Even so, there was a distance there, now that he'd raised his hand to me. Now that he'd exerted his strength and placed himself above me, it was as if our relationship were made of glass which he'd broken. It would never be quite the same, no matter how hard we worked to gather up the pieces and stick them back together.

By Thursday the healing spells had brought the swelling down around my eye and the pulled muscles were working properly again. I left the bruises to deflect questions, and shut down the spells.

Early that evening, I was making plans for surveillance when Bill came to see me.

"Mathew, lecture time, come on mate!" he said, rushing through the door while I was getting some clothes out.

"What lecture?" I asked.

"The magic thing," he replied.

"Had enough magic stuff for a while," I replied, waving him on his way.

And thus began the negotiation.

Bill doesn't like going to these things on his own, and Cathy refuses to gossip and snipe about the presenters afterwards, so he has to have me come along so he has someone to bitch to later.

It always goes the same way. I refuse, he pleads. I refuse again, he tries to bribe me. I refuse a final time before he begs and I give in. Every time. I don't even know why I bother arguing anymore.

"Fine, fine!" came my inevitable reply. I pulled my blazer on and followed him to the auditorium.

It was one of the larger buildings on campus, part of the music complex. It could seat the whole school, and was generally used for things like assemblies, the weekend movie and concerts. Today it was about half full, magic being a hot topic. Bill and I joined Cathy in an empty section near the middle on the left.

"Caved again?" Cathy asked as I sat next to her.

"No," I replied.

Bill stuck his head around me and nodded vigorously with an idiotic grin on his face. Cathy snorted, pulling out a notebook. She selected a pen and got ready to take notes.

"Really?" I asked, "About this?"

She gave me an exasperated look. She always took notes. There was nothing she experienced that she didn't have written down somewhere. Bill had once joked that she'd taken notes on what the doctor was doing as he'd delivered her. I wouldn't be surprised.

"Alright," I said, raising my hands in surrender.

More people were filing in. Belle and Des came in and took seats near the front. My brother nodded at me and Belle smiled, I returned the gestures. Bill noticed the smile and gave me a look and a raised eyebrow, which I ignored. Then there was the Ox and his hangers on, Courtney among them. All in one convenient group. Oh the potential for some surreptitious fun! The ideas were already trickling though my brain...

Then the lecturer came in and the auditorium shut up as Mister Kenilworth introduced her to us. I was only half paying attention, as I was lining up the first of a dozen interesting mental curses when I heard a snippet of his speech.

"-and she is a prominent business owner, operating a variety of clubs and restaurants with ties to the mystical community here and abroad. Please welcome Ms. Tethys Smyth."

Wait, what now?

And Smyth? Really?

I looked up and saw what I least expected. It was her, alright and she was looking insufferably pleased with herself. She was dressed in relatively modest business attire, black and stylish, with a set of black high heels. Her neckline was just plunging enough to be distracting.

"Good evening ladies and gentlemen," she began, looking around the room like a shark eyeing a shoal of particularly slow-moving minnow. I immediately tensed up and cast a set of quick mental shield spells on myself. I held off on Bill and Cathy, I didn't want to risk drawing attention just yet.

I reminded myself that she hadn't seen my face, and I was among a great many other people who would mask my scent... hopefully. There was also still a little bit of swelling and bruising on my face that would help matters further. I made sure that I appeared outwardly calm and decided to wait it out.

"I'm here to talk to you about magic and how it relates to our community," she began. Everyone was already hanging on her every word. What was she doing here? I wasn't arrogant enough to assume that it was about me, but I couldn't imagine a happy reason for her to be in a room full of adolescents, where her particular hormone-inducing powers would have the greatest effect.

"So, who can tell me how magicians are governed?" she asked.

Cathy started to raise her arm. I grabbed it and pulled it back to her hand rest. She turned to look at me, an angry look on her face, but then she saw the naked fear in my eyes and swallowed hard, settling down. Bill saw the gesture and he stopped smiling, too.

Des answered the question.

"The government, just like everyone else," he offered.

"You sound familiar, have we met before?" she asked.

Shit.

"I don't think so," Des answered with a grin, "I'd have remembered that." There were some chuckles from the auditorium.

"Indeed," she said, "and wrong. Her majesty's government would like the general public to think that they are the ultimate authority, but in fact the magical community answers to the Conclave. This is made up of a High Council and a judiciary, which in turn has its own police force. These exist independently of HM government control and oversight, something that has been a constant source of contention."

"So, with that in mind, do any of you know who their head of state is?"

No one did, and actually, neither did I. In spite of myself, I paid attention. She smiled.

"There are five magicians. They are called the Archons. They are the strongest among them, the living embodiments of the five greater elements, Life, Death, Shadow, Time and Space. There are only ever five with this kind of power, when one dies another is born, simple as that."

"How come we've never heard of them?" Des asked.

Good question.

"Because they haven't been seen in almost twenty years, when it was rumoured that one of them died, murdered by the others. It was thought that they all just went away, crippled by their guilt, never to be seen again, and without them around the Conclave decided to transfer their political power to their own organisation, which in turn led to the Great Revelation."

"But how is this of interest to you? It's a good story, but so what? Well, the main job of the Archons was to stop the mages that became too dangerous for the Conclave to handle. The job that is now done by the government-backed SCA. They were the last line of defence against the really nasty stuff. The monsters, the demons, and most dangerous of all, the Shadowborn."

Uh oh.

"What's a Shadowborn?" Belle asked.

Thank you, Belle...

"Monsters in human form," she said, "a magician that can call the very shadows themselves, and use them as he sees fit. Eventually, that power corrupts them. All of them eventually turn into monsters, deformed by power and madness, unable even to step into the light of day."

She paused for effect.

"And if my information is correct, then there's one of them in this very room."

Chapter 24

Well. Crap.

Just be cool. I'm fine. No one would suspect it's me. Cathy had taken my hand and was squeezing it very hard. I didn't mind, I was squeezing right back.

Tethys was looking out at the crowd, who were themselves looking around frantically, as if a monster was about to leap out from under a chair.

"This Shadowborn is clever, meticulous and a very skilled mage. He'll hide in plain sight, and will conceal the full extent of his powers. Is there anyone in here that fits that description?"

Hee hee! I'm in the clear! No one here even knows I have powers, except for Cathy.

"It's Graves!" Courtney said, "He never should have won that duel the other night! We all thought it was too convenient!"

Ah damn it!

"Who's Graves?" Tethys asked, staring at the crowd.

Courtney pointed Desmond out, and Tethys' eyes bored in on him.

"Stand up, Mister Graves," Tethys said. I may not have known the woman all that well, but the look in her eye said that she was thoroughly enjoying this far too much.

Desmond stood up, his face showing how scared he was, though he tried to conceal it. Belle stayed seated, but she kept glancing up at where I was sitting.

"Come up here," she said with a beckoning gesture that somehow managed to look dirty. Des obeyed.

"Are you a shadow mage?" she asked, an evil smile playing over her face.

"No, of course not!" he said, a little tremble in his voice that made him sound guilty. Des didn't really have the social skills to deal with situations like this. Neither did I, but he was worse.

"I don't know," Tethys said, "that's just what one would say. What about the rest of you, any doubts about this young man?"

"He was there when the monster attacked the party!" Courtney shouted. The rest of the students started muttering, Tethys was turning the crowd against him, and *far* too easily.

"He's always acting shifty!" Ox bellowed. The crowd muttered their approval.

They were getting rowdy, and that was dangerous. They were one good push away from turning into an angry mob, and *yet again* there was Mister Kenilworth ignoring everything, letting this bullshit happen in his school.

"You know, there is a test we could do, almost like a trial," Tethys said.

"Yeah!" one of the girls shouted.

"Trial! Trial!" another chanted.

A few of the boys were getting up, moving forward.

"But, I'm not!" Des cried out, "I'm a light-mage. I've never even touched the shadows!"

He looked so scared. Des had never been good at dealing with confrontation like this; he'd never had to face something even remotely like this before. I wasn't having that.

"ENOUGH!" a voice bellowed through the room. It was a second before I realised it was mine. I was on my feet, and I'd never been so angry in my entire life.

"Oh yes, and what do you have to-" Tethys began.

"QUIET!" I shouted.

My voice had never sounded like that before. It was deep and commanding; I wish I could do it on cue.

"Mister Graves!" Kenilworth was on his feet and glaring at me, "This woman is a guest speaker, and you will-"

"One more word, sir, and I'll have every lawyer within fifty miles breathing down your neck. You almost presided over a witch-trial, do you understand what that means?!"

He shut up, and I walked down the stairs, keeping my eyes on Tethys. She looked me over and smiled once.

"Good to see you again, Mister...? Graves was it? I can see the resemblance. Your brother, I presume?"

"Des is not a shadow mage. I would know, and anyone who would look to prove otherwise would have me to deal with, am I understood?" I asked looking her square in the eye. The threat was clear. Secrecy was no longer a priority, back off or be prepared for round three.

"Oh yeah, you and what army?" Ox bellowed from the stands, raising more laughter.

"Be quiet, you small minded, pathetic excuse for a child, or so help me God I will reveal to these people just how much of a coward you really are!"

He went puce, but he sat down. The rest of his group looked shifty too, and they kept quiet.

"Ms Smyth, I asked you a question," I said, turning back to her.

"Yes you did. I agree, your brother is not the mage I'm looking for," she said, smiling broadly at me.

"Glad we have that sorted," I said, "Des, come on, we're leaving."

He nodded, and he walked over to me, his eyes downcast. Belle got up and followed, Cathy and Bill soon after. I gestured them out a side door, keeping myself between them and Tethys, who was still grinning broadly at me. I glared at her once and backed out into the night air.

They were all waiting for me out there, and suddenly I felt dizzy.

Oh crap! What had I done? I'd threatened the headmaster in front of witnesses! I'd publicly faced down the one creature willing and able to reveal my secret to the whole school! And I'd re-pissed off the school bully, humiliating him in front of an audience.

Shiiiiit!

I was in so much trouble! What the hell was I going to do now?

My thoughts were interrupted when Des pulled me into a crushing hug that stopped me breathing properly.

"I'm so sorry for everything Matty, so sorry! I've been such an idiot. I wasn't thinking straight, and I never should have hit you. You've always been the one that took care of me, and I'm sorry I forgot that."

I mumbled something that was probably sappy, but there were tears in my eyes, so there was enough embarrassment to cover it up.

"So, who the hell was that bitch?" Belle asked, "She knew you, Matthew."

Des broke the hug, and I stood for a moment trying to think up a good explanation.

"She's one of the people I went to for information about the creature that attacked you the other night."

"But what is she doing here? Trying to start a riot?" Cathy asked.

"We didn't part on the best terms," I said, "and I met her anonymously. After that performance, I have to guess that she was likely here to find me, disabuse me of the notion that I was off her radar and to inform me that there are repercussions to pissing off an information broker. Incidentally, I'd prefer it if no one told anyone any of this, I'd rather she didn't take any more of the hump with me."

"What was all that "shadow mage" stuff?" Bill asked.

"Probably just an excuse for a witch hunt," Cathy said, covering for me neatly.

"Seems a little excessive to me. Matty, what the hell did you do to her?" Des asked.

"Broke into her strip club, tricked her bouncer and bartender, interrupted her sexual gymnastics with a couple of her dancers, threatened her with physical violence, tried to blackmail her for the information I needed, take your pick. In my defence, she's really not a very nice person, and she almost had me sold to human traffickers, so really, I'm in a morally neutral position, here."

"Wait, wait, wait a minute," Bill said, looking me square in the eye, "you went to a strip club, and you didn't invite me?!"

"Billy!" Cathy snapped, smacking him on the arm.

Chapter 25

I persuaded them to head off to their rooms, and I went to mine, where I donned the same hoody-jacket combination that had kept me anonymous the last time I'd set off to do something stupid (washed since then, though).

Then I went into the woods and waited.

It was almost two hours later when I heard the car coming. I cast mage sight and looked at it. A Bentley? Really? With a driver, too.

Maybe I'll wreck it.

I called my shadows and threw a wall of them across the road a good fifty metres in front of the car. It slowed and then came to a halt when the headlights stopped cutting through the darkness.

A couple of minutes passed, and the driver stepped out, opening the door for her. Tethys slid out of the car, smiling broadly.

"Am I to just stand here all night?" she asked with a smile on her face after a few minutes.

I stepped from the shadows and into the glare of the headlights.

"Ah, there you are," she said, turning to look at me.

The driver turned, reaching for something in his jacket. I released the sleep spell I'd been holding and he dropped slackly to the ground.

"I told him not to go for the gun," she said with a sigh, walking around the prone driver, who was now snoring gently, "and you should really up your game. There's nothing intimidating about a good night's sleep."

The shadows advanced, coiling and sharpening as they swept towards her, snapping and darting around her.

"Better," she said, her smile only growing wider as she kept walking towards me, "but we are both well aware of your limitations, so why don't you just tell me what you're after?"

"I thought we had an agreement," I said softly, staring her down.

"We do!" she said, still advancing, "But you can't blame a girl for having a little fun."

"That's close enough, and yes I can. You come into my world and try to bring it down around my ears, and you expect to walk away without any retribution?"

"Oh relax, I've already squared the whole thing with your headmaster. The man's so pent up he'd have jumped into a volcano if I told him to. I told him that it was all part of a social experiment, and that you thought he was in on it. Smoothed the whole thing over."

Well that did save me a memory charm, but I was still a bit mad.

"And my brother?"

"Really, what would have happened? He's a battle mage isn't he? What could that crowd have done to him?"

Well, she had a point.

"And if he'd hurt or killed someone trying to escape?"

"That would have been unfortunate, and hilarious. And repayment in full for my ruined evening."

"That's what this has been about?" I asked, incredulous.

"That, and I thought it might be fun."

I rubbed my eyes in exasperation, and when I opened them again she was two steps away from me.

"Would you stop doing that?" I asked, opening up the range again.

"What's the matter? Don't trust yourself around me?" she asked, giving me a sultry look.

"No, as a matter of fact. I've already proven myself to be something of a sucker for a pretty face once this week, and I paid a very high price for that little piece of self-discovery. I try not to repeat my mistakes."

"And yet here you are again, confronting me in the dark. You all tense, me all naked..."

"You're not naked," I pointed out.

"Would you like me to be?"

Good grief.

"Oh stop it, would you? It's just not convincing," I said.

"Yes it is," she replied, another step forward, she thought I didn't notice.

"Look, just stay out of my business, and I'll stay out of yours, alright?"

"Would love to, but I have three more lectures to give, and I'd hate to have to try and explain to dear Mister Kenilworth why I suddenly have to cancel."

"There will come a day when you push me too far, you know that, don't you?"

"Yes. But that's not today, is it?" she asked.

I groaned. This woman was going to be the death of me.

"There we are," she said, "now why don't we shake hands, nice and civilised, and agree to just try and have fun."

She extended her hand. I remembered what happened the last time I let my guard down. I just stared at her.

"Oh come on, I don't bite... unless you ask me to."

"No funny business," I said, taking her hand. She covered mine with her other hand, and her eyes sparkled. My heartbeat tripled again as she used whatever chemical-based power she had, but she didn't make any moves, just stood there holding my hand. It was another show of dominance, though I still didn't know why she was trying so hard.

"That counts as funny business," I said through clenched teeth.

"Fun though, isn't it?"

"So much fun that it just has to be bad for me," I said, gently pulling my hand away.

I started walking backwards into the shadows, which gathered around me.

"There is one more little thing..." she said in a tempting voice.

I know I'll regret this...

"Yes?"

"A present for you, a gesture of trust, and a down payment on what I hope will be a pleasant future."

"So you're not still planning to sell me if you can ever get me in a vulnerable position?" I asked.

"Not anymore. I think you'll be so much more fun to have around, and you can't very well be around if you've been sold as cannon fodder."

"What's the present?" I asked.

She smiled, a delightfully naughty one at that. I can think of no other phrase that describes it better.

"A memory card, it's here, in my pocket," she said, gesturing at the inside pocket of her jacket, "why don't you come get it?"

I stepped forward and smiled as I called my shadows. They coiled gently around her feet, slinking their way up and around her waist before a small tendril made its way into her jacket and wrapped itself around the small piece of plastic in her pocket.

"That's cheating!" she complained, but she was still grinning.

"That's the way I prefer to play," I answered as the shadows deposited the tiny memory card in my hand. The coils were still around her, their touch delicate and gentle. She was even tickling one of them, which sent a tingle through the link and up my spine.

"You'll attend the next lecture, I trust? You never know what diabolical thing I'll do if you're not there," she said as my shadows retreated.

"We'll see," I said, "what's this?"

"Have a look. And use it wisely, the information becomes useless after it's been acted on."

"Thank you," I said.

She smiled, batting her eyes, "It was my pleasure..."

Chapter 26

As soon as I could haul my tired carcass back from the woods, I made my way to my computer to see what the memory card contained. I sat there staring at a single document for a good twenty minutes, rereading it several times. Unless I was badly wrong, it was very useful indeed, that is if it could be relied upon. I had to consider the source, after all.

I sat there for a while, thinking it through. The problem was that verifying the information could lead to it being invalidated. I am, after all, inexperienced at this sort of skulduggery. What I needed was someone who could verify my information without giving the game away...

So, ten minutes later I was on top of the chapel, trying to surreptitiously shout for Jeremiah. Thankfully his ears are better than a bat's, so it didn't take long for him to turn up.

"Alright, alright!" he said, appearing behind me, "This had better be good, I was about to get my leg over that saucy little Michelangelo replica on the main building."

"You've been telling tales to strange people, Jeremiah," I said, "You almost got me auctioned off!"

"What? Don't be ridiculous, I never told anyone anything about you."

"What about the gargoyles living on Professor Wilks' roof?"

He looked like he was about to say something, but then his mouth just hung open for a moment. A guilty look came over his face.

"Oops."

"Yes indeed, oops."

Jeremiah sat on one of his handkerchiefs and smoothed out his little trousers.

"I'm sorry?" he said.

"Don't worry, you can make it up to me," I said, pulling out a printout of the document Tethys had given me. I unfolded it carefully and handed it to him.

"What's this?" he asked, pulling a pair of half-moon reading glassed from his pocket and pulling them on.

"I need this information verified as soon as possible," I said.

"You will pay the usual fee, I assume?" he asked, licking his lips.

I pulled a plastic bag full of chocolate bars from my book bag and handed it to him.

"By tomorrow night, please, Jeremiah, my window is closing quickly."

He was looking through the bag with open avarice.

"No problem, no problem at all," he said, already beginning to drool.

We chatted for a bit longer, but it was a losing proposition with his focus elsewhere, so I left him to his sugar-gorging and went to bed. One step closer to the information I required. I have to hand it to Tethys, getting me Professor Wilks' itinerary was very helpful, that is if it turned out to be real.

Friday.

They started throwing things at me. And not soft things either, pencils, sharpeners, books. Some of it hurt. And this wasn't just the in-crowd anymore, even the outcasts were getting mean. One of the projectiles meant for me missed and hit Cathy, so I hexed the offender right there on the spot, and he spent the next ninety minutes throwing up everything he'd ever eaten.

He's fine now, the hex only lasted a couple of hours. A little piece of mental magic, nothing dangerous, I assure you. Distracted the crowd, though, and Cathy was grinning evilly all the way to our next class, so that was certainly worth it. I liked it when she smiled.

The wait for the day to end was miserable and tedious, and my friends had started to notice how antsy I was getting. In the end I had to tell them what I was planning (or parts of it anyway). They told me I was an idiot. I agreed with them, promised that I wouldn't do anything stupid, and then once it had gotten dark, I set out to do something stupid.

Jeremiah came through for me, verifying the information with Wilks' gargoyles (hopefully subtly). I dressed in a decent set of clothes and headed out of the school grounds, where a cab was waiting for me. I didn't bother with a pass this time, after all I wouldn't be granted one. Besides, it was Friday night, when it was almost expected for students to get up to mischief.

The cab took me straight into town and dropped me off right in front of *Bella Note*, a very nice little Italian place I'd been meaning to try. The restaurant was on the ground level of an older building in the newer part of the city, pale stone with wooden windows about five stories high. The restaurant was marked out by its tinted windows bearing the name picked out in gold.

I approached confidently, as attitude is everything when attempting to gain access to a place you aren't supposed to be in. This was not somewhere you got into without a reservation, generally booked months in advance, unless you had power of some sort (not even necessarily the magical variety).

The door was pulled open for me by someone actually employed solely for the purpose, which seemed like a waste of money to me, but what do I know. And it was quite impressive. I nodded my thanks to the young man, who was dressed immaculately in a black suite with white gloves. There was a small wooden pedestal at the end of a slim hallway, manned by a pretty young woman who smiled as I approached.

"Good evening, sir. Do you have a reservation?"

"I'm meeting my friend, Professor Wilks," I said.

She looked at the book.

"I'm sorry, sir, but it looks like the Professor's party has already arrived, additional seating will not be possible."

"Oh, that's a shame. May I have a brief word with the Professor before I go, just to wish him a good evening, you understand?"

"I don't think so, sir. The arrangements of our guests are made some time in advance, and they dislike sudden changes."

This wasn't getting me anywhere. I cast a perception charm that blocked me from her mind, sight and memory before taking a peek at her appointment book. Private room, very nice. Number... three. I walked through the door to the restaurant proper at a leisurely pace.

The main room was impressive. There was a wide black and white marble bar running down the centre, at which half a dozen men and women were chatting. The dinner tables were scattered around the room, with a few intimate booths along one wall. The tables were covered in thick white table cloths, cotton and expensive. The diners all looked wealthy, their dates attractive. Jewels and silks were everywhere; expensive vintages accompanied dishes made with lobster, Kobe beef or caviar. Pristinely dressed waiters darted hither and thither, looking very industrious. I walked past them slowly, casting around for the private rooms. It's surprisingly hard to look for something effectively while trying to look like you're not.

Thankfully I found what I was looking for before someone became suspicious: a small plaque that said "Private Rooms" was above an arch leading deeper into the building. I went through the doorway and up a set of marble stairs. At the end of a white-walled hall was a door with the number three on it picked out in black.

I knocked on the door and opened it.

The room was warm and large, heavy carpeting on the floor and a wide, circular table in the middle, covered in a black table cloth chased with gold and the remains of a large dinner. There were ten men and a single woman seated around the table. The woman was young and elegant, dressed in black, her skin had a Mediterranean bronze to it, her hair a lustrous black. The men all seemed of an age with Wilks (though if they were mages, then looks tell you very little), and were all very expensively dressed. Their suits were black silk, gold and platinum was everywhere, the cufflinks, the watches, the tie pins. They could have been a collection of rich bankers, middle aged, clearly wealthy, high, aristocratic bone structure, pencil-thin immaculately groomed facial hair, what I could see of them.

Half of the diners' faces were... obscured somehow. As if the air was warping around them and my perceptions were directed away from their features. I might have penetrated the disguises with mage sight, but if there were magicians in the room, then I didn't want to give myself away...

What I could see of their faces wasn't much to write home about, but their eyes...

When they turned to look at me, I saw something awful in those eyes. Not evil, per se, but completely apathetic. I saw my own insignificance in those eyes, and I didn't like it, not one bit. They considered me nothing, something not even worth their notice.

Not even worth killing. I almost shivered at that insight, but I got control of myself just in time. I saw a flicker of fear in Wilks' eyes as he saw me, but he had the sense to stay quiet and not give his game away, and so did I. After having seen the crowd in that room, and the way they looked, I was struck by the sudden feeling of... well, danger is the best way to describe it, and so I was disinclined towards any sort of flashy display or indelicate reveal.

I changed my plan on the spot and threw out the first thing I could think of.

"Professor Wilks?" I said, "Is there a Professor Wilks in here?"

Wilks looked a little dumbfounded for a moment before he stood up and took a step towards me, a look of anger on his face.

"Yes?" he said.

"You have a telephone call, sir," I said, looking pointedly at him, "you can take it in our manager's office."

He looked around at the room, glancing briefly at the woman before settling his eyes on an older gentleman, one of the ones with an obscured face. His hair was a little greyer than the rest, and his very posture and position practically screamed "Obey".

"Forgive me, sir, may I?"

Faceless Boss nodded, and Wilks followed me out into the corridor. He shut the door behind him carefully and rounded on my, speaking in a rasping hiss.

"What are you doing here?" he asked.

"You sure you don't mean "how did I escape from Tethys?"," I asked, my eyes narrowing as I stared the scholar down.

"I don't know what that bitch told you-" he began. I cut him off.

"She showed me the letter of introduction you wrote," I said.

His mouth opened and closed a few times, like a fish pulled out of the water.

"What do you want?" he finally asked.

"The information I came to you for," I replied.

"I still don't know what you're talking about!" he whispered, now sweating heavily. No doubt he was wondering how I escaped from Tethys, and just how capable that made me. He didn't know I relied mostly on dumb luck and a blatant lack of sportsmanship.

"I think you do. I ripped the image of your face from the mind of a courier," I said, "It was quite impossible for him to fabricate it."

"Which courier?" he asked.

"You'll find out soon enough. He won't be coming back to work. Ever."

He gulped. Utter drivel of course, but I've all but perfected the art of "creative conversation", and my delivery is impressive, though I do say so myself.

"So, where did the Shaadre come from, where was it going, and why did it go after my brother?"

"Please, don't ask me that," he said, pleading with me, gesturing at the room behind him, "they'll kill me!"

"Give me a name, that's all I want, and then you never have to see me again."

He stood there, weighing up his options. I allowed my shadows to slink out from the cracks and crevices in the corridor, coiling towards him. He looked at them with naked fear and then he started to talk.

"One of my people delivered the Shaadre to a small warehouse on Compton Road, number seventeen."

"When did you sell them the creature?"

"More than three years ago, I thought that they wanted it for research purposes."

"What kind of research purposes?" I asked.

"I don't know, that's just what they told me, and that's all, I swear. They contacted me by letter, untraceable by magic or any other means. Nobody ever uses their real names, I promise."

I used a subtle telepathic spell to check his veracity, and he seemed to be telling the truth.

"Why would they attack my brother?"

"I don't know! I just sold them the creature, that's all I know, please!" he was looking anxiously back at the door.

"Alright. I accept your information, but it's not good enough. As of now, you owe me, Professor. You almost had me sold into some unspeakable fate, and I think that requires some recompense. One day I will call on you for something, and if you refuse me, then I shall be forced to transfer the letter you wrote to the Conclave, do we understand one another?"

He nodded vigorously and I backed away, keeping him in sight.

"Have a nice evening, Professor Wilks," I said. He nodded once more and went back through the door.

I let out a heavy sigh and released the shadows.

Damn, but I wasn't cut out for this stuff...

Chapter 27

I left the restaurant as subtly as I could, not drawing any attention (why would I?). I breathed a little more easily now that I was away from those people. If I ever saw them again it would be about a hundred years too soon, they gave me the thundering creeps.

I started walking away, breathing heavily, adrenaline pumping after my own brazenness. I slowed my walk down, getting my breathing under control. I sighed, watching my breath mist in the air. I rubbed my hands together against the cold before I started heading back to where I might be able to get a cab.

I was about five minutes away when I first felt the stirrings of a familiar power at the edge of my senses. It disappeared, and I walked on, thinking I'd imagined it, and then I noticed the shadow following me.

I stopped, and looked at it. It slithered away.

And no, it definitely wasn't mine; my link to the shadows wasn't even active in more than the most basic way. There was another shadow mage around. I started walking again, this time a little faster. I re-linked to my shadows properly and felt the other mage's constructs squirming off to my right.

He sent them coiling towards me, probing and seeking. I kept my own ready, but didn't interfere. I walked around a corner and away from the street the restaurant was on. This road was empty, and that worried me. Within a few seconds that fear was justified, as the other mage's shadows surged.

I was worried for maybe a second, and then I almost fell over laughing.

It was barely a single coil of darkness, attached to a thin veil. And when it got within a few feet of me it simply stopped and then merged with my own, the shadow dragging itself into my mass of darkness, stripping the mage of his screen.

Well, *her* screen.

It was the woman from the restaurant, and she looked surprised. She was already waving her hands, conjuring more shadows. I took a handful of steps towards her and simply took them away as she called them. The spells were quite elegant really, but she wasn't like me, she wasn't part of the shadows.

The best comparison is between an Olympic diver and a blue whale. The diver is impressive, skilled and far better in the water than 99.99% of the human race, but a whale is *born* to the ocean. The comparison is that there is no comparison.

"Something I can help you with?" I asked.

She didn't answer, instead she switched tactics, and conjured a sphere of intense white light. The alley lit up with it, and my shadows evaporated. I hissed as the darkness parted, leaving me with a sudden feeling of vertigo.

I channelled more power into the shadows while I readied a dispel. The darkness came back, coiling and flowing towards her. I empowered the dispel and cast it, sending it hurtling towards the woman, who ducked and spun, hurling the ball of light towards me.

My dispel missed, her ball didn't. It exploded, ripping into my shadows, tearing them to pieces, but there were always more, and I just kept adding them to the heap. It hurt me a little when the light ripped into the dark, though; it left me feeling lightheaded and queasy.

And it was making me lose concentration.

So, with a reluctance that surprised me, I dropped the shadows and brought up a shield, just like the one I'd made when I interfered in Des' duel, only this one worked against physical attacks as well as magical ones. The glittering barrier stood between us, and her next ball of light glanced off and exploded harmlessly.

I had my eyes closed, my mage sight telling me everything I needed to know. If they'd been open, I'd likely have been partially blind by now.

I didn't know what to do. I didn't want to hurt anyone, but I didn't want to give the woman any more free shots. I threw a sleep spell her way, but all it did was stagger her slightly, so I stepped back, expanding the shield to block the alley between us. I made it self-sustaining, boosting its power before I simply turned and bolted, recalling my shadows and wrapping them around myself.

I felt her calling an immense amount of power, smashing it into my shield, but I was already fifty metres away and opening up the distance. And the shield was still holding. Say what you like about my skills as a combat mage, you must admit I know how to conjure a defence.

She was still trying to batter it down while I was in a cab on my way back to school. I left the range at which I could feel my spell, and the connection broke, shutting everything down. That must have been quite the surprise for the woman. I smirked when I thought of her running around trying to find me in the dark.

I shook my head to clear it, I was *tired*!

And I'd been stupid. I done everything I'd always told Des not to do in a duel. I'd kept up a losing strategy at the expense of power, I'd used shadows as a defence against a light spell, I'd defended when I should have attacked...

And what the hell was wrong with that woman? Why would she just attack, right out of the blue? The only thing I could think of was that Wilks had ratted me out (though why I thought he would do anything else at this point is beyond me).

But why the attack? Surely she could have learned more by following me, or simply asking me what I was doing? An attack seemed unnecessary and crass.

A problem for another day, though.

I thought about it, and I was forced to conclude that I was now officially in over my head. Those people looked like heavy hitters to me, and the impression I got from Wilks was that they were involved in the Shaadre business. Even leaving the woman's attack aside, I really needed to hand this over to the SCA, something I would rather avoid, but they had the skills for this sort of thing and I very definitely did not.

And yet, I was curious about that warehouse Wilks had mentioned. I wanted to know what was in there, and I was now rather concerned that the woman (and the room full of scary men) might well shift their operations if Wilks did a thorough job of his blabbing.

And that was another thing, she didn't use any serious attack spells on me. She barely tried to scratch me with that light and her rather minimalist shadows. The most dangerous thing about those attempts would have been to my eyes, she wouldn't have been able to seriously injure me that way.

None of this made any sense at all...

Better just to forget about this whole mess, pretend I hadn't found anything out, rely on the government and just head back to school and go to sleep.

You know what, that's what I'm going to do. I'm done.

Chapter 28

So, half an hour later my cab pulled up to the edge of the warehouse district.

I'd changed my mind.

Yes, I know that wasn't smart, and the cabbie was not impressed about the sudden change of direction. I had to promise him double to drive me there as it's not a nice part of the city. The whole district is about fifty years old, and there haven't been any new developments since then. Almost half the buildings were empty, and most of those were starting to fall down, it's a rat's nest for thieves and other criminals to conduct nasty business.

The police did their best, but there are an uncomfortably large number of magicians in the area, and policing them is a tricky business with so few mages on the force. Ironically, in the most magical town in the country, the numbers of mage volunteers for official services (government, police, fire department, etc.) is the lowest. It's something to do with the community here, they don't approve of official things (something I can't blame them for).

Anyway, the warehouse I'd come to was very well maintained, a clean exterior with a modern electric fence and security cameras at all the corners. There was a significant gap between that fence and any nearby buildings, so anyone monitoring the cameras could easily see an unwanted visitor coming.

I made my way into a warehouse close by. This one was almost a wreck, the front and part of the roof had fallen in, the metal fence was rusted and torn. I linked to my shadows and let them fan out around me. I activated my mage sight and looked carefully for threats, before going any further. There was a small clutch of life forces deeper in the building, behind some inner walls, but they were just Pureborn, not a threat to me. I ignored them and made my way to a set of stairs leading upwards.

I emerged onto the roof and warded the door behind me with a simple alarm, then I spent a few minutes casting the spell I needed. I'd only practiced it a couple of times, and only recently gotten it right, but it would be just the ticket for this situation.

The spell took shape, a small sphere of energy no larger than my closed fist, a core of mental magic surrounded by a shell of light refracting wards. At the centre was a direct link between the orb and my senses, which would hopefully let me see and hear things away from my body. When I cast the spell I was disoriented for a second as my vision shifted forward a few feet.

I sat down carefully, fully releasing my focus into the spell. It was a remote observation enchantment, and quite a complex one, combining about seven smaller spells into the whole, not including the light refracting shell, which functioned as basic invisibility (to my frustration, I hadn't been able to figure out how to make it work on a human body).

I took control, and the construct shot forward faster than I would have thought, nearly smacking into the wall of the target warehouse. I pulled it up and slowed it down, moving it slowly around to look for a way in. There was nothing on that wall, which was annoying, so I flew it up to the roof and saw nothing there either.

By now I was getting progressively more annoyed, and so I pulled the sphere around and darted it around to the front door. No bell, no buzzer, and it was locked. I saw a security guard at the front desk, looking bored. I pulled the sphere back and darted it forward to knock on the glass.

The feedback made my head ache, but the guard looked up. Seeing nothing he looked back down again, so I hit the glass one more time.

Same thing. It took four more bangs (and an increasingly sore head) to make the lazy twit get up and actually check what was going on, at which point I slipped my spell through the door he opened, and headed in.

There were security cameras in there too, but they didn't see my probe. I really must figure out how to make that invisibility spell work more widely, it would have made this much simpler. Yet another thing to add to the to-do list.

There was a door on either side of the entrance hall; the one to the left was open so I sent my spell that way. There was a short corridor at the end of which was a security door. I really hadn't thought this one through; I can pick a mechanical lock with magic, but I don't know the spell for a card reader, even assuming I could make the probe act as a conduit for the magic.

I was stumped, but then the door snapped open and hit my probe square in the "face". My vision swam and I felt warm blood trickling down from my nose (damn but feedback's a bitch). I recovered in time to see a guard walking through. The door behind him was open and I darted through it as quickly as I could.

The warehouse was larger than it looked. There was a wide ramp leading from a loading door to my right down into the ground. Opposite me I could see an open plan office with another six guards sitting at desks or on sofas.

These ones were armed, and not with tasers, I saw *guns*; pistols in holsters and submachine guns propped within easy reach. These people meant business, and I was suddenly glad that I was nowhere near them. I spent some time looking around, trying to glean anything from the few documents on the tables, but there was nothing useful. So I turned around and headed down the ramp.

The ramp led to a wide corridor. It was dark, but my probe still showed me what was down there. And a fat lot of good that did me. The corridor was lined on both sides with heavy steel bars, creating large segmented cages containing... large wooden boxes.

Couldn't see a damn thing.

Now that was just annoying. All this bloody trouble and I couldn't see what was in the boxes. Now what was I supposed to do?

I was just contemplating something *really* stupid when the alarm spell guarding my rear went off, and my head suddenly felt like it exploded. My face hit the corrugated iron of the roof and my vision went white as the alarm spell interacted disastrously with the remote viewing construct. I could feel blood trickling from my eyes, nose and ears and my head was agony.

Suddenly it occurred to me what I'd done wrong, and even for me, it was pretty stupid. You never mix spells with sensory input components without a buffer enchantment. Never. It's on page *one* of the bloody spell book, and I'd forgotten in my haste, and now there was someone potentially dangerous behind me and I couldn't even see them.

Somehow my ears still worked, though barely, and I heard a gravelly voice moving closer.

"What is it, mate?" it asked.

"Well, well, well. Looks like the fates smiled on us tonight Barnaby, old son. We've got ourselves a lost little lamb. Rich, too by the looks of him."

As you can imagine, this scared me but good, and I was suddenly on the verge of panic. When you're blind and half-deaf, it's not a good idea to find yourself among predators.

"If he's rich, won't someone be looking for him?" Barnaby asked.

"We'll take him downstairs, no one will look there," the other one said. I heard the scrape of a boot and a ghastly mixture of scents including garbage and stale booze. I thought that they were probably the life signs I'd detected deeper in the warehouse. They must have heard me moving about.

"Leave me alone," I said, desperately focussing, calling on energy.

"Don't worry my little lamb," the other voice whispered with a dark chuckle, "it'll only hurt the first time."

While I didn't know exactly what he meant, I could infer certain things from context, and I was suddenly left feeling horrified. I heard them coming closer.

"Stay back!" I ordered, my horror merging with growing fear.

Another ugly laugh.

"No," Barnaby said.

The whole situation just pressed down on me; the idea that I was about to be taken by two Pureborn criminals because of my own stupidity just slammed into my mind and my terror just... transformed. I was suddenly angry, enraged really. It was an awful hateful rage, though still mixed with a healthy dose of terror. I still couldn't see, but then I didn't really have to. My shadows responded to my tempestuous emotions. I soon heard crunches, flailing smacks, the wet sounds of heavy impacts on soft flesh.

And then screaming. Dreadful, horrible screaming. I had to focus so hard to call my shadows off them because I was still so afraid and terribly angry at what they'd been planning. The link I create makes a direct connection between my mind and the shadows, subconscious and all. That's what allows them to assume such complex shapes without my having to focus on every tendril. This situation was the potential downside. When I'm angry or terrified, they respond to my hindbrain, the part that's wired for fighting, fleeing and mating, the savage core at the centre of every man.

The voices were begging now, and my terror slowly abated, transforming into remorse. I'd been fighting the shadows as they attacked, so I could only hope that they hadn't done anything permanent, but I had no way to know, not being able to see.

And truth be told, from what they'd said, I'm not sure that I didn't want them to suffer. Plus, there is the very real truth that if I didn't want them hurt, on some level, then the shadows wouldn't have done it. I felt warm fluid collecting around my knees, I dipped my finger into it and sniffed at it.

Copper. Blood. I fought past the awful headache and sent my shadows out, having them act as feelers to help me navigate my way out of this horrible mess. The shadows guided me like a blind man's cane as I stumbled down the stairs and out of the warehouse. I'd ignored the twitching and groaning piles of meat that was all that remained of those two men as I left. Barnaby was till screaming occasionally. My hands were shaking as I reached into my pocket for my phone. Thankfully it has voice activation.

I called direct enquiries, and then a cab, promising a significant tip. One came some time later, and I told him to take me to the nearest hospital, it was the only thing I could think to do. I was simply in too much trouble to handle alone; blind, half-deaf and possibly guilty of murdering two people by magic.

It hadn't been my best night.

Chapter 29

Now, I didn't actually *see* much of what happened next, so I'm forced to extrapolate.

The cabbie dropped me off at St Jeremiah's Hospital. It was a good one, but it's a religious hospital (Catholic), and so there aren't any mages on the staff. My fault, I should have specified. Of course I didn't know that it was Jeremiah's at the time, and when I found out, it was too late to change my mind.

The cabbie (a very friendly fellow called Brick), helped me out of the cab and into the emergency room, where he deposited me into the very capable hands of Sister Celeste, who promptly squeaked at the sight of me (not something you necessarily want from an emergency room nurse), and went to get a doctor. She came back with a professional sounding fellow who wheeled me to an exam room and asked me a variety of increasingly insulting questions that I answered with as much good grace as I could muster.

I told him a cock and bull story about getting hit by some sort of magic while I was out for a walk. I won't bore you with the details; it wasn't some of my best work. I was still in some considerable pain, after all.

"Can you see this?" he asked.

"No," I replied, I saw nothing but black, and my ears were still ringing.

"I think we're going to need to do some tests, do you have a contact number for your parents?"

"I take it there's no way you could just fix this without involving... well anyone?" I asked.

"I'm sorry, Matthew, but you are not well, and I can't in good conscience act without parental consent. Your sight is at stake, here."

Damn it. I was going to be in so much trouble.

They gave me a room, and I settled down while I waited for the large ton of parental and educational bricks to fall on my head.

What was worse was the fact that this was all my fault. I *knew* that you don't mix and match sensory input spells, at least not without careful preparation because... well because you can get some very nasty feedback.

I read something about it a while ago, but I couldn't remember how quickly this problem goes away, I thought that I remembered something about permanent injury, but I couldn't be sure. I wasn't in there long before a new nurse came in and helped me into a hospital gown (humiliating), from there she took me to various rooms where they tested my eyes, scanned my head and generally poked and prodded me until I couldn't take it anymore.

Eventually they took me back to my room, where I slept fitfully for a while before the door belted open and I heard a familiar voice calling my name.

"Damn it, Matthew, what did I just say?" Mother said. She took my hand, and I grinned for the first time since I'd got to the hospital.

"Sorry," I said.

What followed was that unique blend of anger and affection that only a mother can provide to a child that's been hurt doing something he shouldn't have been. It made me feel better, and it helped to engage my mind in telling a plausible story. I told her most of the truth, at which point she yelled at me for putting myself in danger and hugged me for taking care of my brother. She can get confused at times like this, can my mother.

She kept me company through the night, telling me it was alright when I woke up in the dark. She helped me eat breakfast the next day. I told her my fake story again, and she believed me (I think), and then she started yelling at doctors, who finally came in to see me after another battery of tests.

"There's definitely a problem in there," he said.

"Very insightful," my mother growled, "how do you fix it?"

"We have a series of injections. There's not too much damage, but we have no idea what caused it. The swelling, which we think is the source of the blindness, is going down, and the optical nerve is intact. That means we just need for the inflammation in the eyeball itself to go down, and he should be fine. Though the pigment change appears to be permanent, I'm afraid."

He moved around with a small tray which he placed on the table. He explained what he was doing as he gave me an injection (with a bloody horse's needle, it felt like).

"How is that possible?" Mother asked.

"The blood was almost burned into the iris and sclera, I can't explain it exactly, I've never seen anything like that without there being some sort of scarring, but there isn't any."

"Pigment change?" I asked after he was done.

The doctor harrumphed and made an excuse about something before leaving.

I repeated myself.

"Sweetheart, your eyes..." then she stopped.

"Yes?" I prodded, not really all that concerned after the doctor's "he should be fine".

"It's fine, they just look a little different that's all, the colour's a little darker."

"Well, that I can live with, as long as I can see out of the things..."

At that point there was a knock at the door.

"Come in," Mother said, and I heard two pairs of footsteps approach me.

"You! What do you want?!" Mother said, standing up.

"We're here to interview your son," a familiar voice said.

"You leave this minute, or I'll drop so many lawyers on your heads that you'll drown in wigs," Mother almost growled.

Not the best smack-talk, but I'll take it.

"We will not leave," Kraab said, "you see, young Mister Graves has some explaining to do."

"About what?" she asked, I heard rustling in her purse as she rummaged for her phone, no doubt.

"About the two men who were skinned alive last night."

Chapter 30

Alright, leaving aside the fact that someone got skinned for a moment, there is no way that it could be traced back to me, or that anyone would even suspect that it *was* me. I kept my expression neutral.

"What are you talking about?" Mother asked.

"Last night the police were called to the scene of a crime. Two men were screaming their lungs out, and the police found them on the roof of a factory building. Each of them had been cut more than three hundred times, their skin was in shreds. Their eyes, ears and lips are unrecognisable, it's likely that they'll be permanently blind, and they won't be able to smell properly."

They already smelled pretty bad, I refrained from saying, barely managing not to grin at my own awful internal pun.

"What makes you think that my son knows anything about this?" Mother asked.

I heard the rustle of paper.

"This photograph was taken last night, in front of the building where the victims were found."

I heard flapping and felt air brush my face.

"He can't see, Agent," Mother said, "he was attacked last night as well."

Silence for a moment. And then I felt someone getting closer to me.

"What happened?" Kraab asked, his tone a little softer.

"Matthew?" Mother asked. I nodded.

"I can honestly say that I didn't see anything happen to them," I said, after taking a moment to think, "but I think I heard it happen. After I went blind there were some loud noises, and then I heard them screaming. I think that their blood is on my trousers, if they're the same people."

"Can you remember anything else? A sound, or anyone that might have had a reason to harm them?"

"After I went blind, they came up to the roof and talked about taking me. They said that they were going to hurt me," I said. Mother gasped, I hadn't told her about this part.

"What happened then?" Knowles asked (she hadn't spoken up till that point).

"No idea. Just darkness and screaming and I left as quickly as I could."

"And what were you doing there in the first place?" Kraab asked.

"Looking at a warehouse."

"Why?"

"The source you took from my head gave me the address."

No point in lying, they'd just take the information from my head anyway, and I was still too tired and hurt to put up any sort of resistance.

"The one across the street from where we found the victims?"

"That's the one," I replied.

There were a few minutes of silence and then the sound of receding footsteps.

"We'll let you know if we have any other questions," Kraab said, "don't leave town, please."

I nodded, and I heard the door close. Well, it was now officially someone else's problem.

"Would you care to explain to me why you left out those little details from the story you told me?"

I sighed inwardly. Can't I catch a break?

After yet another retelling, and what felt like hours of cross-examination, Mother accepted my version of events at last and settled down again. She went to the shop and came back with a battery powered radio for me before heading out to speak to Des, who would probably be wondering where I'd got to. Who only knew what Bill and Cathy must have thought by now, it must have been at least midday, and I hadn't been to class yet.

I was there for another three hours, scrolling through radio stations, before my eyes started to get better. Once the SCA goons had left I'd cast a few healing spells, and that had sped the process along greatly. Still though, all I got at first was a blur of indistinct shapes, and it stayed like that, it was infuriating.

I got bored and more bored as time went by. Lunch came and went, it was horrible, but at least I knew where the plate was and could see my cutlery. Around five o'clock I was able to see more distinct shapes, and a nurse came in to administer another dose of something or other.

My vision was serviceable about two hours after that, just in time for Mother to come back with Desmond and several bags full of takeaway food.

They clucked and sighed when I told them that my vision was improving. Things were still a touch blurry, but it was much better.

"Cool eyes, Matty, very spooky," Des said after stuffing himself to completion.

"Desmond!" Mother said in her stern voice.

"What?" I asked, standing up and heading for the mirror. I could barely make out my face, but with some effort I got a general look at my eyes. They were red, the sclera anyway. Not blood red, more like that of a half-dried scab, mottled with small patches of lighter red. The irises were black, deep black, darker than the pupil itself.

"And this is permanent?" I asked, aghast. As if I needed additional reasons to be branded a freak.

"I think it looks cool," Des said, patting me on the back.

"Yes, it gives you an aura of mystery," Mother chimed in.

"It gives me the look of an Ebola victim," I replied, pulling the lids away, and yes, the red's all the way in there. Just wonderful.

Chapter 31

It was another two days before they let me out of that hospital, a full twenty-four hours after my eyesight was back to perfectly normal. The colour of my eyes remained the same spooky mess, though.

I turned up for breakfast on Tuesday morning, sitting down in my usual spot. Cathy and Bill stopped talking when I sat down. They were about to launch into questions when I saw their eyes go to mine. Bill gasped, Cathy squeaked, I rolled my eyes.

"What the hell happened to you?" Bill asked. Cathy looked like she was going to cry.

So I had yet another retelling to go through, when I just wanted to forget the whole thing. Naturally Bill was full of questions about my story, and I answered them as best I could (meaning I made stuff up), Cathy was looking at me suspiciously, she knew I was full of crap.

Eventually Bill headed off to his first class and I told Cathy the real story out in the square. She got a little pissy about it.

"Are you out of your mind?" she asked, "You know that the warehouse district is out of bounds."

"That wasn't what caused the problem, Cathy," I said, rubbing my eyes, which had been a little itchy since getting out of the hospital.

"Don't scratch, you'll make it worse, and what caused the problem was you going places you shouldn't have been and doing things you aren't ready for."

"A little bit of forward planning, and I wouldn't have had any problems at all," I said lamely.

"You could have died, or worse," she said with a little tremor in her voice.

"I don't plan on doing anything like that again," I said, "no more sleuthing for me, I'm leaving it to the professionals."

She looked at me suspiciously, "Really?" she asked incredulously.

"Really," I replied, nudging her with my shoulder, "one permanent physical alteration is enough of a lesson for me, thanks very much."

"I don't know, I think it makes you look a little dangerous," she said with a grin.

"Until you find out how it happened, and then I look like an idiot."

"So don't tell anyone that part," Cathy suggested, getting up and stretching, "come on, we've got maths."

And that was the end of that. I mean, I got some strange looks (more than usual anyway), but the eyes were weird enough that people were giving me a wide berth, even the Ox and his crowd were leaving me alone, something for which I was supremely grateful.

I made it all the way to Wednesday without another incident. But then it was time for another "lecture".

Oh, how I would have preferred not to participate in another one of these messes. I could really do without the additional stress.

I tried to persuade Bill and Cathy not to go, but naturally they wouldn't stay away. Des had the good sense to listen to me for a change, so he stayed out.

The three of us took the same seats as we had last week. This time there was a projector set up on a small table. Oh joy, visual aids.

The room filled up quickly, and the block of Ox's thugs seemed to have expanded to almost twice its usual size, some of them glared openly at me, but they stopped once I looked back at them, meeting their eyes with mine. It turns out that there are some advantages to this injury, after all.

"Oooh, movies," Bill said, noticing the projector, "maybe she has a video brochure for her "gentleman's club", what do you think, Matty?"

"Billy!" Cathy's predictable response came right on cue, and Bill grinned even wider.

"Hi Matthew," Belle said from behind us, moving around to sit next to Cathy.

"Belle? Shouldn't you be watching Des?" I asked.

"He's fine, I left him watching gymnastics practice. He's not going anywhere."

"And you're alright with your boyfriend ogling the leotard brigade?" Bill asked with an evil grin.

Belle gave him a glare and simply didn't answer.

"Why are you here? You know she's trouble for magicians," I said.

"No, she's trouble for *you*, so someone should be here to watch your back."

"We're watching his back," Bill chimed in.

"Someone competent," she said with an acidic grunt. Belle just doesn't like Bill, it's understandable, really; he's an acquired taste.

"I'm competent!" Cathy said.

"Someone practiced in battle magic," she said with what I thought was impressive self control.

Well, she had a point, and it was quite nice of her.

"The more the merrier," I said to forestall any further sniping, and she smiled at me in what I thought was an unusually warm manner, before looking forwards.

Mister Kenilworth filed in, leading Tethys again. This time she had an assistant with her, who she introduced as Kandi "with a K", who sat next to the small table with a computer, which she hooked up to the projector.

She was young, red haired and attractive, her outfit, vaguely resembling business attire, was low-cut, tight fitting and made of fine material; she had the figure of an athlete (or a dancer). Another distraction, no doubt. Tethys' eyes lingered on me before taking in the rest of the room (which was even fuller after the drama of the previous lecture).

Kenilworth introduced her, and Tethys took her place at the podium, leaning forward to look at the crowd and drawing attention to her décolletage.

"I see that word of our little play has spread; good," she said with a smile.

I started grinding my teeth a little and Cathy put her hand on my arm.

"For those of you who weren't here, last week was a demonstration of what can happen when magicians and humans mix. The mood right now is very much in favour, mages are popular, even revered in some circles."

She stepped around the podium, getting closer to the seats.

"But as you saw, that mood can change, and on the slightest provocation. Mister Graves was no threat to any of you, had never harmed you, but given a single suspicion, you turned on him like a pack of wolves."

There was muttering, guilty looks, I got angrier.

"This is human nature. We see that which is different, and we attack it. We go for what might be a threat, it's a throwback to the days when the tribe over the next hill may one day come to burn our village to the ground, it's in our DNA."

"But why do we view the mage as separate to the rest of humanity? What makes a Wizard with the power to throw a fireball different from a pilot controlling a warplane, for example? They have the same power at their command, the same capacity for destruction. What's different? Anyone?"

"A magician can kill more people?" Courtney again. God, I hate that bitch.

"No," Tethys said with a grin.

"A magician's power doesn't need the kind of training a pilot does?" Ox offered.

"Definitely untrue, in fact a mage may well need more training than a pilot," Tethys said with a chuckle.

"A warplane can't put out a fire. A pyromage can," I said, wanting an end put to this discussion.

Tethys smiled.

"Exactly right, Mister Graves," she said slowly, as if rolling my name around in her mouth as she said it.

"Beneficial effects. Every skill a magician masters can have a beneficial effect. Magic is a tool. It's only becomes a weapon when someone chooses to make it so. A mage that can cause an earthquake can also raise a mountain of earth to stop a flood, for example."

"But that doesn't make them any less dangerous," another one of Ox's brutes said, glaring over at Belle.

"Of course not," Tethys agreed, "but it also means that it's not down to the power. It's down to the person with it. Allow me to illustrate."

She nodded to Kandi, who smiled and tapped at the computer. The lights went down at the touch of a button and an image appeared on the screen. It looked familiar. It took me a minute, but then I felt a surge of panic rocket through my chest.

It was a wall of shadow, lit up by the lights from a Bentley.

The wall of shadow I conjured a week ago.

The cunning bitch had taped the whole thing.

Chapter 32

I had to try very hard to resist the temptation to bang by head off the floor in sheer frustration at my own stupidity. How did I not see this coming? I mean there's dumb, and then there's *this*.

"Now, last week I told you about shadow mages. Is there anyone here who'd like to see the man I was talking about?"

I slunk slightly lower in my chair, and Cathy looked sideways at me, but she kept her expression neutral. There was general assent from the room. Tethys nodded and Kandi pressed another button.

I saw me step out of the shadow, and there was a collective gasp from the audience. Damn it! Now I could never wear that outfit again, and it was comfortable, too. There wasn't any sound, which was something, and my face was covered by the hood and the dark, so it wasn't all bad. You'd have to know me really well to have any chance of recognising me from that.

"Hey, Matthew, don't you have that hoodie?" Bill whispered.

"Yep," I said, trying to sound as nonchalant as possible.

"See here the shadow magician. Scary isn't he? Now, watch what he does next."

The guard dropped to the ground, and the audience gasped again. Then there was the part where we chatted, she tried to get close, I rubbed my eyes. A personal tic that hopefully no one else would recognise (making me doubly grateful that Des wasn't there).

"What did he do?" Courtney squeaked.

"All in good time," Tethys said.

Then there was that whole bit with the shadows reaching into her pocket, some of the younger members of the audience screamed a little. Cathy had a death-grip on my arm that was going to leave bruises. The footage ended when I disappeared back into the shadows.

Tethys looked insufferably pleased with herself.

"Well, what do you think?" she asked, glancing around the room, her eyes lingering on me for a few seconds.

"That's horrible!" Courtney shrieked.

"Disgusting," one of the younger kids said.

That's a little harsh, I thought to myself.

"What's wrong with that freak?" said someone from the pack whose name I didn't even know.

Okay, now they were starting to piss me off a little bit.

"Absolutely nothing," Tethys answered.

"What?" Ox asked, "that's *normal*?"

"Perfectly, and also very interesting," Tethys answered.

"Why?" Courtney again.

"When he spoke, the voice was young; I'd say about seventeen, maybe eighteen. That means he's one of you, a student," she tapped the computer, and the picture changed to the wall of shadows at the beginning of the film.

"See this? The lights are shining right at it. You know what normally happens to shadows when you shine light at them?"

"They disappear?" Bill offered, getting into the discussion like an idiot.

"Indeed. So, how much power does it take to empower a shadow when a light is shining right at it? I'll save you the trouble of positing an answer. It's a lot. More than a Wizard-level magician can generate, anyway."

I actually frowned at that. She did have a point, but I didn't know enough about what other Shadowborn could do to confirm or deny anything. I needed more knowledge, that was for sure...

There was murmuring and muttering at that.

"That's right. You have a Sorcerer in your midst. A strong one at that. What makes him interesting is that he hides himself. Now, why would someone that powerful, and this skilled, bother to hide himself?"

I didn't know why she was saying this. I was almost certainly a Wizard, not a Sorcerer.

"He's a freak!" this from one Warren Stone, a disagreeable little twit who captains the football team, currently sat next to the Ox.

"And you think that matters to him? That little piece of magic that dropped my driver was all mental. He could have every one of you thinking he was royalty if he put his mind to it. The fact that he hasn't makes me think that he has another reason for keeping himself at arm's length."

She walked around the podium and the lights came up.

"And why mental magic at all? Why not just use the shadows to toss my driver away? Or an attack spell to knock him out? Why a sleeping spell? Ask yourself what you would do with that kind of power. Do any of you seriously think you would keep it under wraps?"

"So what's he doing? Is he scared, or something?" Ox asked, to a wave of snorts and grunting laughs from his lackeys.

"Of you?" Tethys asked, smiling at Ox, she gestured at the screen, "what do you think?"

"I think that whoever he is, he's a coward, and if he weren't, he'd show himself," Ox replied smugly.

"Or maybe he genuinely doesn't care about what you think. This is my point. Magic is neither good nor evil, it is what its users make it. Shadow mages are feared by the vast majority of people, magicians and humans both, for obvious reasons. But this man, whoever he is, goes out of his way not to hurt people. He lives among you carefully and quietly, never revealing himself."

"So, what, we should just ignore him, then?" Ox asked.

"Well, he's either a quiet soul, just wanting to live a normal life, or...," she let the dramatic pause stretch on.

"Or what?" Courtney asked.

"Or he's just biding his time until he can put his own plans into effect, and no one but him knows what those are, for good or ill."

For heaven's sake, would she like some eggs to go with that *ham*?

More muttering, more fear. I was getting ready to flee the building, fully expecting that at any moment she was going to point at me and say, "Get him!".

"Do you know who it is?" Ox asked, his muscles were bunched, like he was ready to run, or pounce on someone.

"No," she said, I had to restrain myself from sighing in relief, "and I don't recommend anyone looking too hard. He seems to have a penchant for hiding his tracks."

It wound down after that. She told us a little more about shadow mages and their role in historical events, nothing I didn't already know, but still interesting enough coming from a beautiful woman.

Don't look at me like that, I'm still seventeen, common sense only goes so far.

The lecture wrapped up at last and everyone started filing out, some of the bolder ones pausing to have a word with Tethys.

"You guys head out, I need a word with her," I said.

"I'm not sure that's a good idea," Belle said, looking concerned.

"I agree with the muscle, Matthew," Cathy said. Belle frowned at the characterisation.

"I'll be fine, it'll just be a quick conversation," I replied. They looked incredulous, but I smiled back reassuringly and they filed out, though Belle looked back at me, the concerned look never leaving her face. Strange, she was almost starting to be nice...

I shook the thought off. The real problem beckoned...

My friends finally left, and I walked down to the podium, where Mister Kenilworth was chatting (red faced, I might add) to Kandi while Tethys watched me walk towards her. I arrived and opened the proceedings with my best glare, which she countered with a mischievous smile before turning around to talk to Kenilworth.

"James? You mind if I have a word with my dramatic assistant in private? I want to discuss some of next week's lecture with him and wouldn't want to spoil the surprise for you."

"Of course, of course," he said, looking bewildered for a moment.

"Perhaps you would be willing to show my lovely associate some of the grounds while we talk?"

"Yes! Which is to say, with pleasure," he recovered, offering Kandi his arm, which she took with an endearing giggle.

They left through a side door and I turned back to Tethys.

"Kandi? Really?"

"Too much?" she asked, sidling up next to me.

"If that top she's wearing was cut any lower we'd have been able to see her underpants," I replied, putting a little reinforcement into my mental shields.

"And that's a bad thing?"

I glared at her, and she just stuck her tongue out at me.

"Love the eyes, by the way, very sexy. But I assume you didn't come to comment on my employee's attire?"

"No," I replied, "I came to ask you what it's going to cost me to make you stop doing whatever it is you're trying to do to me."

She put her hands on my shirt, tugging at the fabric. I could smell her perfume, and my defences bent under the strain of another push.

"Subtle as always, I see," I commented, staring her down.

"If it isn't working, then why are your hands on my hips?"

I pulled my offending hands back with a start and took a step away. She just kept smiling at me.

"Don't feel too bad, the last mage I used this much power on was on his knees begging me to take him to my bed. You're surprisingly resilient, for a man."

"But why bother?" I asked, "You must realise that it's not worth the effort by now."

"Maybe I like the challenge. Maybe it's just fun for me. Maybe I really want that second kiss..."

"Funny," I replied, "now, what's it going to cost me to have you stop trying to get me lynched?"

"Why would you want to spoil my fun?" she asked with a pout. I quite liked it when she did that...

"Because if you come here again I may need to start taking blood pressure medication," I quipped.

She tapped her chin thoughtfully, biting her bottom lip in a way that was *not* distracting.

"Well, there is one thing that you could do for me..."

Chapter 33

And that's how I found myself walking down the steps to the Purple Pussycat on the next Friday night. I won't bore you with the details of the previous days, suffice to say I survived them, and let's leave it at that. The only thing different was that Belle had started looking at me strangely, and she went pale when I surprised her that morning, but that was a problem for Saturday.

Tonight was to be an exercise in insanity, I was sure, but I wasn't a complete moron, I managed to extract certain promises from her about safe conduct and the suchlike. I still wasn't completely sure about her promises, but an information broker can't build a reputation on lies, so I was hoping for the best.

I still wasn't happy, though.

I walked down the stairs to a much more pleasant welcome from the bouncer (same one I might add), he told me to "Come right in, sir".

The waitresses and bartender inside were even friendlier, and a very pretty brunette, who couldn't have been more than fifteen minutes older than me, escorted me to Tethys' office. She knocked on the door and opened it for me a crack with a wink before disappearing back the way she came. I pushed the door the rest of the way open and walked in on Tethys and Kandi.

I won't go into details, but I had to turn my back *again*.

"Don't you do anything else in here?" I called over my shoulder.

I heard a moaning sigh followed by a thump as someone hit the floor.

"You are so British, you know that?" Tethys asked me.

"That's what it says on my passport. Clothes, please?"

"Alright, alright, keep *your* pants on," she said. I rolled my eyes.

"Or don't," Kandi muttered from somewhere. I heard Tethys snigger.

"Alright, I'm decent," she said.

"Somehow I doubt that," I muttered.

I turned around. Tethys was standing behind me; Kandi was lying face down on the carpet, a look of pleasured exhaustion on her face. She hadn't put any clothes on.

"So, what's the favour?" I asked.

"What, no foreplay?" she said.

"Tethys, blood pressure," I said.

She sighed, "Fine. Kandi, get the bag, will you?"

"Do I have to?" she sighed.

"So hard to find good secretaries, these days," Tethys muttered, "Kandi, mush!"

"Oh, alright," she said, standing up slowly and giving me an eyeful.

This was already more interesting than I like my Friday nights to be.

"Isn't she fun?" Tethys asked as Kandi walked to a cupboard at the back of the room and pulled out a suit bag before walking back toward us, "This is for you."

"If I open this up and find a gimp suit inside, then so help me, Tethys..."

"I love that your mind went there first, but no, just open it, will you?"

I did, and found a Kiton bespoke dinner suit inside. Black and ridiculously expensive, with an impressive silk tie. That thing would have cost more than most high end cars.

"Dare I ask?" I asked.

"Get dressed and find out," she said with a smile, "I promise I won't peek. Much."

I changed, and she did peek, but I try not to dwell.

I should state that I have no illusions about Tethys. She's a predator, pure and simple, and there is no good that can come from believing otherwise. I can enjoy the flirting, and God knows it's nice to have female attention, but I don't for a second let myself believe that she's interested in me for anything other than what she can gain from the association.

The day I forget that is the day I become a slave to the whims of a monster.

So, with that firmly in mind, I finished dressing by putting on a hand-made pair of Italian leather shoes (it all fitted *perfectly,* by the way), and waited for Tethys to get dressed. She chose black silk and high heels, pulling her hair back so that Kandi could put it into a simple braid for her. It took her five minutes to get ready, she didn't even bother with makeup.

She was absolutely stunning, shame she's evil.

She led me down a set of stairs opposite her office on the corridor, guiding me down to a small underground garage. We got into her Bentley, where her driver was waiting for us, and we drove off up a steep ramp and into the city streets.

"So, where are we going?" I asked.

"A little soiree," she replied, "nothing to concern yourself with, I just needed a date that wouldn't have his hands all over me the entire evening."

"To tell me a story like that, you must not have even the slightest regard for my intelligence," I said, pointing out her blatant deflection.

She smiled a dazzling smile, linking her arm through mine.

"My apologies, it's just an unusual pleasure not dealing with a man that wants to sleep with me, I'm not used to having to be convincing," she answered.

Couldn't say that I agreed with that completely, it's just that my sense of self-preservation outweighs the commanding instincts of my *other* brain, though at times it's a close run thing...

"And yet you still haven't answered my question, although flattery is always a pleasant distraction, I must admit."

"Fine," she said with another of those adorable pouts on her ruby lips, "The party is being organised by Lord Faust, a celebration of his great-granddaughter's seventeenth birthday.

At least on paper; really it's an occasion to show his lordship's power and wealth to the other authorities in the city."

"So why are you going?" I asked.

"It never hurts to have people remember who holds the puppet strings around here," she said, looking smug.

"Was I supposed to bring a gift?" I asked, feeling foolish.

"For who?"

"The birthday girl," I replied in exasperation.

"Did I not mention the true purpose of the party? No one brings gifts to these things."

"That's just sad," I said, looking out the window and recognising the street names.

"Could you have your driver pull over two streets down for a moment?"

"Why?" she asked with naked suspicion in her eyes.

"There's a flower stall at the night market. I'm not showing up to someone's birthday party empty handed."

"Matthew, you're not showing up with a bunch of flowers, it's tacky."

"I know that, I have an idea," I said.

"What kind of idea?"

"Just stop the car, would you?"

Tethys gave the order and the ogre at the wheel pulled over. I hopped out and darted down the road to the night market. I loved it there; it was a magnificent collection of brightly coloured stalls selling everything from antiques to hairdryers, nestled in a large plaza between several older buildings.

The area was lit by a motley collection of lights and lamps, some strung between the stalls. I darted to the flower stall and bought a bunch of violets (February's birth flower, in case you were wondering, Cathy is a font of occasionally useful information), before heading to a small paper and stationary kiosk and jogging back towards the car.

"A bunch of violets? Really?" Tethys asked with a peeved expression as we drove off again.

"Wait for it," I replied.

I conjured a small mage-light which floated above my lap, letting me see what I was doing. I selected the nicest looking violet, a large bloom with a bright yellow centre. I carefully pulled the stalk away, leaving only the flower. I put a little power into my Will and lifted the flower up before I started constructing the spell I needed.

I'd done this a couple of times (it's a tricky spell), and it only works properly on inorganic materials, but it should work well enough to look nice. It took most of the rest of the drive to get the spell right in my head, all the while Tethys was watching me intently. Finally, I was ready.

I pulled a piece of the mage-light away and let it drift into the centre of the flower, and then I released a tiny oblong of energy. It drifted down slowly, attaching itself to the centre of the plant. Light flared and the flower shimmered before growing rigid. Slowly the petals changed, growing harder before breaking out with tiny, yet complex geometric shapes as its very molecules rearranged themselves into a crystalline lattice.

Seconds later the spell was complete and the flower was now slightly smaller, but shimmering with the light of the spell I'd trapped within the newly formed crystal. This wasn't so much an enchantment as a transformation; a very tricky piece of magic, because it fundamentally alters the nature of the object. Very difficult to do if the thing is alive, just about doable with a flower that's not connected to the rest of the plant, and that picked hours ago. Can't do it to people, in case you were wondering, not ones that are breathing, anyway. Living beings have an essential anchor to their own shape; permanently changing it is immensely difficult.

But it works just fine as a party trick.

"That's... beautiful," Tethys said, reaching for the floating crystal flower. She gently took it from the air and stared at the violet light as it was refracted by the crystal.

"You really are a Magician, aren't you?" she asked, staring at me in a way that made me uncomfortable.

"The other magic wasn't a giveaway?" I asked, preparing a small white box by placing a piece of coloured tissue paper inside.

"There's magic, like shadows and sleep spells and all that very impressive stuff, and then there's magic," she said, placing the flower into the box with great care, "very few people think to bother using magic to do something beautiful."

"I never liked the idea of magic as a weapon," I admitted, holding up the still pink area of my right hand where I'd burned myself, "and truth be told, I'm just not built for it."

"That's not a bad thing, you know, especially for someone with your particular specialty."

"I know, and once all this is done, I hope I'll never have to use an offensive spell for as long as I live," I wrapped the box up carefully in purple ribbon and cleared up the mess I'd made in the back seat, shoving everything into a paper bag. I extinguished the light and stayed quiet for the last few minutes of the trip.

"Here we are," she said with a smile, though the way she was looking at me was just confusing. It was almost as if she was sad and happy at the same time. Tethys is just plain befuddling, but there wasn't time to ponder anything as the car door was open, and I had a party to go to.

Chapter 34

The building was large and very impressive, Tethys informed me that the Fausts owned the whole thing, ten stories high and fifty metres wide in the richest part of the city. It must have cost a pretty penny. The frontage was white stone with shuttered windows, it almost looked like an ornate gothic fortress.

There was a red carpet leading from the edge of the pavement to the wide front doors, out of which was pouring an inviting light. There were two heavy bouncer-looking types in front of the doors who checked the invitations of a middle aged couple that was ahead of us. Tethys' driver had stopped in front of the red carpet and I hopped out of the far side, moving around to help her out (good manners cost nothing after all).

She smiled her thanks and we headed for the door. The bouncers glared at me and grinned like fools at Tethys, as to be expected, before ushering us through. More security acted as signposts through the wide entrance hall. There was a set of highly polished oak stairs directly ahead of the front doors, intricately carved with woodland scenes. I would have loved to have a look, but there was a red rope in front with a no-entrance sign.

Tethys saw my interest and rolled her eyes, "Can't you at least pretend not to be so... interested in everything?"

"Curiosity is nothing to be ashamed of," I replied as she led me through a side door and into a huge room. What I saw quickly ensured that I forgot all about the stairs.

It was astonishing. The room was softly lit, with stone walls covered in beautiful tapestries. There were glass cases around the walls, containing all sorts of bits and pieces. Just from the entrance I saw a suit of black armour holding a massive silver sword, a pedestal with a black orb perched on it, a book bound in blood-spattered leather, the list went on and on. There were people milling around, chatting and looking around them warily. The mood didn't scream "party" as much as it did "interrogation".

I recognised some of the people from the restaurant and started a little. I never did get a good read on what had happened that night, but for safety it would be best to assume that someone at that gathering sent the psycho woman after me, and just like that I was on my guard again.

"Alright, mingle," Tethys said, "and don't hex anyone."

"This from you?" I asked.

She smiled again and released my arm, heading into the crowd, turning every head as she passed.

I headed for the display cases, no way I'm wasting this opportunity, lingering psychos or not.

Perdition's Orb, the inscription read in the first case, *rumoured to contain the bound essence of the Demon-King Agrammel. Under no circumstances touch, can lead to possession.*

Demons?

There's no such thing. I should state that. Everything I've read states categorically that there's no such thing as demons. I still swallowed nervously.

I cast mage sight, and I really shouldn't have. What I saw nearly made me throw up right there. Whatever was in that thing was... horrifying. I could see it screaming from a thousand mouths, all of them filled with razor-sharp, shark-like teeth. There were hundreds of eyes, and all of them were looking right at me. There were coiling masses of flesh and bone, it was an ugly, ghastly creature, and it was far too big for that orb. I don't know what it was, I'd never heard of anything remotely like it. I only saw it for a second before I had the good sense to look away and shut down the sight, but that was more than enough for me to be seriously worried about the breadth of my general knowledge.

"Ugly little brute, isn't it?" a cultured voice said from behind me.

I turned to see an older gentleman, dressed in an evening suit. His black hair was greying, but his blue eyes were sharp and incisive. He wore a Rolex that would have cost more than Tethys' car, and a heavy signet ring with the image of a rearing dragon on it.

"What is it?" I asked, still trying to blink away the after-image of the creature.

"Did you read the inscription?" he asked with a dry chuckle.

"I did, but I was under the happy impression that there was no such thing," I replied.

He smiled, "So was I, until I looked into that orb. Mage sight has its uses, but damn if it can't also be a curse. Once you can see into the heart of everything, it's very difficult to stop yourself from doing it, I'm sure you'll agree? Mister...?"

"Graves," I said, extending my hand, "and I do agree. Lord Faust, is it?"

No point in lying to this man. Not only had he seen me cast mage sight, but I had no reason to believe I'd ever cross paths with him again after that night.

"Have we met?" he asked, shaking my hand, "I do apologise if we have; I get introduced to a great many people."

"No, I just matched the coat of arms above your fireplace with the ring on your finger and made a logical leap."

"Observant and curious. An unusual combination in people your age. Where did you learn your sight? I don't know more than six magicians who can pull it off successfully."

"I just followed the instructions in one of the government-approved spell books," I replied, "took some practice, though. The first time I tried it, I was seeing in shades of purple for a week."

Lord Faust barked out a laugh that startled a nearby server, nearly causing him to drop his tray of champagne.

"Self taught, eh? Well that's unusual in itself. You never thought of apprenticing yourself?"

"My brother's the real magician in the family, I never really wanted the additional attention," I replied.

He stared at me for a moment, raising a quizzical eyebrow.

"Who did you say you were with tonight?"

"Tethys," I replied somewhat shamefaced.

"Oh dear," he said, taking a step back.

"I know," I replied.

"Really?" Faust asked, seeming to relax again, "Then you two aren't...?"

"Oh, God no. Two words: praying mantis."

Faust smiled again, "Sensible man, though I suppose that someone with the wherewithal to cast mage sight must be able to counter the attentions of a succubus."

"A what?"

"You didn't know?" he asked with a surprised look.

"No, though that would explain a thing or two," I replied, thinking of the wings and the tail, "I thought they were extinct. I remember reading *that* somewhere."

"Word of advice, don't trust everything you read in those government-approved texts. They don't want the general public to know just what's out there, waiting in the dark."

"That has been rather painfully made clear to me lately," I replied.

Faust smiled sadly, then guided me away from the orb.

"But enough about the government, that's a depressing topic. Allow me to introduce you to my granddaughter, she hates these events, perhaps someone her own age can cheer her up a little."

He led me across the room, past some displays that I would have loved to gawp at for a while (damn it) and over behind one of the rows of columns keeping the ceiling up. There was a pretty girl in a rather impressive green gown leaning up against one of the columns, staring disinterestedly at a silver cube in a case, which nearly made me squeak in delight, as it seemed to be a tesseract puzzle box, but I turned my attention back to the girl, it was only polite.

She was a centimetre or two under my height, she had red hair that fell in a sheet down past her shoulders. She had blue eyes and a dainty nose. She would have been lovely but for the scowl on her face. She held a nearly-empty flute of champagne in her hand, swirling it none too gently.

"Jocelyn, dear, I have someone I'd like you to meet," Faust said.

She half turned her head towards me, and I gave her a smile, which was not returned. I extended my hand; she tsk'd before stopping her slouch and taking it half-heatedly. Faust introduced me, and I pulled her present from my pocket.

"Happy Birthday," I said, trying to smile again. The girl's attitude was starting to annoy me, and she was diverting me from my snooping.

She looked at me with a half-sneer, and I felt Lord Faust bristle beside me when he saw her expression. But she took the gift, and unwrapped it distractedly. She pulled the top off, and her eyes lit up for a moment as she pulled out the crystal.

"It's... beautiful," she said, smiling for a change. It made quite a difference.

"Good Lord, it looks like one of Gerhardt Prewst's pieces," Faust said, looking at the flower in Jocelyn's hand in awe, "I thought they'd all been destroyed. Where did you get such a thing?"

That was quite flattering, Prewst had been one of the magical master-sculptors way back when. His work had been gathered up by a single collector, who then ran afoul of the Conclave; all Prewst's works had been destroyed in the resulting cock-up.

"I found it in a little shop I frequent," I said, not wanting to draw attention, "it seemed just the thing for a young lady's birthday."

"That's a handsome gift," Faust said, still gazing at the flower.

"Thank you," Jocelyn said, gazing into the crystal.

"My pleasure," I said, sidling past the admiring duo to look at the puzzle box. I couldn't resist casting image sight again to look at the mechanism. These were designed to be impregnable to someone who didn't know how to solve a four dimensional puzzle (meaning you had to time the attempted solution to coincide with the conditions on the puzzle).

I'd always wanted to try and solve one of those. The thing was massively complex, I would have guessed at least a hundred moves over half an hour, just at a look. I wondered what was in there that would be worth that much security.

I turned back to the Fausts, Jocelyn had placed the flower back in the box and was holding it carefully in her hands like it would break. It wouldn't; there was a subtle strengthening charm on it that would protect it from drops, falls and accidental sit-squashing. Deliberate attempts to destroy the thing would probably wreck it, but they'd need extra oomph.

"Perhaps Jocelyn would be willing to show you around some of our collection?" Faust offered, looking over at his granddaughter.

She nodded, smiling at me. Faust grinned and excused himself, heading back into the crowd.

"So, what would you like to see first?" she asked.

And so it turned out to be a great evening after all. Not that I got to see much of the collection, but Jocelyn and I talked for about three hours. We found our way to a small sofa, and we just stayed there for the rest of the party.

She told me about herself. She'd been homeschooled, rarely had the chance to make friends; raised to inherit the Faust legacy. Her parents had died years earlier, so her great-grandfather had raised her. She seemed not to be too fond of him, so I kept clear of that topic. She enjoyed horseback riding, sailing and martial arts. She was a skilled water magician, a high-end Wizard in power.

She followed duelling, and was no slouch herself. I told her my brother was a duellist, and I described Windward Academy to her, told her about my friends, told her a little about my own magic, explaining why I kept it to myself. She was impressed by the shadow-mage thing, and made me demonstrate a little shadow tendril that made her giggle cutely.

I was sorry when the night wound down to a close and Tethys came to collect me. Truth be told, I'd almost forgotten she was there.

"Time to go, Matthew," she said, looking between me and Jocelyn with naked amusement.

I found myself quite reluctant, but I did agree to Tethys' terms, so I stood up and stretched a kink out of my back before smiling at Jocelyn.

"Happy Birthday again," I said, "and it was great to meet you."

"You too," she said, returning the smile. She stood and gave me a peck on the cheek, which made me blush, and I followed Tethys out of the hall, past Lord Faust, who wished us a good evening and thanked us for coming. We left the building and found Tethys' car waiting for us.

The drive back towards her club was... uncomfortable, as Tethys kept smirking at me. In the end I just had to ask.

"What?" I said after I couldn't take it anymore.

"If I'd known you liked redheads so much, I would have had a couple laid on for you," she said with a wide grin.

"I thought you had," I said, thinking of Kandi, which made Tethys grin, "And she's a nice girl; must you make everything tawdry?"

"You've spent a little time in my company, how would you think I'd answer that question?" she said with an even wider grin.

"Now look-" I started, but never got to finish, as a streak of orange light shot from the street in front of us and carved a hole straight through the bonnet of her Bentley. The car flipped, and all I heard was a series of rending screeches as we hurtled towards the side of a nearby building.

Chapter 35

Tethys saved my life.

In a flash she had her wings out through her dress and had wrapped me up tightly. Just in time, too, as the car's roof hit the road with a rending crash. I was cushioned from damage, but I felt Tethys' bones break all around me as we hit. I heard her yelp in pain before slumping against me.

Finally we screeched to a stop. I was badly dazed and terrified and I could see the flickers of flames starting all around us. Tethys was barely breathing, and I could see blood trickling down the side of her mouth. I activated my mage sight and looked her over. She was badly hurt, a couple of *dozen* broken bones, and a punctured lung, too.

The driver was dead, neck broken, and I nearly panicked, probably would have too if I hadn't seen a set of booted feet through the broken window, the glow of flames lighting up the street around him.

"Come out, whore, there's no way that killed you," he said. The voice was deep and throaty, like he was fighting a bad cough.

I focussed, seeing through the metal of the car. He was short and broad, wearing a hood and loose clothing. His hands were wreathed in flames, and he was radiating power from a strong shield surrounding his body.

Alright, no time for panic, this fellow obviously meant business. I had to get us away from this collection of metal and explosive fuel, before he threw any of that fire, and then I had to keep Tethys alive long enough for her own healing to kick in.

Piece of cake...

I called my shadows, and they surrounded us, filling the cab and pushing out, barbs of power tearing into the metal until the remains of the car screeched and ripped apart, splitting to leave Tethys and me in an empty space. Once we were clear of the wreckage, I sent a group of tendrils at the man to keep him busy as I started working on Tethys.

I cast a basic stabilisation charm to keep her lungs inflating and her heart pumping, then I applied a small, but potent regeneration spell to complement her own natural healing, which was demonstrably impressive. All the while my shadows were darting and striking at the Wizard, smacking into his defences again and again and raising showers of sparks.

I should confess something at this point.

You know all those books on duelling I keep getting for Des, and insisting he reads? I never read them myself. Like an idiot, I never thought I'd need that sort of thing. I'd read the sections on shielding, and I'd paid loose attention when Des was practicing, answering his basic questions about spellcraft, but I didn't know anything about duelling, not really; not in a way that matters in a situation like this.

That probably saved my life.

Because duels work around rules, certain things you can and can't do, every book is very clear on that. This man wasn't playing by any rules, and if I'd gone into this fight thinking it was a duel, he'd probably have burned me to a crisp. As it was, I was woefully lacking in offensive versatility, but I wasn't constrained by a rulebook either.

He launched half a dozen flaming projectiles into the mass of shadows, which absorbed them easily before the little orbs could get within ten feet of me. It was stressful keeping up a defence while casting healing spells, but I kept at it, leaving control of the shadows to my subconscious.

"Nice try, Tethys, but your little parlour tricks won't keep you safe forever," he said. He paused for a minute and threw a wall of white fire straight at my shadows. They absorbed the hit, but the light and the force of the attack ripped them to pieces just as I was finishing my healing charms.

"Who the hell are *you*?" the magician sneered as he saw me standing over Tethys, my shadows temporarily broken. I called my Will and put power into grabbing the back of the car. There was a groan of tortured metal as it left the ground, a wave of my hand and a pulse of energy sent the improvised projectile shooting towards him.

He jumped away in panic, reinforcing his shield, but it took a glancing blow and sent him to the ground, hard. I eased Tethys out of the line of fire and into a nearby alley before bringing up a dispel shield between me and the mage. Just in time, as he recovered enough to hurl another wall of flame at me.

The attack met my dispels and exploded outwards from me, heat and light everywhere. Damned fire mages, they make shadow magic too costly to maintain. It's annoying.

I fell back on Force Magic, bolstering my shield with additional overlapping layers. I focussed and a hair thin beam of kinetic energy lashed out, ripping into his flame shield and tearing great gouts of fire out of it when the energy unravelled.

He darted backwards, throwing up another wall of heat as I followed him with the kinetic beam. It struck the building behind him and stone shattered along with wood and glass. I shut it off and waited for him to stand still rather than risk knocking anything down.

He threw a ball of white-hot fire. I countered with a quick dispel and expanded my shield, making it wider and thicker, the dispels more complex and powerful. I felt him pull in an immense amount of energy, and I focussed, getting to the draw first.

I lashed out with sheer Will, and sent my shield construct flying right into his face. He tried to dodge, but the construct was too wide. His shields and mine collided and exploded. The stonework around him was scorched, and the sheer force of the blow sent him flying to land in a smoking heap on the opposite side of the street, dazed but not down for the count just yet.

"Stay down!" I shouted. He glared at me, flames still flickering in his eyes.

He groaned, and slowly sat up, fire starting up again in his hands. I concentrated more Force into a single ball of blue light and let it go just as he was getting to his feet. He sent a lance of fire back at the same time as the ball struck him hard enough to bounce his head off the stone wall, leaving a smear of blood as he slid down to the ground.

The flame screamed towards me, and I barely deflected it with a single plane of energy, which sent it into the pavement with a *whump* of burning air. The man didn't get up again, and I fell to my knees, exhausted.

I shut everything down, feeling drained. I'd used too much magic in such a short time, and I wasn't really used to this sort of thing (though I have to say that it was getting easier as I used my powers more and more openly). I was shaking from exertion and adrenaline, but I pulled myself to my feet and went back to Tethys, who was sitting up on her own, looking shocked at the destruction.

"So, what did I miss?" she asked, looking a little dazed.

"Oh, nothing much," I replied, flopping down next to her, "some crazy man tried to barbecue us."

"And?" she asked, looking around.

"He was unsuccessful," I replied.

"Evidently," she said, "did you just save my life?"

"You saved mine first, so it was only fair. Sorry about your driver."

"It's alright, he was always pawing at my girls," she said with a disgusted look.

"Not sure the punishment fits the crime, there, Tethys."

"One has nothing to do with the other; it just means that I won't waste too much time mourning the ape."

I heard sirens getting closer, and I slowly hefted myself to my feet. I looked around at the small fires and the shattered stone. There was melted tarmac everywhere, and torn metal from the car all over the place. It looked like a warzone, doubly so with the blood and the slumped magician, who was hopefully not dead, but I didn't have the energy to waste checking.

"I have no way to explain any of this when the police turns up," I said.

"Relax. I've got this, you stay out of sight," Tethys said with a smile.

I moved into the alley and decided that I could sit back down while I waited.

It took the police another three minutes to arrive, and then Tethys *really* put on a show. By this time she looked completely human again, wearing a torn dress and looking quite dishevelled as the pair of police cars came around the corner, sirens screaming.

Tethys ran towards them, waving her hands. The cars screeched to a halt and a number of officers jumped out, heading for Tethys.

"Help! Please help!" she screamed in a very convincing manner.

She all but collapsed into the arms of a police officer with sergeant stripes on his armoured vest. He caught her neatly.

"Easy, Miss, you're safe now. What happened?" he asked, his tone very professional even as he was blushing from chin to ears over the woman in his arms.

"That man!" she said, pointing at the fallen pyro, "He tried to kill me!"

I could already see her powers working on the three men and even the woman, as two of them darted forwards, drawing their batons and handcuffs.

"Careful! He's a magician!" she shouted with just a hint of concerned desperation. The constable at the back of the group paused and withdrew a spell-eater from a pouch, slipping it around her neck.

"Ready?" the copper in the lead asked. The woman nodded, and they proceeded. The mage had barely started to stir before taking half a dozen hard hits to the head and body, dropping him back to the ground. Can't say I felt too bad about that, but I was still a little uncomfortable about how quickly Tethys could make four complete strangers beat the crap out of another human being. Still though, he had almost killed me, so I supposed that I could live with it.

Until the day she has something similar done to me, anyway.

It was another few minutes before the cleanup crew arrived, and by then the mage was efficiently trussed up in the back of one police car, and Tethys was happily ensconced in the other. I watched as the fire truck turned up, along with a third car, after which the first two drove away.

It was at that point that I realised that there was a slight flaw in Tethys' plan, in that I was now alone, without transport, and with police officers beginning to spread out, looking for evidence. Thankfully I'd had the foresight to include my wallet in my borrowed clothing or the trip back to the club would have been taken quite a bit longer.

Chapter 36

Eventually I was able to flag down a cab that smelt faintly of fish, and was driven back to the club, a wide and knowing smile on the cabby's face that was almost enough, after my evening, to make me hex him on the spot. I paid him and he wished me a good night with a snicker before driving away.

Naturally Tethys wasn't back yet, police statements require some time, after all, but her staff was still being very friendly, and they escorted me back to the office, where Kandi fetched my clothes and tsk'd at the state of the ludicrously expensive dinner suit.

I explained where Tethys was, and Kandi squeaked with worry, necessitating me explaining the situation. After twenty minutes, she calmed down enough that I was able to slip out and back to school.

The short trip allowed me some time to think about what had happened, and about the rather convenient way that the fire mage had found Tethys. How had he known where she would be with enough foreknowledge to set an ambush, but not know about the second passenger who might be there (me), he'd been surprised when he saw me.

That led me to some conclusions, but there was one particularly nasty one that I just couldn't let go of; that she'd set him up to go head to head with me (which also begged the further question of how she knew I'd win). There wasn't a huge amount of evidence to support the theory, and she had gotten hurt in the ambush, which tended to indicate a different explanation... but the more I thought about it, the more it made a kind of twisted sense.

If she had been truly surprised by the attack, her first instinct, anyone's for that matter, would have been self preservation, seeing to herself. Instead she'd saved *me,* getting injured in the process. Don't get me wrong, I'm not objecting to the saving, but it does make me rather concerned about the depths of that woman's Machiavellian streak.

Because whether I liked it or not, she seemed to be determined to make herself part of my life, and I was too much of a sap (and yes, if I'm honest, probably too smitten with her) to do anything about it.

I let out a long sigh, and rubbed my eyes, which still ached from time to time. It had all been a bit much, so I leant my head back in the cab and napped until I got back to Windward.

The next morning found me half dead with fatigue, which is never a good state for learning. I cast a small nerve stimulant spell that worked much the same way as eight cups of espresso. As a result, I was in fairly good nick for the day's lessons.

Cathy was eyeing me strangely through most of the classes, until we finally got a break and she made me spill the beans on my evening.

"So, was she pretty?" Cathy asked slyly.

"That's your takeaway?" I asked, "Nothing about the duel, the car crash, the existence of demons and succubae, you want to know if Tethys looked good?"

"No, not *her*! The birthday girl, the one you like."

"Oh stop it," I replied, quickening my pace.

"That's cute, thinking you can stop me nosing by walking faster," she said, easily catching up to me.

"Cathy, it's not like that," I said, feeling my cheeks go red and showing the lie.

"What's not like what?" Bill asked, sidling up to us from behind a nearby corner.

"Matthew met a girl last night, and he's smitten," Cathy said.

"You met a what?" Des' voice said from up ahead, where he and Belle were crouched behind a tree.

"Yeah, what he said," Bill chimed in, "spill. Pretty? Hair? Legs? Boobs?"

"Billy!" Cathy squeaked.

Belle looked miffed for some reason, her expression souring as she heard more.

"Sorry," Bill said to Cathy, and while they were distracted I slipped through a side door and into the main corridor.

"Oh no," Des said, following at a fair clip with a wide grin on his face, "you tell me all about it, and give me a chance to approve your choice."

"It's not like that, she's just a nice girl I spent a pleasant evening with," I replied.

"And you'd like to see her again?" Des asked, not letting up.

"Maybe," I admitted, feeling my face go even redder.

That made them want to hear the whole story, and I had to come up with a convincing lie or two, as per bloody usual.

"The Fausts?" Belle asked once I'd finished.

"Apparently Tethys gets invited to all the fun parties," I replied dryly.

"And she invited you? Why?" Belle asked.

"I'm still working on that," I said as we arrived at the central courtyard opposite Kimmel.

"Of course," Belle said in a tone of voice laced with suspicion. Cathy must have noticed, because I saw her frown. She let it go, though, and Des led Belle away with a wide grin and a wave. Bill sat down under our favourite tree and Cathy and I joined him.

I leaned my back against the ancient oak and slowly drifted off while my friends chatted away. I needed to relax; I was tired and pent up with worry. I seemed to have been distracted by a wide array of things that were preventing me from focussing on the problem, namely that I still didn't know for sure who had targeted my brother or why. That had to be my concern, but I had hit more or less a dead end as far as that went. I couldn't go back to the warehouse, the professor was tapped out, I didn't have anyone else to ask, and I was damned if I was going into debt with Tethys again.

So that was more or less that, then. I had done my best, and had passed the information on to the authorities. And if there was one thing the last few weeks had shown me, it was that I wasn't cut out for these sorts of escapades. So, back to normal I would go. Watch over Des, try to keep from getting lynched, continue getting better at magic, go back to being anonymous.

It was decided. Plan made. Story over!

Naturally that was when the sky exploded.

Chapter 37

I exaggerate a touch for effect, but that's what it seemed like at the time. The sky that day was unusually blue, and the sun was climbing to its winter zenith, not a cloud in it. But then there was a thunderous boom from directly above us, and the sky split in a thousand colours as titanic energies were released.

A wave of Magic spread out, thousands of feet above me, and behind it a sheet of black cloud came from nothing, darkening the sky and plunging us all into a darkness as black as night. Bill and Cathy jumped up in surprise, and I wasn't far behind, leaping to my own feet.

I looked with my mage sight and saw a spell of staggering complexity and impressive power. It was the kind of thing that would have taken me an hour to cast, even supposing that I knew exactly what I was doing, and I had no idea how I would even begin such a thing.

The cloud was deepening and spreading, the last of the day's sunlight had vanished behind the formation that now covered more than a hundred square miles.

"Cathy, take Bill and head to the catacombs, stay there until I come get you, understand?"

The catacombs, which was a very melodramatic name for a very boring place which amounted to little more than a sub-basement to the chapel undercroft, was none the less the safest place that anyone could wish to hide in, being both almost unknown to someone who doesn't snoop as much as me, and far enough underground to qualify as a bomb shelter.

"What's happening?" she asked.

"I don't know, but it's something very odd and I've rarely found sudden bouts of mystical darkness to be associated with good things. So, I think it's better to be safe than sorry, don't you agree?"

By this point the school's automatic lights had kicked in and the courtyard had lit up as motion sensors spotted moving students.

"What about you?" she asked.

"I'm going to get Des and meet you there," I replied, already moving and trusting Cathy to do the same.

I went in the direction of the gym, where I knew Des would have gone for his practice session, darting through corridors past frightened students. I ran out past the dining hall, darting through a side passage between the science building and the theatre, breaking out onto open grass. I could see the gym up ahead, wreathed in light.

That's where I met the first of *them*.

He wore a black suit and tie and carried a silver topped cane that glowed with red-tinged energy. He wore leather gloves and a silver lapel pin in the shape of an ouroboros, a snake eating its own tail, the head exaggerated and toothy.

I couldn't see his face; it was behind the concealing spell that I'd seen at the restaurant, the one that warped the space around the caster. I looked with my mage sight, and the image just flexed even further. I didn't know that could even happen! The whole point of mage sight was to see *through* glamours and deceptions. He turned his head a fraction of an inch towards me and raised his cane in an almost contemptuous gesture.

My shadows came up first. They slithered into existence in a fraction of a second and took the kinetic attack that would have broken every bone in my body. The near-total darkness made this so much easier; I could feel the reassuring presence of all that shadow surrounding me, comforting me. Not to mention the simple fact that my opponent simply wouldn't be able to see me. An unfair advantage, perhaps, but I can't say I was really referring to the Marquis of Queensbury at that particular juncture.

The merest mental twitch, and the sea of dark around the magician simply compressed, and I felt a weak shield collapse with a *whump* before my shadows reached the mage and flattened him to the ground, knocking him out cold (and quite probably breaking his shoulder, arm and jaw).

The shadows withdrew and I checked on the man. His "mask" was still in place, which made sense to me after our brief encounter. The man hadn't been particularly powerful, barely a Wizard, though probably more likely to be an acolyte from the strength of his shield, and that warping spell-mask needs Power (with a deliberate capital P), and skill that he just didn't have if barely competent *me* was able to drop him so easily.

I wished that I knew why they were here! What could they possibly want desperately enough to invade a school in the daytime?

In the absence of answers, I examined the concealing spell carefully, letting my mage sight pass around it, and it didn't take me long to realise that it was High Magic, (Space, if I was any judge, you'll recall the five sorts mentioned by Tethys?), and that means at least a weak Sorcerer around here somewhere, and that was very bad. I have no illusions about my skill in a fight, and the ones I've won so far were down to a potent combination of luck and knowledge, and while I can always rely on the latter, the former inevitably runs out, at which point my sub-par duelling skills just aren't going to cut it.

So I needed to get Des away from here very quickly, before my luck ran out and we all died. So I placed a heavy-gauge sleeping spell on the mage and carried on, moving at a decent clip (for me). I kept the shadows going, and I felt them connect to the rest of the dark around me, questing outward, looking for threats.

The gym was lit with a few internal lights. I saw flares of energy that looked like they came from Belle, the power of her ice-spells were blue coloured and had a distinctive signature, perhaps the pair hadn't even realised that it had gone dark outside?

But then I saw streaks of other spells, red and yellows.

But no white.

Nothing from Des at all.

I started sprinting.

As I rounded the edge of the building, I found the doors open, one hanging from a single hinge, the wood splintered and charred. There was a small corridor with connecting halls leading to the swimming pool, the squash courts and the changing rooms, with the gym straight on from where I'd walked in.

I ran straight forward and into the middle of a pitched battle. Belle was stood facing down four other mages, who were dressed in the same suit as the first, though these wore white masks over the top parts of their faces, and each was hurling magic of various types straight at Belle. She was deflecting and dodging like a ballet dancer, and threw four lances of ice out at the mages, but her attacks were too few, and they were too well prepared.

And she was anchored in place, standing over my brother.

I saw blood pooling underneath him.

And then I saw red.

I'd never been so enraged in my entire life. The auditorium and Tethys, the warehouse roof and the pair of criminals were *nothing* compared to this. I didn't have the necessary focus to even put up a shield, which was so asinine, I can barely quantify it. My shadows simply responded to need and surged out in a massive black wave that tore up the floor, scattered the seating and smashed into the first two mages. Their magic was kinetic or water based, with minimal light and woefully weak shields. The dark hit them like a bloody truck and they flew back into the walls, which shattered as they impacted. Smears of blood marked their passage to the ground. The shadows had been sharp and vicious, tearing their flesh as it tossed them away.

The last two were stronger, their magic brighter. One was a fire mage (it was annoying just how many of them I was meeting lately), the other flesh, judging by the way his form was bulging and the faintly orange power that flowed out of his pores. They were surrounded by light as they powered their spells, light that was only growing brighter as they saw my oncoming shadows.

They had been prepared for me. Well fine, I had other tricks.

I knew on some level that I didn't have the fine control I'd need to make the shadows strong enough to punch through that much magical light (I was simply too angry), and simply piling in the power wouldn't cut it, so I did what I'd done the night I'd met the Shaadre. I pulled it all in, power by the bucket from everywhere around me, letting it coalesce in my outstretched hands.

No feedback this time. Practice makes perfect.

It hadn't taken long, a few seconds, and I could see Belle cowering in the shadows, protecting my brother even when she couldn't see what was happening around her. She was keeping still, rebuilding her defences; I was quite impressed within the small part of my mind still capable of positive emotion.

I aimed in the general direction of the two mages, who were desperately trying to conjure enough light to banish my shadows (and failing dismally), the best they were doing was causing us to maintain our distance. 'Its' distance. I meant 'its'.

I released my spell, and a wave of every energy type darted towards them. They felt it coming, and hastily shoved more power into their shields. The barriers caught a certain amount of the attack, mostly the light and heat, but the rest got through. Electricity shocked them, chemical energy melted their clothes into their flesh, gravitational energy broke their bones, kinetic energy sliced into their skin down to the muscle and the residual heat set their hair and clothes on fire before the atomic energy decayed and soaked them in radiation.

The blistered, broken figures that fell to the floor barely resembled men, and were only just alive, but I didn't care. I was already running for my brother, heedless to what Belle might see. My shadows parted and I dropped to his side, mage sight looking him over. Belle was looking at me in pure shock, taking in the inky shadows leaking from my sleeves and from the dark recesses of my collar and jacket.

"I bloody knew it!" she said, glaring at me as I pulled Des' shirt up to reveal a long, gaping wound in his side. I ignored her, pressing my hands to the injury while I tried to recall everything I'd ever read about triage and medical magics. In addition to the large wound, I saw three dark bruises that covered broken ribs and a little internal bleeding. There were also some smaller injuries and fractures, but they weren't too pressing in the moment.

"We need to get him to a doctor," Belle said.

"Please be quiet," I asked, focussing my mind. She was still chattering, but I was already working. One problem at a time, that's how triage works. First the big wound. Will to keep the blood in while building the flesh-magic lattice that would close it. As my mental hands slid into place, the blood started to pool at the edge of the injury, flowing against the blue barrier. I focussed, building the spell slowly and carefully in my mind, matching it precisely to the wound. I cast it as soon as I thought it was ready, empowering it with a gathered jolt of chemical energy.

The wound began to close, and Belle stopped wittering to watch. Next, the internal bleeding. Another small application of Will energy brought the bones away from the injuries. Then I cast small, but complex, spells designed to knit them back together before I upped the local metabolism enough to close the internal injuries one by one.

By then, the wound in his side was covered by a new layer of pink skin, and the injury to the muscle and blood vessels underneath was repairing itself swiftly and surely. I was tiring quickly but it wasn't the energy use. I still had plenty left in the tank, it was the sheer concentration required for medical magic that was tiring me out. Not to mention the fact that channelling this much energy is itself tiring.

Des' breathing normalised, and I slumped to the floor, a cluster of shadows coming in to keep me upright and support my weight.

"He'll be alright now," I said, but Belle wasn't looking at Des anymore, she was staring at me like I was some sort of alien.

"So it *was* you?" she asked finally, "All this time?"

I shrugged, not really interested in explaining myself.

"You're the Sorcerer? The one Tethys mentioned?"

Another shrug.

"You're stronger than Des, hell, you're stronger than me, and you let me push you around, let Des have all the glory?"

"Magic is his thing," I replied, needing to defend myself, I suppose, "who was I to take that away from him? What was I going to say? Hey, Des, you know that thing you do that no one else in the family can? The thing that makes you feel special? Well I can do ten times as much with a fraction of the effort."

Now that I'd actually been considering such things from a more balanced perspective, I'd realised that I really *was* much better at this than Des. I *was* stronger, I was much more skilled and I was far more versatile. I may well actually be a Sorcerer, which should be impossible, and that came with its own worries if what Wilks had said about Shadowborn Sorcerers was true.

"That was you at the duel, wasn't it? That shield? It was way beyond Des on his best day, let alone in the middle of a fight. I felt it as you cast it, but I didn't believe it."

"What was I going to do, just let that behemoth cave his skull in?"

She snorted at me and we sat for a moment in an uncomfortable silence.

"So, now what? I can't lie to him about this," she said, eyes still on me.

"Sure you can," I replied, getting a little annoyed, "and if you really can't, just let me know, and I can erase your memory for you."

It came out a lot harsher than I meant it to sound, but she surprised me by smiling.

"I always thought you were a weed, you know that?" she said.

"You didn't think wrong," I replied, "you've just caught me on an unusually resolute day."

She chuckled and Des stirred, his eyes slowly opening. I dropped the shadows and they revealed an almost destroyed room. Belle gave me an impressed look and helped my brother sit up.

"What happened?" he asked.

"They turned on each other," I replied, "Belle mopped up what was left."

She frowned at me including her in my lies, but Des looked impressed.

"That's my girl," he said with a grin, "was I bleeding?"

"No," Belle said, "some of theirs got on you during the fight."

"Disgusting, but I'm not complaining," he said. Belle helped him up, and they in turn helped me. I was shaky on my feet from shock and exhaustion, and the growing realisation that I'd mutilated four *more* people.

"You go on ahead, make for the catacombs, Bill and Cathy are already there, I'll catch up. Make sure you call your friends at the SCA as soon as you can," I said.

"But what about the mages? What if there are more?" Belle asked.

"Then we don't want to get in the way of the hopefully rapid SCA response, do we?" I pointed out.

"He's right Des, come on," she said, giving me a wink before leading him out the door.

I stood there, among the ruin I had made, and walked towards the fallen mages, gathering them in the centre of the room with shadow tendrils. Something dark in the back of my mind told me that I could snuff them out then and there; no one would know. And then they could never threaten me and mine again. I fought that part of me back with everything I had, and instead used my magic to make them sleep, a deep sleep, very deep, more like a coma, actually. Unless I removed the spell, they simply wouldn't wake up, *that* deep, bound to their very life forces.

Maybe I'd wake them up one day.

Maybe I wouldn't.

Chapter 38

With that done I staggered out of the gym, my shadows coiling around me as I walked away. I felt a growing unease as I made my way towards the catacombs, retracing my steps for the most part. I could *feel* something watching me. Something nasty, too. I looked around with my mage sight, but couldn't see anything close by. I knew that there had to be something somewhere, and it was scaring me that I couldn't see it.

That's the thing about a mage's senses, they tell you things that a normal person's wouldn't, so listening to your instincts is important, that's on page one of Des' "Duelling for Beginners" textbook (which I had started looking at since my recent misadventures).

I stopped walking and extended the coverage of my shadows, relying on them to conceal me. Anyone launching an attack would be taking a guess as to where I actually was. I made the shape irregular, so that there would be no clear "centre" to the formation, and I began a more complex sensory spell, to which I carefully spliced my mage sight.

I cast the spell and as my vision suddenly expanded, I saw everything around me. It was a little disorientating at first, but I let go of the idea of direction and avoided the spinning feeling that would have made me thoroughly sick. Instant, total coverage removed the need to focus on details, they were all there, dumped into my brain. It was intense, but I got it working and soon noticed, a faint, tiny ripple of power behind me.

I released the spell and recast standard mage sight, turning around so that I could examine that ripple more carefully. It slowly moved towards my shadows, like it was trying to sneak up on me. It was like a hair-thin streak of compressed air, barely noticeable unless you knew what to look for. I prepared a dispel, as powerful as I could make it, and released it in the streak's direction. My shadows opened to let my spell through, and the wall of magic washed over the foreign energy.

Where the energies connected, there was an arching fizz which built to a roar as energy discharged all around the spell. Lightning scorched the grass, and I raised a shield in time to take an arc of electricity that had ripped its way through my shadows (*light*ning, as the name implies, releases a hell of a lot of light on impact, and is quite bad for shadows).

A gaping hole in reality opened and another be-suited figure flew out, his clothes on fire. He desperately rolled on the ground to put out the flames. I let him, I'm not a monster, but when he wasn't burning, I made my move. My shadows darted forward, wrapping around his limbs and neck, squeezing tightly but not lethally. He struggled, and I could feel him gathering energy for a spell.

"Stop, or I'll pop you like a balloon," I said in my most resolute tone of voice, trying hard not to let my hands shake from fear and tiredness.

He carried on gathering energy, and I made the shadows tighter, introducing a few points and barbs to the mix. He grunted at the sudden pressure and pain.

"Alright, alright!" he said, fear entering his voice as he eyed up the shadows grasping him.

His accent was strange, with a faint touch of Manchester, or maybe Liverpool, his eyes were slate-grey and glaring, filled with hatred, all of it for me. He was far short of handsome, his nose was a touch large, his lips just a little too wide, but he held himself with confidence, and I could feel the power he commanded. This was certainly the Space mage I was worried about. I wasn't entirely sure on this point, but I was fairly certain he'd managed to warp reality enough to create a pocket where I couldn't see him, even with my mage sight. That's *heavy* magic, I was years away from being able to attempt something like that.

"What are you doing here?" I asked finally, casting an observation spell that would allow me to see how truthful he was.

He swore before spitting at me. One of my shadows caught the glob before it could land on my face, I *hate* being spat on. That simple defensive gesture made his eyes go wide for some reason, and he shut his mouth tightly.

"Look, I'll level with you," I said, putting an earnest look on my face, "my knowledge of mental magic is extensive, but I've only just begun to study mind reading, and so if I try, while I have no doubt that I'll get the information I require, I'm not sure how intact you'll be when I'm done."

A look of doubt crossed his face as he glared at me, "You're bluffing," he said.

I sighed theatrically and reached forward, building a little telepathic spell. I *can* read minds, it just takes a lot of effort, and the deeper I go the harder it is not to break something. By the time I would be done I could be badly drained, and he could be a vegetable. The mind is not like a book, like people seem to think, it's more like a radio, with dozens of different frequencies all jumbled together representing different layers of the brain and its functions, and then each section of the brain has its own separate sub-frequency, it's a mess that you only really understand once you've played with a living mind a few times (I refer you to the Uncle I mentioned earlier). The easiest to read is current thoughts, which means that if you want them to tell you something useful, you have to make them think about what you want to know.

"Stop! Stop!" he said, flinching back from my hand.

"You have something to tell me?" I asked politely.

"We're only here to talk," he said, "we heard about a powerful shadow mage, and wanted to meet him."

I thought about his answer for a minute before speaking.

"Now, I hardly need to read your mind to know that that's a lie," I said, casting the telepathy spell while he was distracted, "if you came to talk, then you wouldn't have blacked out the sky, and you wouldn't have attacked my brother."

He knows! He knows! What am I going to do? The monster will kill me if I tell it the truth, his thoughts came through loud and clear.

"I'm not sure what you mean," he said calmly.

"And whose idea was the whole 'blackout' thing? You do realise that coming after a Shadowborn *in the dark* is like coming after a giant squid in deep water? Which is to say, idiotic? If I were you, I would be seriously considering the idea that I'd been set up."

The Master would never do that, he'd never betray us like that. The monster is trying to confuse me, that's all.

"I know," I said, "you shouldn't worry, after all, your people will be right over to help. Your group stands together, after all."

I took a shot, it's all about associations in the mind.

That's right! The Sons of the Dark Moon always stand together! The rest of the brotherhood will descend on the creature and take it, as we always have.

Oh ho! Those idiots Tethys referenced in her e-mail when I first asked her to snoop for me. The ones who'd bought the Shaadre! Finally we were making progress!

"So tell me," I said, trying to keep my temper in check, "why are you here?"

"I told you, we came to talk."

Find the abomination.

"And when we were done talking?" I asked.

"We'd go on our way," he replied.

Capture the abomination.

"How many of you came?" I asked.

I think he already got Bruce and his team, so he knows about them and me, but he hasn't found the master and his team, yet.

"Five," he said after a minute.

Eleven.

Crap, four more where he came from. That's my cue to run far away and wait for the cavalry to show up (hopefully the *armoured* cavalry).

"Why do you want shadow mages so much?" I asked.

His face showed confusion, he didn't realise that we were actually having two different conversations.

"I don't," he replied.

Because you're living weapons! Taking you and training you is the only way we can be sure you won't slaughter everyone, while still being rather profitable for us...

Well, his mind was a tad melodramatic.

"One final question before I let you go, who told you about me?"

"We have our sources," he said.

Vanessa Knowles.

I only knew one Vanessa Knowles, and she didn't know who I was. That meant that she sicced this bunch of lunatics on my school, and probably my brother, in an attempt to draw me out, and that made me very, very angry. I prepared another coma spell and dropped it into his mind without preamble. He dropped to the floor as my shadows released him.

Des could have died, died because of *her*. Before all this was said and done, there was going to be a reckoning, I swore. My shadows grew barbed and agitated as my anger grew, and it was an effort to wrestle them away from the fallen 'Son'.

So, just to get this whole mess straight in my head as much as anything else, there is an organisation, powerful and well connected, with access to Shaadres. This organisation sent one of their attack dogs after my brother, and now that I've somehow attracted their notice (though goodness knows how I managed that, I've been so subtle, after all!), they seem to want me captured, which is better than dead, but still not that reassuring. This would explain why the woman who'd followed me from the restaurant hadn't used any lethal magic.

Now, for whatever reason, Vanessa Knowles was either working with them or on the take, passing information to them, which added a whole new dimension of complication to an already complicated mess. Oh, and that's another problem. I knew that Knowles was a passable mind mage; she'd probably be able to pull a memory of me from the heads of the mages who'd seen me. I'd need to do something about that before I did anything else.

And those thoughts and worries don't cover Tethys, who may have her finger poked into this pie in some shape or form, and may well decide to sell me down the river at some point.

It was all a bit of a situation, and I felt a bit overwhelmed, but what could I do? Sit and cry? No. I took a breath, and calmed myself. As with triage, a problem like this is best solved one step at a time.

It was a relatively simple matter to find the man's (maybe I should have asked his name?) memory and erase the last few hours, I'm not skilful enough yet to erase blocks of time smaller than that. I backtracked a bit along my route and did the same thing to the guy I'd knocked out earlier.

Thank goodness I'd come upon this guy, or I'd never have thought to do that, and I would have been deep in some governmental crap at some point in the very near future.

Oh, this is far more than I really want to have to deal with. Maybe it's time I took a holiday? I hear Antarctica's nice this time of year...

Chapter 39

So, with my short term problems sorted (sort of), I started making my way to the catacombs with as much speed as my tired body would allow me. It was still very dark, so I kept my mage sight active, casting around me to make sure that I wasn't being followed or observed. There was nothing, and I wasn't even really anxious, which I hoped meant that I wasn't under threat.

I found the chapel easily enough. Some people find themselves disoriented in the dark; I'm not one of them, as you might guess. I opened the door to the lower levels, walking down to where I sent my friends. I was starting to relax a little bit, believing that for the moment, the situation was contained. Hardly anyone knew about this bolt hole, and if these "Sons of the Dark Moon" twits couldn't find Des, they couldn't attack him, and thus me. So I was tentatively willing to say that things were starting to look up. All we needed to do was wait for the SCA, and that was assuming that any of the Mooners were still here after losing contact with more than half their numbers.

The catacombs were stone-lined corridors, built into the chapel's foundations, back when it was supposed to be the core of an expanding monastery. That was two hundred years before the whole property was sold off and was renovated into a school. There were more than two hundred holy men buried down there in stone caskets, which made it a little creepy, but which would also help to conceal our life signatures. There were a few wall-mounted lights, but it was still quite dark down there, so it's often avoided except by people wanting to give themselves a scare around Halloween.

They used it as a bomb shelter during the war, and there is enough space down there to fit the school's population in the event of an emergency like that, though I think that I'm the only person who would think to go there in a crisis in this day and age. One of the benefits of long-reaching paranoia, you always know where the best boltholes are.

I made my way carefully, releasing my shadows and shutting down my mage sight. The dark surrounded me, and I felt my heart rate increase as my fear of the dark came back with a vengeance. Yes, I'm aware that's strange, but when my shadows are around me, it doesn't *feel* like it's dark, after all, I can see right through them.

I tripped on a few loose stones and fell to the ground with a heavy thump and a bruised knee. I swore volubly for several seconds before I heard Des' voice calling my name. He came around a corner up ahead with a handful of light.

"Not again," he said, moving around to help me up, releasing the light to float in a ball above his head.

"It's not my fault," I replied, dusting myself off, "it's dark down here."

There was a snort from around the corner as Belle showed herself, which I replied to with my best glare. She just grinned back at me. Seriously reconsidering a little memory wipe. After all, what's the harm? Just a teeny little bit of brain damage...

"I called the SCA," Des said, which made me wince in light of recent revelations, but it was still our best move.

"What now?" he asked, seeing the wince, "You told me to!"

"I know, I know," I replied, "but I just overheard some of them talking, and it would appear as if we have reason not to trust your friend, Agent Knowles."

"Not this again," Des said, turning away, a scowl on his face.

I sighed and sat down on the floor. I was tired, and I couldn't be bothered to go another five rounds with Des on the trustworthiness of his new crush. Cathy and Bill sat down next to me as I leaned my head back.

"What did you hear?" Belle asked, sitting opposite me with her back against the other side of the corridor.

"I don't suppose it really matters," I replied, closing my eyes briefly before Belle kicked my foot.

"Spill," she said, a grin on her face.

"Fine."

So I told an edited version of my story, saying that the space mage had been speaking with the warped face guy, and that they had been looking for the shadow mage that had been protecting Des. I almost don't know why I bothered, half the people in the room with me knew the story was full of crap, and I'd have to tell the real one sometime soon, at least once. Belle looked smug. Des started pacing, he didn't look happy.

"Why would she do that?" he asked, flopping down next to Belle, linking his arm with hers, though she seemed annoyed by the gesture.

"Far be it for me to defend the witch-hunters," I said, "but it's quite possible that she didn't know that they were going to use you as bait, she could just have passed on the information to someone she thought was perfectly trustworthy."

"There's no way to know that, and it would be dangerous to assume benign ignorance, for a variety of reasons," Cathy said, scratching idly at a patch of dirt on her skirt. Cathy hates dirt, that spot would be driving her steadily insane until it was gone. I cast a tiny spell and the dirt lifted itself away, gathering itself into a ball before falling to the floor (funnily enough, that spell is actually meant to be used for cleaning wounds, but it works just as well as a fabric cleanser). Cathy went back to scratching to discover that the spot wasn't there anymore, and I looked away as she turned to stare at me. She elbowed me gently in the ribs, which made me jump. She sniggered.

Cathy and Bill started chatting while Belle and Des stayed quiet. I managed to pay attention for about a minute before I simply fell asleep.

I awoke to the sound of heavy footsteps, and then yelling. Lots and lots of yelling. I was ridiculously close to a panic-induced magical indiscretion when Cathy took my hand and whispered in my ear to be calm.

"It's just the police," she said as I got to my feet just in time to be knocked off them again by a colossal man wearing black fatigues with 'SCA' stencilled on the front and back. He was sporting what appeared to be some sort of hand-held cannon (I exaggerate, it was a shotgun, but at the time it looked pretty huge). He'd come around the corner and socked me in the chest with the stock of his gun, which hurt, sending me back to the floor. Another four guys came around the corner, wearing the same thing, also armed. One of them pointed his gun at me. They started shouting for us not to move, and I obeyed with gusto, raising my hands to show I meant no harm, feeling a little panicked that my shadows hadn't come to help.

I reached for magic, any magic, and found that while it *was* there, it was dampened, somehow. I must have still been a little foggy from my brief nap, because it took me a while to notice that the bruisers were all wearing anti-magic amulets, Spelleaters, and they were right on top of me. I was down for the count, magically speaking. Des and Belle were on their feet for about a second before they received the same treatment. Both had taken steps towards me, readying their own spells before the amulets got too close and the magic simply fizzled away.

"Names!" the gunman who'd knocked me down shouted.

"You first!" I shouted back. He turned to look at me, bending over menacingly.

"Don't test me, boy, my patience doesn't cover uppity little shits."

"We are minors under the guardianship of the school you're currently standing in. Just *talking* to us without a teacher or parent present is grounds for dumping you in a media-fuelled shitstor-"

He hit me.

The son of a bitch actually hit me. Me!

He smacked the butt of his rifle into my face and my lip split as my head flew back into the wall, where it received a nice bump. At that point things got a little confused as everyone did a whole bunch of very foolish things all at once. Des and Belle were on their feet again, making for the thug, Cathy had started crying while Bill actually thumped one of the gunmen in the arm with his pocket pencil case, bless his loyal stupidity.

Two of the gunmen stepped towards my brother, shoving him back, at which point I made my biggest mistake of the night (sorry, day, the artificial darkness had me confused), I stood up. It added just enough to the confusion, so that when I stepped towards the guy who clobbered me, he saw me out of the corner of his eye, and was startled enough that he turned towards me, his gun with him. Then Des shoved past the guy who was covering him and Belle, who fell back into the brute who was covering me, causing him to be additionally startled in the already tense situation.

He pulled the trigger on reflex.

There was a bang, and my abdomen exploded in agony as I flew the six inches back into the wall before slowly sliding to the ground.

My hands went to what I was expecting to be a huge hole in my side, but turned out to be more of a dent with a tiny bean bag in it. Don't get me wrong, it HURT, but I could have laughed like a maniac when I discovered that I wasn't going to need a trauma team and nine weeks of recovery (or possibly a coffin).

Des and Belle both shouted, going berserk trying to get to me. Cathy continued her useful streak and started screaming, with Bill's able assistance (after the bruiser he'd thwapped with his pocket protector had smacked him right back, he had crawled away, and was cowering around the corner, sensible fellow; wish I'd been there with him). The bruisers knocked the others down, Belle's lip started bleeding.

I felt something then, looking at my friends and my brother, afraid and hurt, trying to help me. I was suddenly furious again. This was happening a lot more than I was really comfortable with.

I screamed, well, actually it was more of a roar, it was a horrible sound now I remember it. And magic flowed. In a time and place where it never should have been able to, impossibly, magic flowed. My shadows felt my rage, and they came for me, leeching from everywhere as I screamed out my hatred. Colour drained from the room, filling it with comforting and familiar grey, and the shadows lanced and stabbed, thrashing against the bruisers. The amulets drained a lot of my power away, but they could only take so much at a time, and the leftovers were more than enough to break bone and lacerate flesh through their body armour. I felt my depleted Well drain out through my Shadows and into the amulets, but the goons were still fighting and I needed more. In an instant, something inside me sort of tore and I suddenly had more power to hand. Lots more. The soldiers were slammed back, smashing off the walls to land on the floor, three unconscious, two screaming.

I never wanted that, truly I didn't. I don't know where all that hate came from. And now that they were down, I found that I'd never felt so awful before...

And how did I do that?! It shouldn't have been possible to plough through one of those amulets, much less five; not that it really mattered at that moment, there were now five bleeding, injured government agents on the floor, and it was my fault.

After all, I'd been the one to talk back to the bloody SCA goon. I should have just answered his damned question. I'm beginning to wonder if I have some sort of brain damage...

Chapter 40

I have to admit, it took me a minute to get my shit together after all that. I'd stopped screaming, and it took a supreme effort to wrestle both my temper and my shadows back under control. They were still snapping and coiling around the prone figures, leeching my energy into them, but I was able to drag them back under control and send them away. Standing up took a little more work. Something was... wrong. I felt like something had broken inside me. I felt physically weak, and horribly drained, like I was fighting off a bad flu. Add to that the beanbag bullet, and my chest felt like one colossal bruise, and moving was less than pleasant. Still, I clambered to my feet just as my shadows receded.

I looked over at Des and Belle, who still looked shocked, but both gave me a thumbs up. They were alright, but Cathy was still screaming, so she was my first port of call. I knelt down beside her and rubbed her back until she stopped. She turned around and threw her arms around my neck, sobbing into my shoulder. Bill appeared from around the corner, looking sheepish.

He took a long look at the carnage before clapping his hands with finality.

"Well," he said, "looks like my work here is done."

I couldn't help it; I started laughing like an idiot, great guffaws of noise, while Des and Belle looked at us like we were insane people.

"Did anyone see the mage?" Des asked, darting up the corridor, and looking around, "Matty?"

"Nope, sorry," I replied, holding on to Cathy, almost as much for my own reassurance as for hers, if I'm honest.

"Belle?" he asked, almost frantic now.

At this point I'd normally make a crack to the effect that if he'd learned to cast mage sight, he might actually be able to see the man he was looking for, but the last thing I wanted these days is for him to actually do it. It would make my life considerably more complicated. And, to be honest, mage sight might actually be beyond him, it's a very complicated spell, and messing around with your perceptions is dangerous unless you know *exactly* what you're doing (I mentioned seeing everything in purple for a week?). The last time I tried to teach him a spell with *half* as many variables as mage sight, he detonated several hundred cubic metres of air (I was trying to teach him to draw water out of it), so naturally a complex mental spell may be something of a bad idea, but I digress.

"No more mages here than there were a second ago," Belle said, winking at me in a way that I found annoying in my current state. I'd started to shake a little, I was horribly weak. I managed a glare before Cathy started to come out of her daze.

"Is it over yet?" she asked in a little whisper.

"Yup," I answered, relaxing a little.

Suddenly there was shouting from around the corner again. Seconds later, Knowles came bolting towards us, her hands surrounded by purple light, eyes blazing.

Spoke too soon. My bad. I tried to call my shadows again, but I nearly threw up, so I had to stop. It appeared that I wasn't going to be any use to man or beast for a while (a year or so by the way I felt), so over to Des.

God help us.

"Ms. Knowles, the mage- the shadows and attackers! He saved me again, more of them out there, and the security guys..." he blabbered like a buffoon on LSD, articulate as ever.

"Calm down Mister Graves, and take it one step at a time," she said, letting her magic bleed away. She gave a short, sharp whistle, and three more armed men barrelled in, making for the wounded soldiers.

That reassured me. She wasn't likely to do anything to us with witnesses around, hopefully. Truthfully, the second the men arrived, I stopped worrying about betrayal. Whatever extra nonsense she was involved with, she wasn't likely to be a hands-on kidnapper or murderer. No, she was likely just an informant, or she would have been with the Mooner's teams, providing direct intelligence.

"Um," Des said, confused for a moment.

I sighed, and helped the poor idiot out, explaining briefly what had happened, leaving out anything that could get me into trouble, all the while Cathy had to help keeping me upright.

"Are you alright, Mister Graves?" Knowles asked looking me over, "You aren't looking terribly well." I saw the slightly glazed look that comes over someone using mage sight. I would have preferred it if she hadn't done that, but what could I do?

She hissed.

"I'm no life mage, but I think something took a bite out of your living energy, how are you feeling?"

"Sick," I managed, starting to see spots.

"Just breathe. It'll grow back eventually," she said, kneeling next to me, "may take a while, though."

She looked intently at me again, wincing now and then. I must have done some serious damage, though I was damned if I knew how. If I had to guess, I just got a massive boost of power by *eating* a piece of myself (or consuming; however you want to put it, it's still disgusting). Living energy is associated with vitality and health (not to be confused with life force, which is the very energy that runs a living being, determines how long you live, and is easily filled up from a store of magic; different thing entirely). Living energy is what keeps you strong and healthy, it's tied up with your bodily functions, the chemical energy of the food you eat increases it, getting sick or hurt expends it. My baseline was already low on account of that life-link that saved my brother all those years ago, so losing any more tends to cause me problems, and I don't have the faintest idea how to refill it with magic.

So I just sat there, waiting for my body to catch up with the energy deficit, and feeling steadily sicker and weaker as time went on. My breathing was getting harder, and I was growing lightheaded. That does it, never again, I'm swearing off sticking my nose where it doesn't belong. Next time, I'm taking my own advice and heading indoors and staying there until the lights turn back on. Come to think about it, why was I even bothering? It's not like any of this is even *my* problem. Well, that first Shaadre was after Des, so that, but everything else had come exclusively from my meddling and prodding. So, lesson learned, nose firmly removed from other people's business. I'm moving on to quieter pursuits.

But first, there's the little matter of staying conscious.

I just about managed, staying awake while Knowles and her three goons helped the five others. The ones that had stayed awake had passed out, and the ones that had been knocked out had woken up screaming, it was a very confused mess. They were still being treated when Des helped me stumble out into restored daylight. It blinded me and made my eyes ache something vicious. This had been something of a bad day, one that I was very keen to forget. It took a while before I could walk properly again, but I started moving off, leaving Des to answer questions. He didn't know anything that could cause me problems, after all.

I made it to my room almost unnoticed and simply fell into bed, shivering and clammy. I was actually sick! Wasn't that just the cherry on the cake baked from crap that was this day?

I woke up quite some time later, when there was a knocking at my door. I felt so horrible, I just pulled a blanket over my head and hoped they would go away. Of course they didn't.

"Matty?" Des said, opening my door a crack.

I tried for "What do you want now, you life-complicating ignoramus?", but what actually came out was closer to "Maarglfluum...".

"Are you alive?" he asked, flopping himself down on a chair.

"No, go away and plan the funeral," I replied, shoving a pillow over my aching head.

"I have news," Des said, seemingly unwilling to just let me die in peace like I wanted, so I shoved the sheets and blankets back and sat up.

"Yah!" he said with a grimace after looking at me.

"That's just the confidence boost I was looking for, thanks Des."

I levered myself up and saw stars. I hadn't been this sick in years, my head was aching, my chest was a mass of bruises my stomach was... oh no.

I barely made it to the sink. I was throwing up as I got there. Oh that was horrible, and the sight of all that vomit made me throw up again in an awful cycle of sight, smell and vomit until everything I'd eaten since I moved onto solid foods was making its awful way down the sink. Des was holding me up by that point, looking a little green himself as he helped me back to bed (after I'd rinsed my mouth out at least a dozen times), where I propped myself up against the wall.

"Have you seen a matron yet?" he asked, concern all over his face.

"Yes, she said bed rest," I lied.

"Like hell you did," Des said, looking to launch into a diatribe by the looks of it.

"So, you had news?" I asked, in a blatant attempt to change the subject.

"Knowles and Kraab are back at the school," he said, falling for it and opening the window to let some of the vomit stench out.

Noooooooo! Now I couldn't use any bloody healing magic! AGAIN! And I really needed a pick-me-up. I almost cried, don't tell anyone.

"For how long, this time?" I asked, concealing my distress.

"They say until the perpetrators are found," Des said.

"Did you get a chance to ask about what I'd discovered?" I asked, now clutching at an empty and cramping stomach.

"Of course not," he said, "no way she's in league with those people."

I rolled my eyes, but let it go. When I was able to move, I'd go and have a word myself, but that was going to have to wait a while. Like a week, or two. Yeah, two sounds better.

Chapter 41

Des, being the concerned sibling that he was, called the bloody matron. Her name was Ulrika, she was a portly, cheerful-*looking* woman in her mid to late forties, with greying hair and brown eyes. She looked like she cared about the wellbeing of young people.

Don't be fooled, she was *evil*.

She was from the "tough love" school of medical care, which is to say, if it doesn't hurt, then it doesn't count. She's the sort of matron that rips the plaster all the way off in one wrenching tear, rather than letting you peel it off carefully one corner at a time. Everyone's met a nurse like that; they're a fact of life.

Anyway, she turned up at my door and came in without knocking (as bloody usual), and made straight for my prone body. She woke me all the way up without preamble and started diagnosing.

"Wake up," she growled, dragging the duvet off me.

"Wha-?" I managed before she shoved a thermometer in my mouth and pulled my mutated eyes open for a look (though goodness only knows what she was expected to divine from there).

"You have a temperature," she said, looking at the thermometer, "quite likely a bad flu stay in bed and drink plenty of fluids. I'll be back to check on you later."

With that, she dropped two paracetamol down my throat, along with some water that made me choke, inspiring her to slap my back hard enough to make me see sparks. Then she left, leaving me brutally awake, sore and feeling a little violated. Par for the course with Ulrika, good grief.

And that was that week gone.

I spent four days getting worse, throwing up and getting sicker and weaker with that wretched matron dropping off inedible food from the cafeteria and making me eat it. She gave me over the counter meds and otherwise pretty much left me to it, for which I was grateful. Des, Bill and Cathy spent a lot of time with me (Cathy in a face mask so she would 'catch the pox'), keeping me company and my spirits up as best they could. Mostly I just slept. My fever broke on the Thursday, but it wasn't until Saturday that I was in any nick to start moving in any coordinated way. I emerged into what felt more like an armed camp than a school. I saw "discreet" police walking around in pairs, glaring around them at the students and teachers. Des hadn't told me about any of this, and I couldn't say that I found it pleasing.

It turned out that the whole thing had been hushed up by the SCA. No one had the first idea what had happened, other than 'strange, short lived, sky blackout'. Apparently everyone who'd seen anything had been told in no uncertain terms to shut the hell up.

I found Bill and Cathy in their usual spot under the tree, and they waved at me as I approached.

"It's alive!" Bill said, causing me to glare. I sat down, still a little shaky, but otherwise recovered. Cathy looked me over and gave a single nod of approval. I sighed and relaxed, glad to be healthy(-ish) again, it had been a really long week. Though as fully recovered as I was going to get, I felt as if I'd lost another little chunk of me, not as much as I had when I'd used the life-link spell on Des, but enough that I noticed, I was just that little bit slower, just that little bit easier to tire, but my magic... it had somehow gotten stronger, easier to get to, if that makes any sense, not that I could risk using it if Knowles the magic detector was around.

We chatted, they caught me up on all the gossip, and a couple of juicy rumours that were circulating. Apparently Courtney Wilcox was pregnant, and one of the teachers was the father (utter crap, and Bill was very pleased with his work on that one; if there's a particularly good and juicy rumour, you can bet that Bill started it, and almost certainly made it up), the Ox was engaged in a "physical" relationship with one of his male teammates (not one of Bill's stories, which made him jealous, and a little peeved), and also there was a lesser series of rumours that I was engaged in some sort of twisted sexualised game of cat and mouse with Tethys, which Bill swore he hadn't started, but which had his grubby little fingerprints all over it, the prick.

I was just beginning to contemplate an appropriate punishment when one of Kraab's security people walked over. This one looked a little more friendly that the others as he wasn't wearing his sunglasses, even though he was wearing the regulation dark suit. He was young, early twenties, handsome enough with a crooked smile that made Cathy squeak at his approach.

"Really?" I asked with a smirk that made her face go bright red.

"Matthew Graves?" the man asked as he arrived, wincing a little as he saw the eyes (still haven't gotten used to that reaction), though he covered it well enough.

"Yes?" I asked with trepidation, that the fellow must have noticed.

He smiled disarmingly, putting up his hands to show that he meant no harm.

"I'm Agent Stevens, I work with Agent Kraab. He would like a word with you, if it's convenient?"

"Are you aware of what happened the last time Agent Kraab wanted a word with me?" I asked with narrowed eyes.

"He said you'd mention that, and that I should tell you that he promises no funny business, on his word of honour," Stevens said.

I puffed out my cheeks with annoyance, but I stood up and gestured for Stevens to lead the way. Cathy and Bill stood too, following us along, which I found oddly comforting. Kraab was set up in the same conference room, this time filled with technology and four other fellows operating radios and computers.

"Ah, Mister Graves," Kraab said, waving me over to the seat I had previously occupied. He looked over my friends briefly, but said nothing as they filed in behind me and flopped down on a convenient sofa next to the wall.

"Agent Kraab," I replied.

"First, allow me to apologise on behalf of the SCA for the unfortunate incident last week. I assure you that the man who shot you has been suitably disciplined."

I can't say I was expecting an apology, and it took me slightly aback.

"Accidents happen," I said finally (and magnanimously, I thought).

"Very good of you," Kraab said, "but that's not why I asked to see you. Agent Knowles and I have spoken to your friends and brother, and they mentioned that you had overheard something important? Something regarding my colleague?"

What to do about this? Telling him the truth might get me into trouble, or certainly put me in front of people who would only ask more questions. But actively lying to the SCA? That would probably be worse, especially since I'd already spilled the beans to my friends. Crap.

I told him everything. Well, an edited version.

I told him that I'd overheard two of the mages mention Knowles as their source before turning on each other, and then arriving at the gym just as the "shadow mage" had finished with the other four (a story settled on after a brief conversation with Belle a few days ago), before running to the catacombs.

"I will investigate your story, and see what there is to be seen, but rest assured that I will get to the bottom of this. One final thing? Your brother informs me that you stayed behind briefly before joining them, for..." he looked through a stack of papers, "about twenty minutes. What were you doing?"

I looked down, affecting shame, "As you know, my brother has become somewhat obsessed with finding the man who's protecting him. I thought I might be able to find him myself, maybe help him get some closure, move on. It was foolish, given the circumstances."

Kraab smiled a little, "We all do foolish things for our family, Mister Graves. It's nothing to be ashamed of, though you have been getting yourself into unnecessary amounts of trouble lately. This is the magical world, young man. It's too dangerous for a non-magical person."

"I have to agree with you. In fact I have already made the decision to keep my nose well and truly out of things that are none of my concern."

"That is a wise decision," Kraab agreed with a smile.

"Did you get anything out of the people you captured? If you don't mind my asking," I said.

"No harm in telling you that we haven't. There were some very complex sleeping spells on them, almost certainly put in place by that mage looking out for your brother. Knowles is stumped. She exhausted herself trying to remove even one of them, and failed, repeatedly. It's actually rather frustrating."

Well, that did my ego no harm, I have to tell you, not that it really needed bulking up.

The conversation wound down, and I was on my way, quite happy with the result. Bill and Cathy followed me, staying quiet until we were well out of earshot.

"That went well!" Cathy said brightly.

"And no probing this time," Bill added, "though some people like that kind of thing, if you know what I mean."

"Billy!"

Those two are going to be the death of me, I swear.

Chapter 42

Well, there we go, loose ends tied up, decision made, problems solved, gosh it would be nice if *any* of those things were true.

But things did quiet down a bit. So that's something.

For three days.

The next Tuesday. It was now mid-March, and the weather was somehow even worse. It was freezing cold; just cold enough to make the rain biting, but not so cold that it could turn into tolerable snow. Nope, just cold, lots and lots of cold. And I wasn't as able to bear it as I used to be. I would have done some research into just what I had managed to do to myself, but I was still not quite up to anything energetic, and had no urge to go wandering around when I'd have to use magic just to avoid exhausting myself.

I was willing to do the research, more or less, but the problem was that I didn't trust the SCA, and I was sure that they had Windward under a magnifying glass, so it wouldn't be the best idea in the world to attract attention to myself.

So, lying low.

And then I got the letter.

An actual, honest to goodness letter, hand delivered (in the middle of Chemistry, I might add). There was a seal made from black wax on the back, stamped with an hour glass and the words *Victoria in Umbra* in tiny print. It had my name written on the front on a flowing hand.

I tucked the letter into my satchel until I had a moment to myself, which took a while, as Bill and Cathy saw me get it. Thankfully Cathy was able to steer him away, giving me the peace and quiet I needed. The wax snapped away, and I unfolded the letter.

Mister Graves,

Please forgive the manner of this communication, but after your encounter with our associates, and your difficulties outside our storage facility, it was thought best to send a letter, rather than a representative, I'm sure you will agree?

My brotherhood has followed your recent activities with interest. Our friends among the SCA have also informed us of your latest run-in with their puppet organisation, and it is our hope that you and we might come to an understanding to our mutual benefit and future profit.

I am authorised to offer you an invitation to a meeting, this Thursday at the Palm Orchid Hotel, 8pm, the Grill. I am sure that you will have your reservations, which is why a public place was selected, for your comfort.

As further incentive for your attendance, I offer you information about the creature that attacked you brother, and the reasons for it. If you choose to come, then the information will be provided, free from any reciprocity.

A refusal would be understood, but greatly regretted. We look forward to meeting you.

F.

F? Who the hell was F?

No. Don't get drawn in, leave it alone.

Not going.

Not happening. I've learned my lesson and I'm not going. The end.

Alright, I went, but I didn't *want* to.

Apart from anything else, I needed to know who this "F" was, and, if at all possible, what he thought he was up to.

I mentioned it to Cathy, along with some "in the event of my death" instructions, and made sure I was dressed for dinner. I have a half-decent suit I'd bought for my cousin's christening, black and grey, a little drab, but well made. I had my Sunday shoes, which did very well, and I pulled a dark overcoat over the ensemble. I didn't bother with a pass this time, but I was having Des run some interference for me (after I'd taken the trouble to extract some promises for his silence).

Ever since the "Day of Shadows" (wretched Bill's damned gossip mill's name, not mine), security had been a little tighter, and prefects were actually expected to enforce a curfew for a change, which amounted to nothing more than an increase in the going rate of bribery.

So I took the bus into town and flagged down a cab from there, arriving at the hotel at about seven forty-five, allowing me a little time to do some snooping. I cast my remote surveillance spell, making sure to cast a couple of buffers this time, I may not be the best in a practical situation, but I do learn from my mistakes (most of the time).

My little orb flew carefully into the lobby, which was impressive, to say the least. It was a long, thin room, with a polished black and white marble floor. There was a dark-wood mahogany desk at the far end between two staircases which met at the next floor. I followed the sign for the Grill, written in flowing gold. The door was open and I flew through, drifting towards the ceiling for a good look. There was nothing to see, no mages that I could spot (but I didn't have mage sight through the construct), which is to say that there was no one obviously magical, no single people who looked like they were waiting, no serious looking people who looked menacing. I didn't recognise anyone.

Oh... what the hell? It's a public place, what's the worst that could happen?

I released the spell and my perceptions shot back into my body, which made me blink hard a few times, I'd left my eyes open, and they were a little dry, my fault, should have known better, which is a statement I am badly overusing. So far the thing that has come closest to killing me is my own stupidity, and that just *has* to change.

I took a moment to straighten my shirt and tie before heading in. I had taken the trouble to weave a number of subtle protective spells into my clothes, invisible to the naked eye, but they should repel a surprise attack long enough to get a real shield going (hopefully, anyway, this stuff was a variation on some charms I'd learned in Des' books, and were untested in their current form, they might not work at all, or worse set me on fire or something).

I walked through the lobby and into the grill, where there was a young man in full evening attire waiting behind a small podium. I gave him my name, and he snapped his fingers to get the attention of an attractive young woman dressed in perfectly pressed whites and a tiny bow-tie. She led me to a table and I sat next to the wall to give myself a view of the room. I was feeling badly paranoid and already had enough to worry about without exposing my back to strangers as well.

I waited there, keeping an eagle eye out, but nothing happened until eight. To the second (I kid you not), the greeter started bowing and scraping as a man I recognised walked into the grill, took one look around and smiled warmly in my direction. A single twitch of his wrist, and the greeter darted away, and he strode towards me. I groaned quietly in irritation and stood to meet him (only polite, after all).

I knew on the spot that this was the man I was here to meet, and I was instantly mad (again) with Tethys, because I just *knew* that this was her fault somehow.

"Mister Graves, how good to see you again," he said with a wide grin, extending his hand.

"Lord Faust," I replied, extending my own, "fancy seeing you here."

"Have you been here long?" he asked, sitting down, the greeter had scuttled along in his wake, and shoved the chair in under him as he sat down.

"Not long," I replied.

He sat back in his chair, his posture perfectly relaxed, but then why wouldn't he be? It was just ridiculous how little a threat I was to this man.

"You seem unsurprised to see me," he said.

"Spending time with Tethys burned out the surprise portion of my brain," I replied, rubbing my forehead.

"I can sympathise, that woman had me on the hook from our first meeting, I would hate to tell you the sheer quantity of resources I spent trying to win her over. I essentially paid for half her current business empire, it's ridiculous."

Got to say, *that* was an ego boost. The great Lord Faust, ensnared by the woman who'd failed to ensnare me. Naturally I wasn't going to *tell* him that.

"Sorry to hear that," I said instead.

He nodded in acknowledgement, and leaned back, steepling his finger in that clichéd way older mages do when they wish to appear mysterious, incisive eyes watching me closely.

"She seems to be rather... interested in you, it must be said. Strangely so; in fact I'm not certain that she's ever gone to this much trouble over a mage before."

"I'm not sure I really like the sound of that," I said.

Faust smiled, "Wise man. Tethys is like any beautiful woman, her attentions are gratifying, but her agenda is completely her own. And on top of that, she's also a predator, and it's never a good idea to turn your back on such a thing."

His eyes took on a faraway look for a moment before he smiled a sad smile and turned his attention back to me.

"Bah, old times. You're not here to talk about my tragic dating life. You want to know about your brother's pursuers."

"Your letter said that you could tell me something about the Shaadre," I replied carefully, not willing to commit myself too much, or appear too eager.

"Yes, and my word is my bond," he said.

A waitress came along and placed a menu in front of us before pouring two glasses of water. She took Faust's drink order before backing away. I continued to wait for him to speak, perusing a menu that made my mouth water. Focus, dammit!

"The Shaadre belonged to me," he began, placing the menu down in front of him.

"That had better not be it," I replied after a moment, feeling anger pooling inside me.

"It's not, but the explanation is somewhat convoluted, and I wanted to get that out in the open right away, you deserve that much."

I didn't know why I deserved it, but I'd take it. So, this was the man behind the Sons of the Dark Moon? I didn't know him well, but he struck me as the sort who'd never be a subordinate. I was sitting in front of the boss, I had to be.

Simultaneously good, for the information, and bad, because the boss doesn't present himself for nothing, especially with people who hid their faces just to go out for dinner. Had he been there at Bella Note that night? Had he been playing me since then? I knew that he wanted something from me, but I was damned if I was going to give it to him, he'd nearly killed my brother twice, and tried to have me kidnapped at least once.

Somehow I pushed all that aside. I could brood later; I needed to hear what he had to say now.

"Alright," I replied, controlling my temper, "I'm listening."

The waitress came back and took our order, Faust waited until she was well out of earshot before continuing.

"Ever since the Archons departed, my brotherhood has been firmly of the opinion that a war is coming, a big one. The sides are already lining up, soldiers are being recruited, weapons are being stockpiled. The Shaadre was a weapon, one that me and mine spent a great deal of time and capitol acquiring and cultivating."

"And you sent it after my brother?" I asked with a hiss.

"Of course not!" he shot back, "We were training it, that training directs the Shaadre against the most powerful light-mage it can find, but before we could finish its indoctrination, one of our newer trainers made a mistake, and the creature escaped. It was half-mad with rage and hunger, and it did what its half-trained mind told it to do."

He paused as our food arrived. Hand-caught trout for him with fresh vegetables, single steak pie for me. He dug in while I sat there impatiently for a minute before sticking a fork in mine just to be polite.

Oh my God, that was a fantastic bit of food!

I kept eating, distracted for a moment from his explanation, what he'd already told me had greatly relieved my fears, it was a simple mistake, unintentional. He hadn't really meant to hurt my brother.

Oh, I know that I was letting my desire for a quiet life influence my perception, and I soon realised that his story wasn't so much comforting as it was implying far greater problems than a single assault on a student.

"Why are you training creatures to attack light mages?" I asked, my whirling mind rather confirming that I wasn't talking to the right side of this particular argument.

"We like shadow magic, it's very powerful stuff, as you well know. Tethys told us that you had some expertise, a little more than the usual mage, even a Wizard's level of aptitude."

Interesting, Tethys had been downplaying, but why?

"Light mages are the greatest threat to that, not to mention our Shaadres, they have to be dealt with first when the war comes."

There was a certain glint in his eye when he said this, a flicker of some underlying insanity that was starting to worry me not a little. My stomach was starting to turn, and I put my fork down.

"Just how many of those things do you have?" I asked.

"Not enough, and we're one short, now," he answered, looking at me in an intense way that immediately set my heart thudding.

"I think that I've heard quite enough..." I said thickly, trying to stand up. I found to my horror that my legs refused to work, and that a fog was starting to come onto the edge of my thoughts. It was like my blood was cooling, turning my muscles to sludge.

Oh God, I think the bastard poisoned me...

"Relax, Mister Graves, I assure you that the concoction I fed you is quite harmless. You are a valuable commodity after all, and it's only right that you replace the creature you destroyed, though naturally you will require some... training."

I grappled for magic, for my shadows, for anything, but there was nothing, and the dark came in from all sides before I could do any more than glare at the man who'd beat me. If I hadn't been so mad and disgusted with myself, I might have been impressed at the way he'd done it, but alas the last throws of terror wiped away all such rational thoughts and I passed out.

Chapter 43

Well... damn it.

If I could have thought of the *worst* possible way my evening could have gone, I would not have got anywhere near this mess.

Drugged.

Of all the embarrassing ways I could have been taken down... I can never tell anyone about this, I'll never hear the end of it. I can't believe I was so stupid. But that's neither here nor there at the moment. I've been kidnapped due to my own stupidity, and now I have to deal with it.

I woke up to light. It was bright and blinding, and I turned over to get away from it, only to find more of it shining through the glass floor. I blinked hard and looked elsewhere, but the walls of the room were covered in lamps too.

No prizes for guessing what this room is for.

My head was so sore it was ridiculous, and my vision was blurry. I looked around carefully, shielding my eyes as best I could. I found that the room was ten metres by ten, another ten tall, a perfect cube with a glass floor, walls and ceiling. Light came from everywhere, and there was nary a shadow to be seen, not that there weren't plenty under my clothes... which I wasn't wearing.

Oh damn it, those sickos stripped me down! They didn't even leave me with my underwear, the bastards. Again, not insurmountable, plenty of shadow in my mouth, push comes to shove, but let's give it a minute. I reached for my magic and found, to my horror, that there was very little there, the Well wasn't empty, but there was barely a bucket full left in it. I could feel it coming back slowly, but not as quickly as it should. What had been in that poison? I knew that there were brews that could drain magic from the victim, but they were rare and stupidly expensive, but then this was Faust, so money wasn't exactly an obstacle going by his house and what he kept in it.

My mind was foggy, so I forced it to focus. I discovered quickly that my foot was chained to the floor. I examined the lock with my fingers and found that it was ludicrously simple. Even with my pathetic store of magic, I'd easily get out of it. But I held back for the moment, and thought carefully instead.

Alright, from my current state I could draw a number of conclusions: firstly, they're used to shadow mages without my particular level of proficiency, which means that they don't know that I can manifest my powers in this light (draining though it would be), secondly, they're also assuming that cutting me off from shadows cuts me off from the rest of my magic completely, which seems to be a strange assumption for them to make.

And then it occurred to me. The lights. I took a look at them, reaching out with just a whisper of power. There we go... the lights were enchanted somehow, leeching away magic, that's why my well wasn't filling up as fast as it should be. Not even close, in fact, but still faster than such a drain should allow, surely? I thought about it for a long moment, and the only explanation I could come up with is that I wasn't a Wizard, like I'd thought, I was a Sorcerer.

Faust (from his comments) was under the impression that I was a Wizard level practitioner, and there was no way he would put me in a room where he thought a Wizard would be able to use magic. No, he'd put me in a room that would contain a Wizard and then some. Therefore, Sorcerer.

I found myself a little pleased with that. I wouldn't have thought I would be, but there was something reassuring about the idea, especially in this situation, where power made all the difference. Maybe I should have let myself been tested all those years ago. I'd been blundering about in the dark (no pun intended) for so long, without even knowing what I was truly capable of, assuming so much and making big mistakes because of it.

Things were going to have to change; I couldn't carry on like this. Well, assuming I could escape the box of light...

So, I had some advantages, and for the moment I would keep them to myself, at least until an opportunity presented itself, and I knew a little more. My well was still filling slowly;

at a guess I was at perhaps one-hundredth capacity, not enough for much. I wouldn't be happy trying anything without at least a quarter-tank. So, waiting.

I didn't have to wait long for *something* to happen. I heard a rumbling sound from behind me and turned to see a shape in the haze.

"The creature will turn to face its mistress," said a female voice.

I stayed where I was, too dumbstruck to say anything to that. There was a brief whipping sound, followed by a loud crack, and a line of fire appeared on my arm, making me yelp in pain.

"What the hell?!" I shouted, only to get another whip to my leg, which made me yelp again.

"The creature will speak only when spoken to."

"I was spoken to!" I replied, "*You* spoke to me!"

Another whip. Blood was leaking from three separate places now.

"The creature will be silent!"

I shut up. There would be a time for retribution; this was a time for silent reflection.

"The creature's name is Ninety-seven," she said, stepping forward, "what is its name?"

"Did you mean me?" I asked.

Whip-crack, bleeding chest, you get the idea.

"The creature's name is Ninety-seven," she said again, "what is its name?"

"Bernard?" I replied.

She whipped me twice after that, there seemed to be increasing orders of severity with each repeated wrong answer.

Who the hell was this woman? What was she after? I mean sure, obedience training, but what was the point? I wasn't mindless, so whipping me wasn't going to do the job. Wouldn't she know that? The way she handled that whip showed experience, so I could only assume that she'd done this before, and successfully.

"The creature is only what I say it is. It has no home, no property and no life other than what I say it has. Its world is only obedience and loyalty."

Yep she was trying to train me like an errant labradoodle. And if I was in here long enough, with no powers to call on or people to talk to, it might well work. But I wasn't going to give her that time.

She asked my name again, I replied with: "Yo mama", "Lancelot" and "Puff the magic dragon", before I'd had enough and answered with "Seventy-Nine". The woman screeched and whipped me seven or eight times as I complained of dyslexia (which I certainly don't have) before I finally gave the correct answer.

She stood there, panting and angry, and I felt a little surge of triumph. If there's one thing I can do, it's annoy bullies, and she more than qualified. My power levels were growing with every minute, they were already at three or four percent. I just had to buy time.

"The creature will obey all instructions given to it promptly and perfectly, or the creature will be punished."

"I have a name you know," I said.

Okay, objectively, I probably deserved the hits for that one.

"The creature will stand," she said, I could feel the exasperation growing in her just from the tone of her voice.

"On my head, my feet, what were you going for, here?" I asked.

And then I was bleeding from more than a dozen shallow cuts, and had another dozen lighter grazes and scrapes.

"The creature will stand!" she shrieked.

After that, I just did what I was told for a while, it wasn't much, standing and sitting and walking and the suchlike. It took forever, but all the while, my powers were recharging, five percent and climbing.

"Who is your mistress?" she asked after about another hour of this nonsense.

"Probably Cathy, but don't tell her I told you that," I answered.

"What?" she actually said.

"Ah, ah, ah, you forgot to say "the creature will", you lose," I said, snorting with laughter for about a second before she *really* laid into me. *That* hurt, that hurt a lot, but it was sort of worth it, just to hear the woman's screams of pure frustration.

Ten percent. I was in pain, getting angrier. It was close enough.

A tiny flicker of energy and the ring clicked off my ankle as I activated my mage sight. Oh, that was better. I saw the room as it was, a Plexiglas box in a larger concrete chamber. I saw the magical sinks built into the lights, and the sliding door across the room from me with a heavy locking mechanism built into it. I charged my Will and flung the woman, now revealed to be the one I duelled with outside that restaurant, straight at it. Naturally the magic sinks had stripped away all *her* powers, so she couldn't have raised a shield, even if I hadn't taken her by surprise. She hit that door hard enough to rip it off its runner as well as break her spine in seven places. The breaks weren't high up enough to kill, but she would need some serious magical treatment to ever walk again.

I walked out of the box and the trickle of returning power turned into a deluge. I groaned in relief. The lights out here were dimmer, and my shadows came to me, wrapping me up tightly in a way that made me feel safe. The room filled with them, reaching out at a simple command to destroy the lights from the outside, causing sparks and waves of stolen power to cascade away from the centre and short out every piece of technology within reach. I felt men rush in from doors to my left. The guards ran straight into my shadows, like idiots.

I told the darkness to *squeeze*.

There were nine of them. Seven suffocated into unconsciousness, in short order but the other two continued on, Spelleater amulets around their necks; laughably insufficient at this point.

I repeated my earlier trick from Tethys's club with the wreckage of the lights, hurling them straight at the two men with enough force to crush and mangle. I didn't feel bad this time, not at all.

I stopped briefly by the woman and a wave of hatred filled me as I contemplated the humiliation she put me through. Even though I like to think that I'd put up a good front, I'd been furious and embarrassed while it was happening, and now I just felt dirty. I assembled a little mental spell, subtle and nasty. I dropped it into her mind and carried on. She'd never have a good night's sleep again. I had made her mind a home of nightmares, and I felt no remorse about it, she was *alive* after all.

I walked on through the door, dragging one of the suffocated security guards along on the end of a tendril. I linked my mind to his and started a brief search, stimulating his memory with key words, like a search engine, really. I shoved in things like "way out" and "fresh air". Memories of the path to the exit showed themselves. I dropped a coma spell into his head and carried on, slowly starting to calm down.

I walked into a nearby barracks room and pulled on the first pair of clean trousers and shirt that I could find before stepping out and following the path in my head. It was easy to find, there were clearly marked directions to the exit along with red lighting. I arrived at the end of a long corridor that sloped up to the main level (I'd discovered that I was deep underground, beneath that thrice-damned warehouse where I nearly exploded my brain).

I stopped dead as I felt something closing in on me. It slowed to a halt just beyond my shadows. I had to look with my mage sight three times before I started to believe what I was seeing, and then I very nearly crapped my new trousers.

Fire-mage.

Sorcerer-class.

And he was ready for me.

Chapter 44

"Come on out," he shouted, obviously seeing my shadows from where he stood. He was about twenty metres from where I was hiding behind the doorway. He was wreathed in incandescent fire, to the extent where I couldn't see his body without my mage-sight. With it I saw a man of average build, average height, with a small nose, burn scars on the left side of his face and no eyebrows. He wore a black suit, shirt and tie and carried a short staff in his right hand. He raised it, pointing at the edge of my shadows.

He released a spell.

This would be a potent demonstration of the difference between a fire-Wizard and a fire-Sorcerer. Remember that idiot that threw fireballs at me? The one that tried to kill Tethys? Yeah, he threw balls of fire, which is to say burning air that was heated to the point of ignition, dangerous, painful, the combat-mage stereotype. This guy's attacks weren't fireballs, not really. They were tiny spheres of *plasma*. There are several types, I won't bore you with the details, but this is the stuff you'd find in a fusion reaction, which is to say energetic and ludicrously hot.

The plasma hit the door jamb a few feet to my left and carved a molten hole through the reinforced concrete, causing liquid stone to dribble down and burn the carpet.

"I said, come out!" he bellowed, "I can wait all day, but the rest of my brethren are on their way, and then what will you do? Surrender now and I'll make sure they don't punish you too severely."

Oh dear. I was badly out of my league. On my very best day, I was not equipped to go head to head with a battle mage like that. I could tell just by looking at him that he was well practiced, professional, and utterly deadly. Add to that the fact that he would be used to dealing with shadow mages, and you get to a person that I shouldn't go anywhere near. I backed away, moving towards into the holding area, pulling my shadows back with me, while I tried desperately to think of a solution to this problem.

I should have read those duelling books. Damn it, I had a whole week on my back!

Alright, how do you get rid of fire? You can quench it, strangle it or smother it. I can't quench it, I don't have enough water, I can't strangle it, he's too far away, and I can't control the airflow so I can't smother it, and if I collapse the hallway I'll be trapped down here.

I did have an inkling of an idea, but I needed to get him closer, into the open space where the cell was. I scratched my chin, thinking it through.

How to draw him in?

I took some time preparing the ground, even taking the trouble to draw a circle (not normally something I needed to do, but I was still weak, ridiculously so, and the mage sight and shadows were still draining me steadily). I sliced my palm open with a sharp shadow to get the blood out for the circle. It's part of me, so it makes the best conductor for my magic. I wrapped my palm up in a field dressing stolen from one of the guards when I was done, and made my way to the edge of my shadows.

Then I screamed, as long, high and girly as I could (as you might imagine, I didn't need to apply that much effort to create something like that, what with all my previous experience).

"What's that?!" Smoky (let's call him Smoky for simplicity) bellowed.

I screamed again.

"Whatever you're doing, you stop it now!"

Another scream.

"Pru?! Pru, is that you?"

Pru, eh? The name perhaps of the woman who'd been horse-whipping me?

I screamed again, trying to insert some pain into the noise.

"Pru! Hold on, I'm coming!"

Oh shit, he was really moving!

I had to sprint back through the doors and into the room with the cage, while he continued to blunder around in the dark. That fire-light of his was strong, but my shadows were stronger, so he could only see maybe ten feet in front of him.

"Pru! Where are you?!" he shouted.

I dimly heard voices from up the corridor calling him to come back. I allowed myself a loud and boisterous laugh that drew Smoky onwards before I screamed again. He growled and came on, slamming into the room, leaving a heavy steel door in a semi-solid heap on the floor. The fire around his hands flared brighter as he came on, anger growing.

He was nearly there.

I laughed again, quietly this time, but enough for him to hear, and approach.

"Where is she, you filth?" he said, his voice filled with hatred and disgust.

"Over here," I stage whispered. He crossed the line. Just a few steps more, now until he was right where I wanted him...

There!

"Stop, or I gut her like a fish," I said, shoving as much menace into my tone as I could. Poor idiot, she'd never even been awake, much less screaming. He stopped.

I closed the circle with another little smear of my blood and activated my spell.

"Now, stand down," I said.

"Never. Hand her over and maybe I won't carve out your eyes."

I was actually quite pleased with how this played out.

Do you know how much oxygen a plasma-based fire uses in the course of a second? If you guessed 'a lot', then you'd be right. My spell was actually quite simple. The base was a circle about twenty metres across, drawn in my blood. It had to be so large so that when Smoky was at the centre of it, he'd be far enough away from the edges that my shadows could conceal the magic I'd filled it with. It used my blood as a conduit to create a dome of energy with one simple, low-energy function. All it did had to do was keep any more oxygen getting into the dome. Without the fires he covered himself with, he could have gone on quite happily without even noticing for quite some time.

But with the plasma burning...

The oxygen was all used up pretty quickly, and the poor idiot didn't even really notice until he was on his hands and knees, breathing little more than nitrogen and carbon dioxide, neither of which are of much use to a human body trying not to pass out.

I felt him try to cast something, but the spellwork was sloppy and slow; easily dispelled by yours truly. In an act I'll freely admit was almost entirely spite, I let him nearly complete his spell, and get his hopes up, before breaking it like a plastic cup under a steamroller.

He collapsed a few seconds later. I watched with mage sight to make sure he was out before I shut down my dome. There was a dull 'whump' sound as air rushed back in.

I approached the mage slowly. This was another man eager to kidnap and enslave. I didn't think he should be left any less comfortable than his female accomplice. I allowed myself a nasty smile before I dug into his mind like some rabid mole chasing a worm. A few minutes work wiped his memory of every piece of magical knowledge he had (and probably some other stuff, I didn't really care enough to be careful).

Then I simply started walking out of that place, confident that any other magical heavy hitters would have come after me by now if they were there. I sent my shadows ahead to clear the way for me. The men still waiting at the end of the corridor ran at the sight of the approaching darkness, which was sensible.

I sent a tendril out and caught one of the slower ones, beating him enough so that his screams would carry and drive the others away faster; I wanted a clear route to avoid any further complications. I gathered the rest of the darkness behind me and followed them as they ran, howling and terrified. The shadows carried me around corners, up stairs and straight for the exit, passing by rooms full of texts, equipment and all manner of strange things. I was nearly at the exit when I passed a room with a locked door. Something in there tugged at me, and I almost got whiplash stopping.

My shadows eased me to the ground, and I looked carefully at the door, it wasn't anything special, so I had a shadow smash it open. It was a reading room, and on the one desk was a single book. It was bound in black leather, ancient, but pristine. There was no writing on the cover, and the binding was hand-stitched.

It wasn't much to look at, but that book called to me, whispering in my mind, almost. I touched it, and it warmed a little under my fingers, but I didn't recoil. I picked it up and opened it. It was full of drawings and magical construct equations that I couldn't really understand, all surrounded by text in a language I'd never seen before. But I clearly saw shadows; familiar constructs and shapes.

A book of shadow magic?

Oh, that's nice.

Well, finders keepers, and I think this lot owe me at least a little compensation for tonight. I tucked it into my pocket and carried on.

I found the exit, and it was a circus out there. There had to be more than two dozen people, including at least three mages waiting for me, none more powerful than a strong Acolyte. No sign of Faust, though, so that's something. It would take mage sight to see through my gloomy constructs, and I had no reason to assume that those idiots could manage it. It's generally a Wizard's skill, they simply didn't have the Wells for it.

So, I hardened my shadows, and simply walked out.

The door flew from its hinges and smashed into the outer fence, my shadows followed, flowing across the intervening ground and ripping that same fence apart before advancing on the mob. The entire force opened fire with everything they had, fireballs, bullets, smoke bombs, even a lightning strike. My shadows recoiled, looking ragged and damaged.

It provided a nice distraction.

While they were battling my semi-sentient manifested darkness, I was being gently lifted over the fence on the far side of the building, where there were no guards and easy access to some back streets. I was long gone before those half-wits even realised I wasn't actually fighting them.

I ran through back alleys until I could get to more populated streets, though at that time of night, that was a relative term; it was *very* late, just from a look at the moon. But I soon came to better parts of the city, and was able to hail a cab (in spite of my appearance).

I gave him instructions and settled in, still panting and more than a little afraid. It was quite a while before I started to relax.

What a night. I checked the cabbie's radio, and it said 04:20. Yuck, all that, and I had chapel in five hours. May as well go to a strip club while I wait.

You know what I mean; I needed to have a 'conversation' with Tethys.

Chapter 45

The club was winding down for the morning, only a few half-conscious patrons and tired looking dancers. Quite sad really. I went through the usual rigmarole of giving my name, all the while being stared at by servers and patrons alike on account of my bare feet and short sleeves in a cold month.

Anyway, an attractive young woman led me to Tethy's office, where I actually found her working for a change. She was sitting at the desk, looking energetic and beautiful in a black business suit, making me feel tired and sloppy.

"Matthew, how lovely to see... what happened to you?" she said looking up at me with a smile and then confusion, "I smell blood... and shame. Whatever have you been up to?" She waved the girl away, and I sat down carefully on one of her chairs (I'd been whipped on my sitting parts, and I still wasn't entirely comfortable using them).

"As if you don't know," I said with a wince, "Faust."

"Oh," she said, looking sheepish before biting her lip.

"Yes indeed, oh," I replied with a glare.

"You can't possibly me blaming *me* for something he did?" she asked, attempting an earnest look.

"I can blame you for introducing me to him when you *knew* he had a stable of Shaadres, and was looking to expand."

"How could I possibly know that?" she asked me, looking hurt.

I stared back, waiting for her to speak again. It didn't take long.

She smiled that evil smile of hers.

"Alright, fine, so I pointed you out to Faust, I didn't tell him you were a Sorcerer, though, you've got to give me that much."

"That would be the only reason I'm being so polite," I replied, "that, and I've had a long night, and I'm not looking for another fight. At least tell me what you were hoping to get out of this? I can assume that you were hoping to clear a debt or put one in the bank, but you never have just the one reason, so spill."

She let out a breath, looking me over, "I always said you were smart. Fine. Faust was the last man with something over my head. Now that's gone. I'm clear. He wanted Shadowborn, I gave him one, and it cleared my slate, I also wanted it to be you, because I truly *hate* that man. I hate him more than I can reasonably describe. The *things* he made me do when we first met," she shuddered as she recalled, and it actually looked genuine, "I wanted it to be you because I knew that you were too strong for his cages. He is a thug and a bully, and he only takes those too weak to free themselves. You are not weak. I know you want people to think you're harmless, but I know better. You know better. And I hope you hurt him badly on the way out."

She finished speaking and stared at me, almost daring me to reply.

"He wasn't even there," I said, "just left me in a cage with a sadist and a fire-starter."

"You at least hurt *them*, right?" she asked, an intense look coming over her face.

"Wiped one's memory, implanted never-ending nightmares in the other," I replied.

"You can do that?" she asked, a wary look crossing her features.

"Of course," I said, looking her in her lovely eyes, "something for you to keep in mind if you should ever decide to use me like that again."

"Message received," she said with a smile, mischievous again, her confidence returning quickly after her confession. "I take it that there will be a penance to be paid after my dreadful behaviour? Some sort of corporal punishment, perhaps?"

I winced at that, my hand going reflexively to the worst of the welts on my arm.

"Ah," Tethys said, noticing the gesture, "so *that's* what you meant by bad night."

She was a little too smart for my own good. She asked that seemingly tantalising question suspecting what I'd been through, and looking for confirmation.

"Yes," I replied non-committaly.

"Want me kiss it and make it better?" she asked in that husky voice I enjoyed.

"And that's my cue to head off for the fifteen minutes of sleep I'm going to get before chapel," I said, heaving myself up.

Tethys stood too, walking around to see me out.

"See you at my next lecture," she said, stroking my arm.

"Not again," I groaned.

"Yes indeed, my previous one was postponed on account of my legal troubles, you remember our sparky friend?"

I rolled my eyes and walked out to the intriguing sound of Tethys' giggles.

Well, that answered one question, but not others. Tethys had pointed me out to Faust, painted a target on my back, but he already knew about me from Bella Note and probably Wilks. So he was coming for me one way or another, all Tethys did was speed that along and take advantage of it. But why the attack on Windward? Was that their big play to get at me?

No, not just me; I remembered what Faust said about Light Mages. Des was a known threat to them now; they'd gone for him as well. But that sort of thing just didn't seem like Faust's style, he wasn't the sort to get his hands dirty, even by proxy. Well, organisations can have rebellious elements; maybe that was who came at us? It made a sort of sick sense, and then these were sick people.

They way Faust got me was careful and brilliantly simple in its way. I still don't know how he got me out of a crowded restaurant. But that was elegant, not a brutish strike. So a second faction within his own brotherhood was the most likely explanation.

What a mess! And none of that absolved Tethys. I should hate her; hell, I should burn her club down! But I couldn't, because I believed what she'd said about Faust, and he'd all but confirmed it with what he'd said about her. The oily way he'd talked about Tethys was just a little too possessive, too familiar, now that I had context to compare it to.

And the thing was, horrific manipulations aside, that woman was just the sort of smart that I respected. She really was a spectacular creature, ruthless, clever and cunning, and that's without taking into account the fact that she was utterly gorgeous, which I'll admit played a part in my decision making; I am a teenager, after all.

So I left. She'd won, in her way. From the look in her eye, she'd really needed it, and I understood enough about that feeling not to start a war over it.

By the time I finally got back to Windward, my feet were freezing, I was miserable, and I was shivering like a leaf in a gale. Since I was back on the school grounds, I couldn't use any magic, and boy was *that* getting old. That was assuming that Knowles was around, and awake, though...

Still, better off not taking the chance. The cab dropped me off at the edge of the grounds, and I hobbled my way up. I wasn't even half way back to Kimmel House when I heard the crunch of gravel beside me.

"Well, well, well, what have we here?" said an all too familiar voice. I winced and automatically backed away, heading for the edge of the grounds again. What was the range of Knowles' sense? Alright, I had to assume that Knowles, or whoever had the night shift, was in the central buildings, which was about three hundred metres from the closest edge of the grounds. I was at one of the further edges, so, say about four hundred metres. That might just be enough to get away with a little magic.

And with the way the Ox and his cronies were looking at me, I just might need to.

There was the man himself, the usual block of muscle that was his best friend (I'm gonna go with Max Bert-something, I'm not good with the names of pointless people), Courtney, and naturally Max's squeeze of the minute, whose name was... Patricia? Philomena? P-something, anyway, not bad looking at that, but still overtly hostile.

They were dressed for clubbing, and looked in no better state than me, bedraggled and tired, rings under their eyes and smelling heavily of alcohol. The Ox was weaving slightly; Max and his girlfriend were propping each other up. Courtney looked relatively clear-eyed, but there was a tired look on her face.

"Look, we've all had a long night, we're all tired, why don't we just assume that you threatened me, I countered with an insult about your manhoods, you've undertaken to kill me at the first opportunity, and we parted sufficiently annoyed with one another, alright? Alright."

I turned and walked away, readying a small reflex enhancing spell, a tiny little thing, really. I cast it as I heard the gravel crunch under two pairs of heavy feet, and they seemed to slow. I turned to see P-what's-her-name sitting down where Max had dropped her, while Courtney glared daggers at the two boys' backs. They were moving at a weaving clip towards me, their faces contorted with rage and anticipatory bloodlust. I sidestepped Ox and he tripped over his own feet and went face first into a hedge. I took another step, and Max trod on the prone form of the Ox trying to catch me, causing the hedge-tangled nitwit to yelp in a delightful fashion, making me wish I'd had my phone on me so I could have made that sound into my ringtone. Max then fell on top of the Ox, where they proceeded to slap and claw at each other.

I released the spell, wondering why I'd even bothered with the thing in the first place. Then I threw a light sleep enchantment their way (very light, it would wear off in a few minutes).

"How are those life choices treating you, ladies?" I asked Courtney, while she was busy holding (let's go with Pat) Pat's hair while she threw up. Courtney said something un-ladylike, which made me smile as I walked away. Ox and Max were holding each other while snoring loudly.

Maybe this hadn't been a completely wasted day.

Chapter 46

I woke up with aches and pains in places I didn't even know I had (it's a cliché, but an accurate one, I swear that there was a aching muscle on my thigh that I'd never even known was there before). The alarm clock that woke me would have been in serious danger had I not been so badly drained, and in mortal fear of being carted away by the magic police.

I struggled into my Sunday best, and then to chapel. Bill and Cathy looked at me with questioning eyes as they saw me limping in, but then the service started, so they couldn't speak to me, which was great, because I was too exhausted to speak coherently anyway.

The service allowed me time to think, and by the time it was over, I'd come to an important decision. Cathy and Bill tried to catch me as we filed out. It wasn't fair to them, but I needed to do this before I lost my nerve. I darted past with a wave and a "See you later," and made my way into the main building, where I found the room Kraab had made his nest.

I paced back and forth in front of that door for half an hour, psyching myself up to actually knock on it. Finally I walked away completely, making it more than half way back to my house before I finally sucked it up enough. I knocked on the door, rapping loudly. My heart was pounding, and I'd broken out in a cold sweat. The door opened, revealing one of the various government people I didn't recognise.

"What do you want?" he said with almost naked hostility.

This was going about as well as I thought it would.

"To see Kraab, please," I answered politely.

"He's not here, it's bloody Sunday," he replied, slamming the door.

Right. Didn't think of that. That was uncharacteristically stupid of me (or not, if you've been paying attention).

I knocked again. I was getting this over with, by hook or by bloody crook, so help me.

"What now?" the man asked, even more pissed off than before.

"I need to see Kraab," I said, less politely this time.

"Come back tomorrow," he said through gritted teeth, he started to close the door again. I put my foot in front of it.

"Tell him that I have some information for him," I said, trying not to wince when the door hit my foot.

"Tell him tomorrow!" he said, trying to shove my foot out of the way.

"I know who the shadow mage is," I hissed, trying not to let my eyes water. You'd really think my pain threshold would be higher by now.

The pressure on my foot eased, and the agent opened the door again.

"What did you say?" he asked.

"You heard me," I replied.

"If you're lying..." he began.

"Just get Kraab," I said.

Forty minutes later the door opened and Kraab came bursting in. I was sat in front of the desk, reading a book, the agent was standing behind me. I could practically feel the man glowering.

Kraab sat down, looking a tad rushed, he waved at the agent, and he left. Kraab looked me over carefully as I closed my book and tucked it into a pocket. The silence continued for long minutes as one of us waited for the other to speak.

"Well?" he said finally.

I took a breath.

"First, I want certain assurances," I replied.

Kraab grunted in annoyance, and placed his hands in front of him, clenched tight.

"Don't waste my time, Mister Graves, just spit it out."

"Not until I have your word that what I tell you today doesn't get back to my brother, ever."

"What?" he asked, genuine puzzlement crossing his features.

"Desmond doesn't find out what I tell you, and I also want your guarantee that I won't be prosecuted for anything I say."

"What could I prosecute *you* for?" he asked with a sneer.

"Your word?" I asked.

He sighed, appearing to think it over for a moment before grinning again.

"Very well, I give you my word that I will ensure, to the best of my ability, that nothing you tell me will be revealed to your brother. As for prosecution, I can promise that for myself, but I can't speak for magistrates, or the other police services."

An honest answer, I had to give him that. He could have lied and told me that he had the authority, which I already knew he didn't have. Damn, nothing for it now.

"I'm the mage you're looking for," I said in a gabble, just getting it out as fast as I could.

His eyes went wide, his nostrils flared, and then he started laughing. Then snorting, then he started coughing. My face went red. I hadn't seen that coming.

"Very good, Mister Graves, very good. But seriously now, I came all this way, who's the mage?"

"I just told you," I growled. He stopped laughing.

"Now, let's not be foolish. If you were the mage, Knowles would have known."

I closed my eyes for a moment, and called my shadows. The room turned black as the darkness covered the window. Kraab leapt to his feet, globes of violet power appearing in his hands. I stayed where I was, not moving or giving him reason to consider me a threat.

He stayed quiet for a long while, staring at me, those attack spells held at the ready. I released my shadows, and they slid away, letting the light back in. I raised my hands slowly in a peaceful gesture, watching Kraab carefully. He swallowed hard, but dismissed his own spells, letting the energy drain away. He sat down, looking at me with a great deal more attention this time.

"It would appear that we have a lot to talk about, Mister Graves," he said, taking a pad out of the desk along with a tape recorder.

I smiled sadly, accepting at last that the day I had been dreading was finally here. And it was all my show-off brother's stupid fault (more or less, just let me have this one). I was there for four hours as I told him everything. It was actually quite cathartic. I didn't leave much out, but most prominent of my omissions was Tethys; despite myself, I was actually growing fond of that manipulative bitch.

Kraab actually seemed impressed. He asked probing questions, getting every last detail from me, making frantic notes on his pad. He went red with rage when I got to the parts about Faust. It seemed that he was not enjoying hearing what I was reporting. Finally I was done, slumping back in my chair, I was tired and hungry (I'd missed lunch, but then so had Kraab, so I couldn't complain).

"Do you have any evidence of any of this?" he asked after a while, going through his notes.

"No," I said.

He sighed.

"Well, then you might have some trouble if someone ever decides to press charges," he said with a grimace.

I can't claim any eloquence for this part, because what came out sounded something like "Wha-huh?"

"From an outside perspective, you've committed a rather serious series of crimes," he answered, an unhappy look on his face.

Well, he did have a point.

"Mental manipulation is an iffy enough area as it is without the nightmares, the coma-curses and the memory-wipes, which are covered under assault, so is the other stuff you did to those friends of Knowles. That doesn't even begin to cover what you did to your uncle and your brother. Then there's the issue of those homeless men you nearly eviscerated, the fire mage who's skull you fractured, and the Shaadre you cut in half," he said, making me worry a little.

"I would think that a lot of that could come in under the umbrella of self-defence," I replied with a heavy swallow.

He made an indifferent whining sound, "Maybe, if you're lucky. A better solution would be not to make any of this official at all."

I made that strange sound again. He put the pad to one side and stopped the recorder.

"There are certain things that you will have to do now, you will have to register your powers and demonstrate your level of competence; you will have to complete the basic tests. However, I think that it would be wise if we didn't make any of your actions a matter of public record. I will tell certain trusted members of my organisation, who I will ensure against telling your brother or your family, but otherwise, we should keep this quiet."

"So Faust just gets away with what he's been doing?" I asked.

Kraab frowned before speaking again, "You have no evidence, Mister Graves. And without that, your testimony carries little or no weight, especially against a Faust. My guess would be that the warehouse you saw is already empty, and that we would find nothing incriminating there. Further, if we make this public now, there's no way to predict the fallout."

"That's it?" I asked, incredulously. I knew trusting the government would get me nowhere.

"I will begin building a case against Faust, but he has some very, *very* powerful friends, and there would be considerable difficulty in bringing charges against him without iron-clad proof."

That I could understand. I sighed.

"Between you and me, you have done some impressive things in the last few weeks, but you have also wasted police time, as well as all that other stuff. So, I would advise you here and now not to do anything rash from here on out, because I now know where to look for skulduggery."

That was a badly veiled threat. In other words, don't go looking for trouble, or I'll be prosecuted. That was *absolutely* fine with me; I really had finished with this mess. I nodded.

"One day, if all goes well, I'll need to call you as a witness, and that means that you will need to testify. I advise you to tell your family about yourself before then."

I nodded again, looking at my shoes.

"Come back here tomorrow, during your lunch break, and I'll make sure all the necessary paperwork is ready for your registration."

I nodded and stood up, thoroughly depressed. I walked towards the door; I had my hand on the handle before he spoke again.

"And Mister Graves?" he said.

"Yes?" I said, not turning.

"You made the right choice here. I know it doesn't seem like it, but you'll see that this is for the best."

I nodded again and walked away, trying not to slam the door behind me.

Crap.

Chapter 47

That could have gone better.

But then again, I haven't been arrested, so arguably it could also have gone much worse. Really, I'm no worse off than I was before, and if I do go missing again, at least someone will know where to come looking for me, so I guess I've come out of this ahead.

Still...

Bah. I'll just leave it there for now, nothing more I can do about it.

And now for the prostate exam that is the conversation with Cathy.

That went as well as could be expected. She yelled, and then she cried, and then she yelled some more, and then she hugged me, and then she wouldn't let go, it was a whole thing, I won't bore you with the details, suffice to say it took an hour and I nearly missed dinner. Bill was an easier conversation, I just lied through my teeth.

This was getting really frustrating.

Des, of course hadn't noticed a thing, and after I'd used a little magic to get my healing under way (that at least was a benefit of my conversation with Kraab), there wasn't anything to see anyway.

I saw him and Belle after dinner, they were sitting in the quad, and she did not look happy, in fact she was glaring at him. Then she saw me, and the look dissolved in a way I found disturbing.

"Hi, Mathew!" she said, darting to her feet. When did she get so friendly?

"Belle," I said with a nod before sitting next to my brother.

"Hey Matty! How's it going?" he asked, patting me on the shoulder.

"Oh, can't complain," I replied, idly rubbing at one of the deeper whip gashes on my arm. It was healing well, and had now starting to itch right on bloody schedule.

"Where have you been all day? I was looking for you," he said.

Well, here was my shot. I could spill the beans right now. I almost did, but then I remembered that he had recently done me injuries, and I decided that it would be best to wait until I'd had a chance to drop another Asimov in his head.

"What did you need?" I asked instead, thoroughly chickening out.

"Oh, I wanted to tell you that the SCA has offered me work experience during the Easter holidays, isn't that great?"

Oh yes, abso-bloody-lutely, wasn't it nice of Kraab to leave out that little gem of information?

"That's great," I replied with false enthusiasm, thinking quickly, "just remember that if you work for any police or governmental body, you can't compete in any professional duelling leagues."

His face fell like a skydiver whose parachute I'd confiscated. Heh.

"Really?" he asked.

"You didn't know?" I asked with faked regret that made Belle snort.

"No," he said, "what am I going to do now?"

Ooh, a perfect opportunity to get my idiot brother away from the lunatics that may get him killed. Now, how to go about doing it? (I could say that I was struck by the moral implications of manipulating a close family member, but it was only as a footnote to the enjoyment I get from playing people like a kazoo.)

"Tell you what, go on work experience, see how you like it. But remember, if you choose it as a career, you'll have three years at uni, five years of training and more paperwork than an Andrex factory."

"What? Uni? Five years?! And how much paperwork, really?" he asked aghast.

I suppressed an evil grin.

"Well, I'm just guessing, but I know a couple of cops, and they're always complaining about qualifying for things, completing everything in triplicate, all that stuff, but I'm sure the training years will just fly by."

Des jumped to his feet and started pacing, Belle flopped to the ground next to me.

"That was so evil, I'm a little turned on right now," she whispered in my ear.

"What is wrong with you today?" I asked.

"Huh?"

"Never mind," I replied, trying not to cringe. Don't get me wrong, Belle is hot in a way that defies easy description, but she's my brother's girlfriend, and in the nine months he's been dating her, he has told me *everything* in awful detail, so... nope.

And also, what the hell? She had never spoken to me like that before. I'd enjoy the attention if it wasn't for just how much I knew...

"Matty, what if they ask me to sign on for summer, too?!" he asked, stomping back to us.

"Well, just let them know up front that you aren't looking for a career as a field agent. Once they realise that you aren't great in the office, the problem solves itself."

Belle was breathing hard by this point, and it was starting to get a little distracting. I switched on my mage sight and took a look at her, expecting to see some sort of curse, or hex, or some sort of instability. Nothing, she was perfectly normal. That's not good. I wondered idly what game she was playing. Normally she was quite straight-forward, Des would have told me if she'd played these sorts of games (and I would have told him to dump her like a sack of manure). None the less, here she was, eyeing me up. I didn't like it, not one bit, there is no way this situation ends well for me.

So, it's probably best just to ignore it, and hope it goes away, otherwise I'm going to have to do something to her mind, and nobody wants that. Well, maybe I do a little, she has been a complete bitch to me on and off since I met her...

Yikes, what's happening to me? Ever since all this stuff blew up, my thinking had been growing... I don't know, nastier. Not that I was a saint to begin with, but I should *really* keep an eye on that.

"That's a good idea, Sweetie," Belle said, putting her hand on mine and digging her nails in a little bit, "your brother knows his stuff, you know."

She was practically purring now, and she was rubbing my hand in a very... intimate way. I called a little power and sent a small jolt of electricity through my hand. There was a tiny crack and she yelped. I smiled evilly.

"You shouldn't rub so hard, it generates static," I said in what I hoped was an evil hiss. You'd think that would have done the trick, but I think I only made it worse. She started biting her lip and grinning at me. That's it, I'm out of here before she starts rubbing up against me.

"Try not to worry too much, Des," I said, standing up, "just remember what you want to do with your life, you're going to be the greatest duellist ever-"

(Yeah, right!)

"-keep that in mind and you'll know what you need to do."

I patted his shoulder and made a show of looking at my watch. I made an excuse and bolted, eager to get back to my room and pretend that none of *that* was happening. I think, and I'm sure you'll agree, that it's the healthy thing to do.

No?

Well, tough, I'm still doing it-

"Matty, wait up!"

Damn it all to the bowels of bloody hell, it's that wretched girl again!

"Yes?" I asked, quickening my step before remembering that she makes me look like an asthmatic toddler with coordination issues in the fitness department, and I went back to a walk.

We were in the gravel courtyard between the main building and Kimmel, it was dark and trees blocked the view from the buildings, we were quite alone, and I didn't like it.

"Wanna go for a walk?" she asked.

I stopped, turning to glare at her, "Alright, jig's up, what are you after? Just spit it out, would you?"

"What are you talking about?" she asked, a look of incredulity on her face, which was flushed and she was doing that lip-biting thing again.

"We've been going to this school for more than three years, you've been dating my brother for nine months, and the nicest thing you ever said to me in all that time was that I 'wasn't entirely stupid' after I did Des' prep for the umpteenth time."

"That was then," she said, sidling up to me and running a finger down my arm.

"You are dating my brother," I said, a note of anger entering my voice as I shifted her finger away, it made her pause.

"For now; he's so immature, I'm looking for someone more grounded."

I stood there in silence as my anger grew. I could feel my shadows straining at the walls in my mind. They were coming easier and easier these days, it was actually becoming more of an issue to keep them away than summon them. I got myself under control with an effort and forced myself to meet the eyes of the woman who wanted to cheat on my brother (possibly, I still wasn't one hundred percent on this one).

"Go away before I do something I'll regret," I growled, feeling sick.

Her eyes turned dangerous, I knew that look, and I wasn't afraid anymore.

"Are you sure that's what you meant? Are you sure you didn't mean to say 'your place or mine'?"

"What's that supposed to mean?" I hissed.

"It means that if I'm not happy, then who knows what I might say in a state of distress?"

Did... did she just threaten me? ME?!

My shadows were out before I had a chance to do anything but prevent them from stabbing and tearing. Still, she jumped back with a yelp loud enough for me to enjoy before falling on her arse in a very undignified fashion. I was enraged. That might have something to do with my recent experiences with people attempting to take my free will. I imagine I'm not going to enjoy future attempts to compel me to do things, but that's a problem for later.

She backed away until she hit a tree, my shadows following her, snapping at her heels. She was breathing hard, fear plastered on her face, but mixed with something else, something that only made me angrier. I stayed there for a minute, just glaring at her from within a nest of darkness. She looked back at me, and something she saw there made her look away, down at the ground.

I walked up to her, glaring down.

"Look at me," I growled.

She looked up, most of her fear replaced with something resembling awe. It made me even sicker.

"If you ever threaten me again, I won't be responsible for what happens, do we understand each other?"

I felt her gather her magic, was she actually about to make a fight of it? I formed a quick dispel-field, and tossed it at her gently. Her magic drained away in a flash and she gasped, flopping back against the tree. My experiences since this had begun had done wonders for my instincts. Back then I'd been hesitant with my powers, almost timid. I was getting more confident, which wasn't necessarily the best thing.

"Why are you being like this? I've seen how lonely you are, you should be jumping at the chance to get some actual human contact," she said in a voice that betrayed confusion.

"I really don't know how many ways I can put this, so I'll try once more, and as directly as I can, alright? You are dating my *brother*!"

"So?" she said.

"Really?" I replied, "Even leaving aside the moral implications, which are a-plenty, there is the simple fact that I don't want you near me because Des went to the trouble of telling me where else you've been."

She had a look of shock on her face, which rapidly turned to anger, and then she leapt at me. My shadows moved, but she was too close and they missed, she collided with me and we went down in a tangle of limbs. Before I had a chance to do anything else, she had my shoulders pinned and had fastened her lips to mine.

Ethical implications aside, it was a damn good kiss. I mean, she's no Tethys, but who is? I may have let it go on a bit longer than outraged surprise should allow, I must confess, but I eventually pushed her off and got to my feet. She looked annoyingly smug. I made a disgusted sound and stalked off, her laughter following me back to Kimmel.

Well, that was just an awful mess, how do I break this to Des? How do I avoid that crazy bitch? Alright, one problem at a time. First tell Des. I pulled my phone out (which I'd thankfully left behind before going to meet Faust). I texted:

>*Get your bloody girlfriend under control, will you? She just tackled me for no apparent reason. Said something about you two having relationship problems, which are apparently my fault. Will you fix it, please?*

Yep, that should do it. Might cause some trouble for Belle, but that's hardly my problem, the little tramp.

Then the phone rang, and I realised my mistake.

"Matty? What the hell?" Des asked.

Naturally he wanted to meet me, wouldn't let me attend to it over the phone, damn it. So I met him back in the quad (no sign of that crazy girlfriend of his, thank God). Then I had to embellish my cock and bull story into something that didn't involve the concepts of infidelity and magic use. I think it worked; my brother's trusting and not especially bright. In the end I had him convinced that he was having some relationship issues, and that he should discuss them with Belle so that she wouldn't beat on me again. I even told him that she'd made accidental lip contact with me when she tackled me. I was actually quite pleased with my work.

Damn, I'm a bad person. But not a bad brother, at least. I really didn't know what Belle was after. It never occurred to me that she might actually like me that way. I supposed it might be possible that she simply liked power. I heard somewhere that girls like that stuff, and in our little school-pond, I was likely the biggest fish in terms of sheer magical-wattage.

Yuk, it just seemed so mercenary, which is why I'd never have anything to do with her. If she'd leave my brother just because I knew a few more spells than him, she'd do the same to me as soon as the next Sorcerer came along. No thanks.

So on than note, I'd talked my brother down off a ledge, persuading him to pay more attention to his magical studies (thus helping with what I was calling 'Belle's frustration' over his lack of ambition), which worked both in his favour, as it would help to keep him from getting pounded in his next duel, and mine, as it meant that I wouldn't have to worry as much. With any luck, the uptick in his power would bring that psychotic girlfriend of his scuttling back.

You might suggest that driving an imminent-cheat back to him might be a shitty thing to do, but it would hurt him more if she broke up with him like this. And she *did* have some compromising information that I wasn't ready to have disseminated yet. So, keep her happy, keep him happy, and keep me out of it, what could go wrong?

Yes... everything could go wrong. I know that *now*. What can I say? I was an optimist.

Chapter 48

Monday morning. The day when it all becomes official.
Breakfast was... energetic.

"She did what?!" Cathy squeaked when I told her and Bill
what had happened the previous night, swearing them both to
keep it to themselves.

"You magnificent bastard," Bill said, a look of wild
admiration on his face.

"Shut up," I said, poking my scrambled eggs with my
fork.

"How did you do it?" Bill continued.

"Billy!" Cathy said, swatting at his shoulder.

"It wasn't my fault. The resultant mischief was, but the
first part was definitely not my fault."

"Still, impressive," Bill said.

Cathy gave him her best glare and he subsided with a
grin.

"You need to be very careful, Mathew. You may be
smart, but Belle is just plain dangerous, and she seems to be
the back-stabbing sort."

"I thought of that, but then I realised that if I sicced my
libidinous brother on her, he should keep her under control for
at least a month, by which time I should have come up with a
better way of shutting her up."

"Just a thought," Bill said, "but why don't you just... you
know. That would probably shut her up."

"Billy!" Cathy squeaked, going bright red.

I felt my appetite go at the thought, and gave Bill my
own best glare. He just laughed, and then there was a clatter
as Belle thumped her tray down opposite from me, shoving Bill
along the bench.

"You rat-bastard!" she hissed at me. My smile turned evil
as I felt the mean-spirited tingle of a plan well-executed.

"Whatever do you mean?" I asked, unable to get what
was almost certainly a ghastly sneer under control.

"Your brother is smothering me! He's planned magic practice, special dates, more magic practice, it's suffocating, and I can't say no, he's so bloody determined, he won't take a hint!"

"Oh, no," I said with mock concern that sent Cathy into a giggling fit.

"Fix it, fix it now!"

"I didn't have anything to do with it," I said, "but Des is a perceptive guy. If your eyes are straying, then it's quite likely he knows on some level."

"Oh bullshit. This is your doing, and you will fix it!"

"No it wasn't, and no I won't," I replied, trying to focus on my eggs again.

She leaned forward, her pretty eyes blazing.

"You fix this, or else," she growled.

I leaned in so I was nice and close.

"See if you can make me," I whispered, staring right back at her.

She sucked in a breath and started biting her lip again while she stared at me.

"This isn't over," she panted, picking up her tray and stomping off.

I couldn't help but rub my hands together with malicious glee.

"Are you sure it's wise to antagonise her?" Cathy asked.

"Wise, no. Fun? Oh good God, yes," I replied with a grin. Suddenly I had my appetite back.

I made it through the rest of my morning without anything other problems, and then I was approached on my way to lunch by one of Kraab's lackeys. Not again... I was hungry! I was hoping this would happen *after* I'd eaten.

"Mister Graves?" he asked. I nodded. "Agent Kraab wants to see you; he said you'd know what it was regarding."

I nodded again and made my way to the main house. I was already nervous when I knocked on the door. I nearly had a panic attack when I saw Knowles in there.

"You..." I growled, glaring at her (still mad about the whole Day of Darkness thing).

"Easy, Mister Graves, Agent Knowles had nothing to do with the attack on your brother."

"Really?" I asked, continuing to glare, crossing my arms.

"An organisation I consult for took matters into their own hands, Matthew. They passed the information on to the Sons of the Dark Moon without my permission. I assure you, I would never have allowed harm to come to your brother, he's too important," Knowles said.

"In what way?" I asked, this was not the first time someone had said something like this.

"That's classified," she said with a self-satisfied grin that was tempting me towards stupidity. I looked towards Kraab, raising my eyebrows. He rolled his eyes, leaning forward.

"Your brother demonstrated impressive aptitude with light magic, above what should have been possible for a Wizard-class practitioner. He may even be a low level Sorcerer, at least with light magic. That's rare, and we are in desperate need of light mages of his calibre."

"You don't mean to recruit him, do you?" I asked, pretending surprise.

"In time, perhaps, it would be his choice, of course."

Not if I had anything to do with it, it wasn't. I simply nodded.

"Then I should warn you, he has a mind like a sieve, he's easily distracted by anything with cleavage, and he couldn't keep a secret if the planet depended on it. Just letting you know."

Knowles glared at me, but her expression seemed to darken at the information. She looked like she was going to say something, but Kraab interrupted her before she could.

"Let's leave that for the moment, we're here to talk about you," he opened a drawer and pulled out a sheaf of papers and a black pedestal with an indentation holding a black sphere.

"I still think this is a mistake, Sir," Knowles said, "he should be arrested, charged, and forced to reveal how he hexed my people."

Kraab turned an icy glare on Knowles, "If you can't maintain a civil tone, you can leave the room."

Knowles' eyes went wide, and she subsided into the corner. I looked at them both. That felt... unnatural, almost like it was prepared or rehearsed. A little transparent, but it was a good measure of their opinion of me: they thought I was an idiot. Well, no reason to let them know otherwise, it'll mean that their guard will be a little lower.

"Now, Mister Graves, we have some forms to fill in first. One of my people took the liberty of filling in all the general things, name, address and so forth. We'll just fill in the meat. I understand that your brother has been studying the government-approved books and has passed the exams up to proficiency level three. I presume you've also had the chance to study those texts?"

I nodded.

"Good, then what level would you estimate yourself to be at?" he asked, pen poised over the forms.

I had to think about that for a minute. How much do I reveal? Do I even want to lie to these people anymore? I thought hard, and then realised that honesty was probably the best policy. I was a little sick of having to lie to everyone, if I was honest (for necessities, I mean. I still enjoy *recreational* lying).

"I'm proficient to level nine, and know a dozen or so spells from levels ten through thirteen, a couple from fourteen," I finally said. Knowles actually had the good grace to look impressed. Kraab looked at me sideways, doubtfully, I thought.

"Level nine?" he asked, "Are you quite sure? You've had no formal training, is that correct?"

"Yes, and true," I replied.

"Would you mind a small demonstration?" Kraab asked, raising a doubtful eyebrow, "For the paperwork, you understand?"

I nodded.

"Alright, show me..." he thought for a moment, "Hierdon's Translation, third order. Describe the spell as you go, please."

That was a simple enough spell, designed to transform one form of energy into another for different spell types. Third order was more complicated, transforming raw magic into one of the physical energies. I'd mastered it more than a year ago.

I told him what I was doing as I did it; finally, I brought my hand up and opened it to reveal a little flaring blue ball of kinetic energy. The third order spell was not really all that useful on its own, it's really only used as part of a larger construction. Kraab nodded in appreciation (and not a little surprise), and I let the power dissipate.

"Now, Odrim's Seeker, just the mansion."

More complicated. This was an advanced spell incorporating a phased sonic pulse, a reception field and a light projection element. It was designed to produce a map of the area around the caster using magical sound that was inaudible to human ears, sort of like a submarine's sonar. I had tried this spell once and it just about worked. I preferred Google maps if I'm honest.

I concentrated hard, closing my eyes to create the spell framework, building and empowering each segment one by one. It took me about ten minutes of intense work, but I finally produced a ball of shimmering air containing the various spell portions. I cast it, and the subsonic waves flew out. Rapidly, the reflections came back into the ball in my hand, forming a complete view of the building around us in pale light.

Kraab made an impressed sound. He had me cast increasingly complex level-nine spells for the next hour until he finally filled in the paperwork, and had me sign.

"Congratulations, Mister Graves, you are now a qualified level-nine magician."

"You can do that?" I asked, confused, and quite pleased with myself.

"Sure, you just passed the standard practical exam. Your knowledge of the theory is almost word perfect, so I've signed off on the qualification, and the paperwork should get pushed through in a couple of weeks. I'll make sure that the certificates come to my office, so as to prevent any... situations with your family."

I nodded and said my thanks. Just like that, I was a qualified magician! How about that? That opened up quite a few professional doors that I was sure I'd never get around to opening.

"I don't need to do the previous level tests?" I asked.

"There's a box I can tick, holdover from when the government regulations first came in so that us old codgers didn't have to retake our apprentice trials," he said with a smile.

"And you never had any training?" Knowles asked, "None at all?"

"Just trial and error, and one small house fire that I shamefully blamed on my brother," I replied.

"You realise that the vast majority of Wizards never get past level six? Hell, I'm only qualified to level eight," Knowles said with what sounded like irritation. I shrugged non-committaly. Kraab chuckled and pulled out another sheet.

"This one is the general registration form, denoting your power level, affinity and specialisations. We can put down umbrakinesis for affinity without too much trouble. Any specialisations we should know about?"

Another awkward question, but in for a penny, in for a pound.

"Telepathy, Will and Biomancy," I finally answered.

"Oh come on!" Knowles snapped, throwing up her hands in exasperation before flopping onto a nearby chair.

"Easy, Vanessa," Kraab said, and then to me, "Are you sure about that? It's unusual for a Wizard to have two specialties or affinities, much less four."

"You could be right," I replied, "I only mention them because my level ten-plus spells are in those schools."

I wasn't going to tell him that the consensus was that I was a Sorcerer until he figured it out for himself.

"What's the highest proficiency spell you can cast?" Kraab asked.

I rubbed my head for a moment, thinking, I'd told him that I had a couple of level fourteen spells, and I'd had to flip to the back of the second volume to learn the triage spells I'd used to fix Des during the attack. What were the names of the blasted things?

"General Triage and Intermediate Flesh-craft," I finally answered.

Knowles swallowed hard, "Do you know how *dangerous* those spells are if you don't know exactly what you're doing?"

"Yes," I replied, "and don't worry, I do know what I'm doing."

"You mean you've used biomancy on a human being?!" she asked with explosive outrage.

"You've been eyeing up my brother's torso, you tell me," I replied sourly.

That made her pause, then blink, and then her mouth opened and shut again like she was a beached codfish. That was fun to watch.

"I'd forgotten that," she said finally before sitting back down.

"Yes, you made quite a sacrifice for your brother," Kraab said, looking at me with something like empathy. I shrugged in response.

"Blood is blood," I said, "no matter how stupidly they refuse to listen when you tell them not to do something that will kill them."

Kraab and Knowles both nodded emphatically at that. I guess the stupidity of siblings is one of the universal constants.

"Alright, one last test," Kraab said, placing the black pedestal on the table.

"What's that thing?" I asked.

"Very simple," Kraab said, "using whatever spell, power or ability you choose, but preferably your strongest, you try to affect the sphere. In your case, you would try to move it with your shadows."

He pressed a small crystal on the base and the sphere lifted up about half an inch. There were five more crystals under the one he'd pressed, all dark at the moment.

"That's all?" I asked, waiting for the trick.

"That's all," he replied.

I shrugged and called my shadows. They slid from crevices and under chairs, sliding to cover the walls around me and the ceiling above me before slithering down to coil around the orb. I told them to pull.

The sphere rose a tiny amount. I looked at Kraab.

"Keep going, as hard as you can, you can't break it."

I nodded. I called more and more shadows, they coiled and slithered, expanding the tendril from the size of a grass snake to that of a boa constrictor before pulling. Another small fraction of an inch. Three lights had lit up on the pedestal. I put more and more energy into the darkness, until it was shimmering with purple power. The coils and tendrils became denser, twisting and coiling until it seemed that a whole nest of snakes surrounded the orb. They pulled ever harder, the fourth light lit up, and then the fifth as the orb rose an inch, and then another. At five inches, the device started to glow and shudder.

"That's enough, Mister Graves," Kraab said in a voice that sounded strained.

I let the sphere go, and it floated slowly back to its pedestal. Kraab swallowed heavily before he managed to compose himself properly.

He cleared his throat.

"It would appear that our initial estimation of you was somewhat inaccurate, Mister Graves. We thought, because of your brother, that you would be a Wizard like him, but this test is quite conclusive, you are a Sorcerer-grade practitioner. Very high end, too."

That's quite the ego-boost, but it wasn't anything I didn't know by now. Knowles looked like she was going to be sick.

"How is that possible?" Knowles asked, and then her eyes went wide as she seemed to realise something, "What if they're like the others?"

"Not now, Knowles," Kraab said.

"But, Sir-"

"I said not now!" Kraab growled.

"What others?" I asked.

"It's nothing to concern yourself with," Kraab said, glaring daggers at Knowles.

"Oh, just tell me," I replied, "I'll just pester until you do."

"He should know," Knowles said to Kraab, a miserable look on her face, "he might be able to do something to stop it if he's warned."

Kraab sighed, rubbing his face for a moment. He suddenly looked much older. He nodded seemingly coming to decision.

"As you know, recorded history goes back further for magicians then it does for humans. There are many instances of magical twins, and they are almost exclusively born with an opposing skill set, but similar power level. There have been exactly five exceptions. One brother is a shadow mage, one a light mage, generally one is much stronger than the other, but that never makes a difference."

Kraab took a break, rubbing his face again, swallowing hard, like he could dislodge the tightness from his throat.

"Just tell me," I said, "how bad could it possibly be?"

Kraab smiled sadly.

"Every time twins like you are born, the light mage has, without fail, ended up killing his brother."

My brain just... stalled, like I couldn't wrap my head around it. My mind started spiralled into a grinding mess.

"Wait, you mean that we... that Des..." I managed.

Kraab cleared his throat, looking at the table, "If you hold to the pattern, then it is almost certain that, one day, and probably soon, Desmond is going to kill you."

Chapter 49

"That's not funny," I said finally, once the gears in my head had started turning again.

They looked at me with faces that could only be described as *deadly* serious.

"This isn't a joke, Mister Graves. Every time twins are born with light and shadow powers, the light brother has killed the shadow-mage. Every time."

"That was then. This is the modern age, for heaven's sake. People just don't go round killing one another for no good reason," I said, cranking my brain up to its usual speed by sheer force of will.

"Don't be naive," Kraab said in a superior way that made me angrier, "they always had a good reason, at least to them, it was hardly ever the same, and it still always *happened*."

"Des would never hurt me," I said, not believing my own words. He'd already hurt me.

Knowles looked at me sideways. Naturally she knew. Des would have told her everything.

"Yes, yes, I know," I said before she could rub my nose in it.

"What's this?" Kraab asked.

"When I asked Desmond to persuade Matthew to tell him who his sources were, they fought. I understand that you came off worse in that engagement?"

I nodded. It was really more of a draw, but I didn't want to quibble.

They kept talking, warning me to be careful, going through procedures if Des should ever turn dangerous towards me. I wasn't listening. I was too busy trying to figure this mess out. Des wouldn't really hurt me, would he? He was my brother, he loved me... right?

"Why did the other light mages kill their brothers?" I asked, hoping that there might be some clue there.

"There was never a common motive. One brother thought the other was seducing his wife, another thought his brother was stealing from him. The simple fact is that there is a bond between twins; you know that. When their power sets are so diametrically opposed, with Shadows being a High Element, it works on that bond and creates a resonance in the Light Mage that builds until they snap. And light magic is the most dangerous kind there is to a Shadowborn," Kraab explained.

"I'm rarely magically active around my brother, and when I am it's all mental magic and the occasional bit of biomancy, that should buy me some time, don't you think?" I asked, clutching at straws.

Knowles smiled sadly, like she was watching a train wreck in the making.

"It's already begun," she said, "to go from never laying a finger on you to laying you out is a very bad measure of what's happening right now."

I held my head in my hands and tried not to let despair overwhelm me. What the hell was I going to do? Well, for starters, I was going to put that Asimov back, and I was going to make it extra-tight, too. I'd make it so that they'd need the mental equivalent of a super-tanker to drag it out of there.

There were a few other things I could do, tricks and ideas that could help in case the worst happens; and it would appear that I would now have to plan for that. My own brother was going to kill me? Or at least he was going to give it a damn good try some time in the future. I would have to start studying defensive magic in earnest, and I'd have to learn to attack, and what was the best counter for light magic? But first I'd have to confirm this information. For all I knew, this was a convoluted plot to keep me from stopping Des joining their organisation...

"Mister Graves?" Kraab prodded, it was only then that I realised that they'd stopped talking.

"Yes?" I replied, "Sorry, my mind was miles away."

"I asked if there was anything we could do to help," he said, a kind look on his face.

"No, thank you, that's alright, I have an idea or two that might work," I said, getting to my feet.

"I'm sorry that I burdened you that, but Knowles is right, you *should* know. You are an incredible mage, Mister Graves, and forewarned is forearmed, it might give you enough of an edge to prevent anything... tragic from happening."

"Thank you," I said, shaking their hands, "and thanks for helping with all the paperwork."

He told me I was welcome, and handed me his business card, along with instructions to call him or Knowles if Desmond ever became violent again. I decided then and there that I would. This was... beyond me. Even I had to admit that.

I left the office. It was well past the end of lunch, as well as my two afternoon periods. Unable to think clearly, I went to the pool. On the few occasions I feel the need for physical exercise, this is where I go. Swimming is low impact and it's one of the few sports I can actually do, if not actually compete at. I was at it for an hour, hoping that something would click. Nothing did.

By the time I got back to my room, I was a tense mess. My phone rang and I nearly had a urine based accident, *that* bad. It was Des. I ignored it. My heart was pounding, and I didn't think that I could see him at that moment without embarrassing myself. I sat there for a long time, mulling it over. Coming to a strategy took time, and determining a plan even longer.

Eventually I called Des back, and agreed to meet him in the square. He wanted some help with his prep again, and I set him to a task while I cast my spell. This time I felt disgusted. The first time had almost been a bit of fun, something to show my skills, if only to myself. This time was born of fear and necessity, and it left an ugly taste in my mouth.

The Asimov I implanted this time was a great improvement on the last one. That one had been created when my mind-magic was still relatively new. This time I assembled the spell in half the time with a fraction of the power, and it was a lot more comprehensive, not to mention difficult to remove. I cast it, and my heart sank as it slid into Des' mind, where it attached in its programmed places. If he ever tried to do me harm again, his mind would simply shut down and wipe his memory of the moments before he attacked. I hadn't had the skill to make something like that when I'd cast the first one.

Out of sheer guilt, I cleared his entire backlog of prep, a good six hours work for him (though considerably less for me). He thanked me, thumped me on the back and went off to meet Belle, who had apparently been more interested lately, so that was something. I sat there after he left, letting the pain wash over me along with the fear of impending death. If it came down to a fight, I would assume some sort of rage on Des' part, some loss of control, what could I do in a situation like that? It's one thing to punch him in the crotch to show him who's boss, but I couldn't actually *fight* my brother.

And in a flash of insight, I realised that's how he'd kill me.

That's assuming that the Asimov failed, but I shouldn't worry too much about that. It would take a genius to pry that thing out of his head, and there aren't too many skilled telepaths, even in this country, so that was comforting.

Maybe I *could* relax? Just a little? I sighed. I really needed to talk to someone. Could I risk telling Cathy?

I thought about it, and then I called her.

"Mathew? Where have you been all day?" she asked.

"Long story, can you meet me? It's important."

"Where?" she asked. No hesitation, that's Cathy.

I told her where I was and only had to wait a few minutes for her to arrive. I led her away from the square and past the houses towards the field, where I had a good view and knew we were alone.

I filled her in, and by the time I was done she was in tears and I wasn't far off. In the end, she pulled me into a tight hug and sobbed into my shoulder. Don't you dare tell anyone, but I *may* have shed a few tears myself, hastily wiped away before she could see them.

"But you put the Asimov back?" she asked, her voice muffled by the jacket of mine she had her face buried in.

"Yes, it should do the trick as long as no smart-arse figures out a way to remove it."

"Then you'll be okay? Des won't be able to hurt you?" she asked, trembling a little.

"Hopefully. But that's not the problem, if what the SCA says is true, then he's going to start hating me, and it may have already started. Given enough time and incentive, there may be a way around the Asimov. Just because I haven't thought of them doesn't mean they don't exist."

"What kind of ways?" she asked.

"I can't think of any. I've accounted for everything I could think of, right up to him being unable to write down "Kill Mathew" on a piece of paper."

"Then don't worry, just keep vigilant, and try not to worry about something that might not even be true."

"That was my thinking. I need to get that information verified."

"Can your sources help?" she asked.

I actually managed a smile at that.

"It just so happens that I have a debt I can call in."

Chapter 50

By Wednesday, I'd managed to convince myself that it was all a horrible mistake. And anyway, the Asimov would keep me safe, so I was actually in quite a good mood when lecture time came around. I'd been dreading this ever since my last meeting with Tethys, but goodness only knew what she'd get up to if I wasn't there, and watching her like a hawk.

Cathy was keeping close to me lately, as if she was worried Des was going to leap out of a bush and fry me at any moment. It was sweet, but it was also getting a little much, she accidentally followed me into the loo yesterday.

We took our customary seats and waited for the show to start. I heard the seats behind us squeak, and Des' voice came from behind me, causing me to jump a foot into the air (alright, so I may not be *completely* right in the head yet).

"Whoa, little brother, didn't mean to scare you," he said with a reassuring laugh, before patting me on the shoulder, making me jump again.

"Are you alright? You seem a little jittery today," he said.

"Watched Event Horizon last night, still haven't recovered," I replied, trusting to my well-won reputation for scary-movie cowardice.

"Oh, Matty, you know you can't watch horror after eight pm!" Des said in an admonishing tone that I actually found familiar and reassuring.

Cathy snorted and Bill tried to conceal an evil grin.

"Aw, is the little normal scared of a shiny bit of plastic?" Belle said from directly behind me, making me shudder. Of course she'd be here. My potentially homicidal brother, his potentially unfaithful girlfriend, my two best friends in the world and Tethys all in the same room. Yup, this sounds like the ingredients of a fun, stress-free evening.

This time the auditorium was full, and there was even a few seats laid on at the back where teachers were now sitting, along with Kraab and Knowles (oh, bother).

Tethys came in a few minutes later, looking even more smug than usual before standing at her podium. The headmaster introduced her as normal, and then Tethys began. I was already tense. I really didn't need this sort of stress.

"Good evening everyone," she said, "what a great turnout."

She took a moment to look around the room, eyes settling on me for a moment. She gave me a smile, and I glared back, which only made her smile wider.

"Tonight, I thought we'd discuss telepathy," she said.

Oh no...

"Can anybody tell me a little bit about mental magic?" she asked, looking around the room again.

Belle put up her hand.

"Yes Miss...?"

"Warren, Annabelle Warren. Mental magic is what cowards use when they can't win an honourable duel," she said in a voice that dripped with a sneer, which I could practically *feel* being directed at me. I swear this girl had a multiple personality.

Tethys' musical laugh filled the auditorium as she looked at Belle, "Not quite, but a duellist, such as yourself, would of course feel any non-martial magic to be unworthy. Just try to remember that a man can be struck down by a scalpel just as efficiently as he can by a cannon ball."

How the hell did she know that Belle was a duellist? You know what, never mind, I'm not even surprised anymore.

"Anybody else?" she asked, looking pointedly at me. I shook my head, just a little, and Cathy put up her hand.

"Yes?"

"Telepathy, or mental magic, is the school of magic designed for navigating the mental landscape and altering the thoughts, emotions, memory or brain function of the subject."

Thanks Cathy, way to talk down the angry mob.

"A perfect definition, young lady," Tethys said, "You must tell us some time how you came to know so much."

That smug smile again. I wasn't sure where this was going, but I just *knew* something bad was going to happen to me.

"Now, none of us like the idea of someone messing with our minds, so I thought that I would use this session to teach you a little about how to keep your minds safe from mental intrusion."

She smiled, looking around the room, several sets of eyes had glazed over.

"But I don't expect you to just sit there while I take you through mental exercise. From the looks of some of you even the preparatory stretching might be a challenge."

Despite myself, even I smiled at that.

"Allow me to introduce my assistants for the evening," she said beckoning over to the door, "these are the Wizards Niles Pouer and John Groves."

There was applause, and much more attention now that there were mages in the room.

"These gentlemen are experts at teaching mental defence to both Pureborn and mages alike, and they do it in a very special way," she paused for effect, "can I have a volunteer from the audience?"

Almost every hand went up, even Bill's. Cathy had the good sense to keep her hand down, thank God. I thought I knew where this might be headed.

"For this first demonstration, I need someone with a good imagination, but relatively poor focus... how about you, young man?" she said, pointing at the Ox, who grinned widely and flexed every one of his muscles as he made his way out of his row.

"Now, you stand here," Tethys said, guiding Oxley to a spot opposite Pouer. The mage was tall and thin, he looked about forty, with a thin face and a large nose. His partner was younger, heavyset and of Asian descent, with cold eyes and a thin mouth. He stood between them and back a bit.

"Now, it's quite simple, Mister Groves will project an image of what's happening while Mister Pouer tries to gain access to your mind."

Tethys nodded and Groves put his hands out, producing an image made of light. It showed an empty space with a single bright spark in the centre.

"This is your mindscape," Tethys said, walking around behind Oxley.

"Roomy, ain't it," Bill whispered to me, making me snigger.

"At the moment, it is undefended. The spark at the centre is your mind. You must imagine defences to prevent Pouer from getting in."

"What use are imaginary defences?" Ox asked.

"It's an imaginary attack," Tethys answered. The crowd ooh-ed. Imbeciles.

"What should I use?" Oxley asked.

"Whatever is easiest for you to focus on with your mind, castles, trenches, bunkers, a really big wall, it's entirely up to you. Don't worry, Pouer is very competent, and at no time will anything bad happen to you. He will simply break through the defences and extract a single piece of information from your mind."

"We'll see," Ox said with an arrogant grin that made his cronies laugh. The image changed as his mind moved itself to a flat plain, now surrounded by a large, simple concrete wall with barbed wire on the top. It was big, thick and simple, appropriate to the creator.

"Ready?" Tethys asked.

Ox nodded, gritting his teeth in concentration.

Pouer nodded and a golden tendril appeared on the screen, approaching from Pouer's direction. It slid forward carefully, but inexorably, and then, like a snake, it struck. It smacked into the wall like a battering ram, massive cracks flowed through it, and in a second, it fell. The golden tendril darted out of the way of the collapse, avoiding the rubble, and snaked past the defence straight into the spark.

The Ox gasped, and it was over. The image winked out.

Pouer smiled, "You, Mister Oxley, are currently wearing pink underwear, because you heard your girlfriend say she liked that colour and you wanted to surprise her."

My mouth fell open with utter and complete glee.

Best. Lecture. Ever!

There were bellows of laughter and rounds of applause. Oxley looked *really* mad as he made his way back to his seat.

Once the roar faded away, Tethys spoke again.

"An excellent demonstration," she said, bowing to Oxley, who looked ready for murder, "as you highlighted the most important point. The best defence against a mental intrusion is not just strength; it's also focus, and complexity."

She walked around the podium, and looked into the crowd.

"Take a moment to assemble your own defences, make them as big, sprawling and complex as you can while still being able to visualise them clearly. And when you're done, put up your hand and we'll have another try or two."

Bill's hand went up first, and I face-palmed, trying desperately to mutter out of the side of my mouth not to do it. Thankfully, Tethys didn't pick him; she picked one of the footballers in the front row. He was big in the cadets, so his defences looked more military in style with lines of trenches and bunkers surrounding his spark. Pouer just slid over them, bypassing the trenches completely. The image soon winked out.

"Remember, the world you create has rules. If you create a chasm or gap that you can jump over, you'd better bet your opponent can too," Tethys said after Poeur revealed something about the way Johnson cheats at Mariokart.

She had another half-dozen volunteers come out, and everyone had fun participating and watching. I must say that her lessons and ideas were working, each failure taught everyone something, and they were getting better. The last one was a series of walls made of razor-wire and rebar with deep trenches between them, not a bad set of defences, I must say, for a Pureborn. Pouer made short work of it, though.

"I think we can all agree that you're getting better. But why don't we have one more volunteer. Someone who actually knows what they're doing," she smiled that evil smile of hers, looking over at me, "any takers?"

The hands went up again. She was looking at me as I crossed mine over my chest.

"Come on, someone who thinks they can make a really good defence. Otherwise I'm going to have to pick someone else, and who knows what *they* might tell me?"

She looked at Belle, who also had her hand up. How the hell did Tethys know to target her?!

I groaned quietly, and finally raised my hand. Cathy looked at me in shock, and I could hear Belle and Des gasp behind me.

"Excellent, excellent. Please join me on the stage, Matthew," Tethys said in an unpleasantly self-satisfied purr.

I was readying my defences before I'd even made it to the end of my row. Pouer would know if I was using magic, so I needed to make them as solid as I could without using any power. I'd had the chance to expand my constructs after my encounter with Knowles, and I'd spent some time practicing it while I was laid up, so at least I'd managed that much (the concentration had helped to keep the nausea at bay).

I stepped up opposite Pouer and Tethys walked past me, touching my shoulder, "I'm sure you'll give us a great show, Mathew," she whispered, getting her mouth a little close to my ear and making the hairs stand up on my neck.

"That's not playing fair, Tethys," I whispered as the crowd muttered, looking on excitedly. Many of them would jump at the chance to gain more information on me that they could use to make my life miserable. Let's just hope that I had what it took to keep Pouer out.

"Ready?" Tethys asked me. I grinned evilly and nodded, which seemed to vex her a little.

Pouer nodded and Groves put up the image. They both gasped. The crowd started muttering and commenting. They should, this took a lot of effort.

The mindscape was dominated by the imposing form of a mountain, which had replaced my old keep. It was riddled with passages and traps, dead ends and pitfalls; it was surrounded on all sides by a massive maze, most of it filled with water, pits and other nastiness. Pouer sneered at the challenge and went right in.

I went to work.

I shifted the maze with him as he traversed it, shifting it left and right over and over until I sent him right back out again. He growled in frustration and ploughed back in, breaking through one wall, and smacking hard into another. It took him longer to break that one, and he slammed right into another, and another, all the while I was subtly changing the orientation of the walls with each strike until he once again flopped back out of the maze, and I hastily rebuilt behind him.

With a scowl and a burst of energy, Pouer conjured three tendrils and attacked from different angles. One tried smashing through walls while the others tried to navigate the maze. I concentrated harder and the walls started to shift and turn around his attacks, driving and redirecting until the passive tendrils ran straight into the battering one, and I started directing it around and around on itself. He tried to split off another tendril in the opposite direction, but I directed into a pit and then through a tunnel and out the other side of the maze.

Pouer was growing increasingly frustrated. In a battle like this, all the advantages were with the defender, and if that defender knows what he's doing, the attacker would need overwhelming force, or a face-slapping distraction, to get through. Pouer didn't have either. He also didn't really know what he was doing. He was using a simple brute-force attack. If I'd been him, I would have sent out probes looking for weaknesses before directing a series of attacks to wear down my opponent's concentration all over the perimeter, forcing him to maintain a larger spread of detail before striking at a single point in the defence. He also wasn't consolidating his gains; he should have left smaller energy nodes behind him as he went, which would have at least allowed him to know when I was messing with the orientation of the place. After another ten minutes of this, Pouer was sweating and panting like a dog. I was still quite fresh, after the strain of Knowles' attack, this was nothing. He was so slow, and he was already weakening.

"You can see that Mister Graves is using a multitude of layers and stimuli to keep his opponent at bay, even rearranging his mindscape when it looks like Mister Pouer is making progress, it's very interesting. But concentration is key for his defence. With magic, he could solidify the barriers and make Mister Pouer's job that much harder, but with only his focus to go on, Mister Graves is vulnerable to distraction," Tethys lectured from behind me.

There was a pause as Pouer withdrew and gathered himself for another attack. I looked out the corner of my eye after I'd finished resetting the maze, to see Tethys walking to the edge of the audience.

"Miss Warren, could you come to the front, please?"

Oh no, now what?

She came forward.

"You know Mister Graves?" Tethys asked.

"Oh yes," she answered, her voice just a little too sly for my comfort.

"Think you can distract him from his defence?" Tethys asked. I couldn't see her face, but I had to believe that there was an evil grin on it.

Uh oh.

"Oh, come on!" I said just as Pouer renewed his attack and I had to refocus. The crowd laughed at my comment, and Belle made her way up onto the stage.

"Hi Matty," she said. I ignored her. Pouer made his way through the outer wall, and I had to start shifting. Meanwhile Belle had undone her tie.

Don't pay attention, there's nothing to see there.

Pouer broke through another wall and I had to rapidly rearrange the architecture to keep him from getting further, it diverted him, and his tendrils went flying down the wrong way.

Then Belle undid her top buttons, gently pulling her shirt open and half the maze came crashing down.

It fell straight onto Pouer's tendril, though, so that was something. He hissed in pain and desperately tried to pull back. The crowd laughed as he strained, and I desperately rebuilt around him, pinning him in place while I restored the walls and avenues, slamming my eyes shut.

"Des! Control your woman, will you?!" I shouted, the crowd roared with laughter.

"Would if I could, little brother!" he shouted back, raising more laughter.

"Am I distracting you, Matty?" Belle asked in a sultry voice. I couldn't see her, but I couldn't imagine she was just going to leave me to it.

So I rebuilt while I could, assembling a raised platform, containing Pouer's probe, above the rebuilt maze, constantly moving the exit so he couldn't find his way out. He was getting frustrated again. I couldn't keep him in there forever, just until he realised I'd trapped him and ripped himself clear.

I started moving the platform towards the nearest edge of the maze, a route that crossed briefly over one of the inner walls.

Belle ran her finger along my ear, which surprised me enough to demolish half the cage, nearly letting Pouer out.

"Do you mind?" I asked, "I'm winning here."

"I don't mind at all," she whispered in my ear, her voice throaty and sexy as hell.

The cage fell apart and Pouer dropped back into the maze, well past the third line of defence.

He was right next to the mountain.

Chapter 51

"Damn it, Belle, leave off, will you?" I said in a snarl, desperately shifting the architecture again. This was no longer fun. I built a heavy tower and brought it down in the path of Pouer, who tried to skirt it, giving me time to drop a massive chasm around the mountain. Pouer's tendril hardened and he began the laborious process of stretching across the gap, putting more and more power into it, until he touched the other side. Suddenly he snapped across, but I collapsed the rock face, sending him plummeting into the abyss.

Pouer screeched in fear, and he immediately snapped his attacks out of my head in sheer terror. I immediately started rebuilding, and was done in record time.

"Shit!" Pouer bellowed, looking at the display with my rebuilt defences. Sweat was running down his face in rivulets, his eyes were frantic, and he was breathing hard.

"Watch that first step," I said, getting a little tired myself, now. This had long since gone past the point where it was amusing.

"You little bastard!" he almost shouted, and he threw out a torrent of power.

Just goes to show how good I am at meeting new people.

I barely held the torrent of mental energy back. It brute-forced its way through the two outer mazes and ran smack into the third. I felt my nose bleed from feedback, but saw with a glance that he was in much worse shape, blood flowed from his eyes, nose and ears as he pushed himself too far, too fast. My defence was ripping into his construct as he tore his way onwards, and that was dangerous, that probe was an extension of his mind, and damaging it could seriously hurt him.

Still, better him than me.

I let him through the third maze, and he squealed in delight as he saw the chasm again. This time sheer power flung him across. I heard him cough wetly before red stains appeared on his chin; the idiot was killing himself. If I made him smash through any more barriers he might get brain damage, so I cleared the way.

There were two massive gates on the front of the mountain, they would have held him up forever, but I opened them. His probe stormed into the mountain, heading straight up through passages that I was hastily rebuilding to provide a long, looping and very pointless path through a warren that makes the catacombs under Paris look like Bag End. Eventually, after fifteen minutes moving unobstructed through the maze he emerged through a massive gate at the mountaintop and onto the plateau at the summit.

Where he found absolutely nothing.

"Where is it?!" he screamed, "Where are you?! Tell me!"

"Does anyone else think that this may have gone just a pinky-toe too far?" I asked through gritted teeth as Pouer approached a mental precipice, and not just the one I'd created, either.

"Yes, I rather think that's enough, don't you, Mister Groves?" Tethys asked dangerously. This had obviously not gone according to plan.

"Yes. Po, stand down, mate."

"No! Not until I get in! It's so close."

"No it's not," I replied, "you're at the wrong end of the mountain."

"What?! What?!"

"Sub-basement. You missed the turn at the front door."

He turned his probe around far too fast and ran smack into solid rock without some considerable striking force. I'd shut the door behind him. Woops. The strike threw his head back, and he fell to the ground, quite unconscious. I released the defence and sagged after the effort. The mindscape image showed my spark appear from far below the mountain as the defences dissolved.

The crowd went ballistic as Groves darted to his colleague's side. I saw sparks fly, and the mage shuddered. He sat up with a groan.

"What happened?" I heard him slur over the cheering.

"You lost," Groves said coldly, dragging him to his feet before manhandling him towards the door, presumably before he could do some other stupid thing.

"Well, that was a little more intense than expected," Tethys said as Belle helped me back to my seat. The focus had been surprisingly draining. She took the opportunity to pinch my bottom before she let me go, making me glare at her. She just licked her lips in reply and sat next to my brother who gave me a wide grin and a hearty thumbs-up. Cathy handed me a tissue, gesturing at my nose, while Bill grinned at me and offered a fist for me to bump.

"You saw that, everyone? Versatility, focus and, in Mister Graves' case, sheer bloody-minded stubbornness," that earned a laugh, and she winked at me before continuing, "and all that without a lick of magical energy, I must say that I'm impressed. No mage is getting one over on this young man."

I glared, she smiled; you understand the routine by now.

She spoke some more about the mind and its flexibility, she pointed out aspects of my performance, and made sure that everyone noticed the mental feedback that had hit Pouer like a freight train.

"Well, that's it for tonight. One more to go, I suppose!"

The crowd went wild and I sagged in horror at the idea of another one of these. That had been too close. If Belle had tried one more thing...

Well, best not to dwell. My head was killing me, and I just wanted to sleep, but I still needed to do one more thing. Bill and Cathy filed out with Des and Belle while I waited behind. The last of the crowd left, and Tethys somehow distracted Mister Kenilworth again. She slow-clapped as I walked down the stairs to the podium.

"Very, very nice," she said, looking me up and down.

"Oh, bite me," I replied, "You set me up. Again!"

"Oh hush," she said, flashing me a smile, "you handled that perfectly."

"Why, oh why, did you set up that ludicrous display?"

"I keep telling you. Fun, fun, fun! And just maybe I enjoy watching you dominate me."

"Haven't you inflamed my hormones enough for one evening?" I asked.

"It's never *enough*," she purred, "and if you snap your fingers in just the right way, that young Miss Warren will jump your bones so hard your head will spin."

"Don't even start on that. Do you have any idea how much trouble I've had keeping that girl from doing something stupid?" I replied.

She just laughed, "Why try so hard? Life is difficult enough without passing up on sensual companionship."

"Alright, before my head pops off, I need a favour."

Her eyes glimmered evilly.

"Oh yes?" she said, sidling up next to me and running a finger up and down my lapel, "I am of course at your *complete* disposal."

"I need you to get me everything you can about twin mages, specifically those where one brother is a light mage, and the other is a Shadowborn. I want to know how they died. There should be five, at least."

"This sounds like it's important to you, care to tell me why?" she asked, actually looking concerned.

"Get the information, and you'll see," I answered. She nodded.

"And what of payment for this service?" she asked, looking me up and down.

"Don't you still owe me a couple of favours?" I asked.

She made a frustrated sound, "Fine, but next time, it'll cost you. But don't worry, you'll find my friend's rates to be very reasonable. Just ask Kandi how I like to... *extract payment.*"

"Sure, get me riled up this soon after a mental battle, that'll end well," I replied.

"Getting you riled up is sort of my hobby now."

I rolled my eyes and turned away, "See you next week," I said.

"That was easy," she replied, "Normally I have to exert my womanly wiles to get you to turn up."

"Too tired to go through the motions, just please keep me out of whatever hell you've got planned."

"Can't promise that," she called after me with a giggle.

I wandered out of the auditorium and into the night air, taking in a deep breath. Can I not go one week without making an enemy, getting involved in a pissing match with a complete stranger or coming within a hair's breadth of discovery?

No, apparently not.

"Mister Graves?" Kraab said from behind me. They're always behind me; it's starting to affect my blood pressure. I turned to face him, and saw Knowles was there too.

"Agent Kraab, good evening. Agent Knowles," I said with a nod.

"That was quite the performance tonight," he said, "where did you learn to defend like that?"

"Well, after Agent Knowles showed my castle complex to be woefully inadequate without magic, I had to upgrade. So, from her, I guess."

"Really? No formal training at all?" Knowles asked.

"You keep asking me that," I said, "which tells me that you think I'm lying, but tell me, who gives advanced magical training to a mage without proper government documentation?"

"You can't be serious," Knowles asked with a snort.

My blank look must not have answered her question because I felt her brush up against my mind.

"Hey!" I said, slamming a mental shield into place, a real one this time, not just imaginary.

"He's telling the truth," she said with a disbelieving note in her voice.

"What, really?" Kraab asked.

"Yes, he's really self-taught."

"I feel like I'm missing something," I said.

"We'd assumed that an unregistered mage was teaching you. It's supposed to be illegal, but it happens. And they tend to be rather an... unsavoury type. They don't teach the approved version of magic."

"But I do know the approved magic," I said.

"You also have a *lot* of extracurricular knowledge. We thought you were being groomed. Our mistake, apparently."

"That means that you actually invented those spells by trial and error?" Knowles asked.

"Lots of error, I told you about my Uncle, right?" I answered.

"Yes, but don't tell anybody else," Kraab said, "he could demand prosecution."

I smiled a little too widely.

"You left something in his head didn't you?" Knowles asked with a glare.

"As if I would," I said, affecting a hurt voice.

Knowles actually smiled.

"Don't take this the wrong way," I said, "but why are you still here?"

"Not enjoying the warm embrace of her majesty's government?" Knowles asked.

"Not when her majesty's government sticks her head into mine without asking. Again."

"Sorry, force of habit," Knowles said, still smiling.

"We're still here because... well, there's no way to sugar-coat it, we're using you as bait."

"Why would you tell me that?!" I asked.

"So that you stay close to our agents, don't get involved in any plots or problems, and, I can't stress this part enough, stay *away* from Lord Faust," Kraab said.

"As if I'd ever go near that lunatic again!" I replied hotly.

"And please stop casting telepathic spells on people, we still haven't managed to wake up the Dark Moon mages you hexed," Knowles said, looking at me pointedly.

I said nothing, I wasn't going to play. Knowles stepped forward with a sad look on her face. I exchanged glances with Kraab who shrugged, looking like he was containing a laugh.

I sighed, "Do you want me to wake them up for you?" I asked finally.

"How nice of you to offer, in anticipation of your kindness, we have a car waiting for you," Knowles said with a wide grin.

"You really aren't very nice, are you?" I asked with a glare.

"That hurts, Mathew," she said in such a false way that I had to laugh. I shook my head and followed the agents to the car.

They drove me to the James Sutcliffe Memorial Hospital, which was on the opposite side of the town to St Jeremiah's. They led me through a whole bunch of corridors to a secure wing, where they had to escort me past several guards, and to a closed ward where my victims were 'sleeping'. I was quite tired by this point, but I rolled up my sleeves and headed in. The guards joined us at a signal from Knowles. There were a dozen of them, and they waited around the edge of the room, where their amulets couldn't interfere with what I was doing.

"Any particular order?" I asked Kraab.

"Better be the older gentleman, he's the High Mage you clobbered, I'd imagine that puts him higher in the order than the rest," he replied.

"Alright," I said, moving that way.

"Careful not jog the ones with the radiation burn scars," Knowles said with a half-glare, "We've had a hard time preventing their DNA from twisting into spaghetti."

"I'd point out that they started it," I said. Kraab snorted. Knowles gave him a look.

"The boy's quite right. I've been telling you for years that something like this was going to happen. This time they bit off more than they could chew, and that tickles me a little."

Knowles grunted and started muttering while I went over to the Space Mage. He looked mostly better; the hospital's mages obviously knew their business. I only vaguely recognised him, he'd been a mess the last time I'd seen him.

I used my mage sight just to make sure than my hex was where I'd left it, and then I began plucking at the edges, very carefully. I build these things with a specific deactivation key, so it's a simple matter of exposing the core of the spell and sending the key.

The golden web disassembled itself, detaching from his mind and vanishing. The mage woke up with a scream.

"No! Abomination! Monster!" then he looked around and saw where he was. He didn't recognise me, why would he? I had wiped his memory.

"Where am I?" he asked.

The jackboots took over. They read him his rights and strapped him down with Spelleater manacles on his wrists. These worked much like the amulets, only turned inward on the wearer, leaving everyone else capable of magic. He wasn't happy with the treatment.

I carried on to the next one. Someone had tried to remove his hex, and had only succeeded in mangling the outer edges, so this took me a little longer. I was about half way through when I felt it; something... slick and nasty, tickling the outer edges of my magical senses.

I stopped what I was doing.

"What's the matter?" Knowles asked, looking me over.

"Don't you feel that?" I asked, turning my mage sight in the direction of the feeling. I found myself looking out of the window.

My heart seemed to stop beating for a second as I saw it in the distance, a roiling, awful mass of twisting shadows, dense and horrible. It flattened a path through a nearby wood, crushing everything under an immense bulk. Mouths appeared in the mass along with half-formed bladed limbs and awful staring red eyes.

It looked dreadfully familiar. And then I heard its voice. One for every mouth, each slightly different, melding in a dreadful symphony that chilled me to my core.

It started chanting.
Agrammel!
Agrammel!
Agrammel!

Chapter 52

It jumped towards me. Or it seemed to. One second it has more than a hundred metres away, massacring the shrubbery, and the next it was right in front of me. I called my shadows just as a massive bony limb burst through the wall, reaching for me. It was huge, muscular and misshapen, like a melted waxwork of an arm, with too many fingers, each ending in a pale, jagged talon. It was just one of hundreds, and more reached towards me.

My shadows barely blocked that first arm, coiling around it to deflect it. They hardly worked, it was only by a supreme effort of will and power that the terrible arm slowed down enough for me to jump away. To their credit, Knowles and Kraab reacted ridiculously fast, conjuring energy and readying shields.

"Get that shadow out of the bloody way!" Kraab bellowed, while Knowles ordered the men back, they didn't need the distraction.

I did as I was told, and the arm immediately lurched for me, where it met my hastily built Force plane. Bones crunched, and the arm withdrew, instantly replaced by another. The Space Mage started screaming in terror, and one of the arms darted for him, grabbing with a wet cracking sound that cut off his screams as he was dragged out of the room and dropped into one of the monster's waiting mouths.

I tried not to vomit and scurried backwards, keeping the shield in place while adding to it. I focussed power on my other hand as another arm ploughed through the side of the building. Kraab let loose with twin beams of purple light that scorched the monster's flesh, but didn't do much else. Knowles conjured tiny bolts of power that ripped the creature's limbs down to the bone. The arms pulled back again, and I heard a great rending crash as the wall we were facing came down. Great slabs of stone fell towards us, and I barely grabbed them with my mind before they could crush us. I held the boulders and drew power into them, making them red hot and saturated with kinetic energy before hurling them out the hole in the building and into the mass of flesh, where they exploded.

The creature screamed, and the limbs withdrew again. I stepped forward and threw the Force Lance I'd been preparing. It carved a path through the monster's charred and torn flesh, cutting half a dozen of those dreadful arms off. It howled again and pulled back hard, disappearing around the corner. I was breathing hard from panic and sheer terror.

It was a miracle I hadn't soiled myself.

I began drawing in more and more energy for my multi-energy ball, knowing that the creature would come back.

"Mister Graves, get out of here!" Kraab bellowed, increasing the strength of his barrier.

"I would be very glad to," I replied, "if the bloody thing wasn't waiting around the corner of the building for me to do exactly that."

"You can see it?" Kraab asked before remembering, "Oh yes, you can cast mage sight."

"What was that thing?" Knowles asked, her voice filled with fear. I could relate.

"Extra-planar entity," Kraab said in a businesslike tone, "infernal, class-twelve if I'm any judge."

"A demon?!" Knowles almost screamed, "a bloody demon?!"

"Technically a demon lord, or even a prince by the size of it," Kraab said, keeping his guard pointed towards where I told him the creature was. I didn't want to tell him it was a king. Knowles looked ready to faint as it was.

"What do we do?" she asked, her voice edged with hysteria.

"We call for backup, that's what we do," he said, gesturing at his partner, who recycled one of her attack spells so she would have a free hand. She pulled her phone out of a pocket.

I heard screaming, and the ugly crunching sound of the creature feeding. Kraab heard the same thing and ran for the door.

"Where are you going?" Knowles asked.

"People are dying out there!"

"And you want to make sure that you'll join them?!" she asked.

"Not if I can avoid it. Get that backup here as soon as you can. Graves, come with me," he said.

"What?" I asked, contemplating a shadow-assisted escape out the hole in the wall.

"Your attacks hurt it, I need help and you're the only other Sorcerer I've got."

"But I'm not a battle mage!" I complained, trying not to whine.

"I'll keep you safe, just stay behind me, and blast it when you can. Light magic works best, then fire, force and then everything else. Got it?"

"Light, fire and force?" I said as I followed him, assembling a number of attack spells and drawing in light as we went. I don't generally like to use light, it feels funny to manipulate, but needs must. I cast another spell that started generating the stuff, packing it into small globes that floated around me. I bolstered my shield, layering it and shaping it as we ran. I was out of breath when we got there, and we were too late.

There were eight beds in the ward, all empty except for bloodstains. We got there in time to see the last patient disappear down one of Agrammel's gullets, his screams cut off only after he'd been swallowed. Kraab shouted out a war cry and started blasting it with his beams. I assembled half a dozen of my orbs into a lance of energy, and threw it at the largest concentration of eyes I could see.

They exploded into gelatinous fountains, spraying fluid all over the place. More screams split the air as the beam carved into the demon, releasing an eruption of flesh and viscera. A mouth on a stalk of flesh darted through the gaping hole, straight for Kraab. It darted past his defence, and I had to pause my attack to block it before it could tear his head off.

"Thanks!" he shouted over his shoulder before attacking again. His beams turned orange, and I could almost feel the heat radiating off them. The demon's flesh burned and sizzled, mouths were charred shut, arms and bony protrusions were seared off. But there were always more. I cast another light-spear, and then another. The demon screamed and shook in mortal agony, but it was so *huge*, I couldn't think we'd managed to disable more than a tiny fraction of it. And then it simply turned itself to present more appendages.

"Why doesn't it just crush us?" I asked, "It must have the sheer mass."

"It would need to concentrate its mass just to try, and that would leave it vulnerable, especially while it's still gathering its strength!" he shouted, searing off what looked like a bony spear attached to a triple-jointed arm.

"Why's that?" I replied.

"Wherever it came from, it left a lot of power behind, so, for the moment, the power it can draw is limited. Otherwise I think it would have used its own magic by now. But that's only going to last for so long."

"These things can use magic?!" I asked, nearly shrieking, tossing a few of my light globes straight at the mass, where the energy seared more flesh in the explosion.

"Some of them. The big ones, certainly."

"So what are we going to do? Light isn't my affinity, I can't keep it up forever."

"Don't worry, backup won't be long, and then they can banish the thing and be done."

Knowles came around the corner at that moment, saw the demon and almost screeched to a halt behind me.

"How long? Kraab bellowed.

"Half an hour, minimum, the entity team's on callout."

"That seems remarkably inconvenient, doesn't it?" I asked, as I tried an even larger lance that actually made the creature rear backwards in agony as the light bore its way deeper and deeper into the demon's flesh before igniting what it found. I fed more and more light and power into the spell, expending all of the little orbs floating around my head. The creature flowed backwards, flattening an entire car park and its contents before rolling away in a wave of dark flesh.

It disappeared from sight, no doubt gathering itself for another attack.

"I can't do that too many more times," I panted as little orbs began to reappear around my head.

"We're actually hurting it," Kraab said, "We just need to hold on for another... Knowles?"

"Twenty-eight minutes or so," she said.

I groaned. This really wasn't the place for me. I wasn't a fighter, or anything but a coward truth be told. I wasn't built for facing down the ancient terrors of the universe.

I kept an eye on the creature for Kraab, who led us around the hospital, following it so that it wouldn't have an easy shot at any patients.

"What I'd like to know is what it was even doing here, it seemed to be focussed on you, Mister Graves," Kraab said.

"Well," I began, idly scratching my head.

"Well what?" Kraab asked after I'd stopped.

I reminded him of what I'd seen in Faust's house. At the time of telling I hadn't been able to remember the thing's name, but I sure as hell wouldn't forget it again.

"Faust?!" Kraab said.

"So it would seem," I replied.

"So it's after you?" Knowles said, in a tone that all but screamed 'trade him for the rest of us!'

"Maybe," Kraab interjected, "his presence here could just be a coincidence. And the first one it ate was that Space Mage."

"If it would help, I'd be willing to run away as fast as I could so that we could find out," I said, only half joking. My shadows could move me pretty fast if I needed to run.

"No. If it does follow you, you can't run forever, and then it'll kill you. If it doesn't then our defence is reduced considerably, and all of us die. We have to play the probabilities."

Knowles looked nearly panicked. My underwear was on the verge of needing a change, but at least Kraab looked steady. During the conversation I'd taken my eyes off the creature, and in a second it had leapt back to the attack. I barely had the time to adjust my shield before a massive pseudopod of bone and mouths came smashing down through the ceiling. It bounced off my shield, but the force smashed the floor below me, and I went tumbling down.

Knowles and Kraab darted away as tile and concrete fell on the dome of my shield. Agrammel brought its new limb down again and again. My shield barely held, and cracks were beginning to appear. I pulled the light orbs in, adding them to the shield in triangular planes, like blades. When the pseudopod came down again the little swords of light slashed into it, and all those mouths bellowed in pain. It was yanked wetly out of the building and I flexed my shield, scattering the rubble before jumping out through a door and running for dear life.

Another massive limb smashed down, collapsing the corridor behind me as I bolted, it hit repeatedly as I jumped into the stairway and ran upwards, hoping to find the two SCA Agents again. I got to the upper floor and ran out into another hallway. The creature was right opposite me, hundreds of evil eyes glaring at me. It had a dozen of those awful, massive limbs ready for me. One by one they began to fall.

This was it. I threw all my power and focus into my shields. I ran to my left, back in the direction I'd last seen the two idiots who should have been keeping me alive. I'd never avoid all those limbs, or even most of them, I was demon poop for sure...

But then there was a blinding flash of light, and the creature screamed, slithering away from me. I jumped to the window and saw the most amazing thing I'd even witnessed. Four people in robes stepped out of what looked like a massive purple vortex. One of them had conjured what looked like a miniature sun, which Agrammel was shying away from.

They all had staffs or shorter rods, and were dressed in white robes, concealing their faces. Each weapon practically danced with power to my mage sight. I saw massive amounts of energy being assembled by the quartet. One pointed his staff, and a beam of pure blackness speared at the demon, ripping straight through one side and out the other, the demonic flesh bubbling and rotting away around the wounds. Another raised his hands, and a great, sinuous shape came from a conjured fog, wrapping around the demon, binding it in place. I should have thought of that...

A third pointed at a descending massive tentacle, and it froze in place while the end attached to the creature thrashed in agony. Another massive 'pod raised for a strike, and I assembled a spear that cleaved it clean off. It smashed to the ground next to the fourth, who looked right at me, giving me the slightest of nods before raising his staff.

What looked like a massive portal opened above the demon, and a river of lava poured onto the monster. I didn't believe what I was seeing for a moment, but yes, actual *molten lava!* Bound in place and holed through by the kind of combat magic that would make my brother drool, the creature screamed as it started to cook, shaking and thrashing in utter agony. The molten rock flowed down its screaming throats, and, one by one, they were silenced.

The one who'd tied it in place raised his hands again, and a glittering circle of light appeared around the creature as the others blasted or sliced off its massive attacking limbs. Unrecognisable spells appeared in and around the circle as the lines making it up expanded and grew more complex, spells that made my eyes ache just to look at them. As I watched, the circle stopped shifting and sat above the creature for an instant, and then slammed to the ground with a great thrumming whine, surrounding the demon king.

Agrammel bellowed, this time in fear and rage as the air around it seemed to warp and flex. Then the entire creature seemed to fold in on its centre, screaming all the while. And then, just like that, it and the circle were gone, leaving a long moment of intense silence.

The four mages looked around briefly, nodding to one another and then turned their heads up towards me. Each nodded in turn, and then one of them waved a hand, opening up another vortex. I saw green fields and bright sunshine through the gateway, and then they were gone as quickly as they'd appeared.

"Did you see that?" Kraab asked from beside me. How long had he been there?

"Mm-hm," Knowles managed. Oh, *now* they turn up...

"Who the hell were they?" I asked.

"You don't know?" Kraab asked, shocked.

"Does it sound like I do?" I asked a little testily.

"The Archons," Knowles answered, awe in her voice, "those were the four remaining Archons. They've returned."

Chapter 53

"Did you see, Vanessa? They looked right at me! They nodded at me!" Kraab gushed with excitement.

Ah, that made more sense. And thank God! The last thing I need is four super-powered mages noticing *me*. I have quite enough complications in my life as it is, thank you very much.

I sat on a convenient bench, and shut down my various shields, charms and light generators. Damn but I was bone-tired and more than a little bit terrified now that it was over. How could I have been so utterly stupid? Why didn't I run away when I had the chance? This wasn't like me at all.

Sirens were blaring in the distance, and people were starting to mill about.

"I should probably go if we're to keep me from getting involved in any official entanglements," I said, trying to get through to Kraab and Knowles, who were obviously still star-struck. Can't say the presence of Archons mattered much to me, other than the whole saving my life thing. To me a mage is a mage is a mage.

"Hm?" Kraab said, slowly coming out of it.

"Me, school, hiding from police and attention," I said, keeping it simple.

"Oh! Vanessa, get him to the car and back to the school. We'll finish with the sleepers later."

"Yes, Sir," she said, gesturing for me to follow.

"And Mister Graves?" Kraab said, I turned back towards him, "You were exceptional tonight. No matter what happens from here on in, you have a friend at the SCA, remember that."

"Make that two," Knowles said, smiling at me warmly.

I smiled back, nodded, and Knowles took me back to school.

The journey back was actually pleasant. Knowles and I chatted much more freely. A barrier had been removed; I suppose what they say about shared danger is true. I was still on the verge of wetting myself, and I was exhausted in a way I'd never felt before. I'd expended so much energy that I nearly dozed off half a dozen times.

Finally we pulled up to Kimmel House and Knowles shook my hand before giving me a hug.

"We'll be in touch," she said before getting back in the car and driving off.

I took in a deep, relaxing breath. I was alive! I'd survived an attack by a freaking demon king! Then I remembered all those that didn't, and I threw up explosively in a nearby bush. Well, the warm and fuzzy feeling lasted for about as long as it usually does, so at least I'm consistent. Then I remembered that I had nearly been eaten myself, and out came the rest of what remained in my stomach. After *that* I sat up against the wall for a while, waiting for the terror to dissipate and the stomach cramps to fade away.

What was next?!

Faust was obviously holding a grudge. I would have to deal with that soon, or arrange for that to be dealt with, because who knew what he'd try to follow *that*?

I didn't sleep well. Every time I closed my eyes, I saw the creature, its awful, gaping maws, its staring eyes. I doubt I got more than an hour's sleep the whole night, and I woke up in a cold sweat every time.

The next morning I dragged myself out of bed by some miracle and threw myself into a shower by sheer force of will, turning the heat right up. The scalding water helped wake me up enough to face the day. When I sat down for breakfast, Bill and Cathy looked like they didn't recognise me.

"What the hell happened to you?" Bill asked.

"Oh same old, same old. Big party, much drinking, late night behind the auditorium with that special someone," I replied facetiously.

"So, heavy studying?" Bill sneered, "Damn, Mathew, you should really get a life, you know that?"

"And what did you do last night?" I replied acidly.

That caught him short. Bill can dish it out, but he can't take it.

"That's not important," he said with a dismissive wave, "we're making fun of you right now."

I laughed, and the world seemed a little brighter for a while, and then Cathy brought out the newspaper.

"Have either of you seen this?" she asked, spreading it out for us.

It was the Daily Telegraph, there was a picture of the James Sutcliffe Memorial Hospital. It showed gaping holes in the walls where Agrammel had torn the building apart to get to me.

Dozens slain in terrorist attack, the headline read.

"Apparently a man called Faust released a creature into the city, and it made straight for the hospital," Cathy explained.

Faust? I thought, pulling the paper towards me.

I read silently for a minute.

Oh, it was magnificent! I had to give it to Kraab, he'd done the job perfectly. The paper said that '*the SCA's severe crimes unit*' (meaning Kraab and Knowles) traced the creature's psychic spoor right back to Faust's mansion, though I knew for a fact that he couldn't have done that, as Faust was no one's idiot, which meant that they had to know exactly where to look to get their evidence, and that was thanks to yours truly. Faust must have been under the impression that I was going to keep quiet (or that I'd be too dead to tell anyone anything).

Tee hee hee!

Faust was apparently on the run, though his lawyers made a statement protesting his innocence. His bank accounts had been frozen (lovely), and his assets were now being monitored (even better).

Then there was more filler, sources describe the mages who fought off the demon... gallantly buying time for the specialists to arrive... two identified as Agents Kraab and Knowles... a third remains unknown... sources describe him as a Sorcerer consulting with the SCA, etc. Nothing for me to worry about. I handed it back to Cathy who was looking at me funny again. I really had to work on my poker face.

And that was the beginning of a fantastically boring day. No one tried to kill me, nothing tried to eat me. Nobody tried to tie me to anything in the dark, enslave, beat or otherwise interfere with me, it was terrific. I eventually had to tell Cathy a watered down version of last night's events, and she nearly had a fit. I think I was beginning to worry her.

Over the next couple of days news began to trickle out about Faust. Apparently the SCA had raided his other properties; though naturally they hadn't found anything. Still, Faust was having a very bad week and that was enough for me.

Those were very good days. I felt as if things were finally beginning to wrap up. I didn't even use magic all that time. Well, one little cantrip than dropped the Ox face-first into the tray of pudding he was carrying. Don't tell anyone.

I honestly thought that things would be alright.

Then on Sunday I got a call from Tethys.

"You need to come see me," she said without preamble.

"What is it?" I asked.

"I have that information you asked for. I got it from my good friend Sparky. You remember him?"

That was strange. She didn't sound right, and there's no way she'd get information from Sparky. That guy hated her.

"That's great," I replied, thinking fast, "I'll bring the payment we agreed on."

"I want it in cash, remember," she said.

"Understood," I said, and hung up.

Tethys was in trouble. Remember our earlier discussion?

I dialled Kraab's number, and naturally couldn't get him. Should I risk calling the regular police? If there was a problem Tethys couldn't handle on her own, then what could the police do? She'd warned me that something was wrong, so whoever was there obviously wanted to see *me*. What would happen to Tethys if I didn't turn up?

I got up and left, leaving a quick note on my desk in case... well in case I was a little late coming back. I called a cab, and it met me at the school gates. I pulled off my school tie and stuffed it into my pocket, while at the same time preparing several spell constructs in my head and bolstering my defences.

The cabbie dropped me off in front of Tethys' club and I made my way in slowly, mage sight active, looking around carefully. The bouncer waved me in, and Kandi came to meet me. "Would you like to follow me, Mister Graves?" she asked in a half-dazed voice. I probably wouldn't have noticed if Tethys hadn't warned me.

I looked at her mind and saw a compulsion web wrapped around it. She moved slower, as if resisting. I reached up, sliding my own mind between the gaps, looking for an active tether that would let the caster know his spell had been interfered with. There wasn't one, and I'd looked very thoroughly. I pulled the spell away carefully, one strand at a time, isolating each one from her psyche so it wouldn't hurt her when I finally removed it. It took most of the trip down the back passage for me to do it, and I may have cost her a couple of childhood memories to do it so quickly.

She slumped against the wall, and let out a gasp. I jumped to her side and held her up, whispering in her ear to stay quiet.

"I've removed the compulsion, but I need you to stay with me and keep it together; can you do that?"

She took a shuddering breath, and nodded, grabbing onto my shoulders for support.

"What's going on?" I asked quietly, guiding her into a convenient storage room.

She wiped tears from her eyes, though if I had to guess, they were due to anger rather than fear. Good, anger was useful.

"You're Tethys' friend?" she asked, looking me over, "Her Shadowborn?"

"Dupe might be a better descriptor," I answered with a smile to show I was kidding, she smiled back, "but I'll help if I can, what's going on?"

"That Faust prick came in earlier with two heavy guys. They pushed past security and into Tethys' office, then she called for me, and he did something to my head. It made me follow his commands. I didn't want to, I swear."

"That's okay, you couldn't have helped yourself."

"How did you know I wasn't me?" she asked.

"Tethys gave me a warning over the phone, so I was looking. Does he control Tethys like you?" I asked. I suspected no, but I wanted to be sure.

"No, but those guys have those amulet things on, and they're blocking her from using any of her powers."

"Is Tethys tied up, or bound at all?"

"I don't think so, just sat between the two bruisers with Faust looking on. He's terrifying," she said, her voice getting very small at the end.

"Are the big guys armed?"

"Tasers and knives, I think. I didn't see guns or anything."

I thought hard for a moment. How to fix this? I stood there for a while, mulling over the possibilities, and then I had it. It would require horribly good timing and a bit of luck. I explained my plan to Kandi, while preparing a spell that would help things along a little. We sat on the floor cross-legged while I worked.

"Question," she said as I explained what I needed her to do, "why didn't those amulets dispel the mind control in my head?"

"Mental magic is slightly different. It's not just magic, it's also part imagination given form. You can dispel it when it's in the open, when it's being cast, but when it's in, it becomes part of the subject's mind, rather than a separate piece of magic."

"I think I get it," she said, "so what are you doing now?"

"I'm crafting a spell that will look like the web he put over your mind, but which will actually be a ward to keep him from breaking in again, at least for a while. It'll take him a while to remove, if he even notices the change."

"Can't you make it stronger?" she asked.

"I could, but I daren't risk him seeing what I've done until it's too late. That means you'll have to obey until I've got him distracted. You're clear on what to do?"

She nodded, brandishing the small carving knife, which she tucked into her top under her breasts (it was a very small top, I tried not to stare, really I did). I stood and helped her up. I smiled reassuringly, and she kissed me on the cheek before leading the way to the office. I took a breath, engaging my mental defences, properly this time. Magic flowed through my barriers, locking my mind up behind my mazes and mountain. What with Kandi's mental manipulation, it seemed like a wise preparation.

She opened the door, and in the same half-dazed tone she'd used earlier she announced me.

I entered and saw the scene. Tethys was at her desk, looking incensed with rage. There was a large, heavy-set man to either side of her, each looking big enough to bend me over their legs and snap me like a twig, their heads were almost shaved bare, their eyes were cold, almost reptilian.

"Tethys?" I asked, feigning surprise, "what's going on?"

"Good evening, Mister Graves," said an evil voice from behind me, and before I had a chance to do more than breathe, it was on.

If Knowles was a mental battering ram, Faust was a bloody tank brigade. He *slammed* into my outer line with so much force that the outer maze was torn to pieces in less than a second. I didn't screw around; I opened my well and simply connected it to my constructs. I didn't have concentration or power to spare for anything else. I even lost the mage-sight spell as I put everything into holding Faust off. He bashed into my second maze layer from a dozen different directions, each single probe more powerful than Knowles' entire attack had been.

The wall held, bolstered by sheer power. I rebuilt the maze behind him, sending out counter probes of my own to ensnare the ones he'd left behind, tearing them to pieces by sheer weight of numbers. The air between us crackled as we fought, mental energies rippling to and fro. I sent out a lance at his own defences and smacked ineffectually into his own wall, but it forced him to pull back a little to counter me. I used the time to attack the tendrils he'd left in my mind, ripping them apart, while rebuilding and strengthening the outer maze. I was only half done when he renewed his assault. I ran energy through the outer walls, and they exploded, ripping dozens of his probes apart. Both of us were bleeding freely from our eyes and noses as the feedback played havoc with both of our brains.

Faust was immensely skilled. His probes were powerful and complex and his defences were formidable. This was going to come down to a war of attrition, which one of us was going to break first? Who would run out of energy first?

I was using more, as his attacks were much more finessed, and my defences were comparatively clumsy. But I had more power to use than he did, I could feel it. His well was emptying faster than mine. Then his attacks got even more complex, his probes splitting and flickering, darting around and under walls, churning up the imaginary ground to destroy barriers and hedges. The outer line fell again, and I barely put enough power into the second to hold him while I reinforced the third, and put some rather nasty surprises in place.

It was a losing proposition. He was simply better than I was, and I didn't have the knowledge or experience to win, not on the defensive like this. So, with as good a defence in place as I could manage, I launched an all out attack along the path his tendrils took, forming my own battering ram. His defences were smaller than mine, and much less complex, but they were detailed and strong, resembling the Bastille in Paris, surrounded by an empty field with colossal chasms blocking the way. I piled my attack over the first charm just as I felt Faust smack into my third maze. He smashed and battered it as I made it over drop after drop, sending little waves of mental energy ahead of me in case of traps.

Some exploded, causing me referred pain, but I carried on and ripped into the castle's outer wall, tearing apart the stone. I felt pain as I triggered some nasty surprises, but I persevered, and then I darted back as a huge section fell down. I slid over the rubble and into the castle proper. Then I felt agony as Faust struck my probes from behind, ripping into the tendrils and destroying many of them. I reared them up and smashed into his attack, wrapping around them and hurling them right back. I should have stayed behind my walls. Faust was better at this part than I was, much better. He tore my attack apart, and I barely pulled back in time, hurt and beaten, before he would have torn *me* apart too. I heard him laugh as he pursued. I was weak and vulnerable. He was still strong, and he was going to crush me.

And then I heard him moan in ecstasy (something I found quite disgusting), and suddenly the probes dissolved. So did his defences, they collapsed like a sandcastle in the ocean. I took advantage and went right for his spark.

I was in! A mental flick, and I had a coma spell on him faster than lightning. His mind went quiet, and I fell to my knees, the battle over as suddenly as it had begun.

I came back to myself and saw Tethys, hands covered in blood, let Faust slide to the floor before spitting on him. There was red lipstick on his face, and I smiled gratefully. He couldn't take a war on two fronts, thankfully, and like Tethys had pointed out so eloquently at her last lecture, concentration is everything in a mental duel. The lower half of my face was covered in blood, and my head felt like it was going to explode, but we'd won.

"I was winning, you know," I said with a grin.

She seemed to see me for the first time, and her face broke into a wide and friendly grin. She offered me a hand, and I took it. She helped me to my feet and immediately planted a kiss on my lips. No tricks this time, though. Something I appreciated.

"You're turning out to be quite useful, you know that?" she said with a grin, wiping a little of my blood off her lips. I glared at her, she just smiled back. Kandi grabbed me tightly from behind and hugged me.

"You alright?" I asked her once I could breathe again.

"Never better!" she said brightly, helping me to a sofa. I saw the slumped forms of the two heavies.

I should explain.

Once she'd led me into the expected trap, Kandi then walked slowly around the desk until she could slide between the heavies, who were distracted by Faust's and my duel. She placed the knife in Tethys' hand and then ripped the amulet off the neck of the left hand bruiser. Tethys, quick off the mark, had stabbed the other one before darting over the desk and away, gathering her strength before throwing the knife through the ribcage of the first.

It was at that point that Kandi conveyed my request for a distraction, and Tethys happily obliged. See, I had learned the importance of focus, and after only three painful lessons.

I gave Tethys Kraab's phone number, and she started calling. She wasn't able to get him for a while. I didn't mind, Kandi was sitting next to me, holding my hand. It helped to distract from the whomping headache. The feedback was excruciating, I would be out of magical commission for *days* after this. Eventually Tethys got through and handed me the phone. I told Kraab what had happened. It took him a moment to get over the shock, but he said he'd be there as quickly as he could. Tethys called her bouncer and let him know. She sat on my other side, smiling at me.

"This has certainly been an interesting day," she said, "and I must say that the ending was quite cathartic."

By this point, she'd pulled Faust's trousers down to expose his arse for maximum embarrassment when the authorities arrived. I snorted and Tethys linked her arm with mine, inspecting my nails.

"You really need a manicure, you know that?" she said.

The comment was so ridiculous that it made me burst out laughing, which made my head explode with pain.

"Ow, ow, don't make me laugh!" I said, cradling my head.

"Well it's your own fault if you're going to charge into a fight head first," she answered.

"Seriously, you're going to make my skull cap pop right off," I replied.

They spent the next twenty minutes trying to kill me with laughter before Kraab and company arrived. He took in the scene with a bewildered look before seeing me sat between two stunning women with their hands on me, at which point he seemed to give up trying to understand and just asked me to start from the top, waving emergency personnel in to look at the bruisers (horribly injured, but still alive), Faust (comatose, and likely to be that way for the foreseeable future), and finally me (suffering from mental and magical feedback, but would be fine in a day or two).

I told my story, leaving out how I was verifying the information he'd given me, and casting Tethys and Kandi in the role of innocent(-ish) friends of mine, used to lure me into Faust's trap. I described the battle I'd fought and Kraab looked impressed. I learned later that Faust was one of the best mind-mages in the country and that he had centuries of practice under his belt. If I'd known that ahead of time, I would have come up with a better plan.

I told him how Tethys had saved my life, and how Kandi had saved hers. I told him just about everything.

"Well, young man," he said when I was done, "when you poke your nose in, you shove in your whole head with it, don't you?"

I smiled, exhaustion coming over me, and I yawned, desperate to get back to a nice warm bed. I checked the time and it was only four o'clock in the afternoon. Damn I was getting old before my time.

"I'll get this statement typed up and ready for you to sign tomorrow," he said, standing up. They'd carted the bruisers and Faust away some time ago. I stood too, so did Tethys and Kandi.

"See you around," I said. Before I could turn around they both grabbed me and hugged me tightly, kissing me on either cheek. I went bright red and Tethys laughed. They thanked me again and saw me to the door. I waved and left with Kraab who was looking at me like I was some kind of genius.

"You have some very... interesting friends, Mister Graves," he said with a wide grin.

Chapter 54

It was a couple of days later, and I was sitting in the square, taking a mental inventory. Let's look at the checklist of problems that needed solving.

Find out where the Shaadre came from, done.

Find out who sent it, and make sure it can't happen again, sort of done. I mean, the Shaadres are still out there somewhere, and they'll probably cause someone a problem some time down the way, but that's the government's problem, thank you very much.

My brother's safe, and someone who could have been a real problem for me is locked up tightly in a Mage's prison.

I think that's pretty much it. I mean I can't think of anything else that's a pressing issue. My phone dinged and I looked at the text.

>Found the information you asked for. No, really this time. Come see me when you've got a minute. Kisses, T.

I grinned and texted back that I had a free afternoon.

When I arrived, Kandi gave me a hello hug and led me by the hand to Tethys' office; you'd never have thought that there had been a magical battle. Nothing was out of place. Tethys grinned at me, and Kandi left with a smile, leaving us to it.

"She's a little smitten with you, you know," Tethys said.

"Funny," I said, wondering what new trick she was embarking on.

"You are so hard to corrupt, you know that?" she said with a grin.

"Hardly," I replied, "I'm just not that easy to trick. Corruption and I, however, are old friends."

"Are you trying to get me going with your dirty talk?" she asked, eyes boring into mine.

I crossed my arms and tapped my side, affecting disinterest, even as my eyes wondered to the very interesting, and nicely form-fitting outfit she was wearing.

"Fine," she said, pulling a folder from her desk, "I have a contact at archives, he got the information you requested."

She put it on the desk in front of me, "I haven't had time to read it, but I had Kandi make me a copy, in the interests of honesty."

I shook my head, not able to help smiling. She'd never change, but at least she was on my side (for now).

"You mind if I take a look?" I asked.

"Go ahead," she said, watching me.

I flicked through. It was an essay type document, with references and points by section, dealing with each case in turn. It confirmed what Kraab had told me, and my blood ran cold as I read on. There were, in fact, six records of twins like Des and I. All six Shadowborn were murdered by their siblings. The author of the document even went so far as to theorise the existence of a curse on such brothers, due to the consistent end result.

Damn it.

I'd really thought that it had been a mistake or a hoax, or *something*. But no. The author confirmed what Kraab had said, that a resonance between the shadow mage's powers and the light mage's cause the latter to go slowly mad. Shadow magic being 'high magic', the reverse didn't seem to happen to the Shadowborn, at least. And even if I stopped using my powers, it wouldn't make a difference. Twins were linked as long as they were alive. I would slowly drive my brother insane for as long as I lived. One day, in the next few years or so, he would simply snap, and then he would kill me. I closed the file and handed it back to Tethys, unable to say anything at all.

"Mathew?" she said, concern on her face, "What is it?"

"You'll see," I replied, "Thank you for the information, Tethys. I'll try to put it to good use."

"You're very welcome," she said, standing up to walk me out, seeming to accept that I couldn't talk about it.

"Don't be a stranger, now," she said, kissing me on the cheek. I smiled as best I could, waved goodbye to Kandi, and made my way back to school.

I just knew my good mood couldn't last!

I was in a self-pitying funk for the next three days. Hardly speaking, barely eating, constantly worrying. Here's the thing, I didn't want to die, but I also didn't want Des to go insane. So I had to come up with a cure from somewhere, some way to fix him, prevent him from going nuts, and the clock was ticking. How long did I have? The report said that the youngest had gone insane at fifteen, and the oldest at twenty-three. In the latter case, the mages had spent the previous three years apart, so it could be that proximity was a factor in the equation.

I had to get Des, or me, away for a while, at least until I could fix this.

I got up and went looking for my brother. I had something to tell him. A conversation seventeen years in the making. I found him in the gym, getting ready for a sparring duel with Belle. Probably a good idea, Mister Koenig was nearby with his magic-killing stuff. I walked up to my brother, sweat rolling down my face.

"Des, can I have a quick word?" I asked.

Afterword

Thanks for reading *The Magician's Brother*!

If you liked it, and you have a moment, please leave a review. Any questions or comments can be sent to hdaroberts@gmail.com, I'm always happy to hear from a reader.

Look for The *Magician's Brother, Volume 2: Sorcerer's Loss*, coming soon!

Printed in Great Britain
by Amazon